PRAYER OF THE HANDMAIDEN

What Reviewers Say About
Merry Shannon's Work

Sword of the Guardian
"This is a rollicking fun book and a must-read for those who enjoy courtly light fantasy in a medieval-seeming time. Merry Shannon is a bright new voice in lesbian fantasy fiction, and this one's highly recommended."—*Midwest Book Review*

"*Sword of the Guardian* is a well written book. Merry Shannon has a great gift for story telling and world building."—*C-Spot Reviews*

"First time author Shannon keeps the tension riding high like a pro... Shannon balances personal development, love story and political drama with confidence and a swift, lively style."—*Curve Magazine*

Branded Ann
"Daring, bold and suspenseful are just a few words to describe the latest novel from Merry Shannon...Shannon keeps the story moving swiftly along with traumatic plot twists and turns. Overall a great second novel from Merry Shannon."—*Lambda Literary*

"Treasures abound in this rollicking, high-seas adventure. Lesbian protagonists are not usually featured in pirate exploits, so this extremely well told novel is a treat not soon to be forgotten. With nonstop action and delicious sexual tension, Captain Branded Ann and her fellow pirates take their readers on an unpredictable journey..."—*Curve Magazine*

"*Branded Ann* is a great romp through the time when pirates roamed the Caribbean Sea, and were feared by all who sailed those waters. ... *Branded Ann* is an exciting, edge of your chair read. It keeps pages turning right to the satisfying conclusion."—*Just About Write*

"Merry Shannon's second novel for Bold Strokes Books, Branded Ann, is an amazing story of pirates, romance and adventure. ...For lovers of lesbian pirates, *Branded Ann* is one of the best I've ever read. I strongly recommend it!"—*Rainbow Book Reviews*

Visit us at www.boldstrokesbooks.com

By the Author

Branded Ann

The Legends of Ithyria Series:

Sword of the Guardian

Prayer of the Handmaiden

PRAYER OF THE HANDMAIDEN

by

Merry Shannon

2015

PRAYER OF THE HANDMAIDEN
© 2015 By Merry Shannon. All Rights Reserved.

ISBN 13: 978-1-62639-329-5

This Trade Paperback Original Is Published By
Bold Strokes Books, Inc.
P.O. Box 249
Valley Falls, NY 12185

First Edition: March 2015

Credits
Editor: Cindy Cresap
Production Design: Susan Ramundo
Cover Art By Kaitlin Porter
Cover Design By Sheri (graphicartist2020@hotmail.com)

Acknowledgments

This book would not have been possible without the love and support of the many readers and friends who have been asking, over the course of many years, when the next Ithyria book would be ready. I've had the privilege of chatting with so many of you, whether by e-mail or in person, and those conversations have been my inspiration and motivation to keep on with this series and these characters. I can't wait to share this new story with you all—hope you'll find it worth the wait! I also want to thank my patient and talented fiancée, Kaitlin Porter, for her beautiful artwork on the cover, for taking my author bio photo, and for letting me bounce ideas off her as the story progressed. I love you! And thanks to Sheri for the graphics that make this cover go so nicely with the cover of the first book. Thanks to my editor, Cindy Cresap, for helping to polish the rough spots and always encouraging me to grow as a writer. And of course, to Radclyffe and all of Bold Strokes Books—the BSB family is an amazing group of people and I am so fortunate and proud to be a part of it.

Dedication

For Casper
The best writing companion a girl could have asked for.

CHAPTER ONE

I am Qiturah, Honored Mother of Verdred Temple and humble scribe to the Goddess Ithyris. As the Goddess's historian, it is my responsibility to document the significant events of our generation as they unfold, so that Her wonders may never be lost to memory.

We, the priestesses of Ithyris, know that our Divine Lady's power shines brightest when love is Her instrument. It is our sacred duty to bring this truth to Her people. Perhaps you have already read my first contribution to these chronicles, wherein love served as Her weapon in the Battle of the Ranes. Scarcely a season has passed since Queen Shasta's coronation, yet I have already been given a second such story to relate.

This time, however, I bring you a tale not of royalty, but of faith.

The day had been completely ordinary. In fact, Qiturah might even have described it as tedious. Prayers, chores, mealtimes, and studies had been carried out at their scheduled times, without the slightest anomaly. Certainly she had received no warning, not even the smallest hint, that this afternoon was to be any more remarkable than any other—right up until the moment when the Goddess Ithyris materialized, unheralded, in her private chamber.

She was more beautiful than any mortal woman Qiturah had ever seen. In a single, glorious instant, the Honored Mother of Verdred learned for herself that the legend was true: Ithyris's translucent skin appeared to glow from within, as if the brilliance of Her spirit could not be contained by Her body. Her limbs were slender, Her features delicate, the bridge of Her nose a perfectly straight line. Her mouth was expressive and sweetly sensual, and Her eyes...Qiturah found it impossible to look into those luminous eyes for more than a few seconds before gooseflesh swept her skin.

The shock of Her arrival was soon eclipsed by a sensation of nakedness. Before the Goddess's all-encompassing gaze, Qiturah might as well have dropped her robes to the floor, for all the good they did. Ithyris's ability to view her was not limited to physical attributes, and Qiturah felt Her perusal to the core of her being, her every grace and shortcoming laid bare. The feeling might have been humiliating were it not for the breathtaking tenderness in Her eyes.

Qiturah's knees struck the floor. Her arms came up of their own volition, thrown wide, and her head fell back. This was the traditional Ithyrian prayer position, but Qiturah had never truly understood the reason for it until this moment. *"Y'kurakura nasiaa; y'vysashun lo siriaa. Ah Shaa'Nalusa, nu yi ailo, nu yi ailo..."* The hymn fell naturally from her lips, and the words had never been so true.

My heartbeat dances for You; my blood is singing for You. Oh Divine Lady, You are with me, You are with me...

In all her sixty-seven winters, Qiturah had never felt more alive. Ithyris almost never appeared to the mortal eye. Even the sound of Her voice was a rare and precious gift. Qiturah had never dared to hope for an honor such as this. Yet She was there, bare feet hovering a handbreadth above the floor, pale hair and robes floating as if suspended in water.

"Qiturah, y'ostryn makluran." The ariose syllables chimed like bells. *Qiturah, my beloved daughter.* Qiturah's eyes filled with tears as she tried to form a proper reply, but her lips could only move noiselessly.

"Byrias ai piare," the Goddess said. *You must help me.*

Qiturah gasped and pressed her fingertips to her forehead. What could She possibly want from her, that warranted such an extraordinary personal visit? "Of course, Sweet Ithyris," she replied in the Ithyrian tongue. "You know I will do whatever You ask."

"Yi fuli shaa'din."

Qiturah stared at Ithyris in disbelief. Had she heard correctly? She did her best not to stammer as she asked, "Who, my Lady?"

"Y'ostryn n'nu tana veran. Kadrian."

"It shall be done," Qiturah said, and Ithyris's mouth curved upward. If She had been beautiful before, this small shift in Her expression elevated Her loveliness to inhuman proportions. It was the most wonderful smile Qiturah had ever seen, and she felt light-headed.

"Kurariaa." Thank you.

Ithyris was gone as swiftly as She'd come. She vanished in a whisper, like a candle extinguished by the wind. Qiturah stared longingly at the space where She had been, savoring every detail of that face, that smile, pressing the images into her memory as carefully as she could. She wanted never to forget them, for this was the most momentous day of her life.

"No, thank You," she said to the empty air. "Thank You, oh thank You..."

Her head was spinning, not just with the Goddess's unprecedented visit, but with the intriguing request that had provoked it. A *shaa'din*! Not since the Twelve had the Goddess called a holy warrior into Her service, and the implications were as alarming as they were thrilling.

A millennium ago, Ithyris had bestowed Her spirit on twelve young women in order to drive Her brother-God Ulrike's darkness back into the mountains of Dangar. With an army of the Goddess's devoted followers at their heels, the Twelve had waged war against the disciples of Ulrike. As *shaa'din*, they channeled the Goddess's power into the mortal world, and ultimately they succeeded in carving out a swath of land, bordered to the south by sea and to the north by mountains. There the Goddess's people could live in peace, sheltered from Ulrike's raging lust for dominion. The Twelve had become the first Honored Mothers of Ithyria. Each province of the kingdom inherited one of their names, and their accomplishments were immortalized in folk songs and bedside tales passed down through generations. Even today their influence pervaded almost every aspect of Ithyrian life, and rightfully so, for without them Ithyria would not have been.

Now Ithyris had declared there would be another *shaa'din*, and Qiturah could only imagine what She might have in mind. Just a few moons earlier, a renewed war with Dangar had seemed inevitable. A power-hungry traitor from within the Ithyrian royal house had struck an unholy bargain with the Dangar emperor. A horde of barbarian warriors advanced on the northern provinces, intending to reclaim them in the dark God's name. But Ithyris intervened. The Battle of the Ranes ended in a wondrous spectacle of Her celestial fire, and the death of the traitorous Chancellor Kumire. And, by some strange miracle no one could explain, the barbarian horde had retreated—perhaps because the easy victory they had anticipated no longer seemed certain? With Queen Shasta of Rane restored to the throne, the kingdom had joyfully celebrated its one thousandth winter of freedom from Ulrike's tyranny. There had been fireworks, and feasting, and a great release of tension, as if all of Ithyria had let out a collective sigh of relief. Everyone was looking forward to a time of peace in which to rebuild, but this stunning turn of events seemed to indicate that the Goddess anticipated yet a greater fight ahead.

Qiturah tucked a cushion beneath her knees, which were beginning to smart from the impact with the stone floor. She closed her eyes, tilted her head back, and breathed deeply. Some tremendous darkness must be approaching, for Ithyris to call a *shaa'din* into Her service once more. The need was evidently so great that She had come personally to ask Qiturah to prepare the chosen vessel for Her power. To be called to such a task was the greatest honor Qiturah could imagine. Much research would be necessary, as she was not even certain how a *shaa'din* was created. Such a thing had not been done for a thousand winters.

What an enormous change was about to take place in the life of this fortunate—or perhaps not so fortunate, for the responsibilities to be laid on her shoulders were unimaginable—young woman. Ithyris's choice was curious, for the priestess She had named was quiet and timid. Truthfully, Kadrian did not seem at all like a leader. But Qiturah held absolute faith that no one knew a person's true heart as well as the Goddess. In fact, this was the second time Ithyris had requested the services of this particular priestess by name. Last winter, Ithyris had directed Qiturah to send a letter to the capital city of Ardrenn, and She specified that Kadrian was to carry the message. That mission had resulted in the rescue of the Ithyrian princess. Had those events been a precursor for whatever was happening now?

The news was sure to come as a shock to young Kadrian. How would the other priestesses react? How would the citizens of the kingdom react, for that matter? This was certain to cause as much fear as celebration. Yet like it or not, Qiturah realized, Ithyria was about to witness the birth of a legend.

❖

The infant's distinctive amber-colored eyes brightened with interest at the thick braid dangling a fingerwidth from her face. She shrieked and grasped for it with tiny hands. Erinda laughed and kept her hair out of reach as she finished straightening the bedclothes in the cradle. Then she reached down and took the child in her arms.

"Feeling playful tonight, Your Highness?" she asked the baby, who fisted the end of one of her braids and attempted to stuff it in her mouth.

"She's been a handful all day. One can only hope she'll sleep soundly tonight." The ancient woman who hobbled up behind Erinda had been tending the royal nurseries for four generations. No one even remembered her real name anymore; she was known to everyone simply as "Nurse."

Erinda could hear the weariness in her voice, and smiled. "Why don't you rest for a while, Nurse? I can watch her until the Queen returns. I passed the conference room on my way here, and the viceroys were just adjourning for the day, so it shouldn't be long." She didn't add that the provincial leaders had been red-faced and irate as they shoved their way out into the palace corridor, suggesting that today's session had rubbed more than one man the wrong way. That generally meant that the young Queen had said or done something inflammatory, which was becoming almost a daily occurrence of late.

The haste with which the old woman scuttled from the room was comical. Nurse enjoyed her work, but it was also a well-known fact that the crotchety woman treasured her quiet time alone.

The baby had busied herself with the lacings of Erinda's bodice, gumming the leather thongs into a slippery tangle. She was a cheerfully preoccupied child, interested in everything that passed before her eyes, though her focus shifted as quickly as a honeybee danced between flowers. Her full title, as bestowed by her adopted mother the Queen, was Her Royal Highness the Crown Princess Bria Talon Shastis of Rane; quite a grand name for such a tiny girl. The Queen had taken to calling her "Brita," a contraction of Bria and Talon that was much less of a mouthful.

Hefting the baby in her arms, Erinda looked seriously into her golden eyes. "So it's been a busy day for you, has it, little Princess?"

"She's not the only one," Shasta said from behind them, and Erinda looked up to find the Ithyrian Queen in the nursery doorway, watching them with a smile. The Princess kicked happily at the sound of her adoptive mother's voice, and Erinda delivered her into Shasta's waiting arms.

"Hello, my pretty girl," Shasta murmured, and held out the heavy emerald pendant around her neck for the baby to examine. Giggling, Brita clutched at the gem with chubby fingers, trying to guide it toward her mouth, and Shasta laughed.

Erinda could not help noticing fine lines at the corners of her friend's eyes. Shasta was scarcely twenty winters of age, and had only held her office for a matter of moons, yet the strain of her office was already beginning to show on her face. Erinda worried for her. The responsibilities she bore were heavy, and this evening Shasta's pretty features were even more tense and drawn than usual.

"Difficult day, Your Majesty?"

"Erinda, I've told you time and again that I'd much prefer you to call me by name. For the love of the Goddess, we grew up together."

Erinda cringed. The women of her family had served as maids in the palace for as long as any of them could remember. The proper forms of address were so ingrained in her upbringing that it seemed like treason to refer to the Queen in casual terms, even if she did regard her as a dear friend.

Shasta seemed to read her mind, and her eyes twinkled. "Consider it a royal command, if that makes it easier." She smoothed Brita's sleek black hair and pressed a kiss to one plump cheek. "And yes, it was a very difficult afternoon. Every day I discover that dreaming up great and noble ideas and actually implementing them are two very different things. There are so many things I want to change, but politics are all about maintaining a delicate balance. A small change to one regulation might mean the salvation of one family, but also the starvation of another. No matter how many plans I think up to better equalize wealth and opportunity across the population, those who already have both just find ways of passing the costs down onto the ones whose shoulders they're already standing upon." She shook her head wearily. "I suppose I had this naïve idea that once I gained the crown, I'd be able to clear up all Ithyria's problems with a few strokes of the pen. I never imagined how complicated it would be."

"Haven't you already made a great many improvements?" Erinda had heard enough palace gossip to know that even in her few moons on the throne, Shasta had already gained much public favor.

"Oh, I've managed to change a few things. Replacing a few of the most corrupt viceroys, for a start. But I've had to stop myself on so many occasions to ask if I'm really doing it because they're corrupt, or if I'm just silencing dissenters. Blindly forcing my own will makes me no better than the men I despise." Erinda thought this was an impressively wise statement, but the tension lines deepened around Shasta's eyes. "I have too much power, Erinda. I can use it to keep the nobles in line, but who's going to keep *me* in line if I lose my way?"

Erinda wasn't sure how to answer, so she just squeezed her hand. She knew Shasta well enough to recognize the shadows haunting those famous amber eyes. "They were pushing the heir thing again, weren't they?"

Shasta's lips tightened and she drew the cooing baby closer. "They refuse to take no for an answer, no matter how many times I say it. Princess Brita is my heir. I will have no other. But the nobles are getting bolder with their arguments and insults. This afternoon, the Fynnish viceroy had the audacity to call her a..." she lowered her voice and whispered, as if not wanting the baby to hear, "...a Halflander."

Erinda's mouth dropped open. "He didn't!" It was an insult of the rudest sort, referring to the Princess's half-Outlander heritage. The black-haired, olive-skinned Outlanders were regarded with contempt by many of their fellow Ithyrians. "I hope you pitched something hard and spiky at his head."

"Worse," Shasta said wryly. "I hit him. Just about flew over the conference table, in all my regal glory, and slapped the viceroy of Fyn across the face. It was dreadful."

"I think it sounds magnificent. Wish I could have seen it."

"It certainly felt good at the time, but…oh, Erinda, what was I thinking? I am the Queen of Ithyria, and instead of putting that man in his place with the dignity of my birthright, I let him goad me into brawling like a barmaid in the middle of the royal conference room. The viceroys are in an uproar. We had to adjourn for the day."

"Well, I may not be the Queen of Ithyria, but I say the man had it coming." Erinda caressed Brita's cheek with a fingertip. "Our little Princess is Rane blood, same as you. And I daresay her Outlander mother, may Ithyris grant her peace, would have been right at your side boxing the viceroy's ears if she were alive to do so."

This brought a wistful smile to Shasta's face. Bria, the baby's birth mother and namesake, had been her childhood companion. Bria's free-spirited and somewhat unscrupulous approach to life had caused them all considerable trouble, but in the end she had given her life to save Shasta's, and with her dying breath she had entrusted her infant daughter to Shasta's care. Shasta loved Brita as her own, but unfortunately, that love caused no end of strife with her royal counsel. The provincial viceroys vehemently opposed her decision to make Brita heir to the Ithyrian throne.

"I'm sure you're right." Shasta's features softened as she gazed down at the baby. "But I have decided to leave it all for tomorrow. Business is over for the day, and it's time for happy thoughts."

The nursery's double doors swung open, and the anxiety on her face melted into a radiant smile. "Speaking of happy thoughts…"

A tall, broad-shouldered, olive-skinned soldier strolled into the room and moved to plant a tender kiss on the Queen's lips. Erinda had to grin as the lovers murmured greetings between kisses. Talon was captain of Shasta's royal guard, and adopted "father" to the baby Princess. Most of the kingdom knew Talon as a man; Erinda was one of the few aware of the truth.

"Good evening, Captain." Erinda dropped into a playful curtsy.

Talon winked. "Good evening, yourself." Her deep voice held the faintest hint of flirtation, though no one knew better than Erinda that the Outlander's heart belonged only to Shasta. "And how's our little girl tonight?" she asked as she took the Princess from Shasta's arms. Brita squealed as Talon made a face at her.

"Full of energy, it seems," Shasta replied, letting Brita curl a little hand around her index finger.

The resemblance connecting the three of them was evident. By blood, the child was Talon's niece and Queen Shasta's cousin, and so while she had the dark hair and skin of an Outlander, she also possessed the distinctive golden irises known to legend as the "amber eyes of Rane," the genetic demarcation of the Ithyrian royal house. Together, the three made a beautiful family. Yet as much as Erinda adored them, she still felt a niggling pang of envy.

Talon chuckled, but her eyes searched Shasta's face with concern. "You sound tired."

Erinda could hear the deliberate lift in Shasta's voice. "It's nothing, really. You know how trying these conferences can be."

Erinda was certain Shasta's nonchalance didn't fool Talon any more than it did her. Everyone in the kingdom was aware of the viceroys' impassioned refusal to acknowledge Princess Brita's claim to the throne, and Erinda suspected that the baby's half-Outlander heritage was a large part of the reason. The nobles felt that the Queen, of prime childbearing age, owed the kingdom a more suitable heir—preferably one that was male, lacked any hint of Outlander blood, and was from her own body rather than her traitorous late cousin's. To that end, they pressured her at every possible opportunity to consider the matter of marriage, something Shasta emphatically refused.

Only Erinda knew the extent of the private strain this generated for Shasta and Talon. While their romantic relationship was a common theme of court gossip, most could not imagine how sensitive the subject truly was. The two of them had, in fact, discussed marriage, but Talon was reluctant for many reasons—not the least of which was her guilty fear that perhaps she was preventing Shasta from fulfilling her duty to the kingdom. Talon's love was so absolute that she would sacrifice anything, even her own happiness, to ensure that Shasta's position at court was safe and secure. Erinda had never known anyone so single-mindedly selfless.

Now, Erinda watched every one of those conflicting emotions pass over Talon's handsome features. But after a moment, Talon merely pressed a kiss to Shasta's temple and murmured, "Perhaps you and I should go hold a…*conference* of our own."

Grinning, Erinda took Brita from Talon's arms and waved the lovebirds away. "Go, both of you. Enjoy some time together. You've earned it." She waggled her eyebrows at Shasta. "Do try to keep it down this time though, Your Majesty?"

While Shasta's cheeks flushed crimson, Talon's mouth curved. "Tired of faking those stomachaches for us, Erinda?"

"You both know I'll do anything for you," Erinda said tartly, "including gagging down the healer's awful potions to cover for our Queen's…um…*enthusiasm*." Shasta turned an even deeper shade of red and buried her face in Talon's chest. Erinda laughed, then. "No need to be embarrassed, Your Majesty. I'm glad you're both so happy. You deserve it."

Still, she struggled again with pangs of envy as the two left arm in arm, Talon whispering something in Shasta's ear that made her flush and giggle. Yes, Erinda was pleased that her friends had found such bliss together, especially since the journey to reach this point had been long and painful for each of them. But nonetheless, their happiness was a constant reminder of the life she would never have.

Like Shasta and Talon, Erinda found herself drawn to other women in the way most women were drawn to men. She had embraced this at an early age, and over the winters had taken a handful of discreet lovers—which had even, for a time, included Talon herself. But it was highly improbable that Erinda would ever experience the joy of a relationship like theirs. For one thing, Talon had the distinct advantage of her male disguise. While her affair with the Queen might be considered scandalous because of her station and background, even her Outlander blood, the fact that she was a woman was not part of that scandal. How likely was it that Erinda would find a lover she could be with so openly?

And even if she could…Erinda shook her head sadly and touched her forehead to the baby's. "Ah, little Princess, as you grow up, take great care with your heart. Choose carefully who you give it to, for you may never get it back."

Brita's eyelids drooped sleepily, and Erinda sighed. "Bedtime, is it?" She carried the baby back to the cradle and sat down to rock her. She started to croon a lullaby, and let her attention drift.

This was not something she did very often, as her thoughts, left unchecked, invariably ran to the one topic forbidden to them. Even as she hovered at the fringes of those dangerous memories, she knew there would be a steep price to pay. The emptiness was sure to find her tonight, to keep her awake long after the rest of the palace was asleep, wrapping her in the grief and anguish she deserved for such careless indulgence. But right now, she didn't care.

Green eyes, the vivid hue of grass right after a rainfall, were smiling at her from the depths of her imagination. They were breathtaking, and she couldn't bring herself to force them away as she usually did. Then it was too late, as Kade's entire face came into focus, her laugh echoing through Erinda's mind. She could not have stopped the memory from following then, even if she'd wanted to.

They were lying together beneath the biggest tree in the palace gardens. It was late autumn, and Erinda was seventeen. Kade, nearly a winter older, was stretched out on her stomach next to her, propped on her elbows as she twirled a fallen leaf between her fingers. Her golden hair was cropped in a blunt line just below her jaw—the distinctive hairstyle of a Pledged.

"I can't believe the ceremony's coming up so fast," she said, and Erinda could recall with perfect clarity the melancholy in her tone.

"What's the matter?" she heard herself ask. "I thought you couldn't wait to take your vows. You've wanted to be a priestess your entire life."

"Yes, but..." Kade flipped over, settling her head on Erinda's lap. Her face was pale, her eyes large and serious. "After the ceremony, I won't see you anymore, Rin."

No one else in the world called her that. In another two moons, no one would ever call her that again. The knowledge sat like rocks in her stomach, but for Kade's sake, she couldn't let it show. "Sure you will. I'll be in temple for prayers all the time."

"You hate temple prayers."

"Not when you're there." Kade's hair drifted like corn silk between Erinda's fingers. "In fact, I'm pretty sure that I'll be praying twice as often once it's the only—" *The only way I'll ever get to see you.* Her throat closed around the words.

Their separation was inevitable, but as children their eighteenth birthdays had seemed a comfortable eternity away. According to tradition, families sent their firstborn sons into military service, and firstborn daughters into the service of the Goddess. Erinda's older sister had taken vows eight winters ago, and in spite of her reassurances to Kade, she knew how rare it was to even catch a glimpse of her sister now. The priestesses' shaved heads and filmy veils made them difficult to tell apart. Half the time she wasn't even certain she recognized her sister's face anymore.

The rocks in her gut tumbled around each other, and she swallowed a wave of nausea. How was she going to live with this? Kade was biting her lip, watching her, tears glittering along her lower lashes. The sight of them grounded her at once. She had to be more careful—Kade could read her too easily.

She swept the pad of her thumb under Kade's eyes. "Hey, stop that. At least my mother will be pleased. She's constantly badgering me to spend more time at the temple."

"Well, you *are* practically a heathen."

Oh, thank the Goddess. Teasing was something she could work with. She feigned a gasp. "I am not! Take that back."

"Can't. The Pledged are unable to lie." Kade squeaked as Erinda's deft fingers found the ticklish spot on her ribs.

"Take it back."

Kade hopped up from Erinda's lap, grinning and poised to run. "No way."

The elaborate palace gardens had always made for a fine game of chase. Such childish antics might be undignified for young women their age, but right now it was comforting to forget that the lonely world of adulthood was looming so close. For a few minutes they could be seven winters old again, happy and silly, free of painful grownup concerns. Kade's laughter rang in her ears, leading her around trees and under bushes and over the smooth stone pathways that looped through the flowerbeds, until Erinda finally caught the back of her robe and they both tumbled to the grass.

She pinned Kade beneath her, trapping her wrists together with one hand and securing them over Kade's head. With the other hand, she threatened the ticklish spot again. Kade struggled, giggling, but they both knew she had lost. Erinda was younger and shorter, but she had always been stronger.

"Take it back," she said.

Kade's chest heaved as she tried to catch her breath. "Whatever you say." She squealed again as Erinda's fingertips skimmed her ribs. "All right, all right! You're so mean."

Erinda relaxed her hand, feeling the delicate bones of Kade's ribcage curve beneath her palm, too close to the skin. After more than a decade of friendship, this fragility was something she probably ought to be used to, but every now and then it still managed to take her by surprise. She squeezed with her fingers, just a little bit. "Ah, but you love me anyway."

Ugh. The cheeky quip was underscored by an inflection that sounded plaintive, even to her own ears. What was she doing? This was madness.

The expression on Kade's face shifted. One moment her mock-pout was buoyant and playful; then she was gazing at Erinda so intently that Erinda felt the air hitch in her lungs. Kade's eyes were set just a little too close together, her nose slightly too pointed, her chin a bit too narrow for most people to consider her pretty. But the sharpness of her features had always reminded Erinda of a hawk, or maybe a fox. Sleek. Intelligent. Elegant. She found herself possessed by the need to memorize this face, before it was gone forever. Greedily, she drank in the sight of her: the faintly freckled skin, the perfectly arched eyebrows, the tiny mole just below her left eye.

Beneath her, Kade's heart was thudding. Erinda could see the pulse in her throat. Her hair was spread in the grass, a halo of gold and green, and she held Erinda's eyes without seeming to breathe. Something inside Erinda quivered and warmed, weighing her down over Kade's body as if she could melt them both into the ground. As if she might be able to keep her from leaving, if only she could wish it hard enough. Kade was staring at her with such uneasiness, like she was struggling to work out the answer to a hopeless riddle. Transfixed, she felt her grip on Kade's wrists go slack. Kade didn't try to move away, but one of her hands freed itself and threaded into Erinda's hair.

She brought Erinda's face close, until her breath fanned softly against her lips. "Of course I do."

But when Erinda leaned down toward her, Kade's other hand pressed her chest, stopping her descent. She wasn't pushing her away, but for a long moment she held Erinda's face a fingerwidth from hers, one hand trembling in her hair, the other splayed against her breastbone. Such deep sadness filled her eyes, warring with another darker emotion that Erinda couldn't identify.

Gently, Kade released her hair and maneuvered out from under her. "Afternoon meditation will begin soon. I have to go."

The words filled Erinda with inexplicable dread. "Kade, wait." But Kade was already walking away, into a cloud of mist that was curling through the hedges. Erinda leapt to her feet and followed, anxiety increasing with every step.

"Wait, please!" The mist swirled into the space between them, wrapping around Kade's silhouette, obscuring her from view. Erinda broke into a run. "No!"

The fog was so thick that it was like trying to run through water. Her legs strained in vain to keep up. Kade got farther and farther away, until all Erinda could see was the contrast of her pale hair against the deepening gray.

Then, even that was gone. There was nothing but the mist, cold and empty. It enveloped her, wisping into her throat, cutting off her breath. She tried to shout for Kade again, but the words never left her lips—or if they did, they were swallowed by the silence. She could feel herself dissipating, thoughts and emotions dulling around the edges. Soon she, too, would disappear.

The hazy light was fading. She wheezed for air that was no longer there, reaching blindly into the empty void, trying to remember what it was she was even chasing. Her fingertips, then her hands, then her wrists vanished in front of her eyes.

"Erinda?"

A voice pierced the dark, drawing her up through the shadows until her head broke the surface. With an enormous, painful gasp, Erinda's lungs filled, and her eyes opened. Shasta was standing over her, worry creasing her forehead.

"Goddess, Erinda, are you all right? What's the matter?"

Dazed, Erinda shook her head. "I'm sorry, Your Majesty. I must have fallen asleep. I didn't wake the baby, did I?"

Shasta scooped the sleeping Princess into her arms. "No, no, she's fine." But she eyed Erinda with concern. "Are you?"

Her heart was pounding so hard that she felt dizzy, and her mouth was dry, but Erinda summoned a sheepish smile. "I'm all right. Just a nightmare." When Shasta didn't seem reassured, she elaborated. "You know, lots of hairy, stinking men with huge bloody axes. The usual."

At that, Shasta's expression turned sympathetic. "I think we're all still having those." Just about everyone in the royal court shared a residual terror of the barbarian army that had overrun the palace six moons earlier.

Erinda didn't like misleading her, but she couldn't bear to share the truth either. Kade was a personal grief. There was nothing Shasta could do, so there was no point bringing her into it. Besides, she'd brought the nightmare on herself with all that foolish reminiscing. Erinda stood with an exaggerated stretch.

"The Princess will be in your room for the night, Majesty?"

"Of course. You should go get some rest."

Erinda curtsied and took a candle from the nearby table as she left the nursery. The palace chambermaids shared a dormitory just down the hall from the Queen's childhood bedchamber, which the little Princess would likely inherit once she'd outgrown the nursery. When Erinda's mother had taken sick last winter, Erinda had been promoted to head of household. As such, she was allowed her own small room, located just behind the larger one shared by the six other maids assigned to the royal chambers. Erinda nodded politely to Alva, the youngest of her staff, who was climbing into her bunk above Hali's. Alva gave her a smile as she settled under her blankets. Erinda couldn't quite muster one in return, and hastened past to her own quarters.

She drew the thick curtain behind her, set the candle on the chest at the foot of her cot, and mechanically went through the motions of preparing for sleep. She kicked off her shoes and stripped out of her apron, split skirts, laced bodice, and chemise, hanging them from pegs on the wall. Though it was the middle of spring, the palace was chilly in the evenings, and she shrugged into a woolen night shift. A basin of water sat on a table under the narrow window, and she splashed her cheeks and neck, drying them with a towel. She left her hair plaited so the wild curls would not tangle themselves into a hopeless snarl during the night. In the morning, she would comb them out and re-braid them for the day's work.

After snuffing the candle, Erinda climbed into bed and pulled the quilts to her chin. Then she closed her eyes and sighed as the first fat drop of moisture escaped her eyelids. There would be many more before she could sleep…if she could sleep at all tonight. The searing tears and miserable ache in her chest were her penance for being so foolish. She accepted them, allowed them to consume her, her body racked with sobs muffled into the pillow beneath her.

Kade was gone. She'd left seven winters ago, when she'd vowed to the Goddess that she would serve the temple for the rest of her life. Erinda had realized, too late, that she was hopelessly in love with someone she would never be allowed to keep. And just as that realization dawned, Kade's departure had torn a gaping hole in her life.

In seven winters, the emptiness had never filled. The raw edges had never quite healed. Yet gradually, the suffering became endurable. The paralyzing despair was pushed back, a little at a time, as she learned to censor her thoughts. She locked away every memory of Kade in the deepest part of her mind and severely refused herself access to them. It was the one thing that worked.

For a time, existence had been manageable. She filled her days with work, friends, and, whenever possible, with the distraction of clandestine lovers. Things were going all right until Talon came along; courageous, gallant Talon with all her carefully guarded secrets, and an impossible love of her own. Erinda found herself breaking her own rules, sharing memories she'd sworn never to bring up again, in her desire to help her friends find the happiness that had eluded her in her own life.

Then, last spring, Kade had appeared on a cabinetmaker's doorstep in the middle of the night. She'd been sent by the Goddess to rescue Princess Shasta from a terrible palace massacre. For two long days, Erinda found herself in unbearable vicinity to the woman who'd broken her heart. Sitting opposite her in the carriage, Kade's vulpine brows and vivid green eyes were recognizable as ever above her priestess's veils. Erinda couldn't stop herself from staring. A thousand things she wanted to say welled up at once, each one choked back by all the others. Yet Kade would not look at her, would not speak so much as a word. Not even after Erinda tracked her down in the Great Temple, and—

She stifled another cry into her pillow. Everything had gotten so much worse after that. Exiled memories and hollow agony plagued her every day, and it was so much harder to rein them in. But she had to. Somehow, she had to, because Kade was never coming back.

CHAPTER TWO

"Mother Qiturah, I don't understand." Kade gaped at the Honored Mother in consternation. "There hasn't been a *shaa'din* since the Twelve."

Qiturah's long golden earrings tinkled as she nodded. "I am aware of that."

"And there are thousands of priestesses in Ithyria now."

"Yes, there are." Not a hint of annoyance tinged the Honored Mother's voice, though of course she knew all of this already. She seemed to be allowing Kade the chance to process her shocking announcement.

"With so many Daughters in Her service, why would Ithyris require another Handmaiden?" A thousand winters ago, there had been only twelve young women standing between Ithyris and Her wicked brother Ulrike, God of the Flesh. But now, surely so many priestesses, armed with the Goddess's celestial fire, were sufficient to protect the kingdom.

"She did not tell me, *Ostryn*. But I am certain you will get the chance to ask Her yourself very soon."

"Your Honor, there has to be some mistake. The Goddess could not have chosen me." After all, she didn't meet one of the most important requirements. The thought brought a flush to her cheeks, and she hoped the Honored Mother would not be able to see the heightened color beneath her veils.

"Oh, She was quite clear. Ithyris specifically requested 'My Daughter with the viridian eyes.' And then She called you by name. No, *Ostryn* Kadrian, there has been no mistake."

"But that's impossible." Kade felt her face getting hotter as panic built. Ithyris knew all, of course. All her guiltiest secrets. She had sworn to spend the rest of her life atoning for her failures, but in her heart she knew that was not enough. Ithyris didn't seem to think so, either. Was this yet another test of her loyalty?

Any other priestess would be overjoyed beyond words to be told they'd been selected by the Goddess for such an elite calling. It was a fantasy, a fairy tale. This kind of thing didn't happen anymore. And instead of demonstrating the appropriate awe and gratitude, she just felt fearful and embarrassed. How could she possibly look the Honored Mother in the eye and explain the truth? The humiliation would be too much to bear.

But then she realized that was probably the point. After how she'd betrayed Ithyris, how wantonly her traitorous heart had failed Her even after so many winters in Her service, she deserved much worse than this. Kade inhaled and closed her eyes. *If this is what You ask of me, Divine Lady, I will obey. I swear I am Yours alone, now and forever.*

"Your Honor, I'm certain that the Goddess does not mean to make me *shaa'din*."

The Honored Mother raised her eyebrows. Kade's entire face was burning. "A person must have certain attributes to become the Goddess's Handmaiden." She'd hoped maybe Qiturah would catch on, but her expression did not change. Kade shuddered as she forced the words out. "That is…Everyone knows that…. Well, the chronicles say that only virgins can be *shaa'din*."

To Qiturah's credit, she didn't so much as twitch an eyelash. But the silence that fell through the study filled Kade with shame. Only through sheer force of will was she able to keep her head up, keep her eyes on the Honored Mother as she considered this statement. The effort made Kade's knees tremble. What would happen now? Qiturah was sure to demand details. Maybe she would even conduct an investigation. Technically, Kade hadn't broken her vows, but that didn't mean that such an inquiry might not result in her excommunication once the whole truth came out. That kind of disgrace was not something Kade would be able to live with.

After what seemed like a quiet eternity, Qiturah laid a hand on the sheaf of paper on her desk. "Do you know what this is, *Ostryn*?"

Kade shook her head miserably, and Qiturah smiled. "This is the Book of Verdred. These are the records penned by Ithyris's very first scribe, Verdred of the Twelve." She traced the neat lines of script with her fingertips.

Kade stared at the sheets of parchment with wide eyes, wondering if Verdred had outlined a procedure for dealing with priestesses whose virtue had been compromised.

Qiturah chuckled, probably mistaking her terror for awe. "Oh, this isn't the original, of course. That's contained in the Ithyrian Treasury, and I doubt even I would be granted access to it. No, this is just a transcription, but it's one of the oldest copies still in existence. I've been poring over it all night in the hope it might guide us through the ceremony required to fulfill the Goddess's command." Qiturah shuffled the sheets until she found the passage she was looking for. It was written in the ancient Ithyrian tongue, of course, but the Honored Mother translated aloud as she read.

"And it came to pass that Ithyris, Divine Goddess of Spirit, chose Twelve from among the daughters of Man—girls of pure heart, untouched by men—to become vessels for Her power. These Twelve were called holy warriors, Handmaidens of the Goddess, and through them Ithyris would manifest Herself within the world of Man."

Qiturah tapped a spot on the page with her finger. "*Bakaryt'dulanu rynzarti da*. Literally, 'bodies of men touched them not.' The use of the male-gendered *bakaryt* is particularly interesting when one considers the previous phrase, *Bak'ostryn*, which we translate to 'daughters of Man,' though the root word *Bak* is not gender specific, and refers to our race as a whole." She must have read the confusion on Kade's face, because she laughed.

"Yes, I know, linguistic intricacies are not as interesting to everyone else as they are to me. The point is, today our translations tend to simplify much of the complexity of the original text. In our modern scripture that first phrase is usually reduced to a single word, 'virgin.'" A knowing light entered her eyes that Kade found unsettling. "Perhaps, however, that is too narrow a summarization."

Kade frowned. She enjoyed studying, but this was over her head.

Qiturah leaned forward and asked patiently, "Child…was it a man?"

Several moments passed before she realized what Qiturah was asking, realized what she must have guessed. She never would have expected the Honored Mother of Verdred, of all people, to have knowledge of such things. At a loss for words, all she could do was shake her head.

Qiturah sat back in her chair. "Ah, I thought not." Though her face was obscured by her veils, Kade was stunned at the smile lines that appeared around her eyes. "Well, *Ostryn*, it appears that you aren't disqualified after all. Ithyris doesn't seem to think so, and Her opinion's the only one that truly counts."

Her astonishment grew as it became apparent that not only was Qiturah unfazed by her mortifying admission of impurity, she didn't even seem shocked by the unusual nature of her indiscretion. Questions buzzed so frantically in her head that she could barely untangle them enough to say anything at all. "Mother Qiturah, isn't it…I mean, aren't you going to…?"

"Aren't I going to punish you?" The smile lines were replaced by a look of sympathy. "No, Kadrian. Something tells me you're doing a fine job of that all on your own."

In the distance came the sound of the temple bell, and Qiturah rose to her feet. "Thank you for meeting with me so early. I wanted to tell you privately, before I shared the news with the rest of the temple this morning. There is so much preparation to be done, and I fear we have little time."

Dismay filled her as she realized that in just a few minutes, every priestess in the temple would learn of her calling to become *shaa'din*. The response would be dreadful. Stares of envy and disbelief, whispered conjecture as she passed in the halls…how was she going to endure all the eyes watching her, all the questions she was sure to face? She hadn't even processed the strangeness of it all herself.

Perhaps Qiturah understood, because she said, "I think you shall be excused from group prayer this morning, child. A period of solitary meditation seems more in order, given what's about to occur for you."

Grateful, Kade bowed. "Thank you, Your Honor." The bell continued to toll overhead, and Qiturah had just enough time to lay a reassuring hand on her shoulder before hurrying from the study to lead the morning prayer service.

Kade headed down the hall in the opposite direction, relieved she wouldn't have to be there when the announcement was made. She didn't know how she would have managed it, standing there trying to look…well, how was she supposed to look? Embarrassed? Delighted? Graciously humble? Every facial expression, every word she spoke, every person whose eyes she met—and anyone's she didn't—every bit of her reaction would be analyzed down to the most minute detail. Every priestess in the temple would be wondering why Kade had been chosen when she herself had not, wondering what made Kade most worthy in the Goddess's eyes. They would all want to know what this meant, the calling of the first *shaa'din* in a thousand winters. They'd have so many questions, none of which she had the answer to.

She reached her room. A beaded curtain draped the doorway, and it clattered back into place behind her. From down the hall she could hear the soft patter of feet on the stone floor; someone was running late to prayers. Kade sat on her cot and closed her eyes.

The Goddess Ithyris wanted her—shy, reclusive, overly-emotional, far too attached to her former life even after seven winters in Her service—to become a vessel for Her power. *Why?* It was the one question that drowned out all the others in her head. *Why me?* She could list fifty women in Verdred Temple alone who were much better candidates. Every one of the Twelve had been powerful, charismatic, a great leader. She was none of those things. What was Ithyris expecting from her?

Qiturah had said she'd be able to ask the Goddess herself soon enough. What would that be like? Up to now, her personal experience of Ithyris had been limited to the loving, blissful spirit that surrounded her during prayers and meditation. Ithyris's aura, in and of itself, was breathtaking. But the chronicles said the Twelve had direct communication with Her. They regularly heard Her voice, even saw Her with their own eyes. Few priestesses were lucky enough to experience such direct contact today, and those occurrences were few and far between. Qiturah was the one person Kade knew of who had heard the Goddess speak more than once. She could not imagine seeing Her face, hearing Her voice for herself. She also knew she wasn't worthy of it.

The Twelve were said to have had extraordinary abilities, channeled by Ithyris through their bodies. The legends described everything from hearing others' thoughts and influencing their emotions, to transforming dust into drinking water and making themselves invisible. How many of the tales were true and how many were exaggeration handed down through generations, no one really knew anymore. But the Twelve's abilities were related to the safety of Ithyris's people and lands. Kade wondered what that might mean now, what it would be like to feel Ithyris's power inside her, accomplishing impossible things according to Her will.

She could imagine nothing more glorious than to feel Ithyris within her so intimately, flowing through her with more life-giving sustenance than her own heart's blood. All Daughters of Ithyris shared the same passion to give themselves to the Goddess, to be one with Her spirit. This insatiable longing, which Kade had felt since childhood, was what had drawn her into the Goddess's service even when it felt like every other part of her would die when she took her vows. She had made the sacrifice because this was where she was meant to be, here in Ithyris's arms.

Yet that certainty hadn't been able to quench the other more selfish cravings of her heart. She had been unfaithful. She had given a piece of herself to another mortal, when all of her should have been reserved for the Goddess alone. Now, try as she might, Kade could not take that piece of herself back. If she was being honest with herself, part of her didn't really want to. Would that even matter anymore, once Ithyris made her *shaa'din*? Was this an answer to her prayers, or was the Goddess just laying claim to that final, tiny part of Kade that rebelled?

She dropped a prayer cushion onto the floor and lowered her knees onto it. Disjointed thoughts tumbled in her head like trapped butterflies. She had been so sure that the consequences of her confession to Qiturah were to be her punishment for betraying Ithyris. It hadn't turned out like she'd feared, but that didn't mean her guilt was absolved. The Honored Mother might be satisfied simply because the Goddess had named Kade *shaa'din*, but Ithyris had to have some other intent. This must be some sort of trial or test, perhaps even retribution for Kade's egregious transgressions last spring.

She winced, remembering how the cabinetmaker in Ardrenn had opened his door and suddenly her greatest temptation was staring her in the face—the same pouting lips, wide gray eyes, and mousy brown braids that she remembered from childhood. But Erinda's cheekbones were more prominent now, her features mature and defined, and her plump, girlish figure had developed into lush curves. The shock of Erinda's presence had been savage, like being kicked in the stomach. It wasn't just bewilderment at seeing her after so long. It was the way her blood heated in an instant, the way she had to use every ounce of self-control she had to stop herself from taking Erinda in her arms and burying her face in those soft curls as if they hadn't even been apart for a day, much less six winters.

That moment had been the Goddess's way of showing her just how empty all her prayers for forgiveness and promises of eternal faithfulness were. Oh, she'd managed to sit silently throughout the torturous, two-day carriage ride to Verdred, as they whisked the Ithyrian Princess from the city. She'd kept her eyes averted from Erinda's, endured being stared at while Erinda's sadness radiated into the space between them, until it felt like she would suffocate with guilt. She had succeeded in remaining firmly seated on her side of the coach, even when every muscle in her body shook with the effort it took.

But her heart had betrayed Her, nonetheless. While Erinda and the Princess slept, her eyes lingered helplessly on Erinda's mouth until her own lips were tingling with longing. Every weary line etched into the pretty face pierced her with remorse. She knew Erinda too well, could see right past the cheerful façade that she knew was for the Princess's benefit. Clearly, she wasn't the only one for whom six winters hadn't made a bit of difference.

Since they were children, Erinda had always been the kind of person who needed companionship and affection, needed them the way other people need food and water. All this time, Kade had consoled herself with the certainty that her beloved had moved on to someone else, someone who was giving her everything Kade could not. Instead, what she saw now was a mask that Erinda kept wrapped around her like armor. She realized that Erinda had not been happy in a very long time, and that discovery led her into anger.

It was one thing for the Goddess to put Kade's resolve to the test, even to discipline her unfaithfulness. Kade had vowed complete submission to Her will. But Erinda had made no such vows. Ithyris had no right to punish her as well.

Such blasphemous thoughts preoccupied her after they reached the Great Temple. Kade did her best to avoid Erinda whenever possible, but there were still times when they passed in the halls, or when the sound of her voice from within the Princess's chambers made Kade halt outside the curtained entrance, straining to hear her again. Every encounter, no matter how small, fueled her furious inner fire. No one else seemed to notice the shadows haunting Erinda's eyes, the calculated lilt in her tone, the forced effort of her laughter. But Kade saw it all, and her anger grew.

Then, one night, she was alone in the temple kitchen scrubbing dishes when Erinda's voice came unexpectedly behind her.

"Need a hand?"

Kade turned to see Erinda's hesitant smile, one that revealed just a hint of the dimple that hid at the corner of her mouth. She swallowed hard. That smile—she hadn't seen it in so long, and it still had the power to disarm her. She moved aside so Erinda could join her over the tubs of soapy water.

For several minutes, they washed dishes side by side, scrubbing the plates and rinsing them before stacking them in a rack to drain. It was a poignantly familiar scenario. How many times had she helped Erinda in the palace kitchens just like this when they were children? She was too conscious of Erinda's presence beside her, the space between them fizzing with the relentless magnetism that had always drawn them to one other. From this proximity, she could feel sorrow and uncertainty pulsing from Erinda in waves. It made her chest ache.

Erinda reached around to fetch the towel hanging from a hook on the table. Her hand came to rest on Kade's hip, and Kade froze. Erinda was on tiptoe, her lips close to Kade's ear. "I miss you."

The confession was so small and broken, so vulnerable, that she felt her stomach turn over in agony. It was her fault Erinda was in so much pain. She must have looked alarmed, because Erinda lifted a hand to her veiled face. "Shh. It's all right."

She flinched as Erinda's fingers brushed her cheek. Erinda quickly withdrew, but Kade reached out and caught her hand. She closed her eyes, struggling for the right thing to say. *Rin, I've never stopped loving you...I think of you every day...* Or even just a simple *I miss you, too.* Surely that would be permissible? But nothing she said was going to take Erinda's pain away, and letting herself admit any of this out loud would just lead her even further from the Goddess than she was already.

Erinda was unpinning one side of the gauzy material that covered Kade's nose and mouth. Her eyes held Kade's anxiously as she drew the veil away, her lips a delicate, dark flush of color. Kade could read the longing in her gaze, and knew exactly what she wanted. Stunned, her legs shook beneath her, though with anticipation or terror she couldn't tell. The blood rang in her ears. Common sense demanded that she put a stop to this, but she didn't move. She didn't protest or struggle as Erinda again rose on tiptoe and kissed her.

She'd forgotten, after so long, just how exquisitely soft Erinda's mouth was. Her memory did no justice to the taste of her kiss, the incredible sensation of her warmth pressed so close. Her lips were full, hot, and satiny as flower petals, and she felt them close around her lower lip with a faint brush of teeth. This felt like coming home to a place she'd never expected to see again. Her stomach dropped and she felt the walls of the kitchen spinning nonsensically around them. How had she lived without this?

Without thinking, Kade let desire overwhelm her, let Erinda's raw need consume them both. She moved her hands up Erinda's sides until her palms brushed the tender curves of her breasts, leaned into her as much as she dared. Moisture dampened Kade's cheeks, but the tears weren't hers. Kade felt her heart constrict so tightly in her chest that she almost whimpered. Erinda didn't cry! Erinda never cried.

Oh Goddess, Rin, what have I done to you?

How long had Erinda lived with this kind of pain? Their physical contact allowed her to feel for herself the incredible depth of Erinda's grief, and her rage flared again. The cruelest part was yet to come, because she knew what she had to do, and it was so much worse than when she'd had to walk away the first time. She pushed Erinda back, her roiling emotions making the action rougher than she meant it to be, and covered her face again with the veil. This wasn't fair. Why should her commitment to the Goddess require her to rip an innocent heart to pieces? Was Ithyris truly that jealous of Her Daughters' affections, that She would condemn Erinda to such suffering just for daring to love one of Her priestesses?

Kade panted softly as an excruciating play of anguish and shame crossed Erinda's tear-streaked features. She watched in horror as flickers of that carefully fabricated nonchalance appeared and then disappeared, as if Erinda was fighting desperately to pull her armor back in place again. But she lost the battle. More tears slid down her cheeks, and Erinda spun around and fled the kitchens altogether.

Kade turned back to the tubs of dishwater and let her own eyes spill over uncontrollably.

Those tears were back again now, hot and dripping down her cheeks as she knelt by her cot and rocked back and forth, chanting. The whole thing had been her fault. If she had kept her focus on the Goddess, where it belonged, she'd have been able to handle it so much better. She might have been able to talk with Erinda, to give them both some comfort and closure. She could have encouraged Erinda to move on with dignity and compassion, instead of tearing her heart wide open again. All the misery Erinda had been through, everything she was undoubtedly still going through now, that was all on Kade's head, because Kade hadn't been willing to let go herself, first.

Please, Divine Lady, don't let her suffer any further on my account. I will do anything You ask. I will gladly be Your Handmaiden. I will follow wherever You lead to the end of my days. Anything You wish of me is Yours for the taking. But please, Sweet Ithyris, give Rin peace. Let her find happiness. Please.

Kade didn't know if she was even permitted to make such a request. After all, it was Erinda who pulled her attention and loyalty away from the Goddess to begin with. But right now, she didn't care. Her life belonged to Ithyris, and she would obey Her until her last breath. There was no reason for Erinda to pay the price for her shortcomings. She continued to rock her body back and forth, tinkling syllables of the Ithyrian tongue dropping from her lips in hypnotic rhythm.

After a while, she began to feel the Goddess's spirit settling around her. A sensation of calm crept over her frantic mind, soothing her tormented thoughts. The hymn's ancient words of adoration and devotion were a reminder that Ithyris was not bound by the same mortal selfishness that afflicted Her children. Ithyris was never cruel, never jealous, and never did anything without reason. Just because Kade didn't understand Her motivations didn't mean She did not have them, or that they were not absolutely pure. Ithyris valued love above all things, and Kade could feel that truth penetrating the deepest, most broken parts of her being.

And then a musical voice spoke in her ear. Though she'd never heard it before, it was impossible not to recognize.

"*Yi kluri, y'Makluran.*"

"Oh!" She turned her head, instinctively looking for the source of the disembodied words, though she knew she would find no one there. She listened, but the voice did not come again. Once was enough, anyway, as Kade had heard Her the first time. *Trust me, my Beloved.* The Goddess's request, so profound in its simplicity, filled her with grateful exhilaration.

"Oh Lady, I do trust You, I do. Forgive me." She lifted her hands in a gesture that was part worship, part surrender, and with her heart open at last, she was able to give herself over to the Goddess's loving presence.

❖

Dawn had not yet crept onto the moors when Erinda awoke, her throat graveled and eyes stinging. She lay still for a few minutes, trying to steady the erratic pounding of her heart. Remnants of the nightmare still threaded her imagination, though in consciousness she could temper them with some measure of reason. At least this one had not been as bad as most, because this time she had felt Kade's bliss and contentment. Her own loss was still as painful as always, but it was easier to bear when she remembered that Kade was happy.

She sat up and gave a little moan as the throbbing in her head flowered into a storm, surging hard against the insides of her skull. Crying herself to sleep at night always made for an equally miserable morning. But it was not yet light outside, and if she was lucky, she might be able to squeeze in a few minutes of rejuvenation before the rest of the palace began to stir.

She dressed impatiently and slipped through the dormitory of sleeping women into the dark hall, eagerness rendering her impervious to the morning chill. The winding stairs of the eastern turret clicked beneath her heels as she scurried down to the kitchens, past the palace laundry, and finally to the small door that led into the servants' gardens.

This was her favorite exit route because it was usually deserted this time of the morning, and she was pleased not to encounter a single person as she made her escape across the palace grounds to the royal stables.

Kallin, the aged constable, was the only person Erinda knew who got up even earlier than she did. He was already shoveling out one of the stalls when Erinda arrived, and he looked up with a grin when the stable doors swung open.

"Mornin', miss. You thinkin' of a ride?"

Erinda returned the smile and nodded, taking up a pair of leather gloves and tugging them on. "How's Ember today?"

"Troublesome as ever, even after you two went through the paces yesterday. Could do with a hard run if you ask me."

"Just what I was hoping for."

Kallin looked her up and down and pursed his lips. "You feelin' all right yourself?" He always seemed to be able to tell when she'd had a rough night.

"I'll be fine. Sometimes I just really feel like I need to get away from all of this, you know?" She waved a hand in the vague direction of the palace. "Especially lately."

Kallin nodded, and then before Erinda could move, he stepped forward and engulfed her in a hug. She was startled, as the gruff stable hand was not usually so affectionate, but the warm, horsey smell of his tunic and rough stubble of his cheeks were welcome comforts. Erinda had been coming out here to help him with the horses for many winters now, and after so much time together Kallin had come to know her well. She was grateful for his kindness.

"You be takin' care of yourself, miss."

Erinda gave him a squeeze before stepping back. "Thank you, Kallin."

"Time's wastin'. Better get back there before Ember knocks the stall down around him."

Erinda walked to the stallion's pen at the back of the stable. Before she even got close enough to see its occupant, she could hear him stamping impatiently inside.

"Shh, boy," she murmured as she let herself into the stall. Ember was her favorite of the royal horses, a tall, lithe stallion with a gleaming red coat and mane. He was the first horse that Kallin had let her break in all by herself, and in the process they'd grown quite attached to one another. Erinda waited for his velvety nose to bump her gloved hand, seeking the little apple he knew was there. His lips plucked it from her fingers and he crunched into it with satisfaction as Erinda threw a blanket across his back, saddling him and tightening the straps just as he liked. She waited for the horse to finish his treat before slipping the bit between his teeth and securing the bridle around his head.

Then she swung onto his back. He shifted his weight in excitement, and Erinda patted his neck. "Yes, boy, we're going for a little run."

Kallin opened the pen and stepped out of the way as Ember surged forward, already at a trot before they'd even reached the stable doors. Erinda allowed him that, though she kept him restrained from greater speed until they'd reached the palace gates. She waved to the guard on duty, who opened the gates for them. Then she barely had to touch her heels to Ember's flanks before they were flying into the long grass of the moors.

The sky was dark on the western horizon, the moon still visible as it hovered above the tops of the distant mountains. To the east, the clouds were shot through with streaks of pale pink and orange that heralded the rising sun. Erinda leaned over the stallion's neck and let the wind whip his fiery mane into her face. She let him run at his pleasure, and he tore through the moor like a giddy dog after a rabbit. The ground streaked by in a blur.

Erinda closed her eyes and lost herself in the torrent of sensation, the morning air rushing raggedly around her body, the horse's warm, seething ribs under her knees, the soothing vibration as his hooves pounded the grass. Her mind cleared, adrenaline burning off all vestiges of unpleasant thoughts. Out here, she was one with the powerful creature beneath her. There was no loneliness, no sorrow, nothing but the solid earth beneath them, the fresh air surrounding them, and the vast sky overhead.

She directed Ember to veer right, toward the edge of Warin Forest. Just before the tree line, several fallen tree trunks lay in random disarray, and Erinda urged the horse forward. She held tightly as Ember gathered himself for the first jump, and they soared over a log. Just a few paces away lay another, and then another that was bigger. They made several circuits through the maze of jumps, Ember's hooves clearing each obstacle and finding the earth again with thunderous surety. He was sweating now, but kept on jumping. Erinda knew he'd happily keep going until he collapsed, and so after running the course six or seven times, she turned him back toward the castle. They made their way home at a slower rate, both reluctant to end the ride, but Erinda had to get back. The Queen would be awake soon, and she was already running later than usual.

At the palace gate, she waved to the guard again. The guards were accustomed to her coming and going in the early hours of the morning, and the man at the gate let her back in without challenge. Ember returned them to the stable where Kallin was waiting. He took the reins as Erinda leapt down from the stallion's back.

"Looks like you two had a good time of it." He ran a hand over the horse's gleaming coat, slick with sweat. "Well done. That ought to calm him some, at least."

"Kallin, would you mind…?"

He eyed her disheveled braids and windblown cheeks and grinned. "I'll get him cleaned up and cooled down, missy. You'd best be gettin' back to Her Majesty quick. She'll be lookin' for you."

Erinda flashed him a grateful smile, and with one last pat to Ember's glossy red shoulder, she took off running toward the palace kitchens.

CHAPTER THREE

The huge oak doors that led to the Queen's chambers were carved with an elaborate representation of the House of Rane's royal crest. A pair of feathered wings stretched from one door to the other, divided down the center by the blade of a long-sword, and the entire thing was encircled by an ornate coronet bearing four jewels: a huge aquamarine the size of a man's fist at the center, and three smaller rubies dripping beneath it. The jewels of the signet were real gemstones set into the wood, the center aquamarine and ruby in perfect halves that, when the doors were closed, appeared seamless, but split into half-circles when they were opened.

These doors were painstaking re-creations of the originals, which had been destroyed when the Queen's traitorous cousin Kumire had overrun the palace with his hired barbarian army. The replacements were a gift to the Queen from the newly-appointed viceroy of Mondera, the jewels retrieved from the personal treasury of his predecessor. The gift had been made as much out of reconciliation as friendship, for Kumire had been a high-ranking official of the Monderan senate.

Erinda skidded to a stop in front of this grand entrance, and patted her hair and clothes to be sure they were free of any stray wisps of grass. She pulled the heavy doors open and stepped into the royal parlor.

Had Shasta been a conventional Ithyrian Queen, by this time of morning the parlor would have been full of the ladies of court, bedecked in glimmering silks and busying themselves with idle gossip while they waited for Her Majesty to emerge from her bedchamber. But Shasta held the throne without a king, and therefore possessed the sole power and responsibility of the royal house. She had neither time nor desire for frivolous entertainment, so the opulent parlor was quiet and empty.

Or at least, so it seemed at first. A flicker of movement caught Erinda's attention as she crossed the room on her way to the bedchamber. She sighed as she recognized one of her staff seated on the floor in a far corner of the parlor. The young woman had turned the page of a book that was nearly twice the size of her lap, so absorbed in her reading that Erinda's entrance had not disturbed her. A tendril of pale blond hair had escaped her cap to brush the pages of her book, which she also seemed not to notice.

"Panna!" Erinda put as much reprimand as she could into the name. She would need more than two hands to count the number of times she had scolded this particular member of her staff for sneaking books from the Queen's study.

The maid's head remained down, and Erinda grumbled under her breath as she marched toward her. Once Panna began reading, the entire palace might collapse around her ears and she would remain oblivious to anything but the book in her hands. Erinda had to bend over in order to take the book from her. The page drifted upward and Panna's eyes followed, still scanning eagerly back and forth over the text. When Erinda's presence registered, her face flushed with guilt.

Erinda snapped the enormous tome shut and sighed in frustration. "Really, Panna, how many times will we have this conversation? It's about time I send you to the kitchens and let Cook try to manage you."

"Oh, no, Miss, please don't!" Panna cried, springing to her feet. The world of scullery maids was entirely different from that of the royal chambers. Kitchen labor was far more physically demanding, and the luxuries of books were nonexistent there, as most of the kitchen staff could not read.

"I'm sorry, Panna, but this kind of repeated theft cannot be tolerated."

"Oh, but I wasn't stealing it, Miss! I swear to the Goddess, I was going to put it right back."

"It doesn't matter if you put it back, Panna. We've talked about this. Her Majesty's things are not to be disturbed, and you know that." Erinda drummed her fingers on the book's cover. "There are any number of kitchen girls who will be more than happy to trade places with you, and will respect the sanctity of the royal chambers."

Panna hung her head, but Erinda glimpsed the crystalline drops that fell from the tip of her nose to the carpet. Any maid of the royal chambers would find it a terrible fate to be demoted to the kitchens, but Erinda knew it was the loss of her precious books that Panna feared. She felt a flash of remorse. Books were to Panna what the horse stables were to her. More than just an escape, they were the reason for rising in the morning and making it through each day's labors. Wasn't she late for her own duties this very morning, having been caught up in personal diversions? This was the same argument that arose within her every time she confronted Panna with a covertly borrowed book, and was the reason she had yet to administer the discipline that she knew was long overdue.

"Please, Miss, please don't send me down there."

Erinda noted that the plea did not include a promise to refrain from taking more books in the future. Panna was an honest girl, if not a particularly reliable one. "I'm truly sorry, but—"

The bedchamber doors opened, interrupting her. Talon entered the parlor, wearing her scarlet uniform, and shoved the doors closed behind her with a little more force than was necessary. The resulting bang sent Erinda's eyebrows up. Talon's face was drawn, her lips pressed into a tense line, and the realization she was not alone in the parlor seemed to startle her.

Erinda dropped into a curtsy, and Panna followed suit beside her. "Good morning, Captain Talon."

Panna's tear-streaked cheeks seemed to distract Talon from whatever was bothering her, because she looked from Erinda to Panna and asked, "Something the matter?"

Talon the Marvel, forever coming to the rescue of a damsel in distress. Erinda held back the remark, knowing it was inappropriate given their current audience. "Nothing to concern yourself with, Captain."

Unsatisfied, Talon turned to Panna. "Panna?"

Panna raised her head only enough to catch a glimpse of Erinda's face, but then she seemed to muster a burst of courage. She straightened to look Talon in the eye. "Please, sir, I was only reading one of the books from Her Majesty's study—just borrowing it. I swear I was going to return it straightaway." She dropped to her knees, bowing until her forehead touched the carpet. If it had been anyone else, the pose would have been ridiculously overdramatic, but Panna's heartfelt plea was genuine, if somewhat theatrical. "Please don't let them send me to the kitchens, sir."

Talon and Erinda exchanged glances, Talon chewing the inside of her lower lip as if trying not to laugh. She reached out for the book in question, which Erinda handed over silently, and read the spine. "*Born of Land and Sky: A Study of the Outlander People.* Are you interested in the Outlanders, Panna?"

"I'm interested in everything, sir," came the muffled reply.

The fact that Talon was of Outlander descent was not lost on Erinda, and mentally she had to congratulate Panna's cleverness. She must have guessed Talon would be sympathetic to her cause. Talon did appear intrigued, and she turned to Erinda. "Are the kitchens really necessary?"

"I'm afraid this isn't the first time a book from the Queen's study has been borrowed, so to speak, Captain, in spite of many admonitions that Her Majesty's personal effects are not subject to the pleasure of her servants."

Talon nodded, looking thoughtful. "And there are many items in the Queen's study of a private and highly confidential nature, which are meant for Her Majesty's eyes only. This, however"—she held up the book—"happens to be from my own collection." She bent and held it out to Panna. "A gift."

Wide-eyed, Panna reached for it, but Talon held it firmly for a moment longer and added, "With your promise never to enter the Queen's study again, from this day forward."

Panna's fingers froze. "Sir…"

"You know of the palace libraries?" At Panna's nod, Talon said, "They are reserved for members of court, but I shall speak with the head of the archives on your behalf. There should be more than enough reading material there to satisfy your appetite."

The joy that filled Panna's face was contagious, and Erinda struggled to subdue her own smile as Talon turned to her.

"Now, as for the other matter, I'm afraid I have no authority to choose who serves the royal chambers. That decision rests with Erinda, as head of Her Majesty's household." Her dark eyes twinkled, and Erinda understood the silent message. Talon was deferring final judgment to her, though she was certainly casting an unspoken vote in Panna's favor.

Erinda focused sternly on Panna, who was clutching the precious book to her chest. Clearly, even the prospect of being sent to the kitchens could not dim the excitement of gaining access to the palace's famed archive of literature, but she still made an admirable effort to compose her face as she awaited the verdict.

"If you enter the Queen's study again for any reason, it will not be to the kitchens with you, but to the streets. You shall be banned from palace service permanently, Panna. Is that understood?"

"My word, Miss, I won't go in there ever again."

Erinda pretended to deliberate a moment more before saying, "Very well. You are dismissed. Take that thing to the dormitory and be quick about it, for Her Majesty's breakfast is likely to get cold before you've fetched it."

Panna rose from her knees and bobbed up and down rather awkwardly, the heavy book in her arms skewing her balance. She turned and dashed out the enormous, signet-carved doors, only to reappear a moment later.

"Thank you, Captain, thank you so much!" Another crooked curtsy, and then they could hear the skittering of her slippers against the stone floor of the hall.

"You indulge them," Erinda said with a little shake of the head. She didn't need to explain what she meant by 'them." Talon was overly benevolent and generous with every one of the servants, even the simple-minded old man who scrubbed the palace chamber pots each day.

"It wasn't so long ago that I was one of them," Talon reminded her gently. "I haven't forgotten. And besides, so few even have the desire to learn to read, much less a hunger for knowledge so powerful that they would risk demotion to the kitchens for the chance to peek at a book."

"She's not bad looking, either," Erinda had to tease.

A slow grin crept over Talon's face. "No, she's not." But then she turned sharp eyes on Erinda and changed the subject. "What I want to know is what's been going on with you. Every day you're looking thinner and more pale."

"Why, Captain, you certainly know how to flatter a girl."

Talon would not be drawn into flirtatious banter. "I'm serious. I'm worried about you."

If she didn't hang on to the coy pretense, she might very well break down into sobs right there in the Queen's parlor. Erinda kept the smile painted to her cheeks. "Really, Captain, there's no need. It's just that too much solitude isn't good for a person, you know? There hasn't been anyone for me since, well…you." She threw in an airy wink for good measure. "And as you're now spoken for, I've had an awful time finding an adequate replacement."

Talon's perceptive gifts far outmatched the Queen's, and she did not appear in any way convinced, but she was too well-mannered to press the issue further. Instead, she took Erinda's hand and pressed it to her lips. "You've always been there for me when I needed an ear, Erinda. If you ever need to talk…"

The warmth of that touch was almost enough to melt her resolve. At that moment, she wanted nothing more than to collapse into Talon's arms, to feel the solid presence of another person holding her up so that she didn't have to keep fighting alone to remain on her feet. But

Talon belonged to someone else now, and it wouldn't be right to use her that way. Anyway, it wasn't Talon that she truly wanted, and not even Talon with all her damsel-rescuing prowess could save her from this pit of unhappiness. So she willed lightness into her voice as she finished Talon's sentence for her. "…I know where to find you, Captain. Thank you." That was the best she could do, and thankfully, it seemed to be enough. Talon gave her another nod, then left the room.

Erinda took a shaky breath. What she'd said to deflect Talon hadn't been entirely untrue. She found her emotional stability slipping the longer she went without intimate companionship. Maybe it was time to begin searching in earnest for a new lover. A bored countess, perhaps, or one of the more adventurous servant girls. For the briefest instant, she tried to imagine the bashful Panna's likely response to such advances, and nearly laughed aloud. Still, the idea had possibilities. She especially enjoyed a challenge, and Panna *was* very much her type. Shy, quiet, blond…

Before that thought could carry her further down its inevitable path, Erinda forced herself to rap at the Queen's bedchamber doors, then pulled them open. "Morning, Your Majesty!"

She stopped short at the sight of Shasta, still sitting in bed, her head resting on her knees and her long golden brown hair draped down the coverlet. "What's wrong?" she asked, sitting next to her on the edge of the massive mattress. Formal decorum was strictly observed when serving Shasta, Queen of Ithyria, but in such moments of despondence, Shasta was just a dear friend in need of consolation.

"Talon," came the muffled, miserable reply.

Erinda recalled the way Talon had nearly slammed the doors in exiting the bedchamber. "Tell me," she said.

"I think she's going to leave me."

"What? That's absurd. Trust me, Your Majesty, Talon is going to worship you with every breath in her body 'til the day she dies." If there was one thing she was certain of, it was the truth of that statement.

But Shasta only flopped over on her side, grabbed a nearby pillow, and covered her face with it. "I'm not so sure anymore."

"Now stop that." She tugged the pillow away. "Just tell me what happened."

"I don't know what happened," Shasta replied with an edge of frustration in her voice. "Nurse came to fetch Brita for her morning feeding. Of course I slept right through it, but Talon was up after that, so she woke me up like she usually does, you know, and it was really nice at first…"

Erinda grinned. "Oh, I'll just bet it was."

Shasta pushed her away playfully, her cheeks flushing. "Hush."

"No, no, I'm listening. So Talon treated you to a lovely morning of carnal delights, and then what? She announced she was leaving you?"

Shasta's blush deepened, but she shook her head. "Not like that, no. But we were lying there, you know, after…and I was telling her how happy I am, how nothing in the whole world is as important to me as she and the baby are now. I was just chattering on about how it doesn't matter what the viceroys think because she and Brita are my family and I won't let anyone divide us. And then Talon said…" Shasta furrowed her brow. "She said maybe I should start listening to the viceroys."

"Did she say why?"

"She thinks we might be putting Brita in danger, because so many of them don't like her and might even see her as a threat to the kingdom. I told her that we could assign Brita a bodyguard, you know, like Talon was for me." Shasta took a breath, her temper clearly building again. "And then she said that I'd better be sure of all my options first, and that maybe it would be best for both me and Brita if she were to leave, so I could find a husband and give the viceroys the heir they want."

Now that sounded like the Talon Erinda knew: self-sacrificial to a fault and utterly attentive to Shasta's interests, whether or not they lined up with her own. But Erinda didn't dare interject because Shasta's fury was in full bloom.

"Can you believe her? As if I could ever, ever be with anybody else! There's no one for me but her. She knows that. Or at least she ought to! I could just never…I mean, could you? Can you *imagine* going to bed with a person while you're completely in love with someone else? Ugh!"

Erinda quirked a smile. A few minutes ago she had been considering that very prospect. Shasta was also quite aware that for a time, Erinda and Talon had engaged in such a relationship. Apparently, Shasta had just recalled that fact, too, because her eyes widened with horror and her hand flew over her mouth.

"Oh, Erinda, I'm sorry. Of course I didn't mean…I wasn't thinking."

"It's all right."

"No, it's not. I'm the most dreadful friend, aren't I? Here I am rambling on about my problems, while you—"

"We're not talking about me right now, my darling Queen. This is about you and Talon. And no, I don't see either of you capable of being intimate with anyone else, not now that you've found each other."

"That's just what I was trying to tell her," Shasta said. "But she kept saying that a Queen must not refuse to listen to the voices of her court." She stopped and blinked at Erinda, waiting for her opinion on the matter.

"Well, I'm not the least bit knowledgeable when it comes to affairs of state, but it does seem to me that Talon has one very good point—the Princess's safety. Even if you succeed in eventually winning over most of the viceroys, you're probably not going to convince everyone in the kingdom of Princess Brita's suitability for the throne. You remember Kumire? Just one nasty person in a position of power could pose very great danger to her."

"I can arrange for a bodyguard, like how Father assigned Talon to me."

"Oh, I definitely think that's a good idea. But Talon's still right. The life your daughter's facing is going to be extremely difficult. She's at the center of a very big mess of politics and prejudice. Have you considered how all of this is going to affect her, growing up in the palace surrounded by whispers and name-calling?"

Shasta's hostility seemed tempered by this thought, and she was quiet for a moment before muttering, "That doesn't mean I have to run off and find a husband to make babies with."

"No, it doesn't. But it sounds to me like Talon's trying, as always, to keep you safe. To make sure you really understand what you're digging your heels in for, before you get dragged down into the mud over this. She needs you to be certain that you're choosing this path because it's the right thing to do, and not just because you're so in love with her and little Brita that you can't think clearly."

"But how can she, I don't know…How can she stand the thought of somebody else touching me? Shouldn't that make her angry? If she loves me, shouldn't she be fighting to keep me instead of offering to walk away?"

Erinda closed her eyes for a moment, the question stirring unwanted memories. *I love you too much to keep you, Rin*…With a mental shake, she opened her eyes again and took Shasta's hands. "Believe me, such a thing would devastate her, and she knows it. But she's willing to let it happen if it turns out to be best for you. That woman would do anything for you. Anything."

Shasta flung herself backward onto the bed, arms out to the sides, staring at the filmy canopy draped overhead. "So what do I *do*?" Her petulant tone was a bit reminiscent of the spoiled Princess Erinda had grown up with.

"You allow her to go her way, as you must go yours. If your fates are truly entangled—and I absolutely believe they are—your paths will never separate you for long." She had never been able to fully convince herself that her own fate wasn't meshed with Kade's, though of course it was impossible. That was probably why the loss still haunted her even after all these winters apart.

"You really believe that?"

"I do." She reached out and patted Shasta's knee. "And now, Your Majesty, we need to get you dressed for breakfast."

This seemed to bring Shasta back into the present, because she sprang from the bed. "Goddess, I forgot how late it is. I have a meeting with the chancellor of Marinland this morning and then a huge stack of levy proposals to review, and the viceroys are expecting me in conference this afternoon, and, oh, *that's* going to be interesting after yesterday's debacle..."

Erinda was only half-listening as she helped lace the Queen into her foundation garments, and then wriggle into heavy petticoats and a gown of rose-colored brocade trimmed in lace and pearls. She adjusted the skirts so they draped properly, ensured that every tiny button down the back of the bodice was properly fastened, brought down the matching brocade slippers from a shelf, and helped Shasta affix large pearl drop earrings to her earlobes and a necklace boasting six strands of pearls and a walnut-sized garnet pendant around her throat. Once she'd maneuvered them both to a silk-upholstered bench before the mirror, Erinda twisted and pinned Shasta's long hair into an impressive confection of loops and swirls.

Attending the Queen's dress and hair were tasks usually assigned to her Majesty's ladies-in-waiting, but Shasta preferred Erinda's services to those of the women at court. More than once she had offered to bestow Erinda with a Lady's title and status, but Erinda wasn't interested in the social obligations that came with such a position. Court ladies had to maintain lavish wardrobes, appear at countless palace banquets, and host extravagant parties in turn, not to mention the expectation that any unmarried women among them should be in near desperate search of a husband from among the eligible nobility. Wealth was the deciding factor in selecting one's mate at court; love was an afterthought, as there were ample affairs to be had should a woman find her husband unsatisfying.

Nothing of court life appealed to Erinda except, perhaps, the occasional scandalous liaison of her own, and she didn't need a title for that. As to the rest, she much preferred the sleek, handsome horses of the royal stables to courtly pageantry.

Through the bedchamber's open doors, she saw Panna enter the parlor with a breakfast tray, carrying it out of sight to the glass-walled dining alcove at the far end of the room. Erinda finished pinning the ends of a small golden circlet into the Queen's elaborate hair, and once Shasta moved into the parlor to enjoy her breakfast, Erinda began making up the bed.

She finished straightening the bedclothes and arranging the pillows, and was turning her attention to the Princess's small cradle at the foot of the bed when Talon unexpectedly reappeared.

"Your Majesty," she said with a formal bow, "please forgive the interruption, but a courier from Mondera has just arrived. He is with the Monderan viceroy and chancellor now, but has requested an audience as soon as possible. He claims his message is of urgent concern to the crown."

"From Mondera?" Shasta repeated through a mouthful of raspberry muffin. Hastily, she swallowed and wiped her hands on a napkin, rising from the table. "I shall meet them in the reception hall at once."

Talon eyed Shasta's full plate. "You haven't finished your breakfast yet." At the Queen's reproachful frown, she added with somewhat more deference, "Your Majesty."

After a moment of consideration, Shasta sat back down. She speared a boiled egg on her fork and raised it to her lips. "Lead them there, Captain, please. I will join you all shortly."

Erinda, pretending to be deaf and blind to all but her chamber duties, grinned to herself nonetheless. Shasta did love her breakfast.

Talon bowed again and left, and Erinda continued her morning routine as the rest of her staff arrived in the royal chambers, ready to begin their daily work. She sent Alva to carry away the chamber pot from the privy, and set Garima and Clio to polishing the parlor furniture. Once Shasta had finished eating and left for the reception hall, Panna cleared the remains of breakfast away. Hali brought an armful of clean towels from the palace laundry, and after restocking the Queen's bath, she took a second set down the hall to the nursery where the sixth member of Erinda's staff, Oralie, was tending to the Princess's needs.

There were fourteen chamber suites on this floor of the palace, all under Erinda's supervision. Only the royal suite, the nursery, and the maids' dormitory were currently occupied, however. The other rooms, reserved for members of the royal family, sat empty. Her grandmother had told her that at one time, when Shasta's mother Talia had been just an infant, the palace had been full to bursting with royalty. Shasta's great-grandfather and his Queen consort had

produced six children—three sets of twins, which were common in the
Rane bloodline. Though Talia was her father's only child, she'd grown
up surrounded by aunts and uncles, cousins and second cousins. The
royal nursery was home to a seemingly endless succession of amber-
eyed Rane babies. Nurse had required a staff of four other nursemaids
just to care for all the children.

But over the course of three decades, an unlucky combination
of illness, infertility, and tragic accidents had caused the royal family
to dwindle in numbers, until only a handful were left. Until recently,
Archduke Fickett, who had been Talia's uncle, and his son, Kumire,
were the only remaining members of the royal bloodline aside from
Shasta and her twin brother, Daric. Then Kumire had assassinated
Daric, and Talon had killed Kumire, and the Archduke had died upon
hearing the news of his son's death; so now Shasta and the baby Brita,
who was Kumire's daughter by birth, were the only living descendants
of the house of Rane.

Many blamed the royal family's misfortunes upon Ulrike, dark
God of the Flesh, brother and sworn enemy of Ithyria's beloved
Goddess. Privately, Erinda thought it far more likely that the power-
hungry Fickett had been responsible for most of the mysterious deaths,
but if she let herself think too much about all the intricate politics
surrounding the royal family, it gave her a headache.

She preferred a simpler existence. Her entire world revolved
around these fourteen suites of rooms, regardless of their present state
of occupancy. She would mop and dust, polish and sweep, stock and
straighten these rooms, keeping them fresh and ready for the royal
family's use whenever they were needed. For the rest of her life,
Erinda would serve Queen Shasta, Princess Brita, and any other Rane
children that might follow them, just as her mother, grandmother, great-
grandmother, and great-great-grandmother had done. That was, after
all, what she had been born to do.

Don't you understand, Rin? I was born for this!

*But you want me. I know you do. Do you think we'd feel this way
about each other if She didn't intend it to happen?*

I'm meant for Her. And this...it's wrong.

*It's not too late, Kade. Just say you'll leave with me. We'll pack
a few clothes, take one of your father's horses, and be gone before
anyone wakes up.*

And then what?

And then we'll start a new life, together!

Where will we go, Rin? How will we live? Do you really think anyone will take us in? Even if they did, how long do you think it would last before they discover us and turn us out again...or worse?

We'll think of something.

Face it. It's impossible. You deserve a better life. You deserve someone who can take care of you, provide for you, someone you can love in the open without fear. I can't give that to you. After a while, you'd start to hate me.

I wouldn't!

You would, and I won't let it come to that. I love you too much to keep you, Rin.

"Erinda, what's wrong? Are you sick?"

Her knees hurt, and she realized she was hunched on the floor, her arms wrapped around a mop handle and her nose nearly resting in the bucket of sudsy water she'd been using to clean the parlor floor. She raised her head to see Clio watching her with a worried crinkle in her forehead. No wonder, since Erinda hadn't even felt herself go down. She swallowed around a hard knot in her throat.

"I..." Using the mop for leverage, she brought herself to her feet. "I'm not feeling very well. Do you think you can manage the other girls for me this morning?"

When Clio nodded, Erinda handed her the mop. She didn't like the way her knees were already threatening to buckle again, and focused all her concentration on putting one foot in front of the other.

She probably should have gone back to her little room, but the need for fresh air was overwhelming. Unsteadily, she descended the turret stairs and made her way to the servants' garden. The moment she was outside she leaned her back against the door, closed her eyes, and took several deep breaths.

Goddess, what's happening to me?

❖

The basement of the Great Temple library was musty and smelled of old leather and candle wax. While the library's upper floors were open to the public, well lit by numerous windows and a majestic, vaulted glass ceiling, these lower levels were restricted. Any visitor who desired access had to obtain a permit from the Honored Mother to peruse its contents. Down here were housed some of the rarest and most valuable documents in all the world, for Verdred province had long been the home of the Goddess's scribes.

Verdred of the Twelve had been the first, charged with recording the events of her time for future generations. She had passed that legacy down to each of the Honored Mothers who succeeded her. The scribes were the keepers of Ithyrian history, and their chronicles dated back a thousand winters, all regularly copied to ensure they would never be lost to time. Even on these restricted floors, nearly all the books were transcribed duplicates. The original documents were too precious to entrust even to the temple librarians, and were carefully preserved in the Ithyrian Treasury along with the kingdom's most priceless artifacts.

Since this floor of the library was underground, there were no windows. Instead, rows of thick yellow candles were mounted across the walls, and when they were all lit, they provided a wash of golden, flickering light. Qiturah directed Kade to sit at a roughhewn table before one such illuminated wall, and then began stacking books and scrolls in front of her until Kade could barely see over the pile.

"These are the ones I've gone through myself, though I've kept a few in my study to gather up the last details for the ritual." She sounded tired, and Kade suspected that she had been poring over these manuscripts all night. Yet excitement filled her voice as she added, "I think we will be ready to begin in just a few days."

This bit of information filled Kade with dismay. She'd rather hoped it would take at least a moon for Qiturah to determine all the proper arrangements. Shouldn't it take more time to prepare for something so momentous? She didn't feel at all ready. In fact, secretly she'd been wishing that when she woke up this morning she would discover the whole thing had been a silly dream. But she'd had no such luck. Right after morning prayers, which she had spent trying desperately to ignore the stares of her sister priestesses, Qiturah had whisked her away and led her down here.

Kade eyed the pile of literature in front of her with trepidation. Qiturah said these books could tell her more about the *shaa'din*— what they were, how they had served the Goddess, perhaps even some insight into what she could expect once she became one herself. Until yesterday, Kade had felt rather well versed on the Twelve. After all, she'd spent most of her life studying Ithyrian history. It wasn't until she'd been told she was about to become a part of that history that she realized how many, many things she didn't know at all.

The corners of Qiturah's eyes crinkled, and Kade sensed the smile beneath her veils. "I realize how overwhelming this must be for you, *Ostryn*. Please, take your time with these, and let me know if you would like to discuss anything in greater detail. I do not pretend to know everything myself, but I am happy to offer my thoughts if you wish to hear them."

The subtle deference of her offer was disconcerting. Kade realized that Qiturah now considered herself outranked. At least she didn't seem overawed like the others, but Kade found it uncomfortable that the Honored Mother she had always obeyed without question would now speak to her with such humility. And by virtue of what, exactly? Just because the Goddess had named her *shaa'din* did not mean she suddenly possessed any greater spiritual insight than she had before. Kade had no idea how to respond, so she just nodded.

After a courteous bow, Qiturah left the room. Kade sighed as she pulled the first book from the top of the stack, a dictionary of the ancient Ithyrian tongue. The Goddess's language was nearly extinct among the public now. Her priestesses kept it alive through study and prayer, in the hopes that they might one day be fortunate enough to hear Her voice. This particular book was clearly very old, and Qiturah had helpfully left small strips of ribbon between the pages, marking passages she'd thought were most important. Kade turned to the first marked section.

Shaa'din—*Combinant of* shaa, *meaning "holy" or "divine," and* din, *"warrior." A mortal woman touched by the Goddess, and who, as a result, may serve as a vessel for Her spirit.*

That was the extent of the entry, and it wasn't particularly enlightening. Far more interesting was the small scrap of parchment tucked between the pages, bearing Qiturah's handwritten notes.

Touched by the Goddess—literal or symbolic?
Vessel—as in receptacle? Or as in vehicle? Perhaps both?

And then, underlined for emphasis:

What changes?

It took Kade a moment to figure out that Qiturah was wondering what it was about the chosen girl that would change when Ithyris touched her. What would suddenly make her a vessel, when she hadn't been one before? Kade thought it was a very good question, though she hadn't an inkling what the answer might be.

Moving on to the next book in the pile, which was a collection of poetry, she opened to the ribbon marker.

Blessed Handmaidens, Mothers of Ithyria
With your lips, She hath given us truth
With your hands, She hath vanquished our enemies
With your blood, She hath purchased peace for Her children
What wonders we have witnessed through your eyes!

Kade had never been much of a poetry reader, and though several more stanzas followed, she couldn't glean much that was useful from any of them. She set that book aside, and took another. As she began reading, she realized that this was the manuscript Qiturah had shown her yesterday morning. The Book of Verdred, the first Ithyrian scribe. She leaned forward eagerly over the pages. Verdred had been *shaa'din,* so this would contain a firsthand account of the experience. The text was written in the Ithyrian tongue, and Kade had always struggled with translation, so she stumbled over the words slowly.

The Twelve were named Aster, Olsta, Verdred, Zarneth, Tabin, Striniste, Marin, Hollis, Daiban, Mondera, Fyn, and Cibli, and the latter three were sisters. To each, She gave a gift of spirit, which was enhanced by Her touch.
To Aster, sister of Rane, She gave wisdom and a quick wit. To Olsta, She granted commune with creatures of land and sky. To Verdred, She gave the gift of story telling. To Zarneth, She gave courage and the capacity to withstand pain. To Tabin and Striniste, She gave great speed and stealth. To Marin, She gave cleverness and invention. To Hollis and Daiban, She granted touch that promotes life and music that heals the heart. And as for Mondera, Fyn, and Cibli, She blessed unto each a sight beyond mortal understanding.
And the Twelve were Her Handmaidens, who carried out Her will. Each, at the Divine Lady's call, left her father's house and took up arms, to drive back the dark from Her lands according to Her command.

Kade reread this passage several times. According to Verdred, each of the *shaa'din* had received a special gift from the Goddess. A gift of spirit, the text said, though Verdred had been maddeningly imprecise when it came to the particulars—what exactly did "a sight beyond mortal understanding" mean? And did this imply that Kade might be given some sort of gift as well?

For the rest of the day, Kade read through the materials that Qiturah had set out for her, checking every marked page, trying to put together as much information as she could. She pored over tales of the Twelve's individual and collective exploits, many of which contradicted one another or included details that were clearly pure fantasy. Some claimed that the Twelve could fly, raise the dead, even command the weather. In one story, Zarneth of the Twelve grew three extra pairs of arms and single-handedly defeated an army of a thousand men. In another, Marin saved an entire village by loading them all into a wagon that floated away into the sky. Many of these were popular children's bedtime stories now, and Kade was familiar with them. But some, mostly the less dramatic ones, Kade had never heard before.

She read for so long that her eyes ached. Repeatedly, she found herself returning to the Book of Verdred, looking for anything in her account that might substantiate the claims of other texts. To her surprise, she discovered that while Verdred never made mention of Zarneth's extra arms, there was what sounded like a description of Marin's floating contraption, as well as confirmation of several other tidbits Kade had considered dubious.

She was also more than a little disturbed by the many graphic battles Verdred recounted. It seemed every one of the *shaa'din*, regardless of her individual gifts, had been involved in very messy, very dangerous fights. And though the Twelve may have been the chosen of the Goddess, they were not invulnerable. According to Verdred, half of Tabin's face was badly deformed after she was struck by an enemy weapon, and Fyn lost her eyesight after a serious head injury. Zarneth seemed to be the favorite for tortures of all sort, and she must have been covered in battle scars from head to toe after the many and various wounds she incurred.

But Olsta—gentle Olsta—had suffered worst of all. Kade took her time in digesting her story, unable to believe that in all her winters of study she had never heard it before. Verdred tried to soften the brutality of her report by using objective language as she wrote of how Olsta had been captured by a tribe of Ulrike's most barbaric and zealous followers. She'd been held for ten days, during which she'd been raped and beaten almost to death, and was barely breathing by the time the others were able to rescue her. In spite of Verdred's carefully dispassionate verbiage, the anguish that the Twelve had felt for their comrade was nonetheless infused in the text, so much so that it seemed Verdred could not help slipping back into a first person narrative as she concluded, *In time, through the grace of Ithyris, our sister healed in body and mind. Yet her spirit was forever changed, and henceforth only the great love of our Divine Lady kept Olsta among us.* Kade wondered if that was Verdred's judicious way of saying that if it hadn't been for the Goddess, Olsta might have taken her own life after her ordeal.

When at last she could no longer decipher the letters that swam before her eyes in the candlelight, Kade closed the book and stretched. She wondered how late it was. Down here it was easy to lose track of time. Her stomach was rumbling, and she suspected that she'd missed the midday meal—possibly the evening meal as well. She wished she could take the Book of Verdred back to her chamber, but knew the precious manuscript was far too valuable to risk removing it from the library. No, she would return tomorrow and pick up where she'd left off. She was determined to read the entire thing, cover to cover. She needed to know what was about to happen to her.

CHAPTER FOUR

Erinda was counting on a good long ride to help clear her head. But when she entered the royal stables, her first impulse was to turn and flee back to the palace again. Before she could make her escape, she'd been spotted, and it was too late.

"Erinda!" a delighted male voice exclaimed. She found herself spinning in the air as the handsome new viceroy of Mondera whisked her off her feet in an embrace.

Smiling in spite of herself, she pounded his shoulders with her fists. "Jen Crossis, you put me down this instant. What would your wife say?"

He set her down, eyes twinkling. "Aw, Minde wouldn't begrudge me a moment to catch up with an old friend. How have you been? You look…" he paused as he looked her over, "terrible."

She smirked at him. "That's very kind of you, Your Lordship."

Tall, blond-haired, green-eyed Jen Crossis was Kade's older brother. He and Erinda had carried on a good-natured rivalry ever since the day when, as children, he'd tried to sneak up on her and Kade with a dead rat, and Erinda had wrestled it from his hands and stuffed it down his pants instead. Though Jen's new appointment to the Monderan senate meant that he often spent extended periods of time at the palace on political business, Erinda didn't see him very often. In truth, she did her best to avoid him, as his resemblance to Kade was difficult to overlook.

"What are you doing out here?" she asked.

"Trying to talk Kallin into lending me use of his stallion over there." He indicated Ember's stall. "I've got a particularly fine mare stabled at Warinsgate that's ready for her first breeding."

"You sure you're not just shirking work? I've heard there are big things going on in Mondera lately." She'd been teasing, but Jen's expression sobered so quickly it was alarming. "It's really that serious?"

"We don't know, exactly, but it's not good. Mondera is used to attacks from Dangar, being so far north. The barbarian tribes are always creeping out of their mountain strongholds to stir up trouble for our villages along the border. Usually our provincial guard can push them out again before they get very far, but about a moon ago, something changed. They say the barbarians have a new leader, but we haven't been able to get much concrete information. The stories going around are impossible to believe. Nonetheless, our guard hasn't been able to force them back, no matter how many reinforcements we send. A horde has already taken at least three of the large northern towns, and they're still advancing."

"Advancing? Are they coming for the palace again?"

Jen shook his head. "They're headed south. Right now it looks like they're on their way to Agar, the Monderan capital, though for what purpose we can't guess."

"Does the Queen know?" Realizing that of course Jen would have gone to Shasta right away with something like this, she revised her question. "What's she going to do?"

"I've requested the assistance of the royal guard, and she's granted it, along with additional battalions from the provincial guards of Aster, Fyn, and Cibli. Captain Talon's planning to lead the first unit out in a matter of days, in fact."

She gaped. "Talon's doing what?"

"Oh, he was the first to volunteer. Seems pretty excited about it too…well, as excited as the captain gets. You know how he is. I think maybe the peace and quiet of court life's getting to him." Jen grinned.

Erinda sincerely doubted that it was the peace and quiet that Talon was thinking of. She recalled Shasta's earlier assertion that Talon was going to leave, and wondered if she'd been too hasty in dismissing her fears. Once Talon got an idea in her head it was difficult to get her to let go of it, at least not until she worried it to death. If she was determined to give Shasta space to consider the marriage-and-babies matter, she'd jump on any opportunity that presented itself, no matter how dangerous.

"Idiot," she muttered. She was going to have to track Talon down and have a few well-chosen words with her. Running off to Mondera to do battle with barbarian hordes was most definitely not the answer to her relationship insecurities.

"Hey, don't be too hard on him," Jen said. "Around here it's all politics and politeness, day in and day out. Every soldier needs a taste of adventure now and then. I'd give my eyeteeth to join him myself, but Minde won't hear of it."

She punched him in the shoulder. "Well, look at you. Only married a few moons and already Minde's got you completely broken in. Good for her."

"Hey, I know when I've gotten lucky. I have no intention of bungling it up."

Her breath caught for a moment at the expression on his face. She'd seen that look before, on another set of all too similar features. Only back then, it had been meant for her. Dizziness eddied dangerously through her head, and she focused on picking an imaginary blade of hay from the sleeve of his uniform. "Your wife is a fortunate woman."

He laughed. "Sorry you missed your chance?"

"What?"

"Oh, come on. You have to know how many winters I spent madly infatuated with you."

This was the first she had heard of any such thing. She squinted at him. "Really?"

"Of course! Kadrian was forever teasing me over it. I can't believe she never said anything. I was desperate for you to notice me back then, but you only ever wanted to spend time with my kid sister." He gave a theatrical sigh. "You have no idea how jealous I was. I tried everything I could think of to get her out of the way."

"Out of the—Jen Crossis, are you telling me that all those awful pranks you pulled on Kade were…?"

"For the sake of winning your heart, my lady," he said with a flourishing bow.

She kicked him in the shin, and he made a startled noise. "Winning my heart, indeed. You really thought that putting spiders in my best friend's hair and worms in her food and frogs in her shoes was going to make me fall in love with you?"

"I never said it was a *good* plan."

She reined in the temptation to kick him again. "You made our lives miserable, you rotten lout."

"Ah, but you two always found a way to pay me back, didn't you? Or have you forgotten the chamber pot incident?"

Her scowl dissolved as she burst out laughing. "Oh, Goddess, I haven't thought about that in winters!"

One morning, instead of taking the palace chamber pots down to be emptied and cleaned as usual, Erinda had smuggled every last one of them into Jen's quarters. She piled them both under and on his bed, stacked them in every corner, and placed them on every available shelf. She even opened his trunk and nestled one in amongst his clothes. Then she made certain the small window was securely closed, while most of the pots' lids were left open. It had been a particularly hot, muggy midsummer day, and Jen, a new recruit in the royal guard, hadn't returned to his quarters until much later that night. By that time, the fetid stench had thoroughly penetrated everything he owned.

The recollection made her laugh so hard she could not stand up straight. "You completely deserved it, though!"

"I'm sure I did. Though I can't for the life of me remember which of my boyhood crimes necessitated such drastic revenge."

"You stained Kade's hair, just two days before her Pledge ceremony. You waited for her to fall asleep and then soaked her hair in that awful stuff and turned most of it green!"

"Oh yeah," he said, his grin widening. "That was one of my best."

"It was downright cruel," Erinda snapped, her humor vanishing at the memory. "Do you have any idea how frightened she was of being up there in front of all those people? And then you went and made it so much worse. She cried for days."

"The high priestess was going to cut her hair off anyway," he said, still smiling. When Erinda continued to glare, he held up his hands. "Hey, at least she always had you to ensure she was well avenged."

That was true. She had taken great satisfaction from the knowledge that Jen had spent days on his hands and knees, scrubbing down the walls and floor of his quarters with buttermilk in an effort to get rid of the smell.

Still, she would never forget Kade's hysterical, panicked sobs. Kade had clung to her neck for hours, her tears soaking Erinda's apron. She was convinced she would die of humiliation when the head priestess and the rest of the Temple got a look at her. The Pledge ceremony was a sacred moment, she'd wailed, and everyone was sure to think she was a disgrace to its solemn dignity. What if they wouldn't allow her to Pledge after all? What if she was to be turned away from the temple forever? Surely the Goddess would not want a girl in Her service with *green hair*. What if everyone laughed at her?

"Kade, my darling, it's going to be all right," Erinda murmured over and over, rocking her in her arms. "No one's going to laugh at you. It's not your fault. Everyone knows what a bully your brother is." And he was going to pay for it. Of all the mean tricks Jen had pulled, this was the most unforgivable. If she were a boy, she would probably challenge him to a fight, but that lacked adequate imagination. No, she was going to come up with something to make Jen suffer at least as long as Kade had.

"I look so ugly!" Kade bawled, burying her nose in Erinda's shoulder. Vengeful thoughts would have to be set aside for the present, as Kade's terror was the more urgent matter.

"You're beautiful." Erinda moved back so she could look Kade in the eye. Kade's face was pale, her eyes red-rimmed, the wet shine of her cheeks causing her skin to look almost translucent. Tears clung to her blond eyelashes, like crystals from a chandelier. Most girls looked terrible when they cried. Somehow Kade managed to look ethereal, like a fairy tale creature too fragile to belong in this world. "You hear me? You will always be beautiful. Anyway, once you take vows your hair will be shaved off, won't it? And even then you will still be beautiful. I promise."

The reminder that priestesses shaved their heads seemed to assuage Kade's distress a little. Erinda used one corner of her apron to wipe Kade's eyes as she sniffled. "I suppose Ithyris won't really mind my hair?"

"Of course She won't." Erinda smoothed back one of Kade's long blond-and-green tresses, tracing the shell of her ear with her index finger, tucking the hair behind it. "And you needn't worry what anyone else might think, either, because I'll be there with you every second, right up front. Anybody even giggles, I'll shut them up with a punch to the nose." She brandished a fist to emphasize her point.

Kade threw her arms around Erinda's neck and kissed her. "Oh, Rin, you're just the dearest friend!"

Erinda smiled and returned the affectionate peck with one of her own.

They both felt it the instant their lips separated. Something powerful crackled into the space between them, bright, hot, and irresistible. Kade let out a surprised puff of breath, and then, hesitantly, her mouth sought Erinda's again. Softer. Slower. So very gently that Erinda thought she could actually feel the caress in the deepest part of her soul. It was like being hugged from the inside, like Kade had somehow taken Erinda's heart into her hands and enveloped it in the most exquisite awareness of being cherished and adored. She'd never, in all her life, experienced anything so amazing.

Erinda drew that sweet sensation as close as she could, and Kade seemed just as eager to share it with her, pressing her slight frame into Erinda's arms. They clutched at one another earnestly, and then Kade's tongue skated lightly over Erinda's lower lip, and Erinda met it with her own. She felt the connection right down to her toes, every part of her weaving itself inextricably with Kade as the kiss deepened. A small cry of pleasure erupted from the back of her throat. Goddess, had anything ever felt so wonderful?

Their mouths lingered together for several long moments before they each pulled back to stare into the other's eyes.

Erinda was abruptly aware of the disconcertingly similar green eyes that were watching her now, with curiosity that was beginning to look a lot like concern. Jen was reaching for her.

"Where'd you go just now? For a minute there it looked like you were going to be—"

Erinda had just enough time to stagger a couple steps away before the bile in her stomach emptied itself into the hay of a nearby stall. Her insides heaved until they were dry, and still she retched for several more painful moments until the wave of nausea passed. Finally, she was able to straighten and wipe her mouth with the back of her hand.

"...sick," Jen finished lamely.

Erinda didn't have the strength to take any more of their conversation. She wished with all her heart that she'd just kept walking when Jen had called her name. Now Kade's beautiful face, the rapture of that first kiss, the lush pleasure of her embrace were frolicking through her memory, slashing through the layers of self-control she'd so carefully wrapped them in, cutting her into agonized pieces so quickly that if this kept up she would surely lose her mind. Where had this come from? Why, after all these winters, was all of this seeping up to torment her again?

Whatever the excuse she'd muttered, Jen must have found it plausible, because when she turned to run back toward the palace, he didn't follow her.

❖

"More, Your Grace?"

Before Kade had the chance to reply, the young Pledged had already plopped a second generous scoop of boiled potatoes on her plate. Kade sighed and tried to sound grateful.

"Thank you, Myka."

"So is it itching yet?"

Kade looked up at the younger girl with shock. "What?"

"Your scalp. I overheard some of the others say you're to let your hair grow out now that you're *shaa'din*."

"I'm not *shaa'din* yet."

"But *Ostryn* Talara didn't shave your head yesterday like everyone else." Without invitation, Myka climbed onto the bench next to her, her blunt-cut, strawberry blond hair swinging around her ears. She propped her chin on one hand and watched Kade take a bite of the potato, her eyes bright with fascination.

It was awkward to chew with Myka's eager gaze following her every move. With effort, she managed to swallow and shrugged her shoulders. Maybe if she didn't reply, the girl would go away.

"They say you won't wear veils anymore either, after it happens. And there's talk of giving you your own private study, right next to Mother Qiturah's."

Kade put another potato in her mouth and chewed a little more aggressively.

"You'll have all kinds of powers. Nobody can even really guess what, exactly, since there hasn't been a Handmaiden for over a thousand winters, but I'll bet it's going to be amazing. Do you think She might make you able to fly?"

The volume of Myka's commentary was increasing with her excitement, and Kade could feel even more eyes gravitating to her as priestesses around the dining hall paused in midst of their own meals. She was quickly losing her appetite. She should have just stayed in the library basement, she thought ruefully, and skipped the communal midday meal.

"Will you just," she wanted to say *go away*, but it seemed too rude, "keep it down? Everyone's looking."

"Well, of course they're looking. Better get used to it. There's going to be a lot of people who want to look at you now. You're famous!"

Kade didn't want to be famous. She just wanted to eat her lunch in peace. The way things were going, she might never have another peaceful meal again, and the prospect was not a happy one.

"Are you scared?"

Kade cast her an irritated sidelong glance.

"Not that I'd blame you if you were, because this is just huge. It's the biggest thing to happen to Ithyria since…well, I don't even know how long since. Course, if it were me, *I* wouldn't be scared. See," she lowered her voice, as if divulging a secret meant only for Kade's ears, "someday I'm going to be famous too. I'm going to do something so great that the scribes will write about it, and people will remember me for centuries afterward. It's my destiny. I know it. It's why I decided to join the Temple in the first place."

Kade wasn't sure which part of Myka's naiveté irked her more: her rather sacrilegious admission that she was entering the Goddess's service in the hopes of garnering fame, or her blind assumption that being *shaa'din* was some great and glamorous adventure. If Myka had spent the last few days studying the countless bloodcurdling evils that the Twelve had endured, and wondering if, very soon, she would be expected to face those same horrors herself, she would probably not be so eager to take Kade's place.

She rose without comment and carried her plate to the offering dish at the front of the temple dining hall. With a prayer of thanks, Kade spooned the remaining potatoes from her plate onto the large silver dish. This was ritual at every meal. Each priestess reserved a portion of her food for this offering. Three times a day, their combined tithes were taken outside and gifted to one of the many impoverished pilgrims that gathered at the Great Temple's doors.

This special meal was considered a sign of Ithyris's favor, though more often than not the recipients weren't nearly as interested in divine benediction as they were in filling their empty bellies. For many, a Temple offering was the only nutrition they had hope of receiving that day, and sadly, there were always far more starving people than there were mealtimes. The ritual had become so ingrained in temple life that many priestesses would just thrust the tithe dish at the closest pair of hands outside the door, but whenever it was Kade's turn to deliver the meal, she always took a moment to seek out the hungriest face in the crowd.

It was that face she prayed for now, invoking the Goddess's providence and grace for whoever would consume this meal, and taking a moment to consider and appreciate her own fortune. As a Daughter of Ithyris, she enjoyed three full meals every day. Many, many Ithyrians were not so lucky.

When she'd finished, Myka was at her side again, ready to take her empty plate back to the temple kitchens. Myka eyed the offering dish with something akin to awe. "Wow, I wonder what the folks out there would do if they knew this plate's been blessed by a real *shaa'din!*"

From the way Myka was ogling the potatoes, Kade got the uncomfortable impression that she wished she could sneak a bite of them herself. She turned away so Myka would not see her roll her eyes.

"I'm not *shaa'din* yet," she repeated.

"You're about to be." Talara, one of the elder priestesses, had glided up silently behind them. She touched her fingertips to her forehead and gave Kade the respectful bow normally reserved for an Honored

Mother. "*Ostryn* Kadrian, it is time to prepare for the ceremony. Will you come with me, please?"

Kade tensed from her jaw all the way to her toes, and beside her, she felt Myka do the same. She inhaled slowly, filling her lungs until they burned, and nodded tightly. At least a dozen pairs of eyes bored into her back as she reluctantly followed Talara from the dining hall.

❖

Erinda couldn't remember the last time she'd seen Shasta so distraught. Alternately sobbing her heart out and shucking priceless works of art across the room to shatter on her parlor carpet, the Queen had worked herself into such a state by the time Erinda got to her that she was having a very difficult time calming her enough to make intelligible sense of her frenzied ranting.

Not that Erinda wasn't certain she already knew what had upset her so. Jen had clearly been right. Talon was planning to join the regiment of royal guard headed for Mondera. Shasta was beside herself, as if her heart couldn't decide whether it was furious or just simply broken.

"Your Majesty...Shasta, darling, breathe. Sit down and breathe."

"I can't!" Shasta shrieked, tears streaking her face as she paced the parlor floor. "Why is she doing this to me? I need her here." She stopped in the center of the room, her shoulders slumping as if her temper had abruptly run out of fuel. "I need her, Erinda."

"I know you do." Erinda moved to take her shoulders and guided her to the silk-upholstered couch. She pulled a handkerchief from her bodice and handed it to Shasta, who dabbed despondently at her eyes.

"I don't understand. What have I done wrong?"

"Nothing, Majesty. This isn't about anything you've done."

"But it has to be. She promised she'd never leave me again. She *promised*! Yet now she's running off to Mondera to get herself killed."

"You could order her to stay."

"I tried that." Shasta gave an exasperated growl. "She said unless I wanted to execute her for treason, she was going. Argh!" She twisted the handkerchief in her hands. "I reminded her that it's not safe. How will she keep up her...you know, her image, roaming across Ithyria with all those men who don't know what she really is? How will she bathe? How will she relieve herself? What will she do every moon when she bleeds? What happens if she gets hurt and..." Shasta's face crumpled. "Oh, Erinda, what if she gets hurt?"

Erinda took her hand and squeezed it, though she couldn't bring herself to offer reassurances she knew might be lies. The fact was, the Dangar barbarians were deadly. Talon had been badly injured in confrontations with them before.

"I just can't believe she'd be doing this if she really loves me," Shasta bawled, melting into a fresh barrage of tears on Erinda's shoulder.

"I'll talk to her, Your Majesty."

"It won't help. She's so damned stubborn. All she'll talk about is how she has to give me space to consider my options. No matter how many times I tell her I already *have* considered my options, and I've made my decision, she won't listen. I don't know what it's going to take to convince her."

"Perhaps you can't, Majesty. It may be that Talon needs to convince herself."

"Well, how's she going to do that by running off to Mondera and getting herself carved up by a bunch of barbarian animals? She'll probably be out there for moons, maybe even a whole winter, and I doubt she'll write to me if she's trying to 'give me space.' I won't know a thing about what's happening to her. I'll have to wait for some messenger to show up at the palace to tell me that the love of my life died on a battlefield somewhere! And...*And*, she'll probably spend the whole time convincing herself that the moment she's out of sight some nobleman at court will have swept me off my feet, so that by the time she gets back I'll be happily married, hugely pregnant, and have forgotten her entirely."

This speech was punctuated with anguished sobs, but dramatic flair aside, Erinda knew Talon well enough to admit that Shasta's predictions were probably not that far from the truth.

"The not knowing's going to kill me, Erinda. I can't handle this! How am I going to wake up every morning to an empty bed, make it through my responsibilities every day all alone, wondering every second if she's still alive out there, if I'll ever even see her again?"

Erinda knew the feeling all too well. Living with that kind of uncertainty was a hell she would never wish on anyone. She embraced her with heartfelt sympathy.

And then, an idea presented itself to her weary mind, a wild, simple solution to both their problems. "Your Majesty, what if I were to accompany Talon to Mondera?"

Shasta broke off in mid-wail. She stared at Erinda with wide eyes. "Are you serious?"

Erinda nodded thoughtfully. Lately, it seemed that every corner she turned, every person she ran into dredged up some unwanted emotion that threatened her sanity. She desperately needed a change of scenery, an escape to some fresh place that held no connection to her childhood memories. Logistically, Mondera might not be safer, but right now she would prefer the dangers of an enemy army to those of her haunted past.

"I could help Talon preserve the secret of her gender. Goddess knows I've been doing it long enough. And I could write to you regularly of her well-being, even if she won't. A courier with a fast horse should only need a quarter moon to get my letters to the palace, so you'd always know where we are and what we're facing. Who knows? Given enough time, maybe I can even get Talon to call off this ridiculousness and come home."

"You would do that for us?" Shasta asked, her voice quivering with hope.

Erinda felt a twinge of guilt. Her offer wasn't exactly selfless. She was thinking of her own interests as much as she was Shasta's. But she nodded again. "Of course, Your Majesty. Maybe neither of us can stop Talon from going, but I know she loves you more than anything else in this world. Eventually, she'll realize what nonsense this is, but in the meantime I'll do everything I can to get you both through it."

Shasta threw her arms around Erinda's neck. "Oh, Erinda, you are just the dearest friend!"

The familiar words struck like knives. Erinda closed her eyes and grappled with every last ounce of her battered willpower to keep the contents of her stomach down where they belonged. Frantically, she promised her churning gut that its abuses would be over soon. *Just hold out a little longer. Once I get out of here, everything's going to be all right.*

CHAPTER FIVE

*A*s preparations began for the ceremony that would transform *one of our own into the Goddess's chosen vessel, every priestess in Ithyria shared the same breathless anticipation. Even the youngest of those who had lived during the time of the Twelve had long since departed this world, as had their grandchildren and great-grandchildren, but soon, we would have among us a holy warrior the likes of which Ithyria had not seen in a millennium. We would witness with our own eyes the power and glory of a true Handmaiden of Ithyris.*

As word spread, visitors began to flood the temple in the hopes of attending the historic birth of a shaa'din. The Honored Mothers of Olsta, Zarneth, and Striniste arrived with select delegations from each of their provinces, and I am sure more would have come had there been time. As it was, Verdred Temple could scarcely hold all its guests.

For my part, I wondered if all the attention was truly necessary. I find it doubtful that the individual callings of the Twelve were met with such fanfare a thousand winters ago. Nonetheless, I could hardly begrudge my sister priestesses their excitement. I, too, found it difficult to contain my enthusiasm, even as I directed the cleansing rituals...

For two days, Kade was steamed, scrubbed, oiled, and perfumed. Every part of her anatomy was meticulously cleaned, from her fingernails and toenails to her teeth and the inside of her ears. After spending hours sweating in a cramped stone steam room, then soaking in a scalding bathing tub, her entire body was slathered with reddish clay, and she had to lie perfectly motionless for what seemed like a century in order for it to dry. Once this was rinsed from her skin, it was followed by a clear, gooey substance that smelled of lemons. That too was allowed to dry into a waxy coating that was snatched off in strips—

taking with it every last bit of her body hair, which was possibly one of the most disagreeable experiences of her life. Her feet and hands were soaked in various sweet-smelling concoctions, the nails neatly filed and calluses scraped away. She was rubbed down with so many different oils and potions she lost track of which were supposed to do what. As her purification was to be internal as well as external, she was permitted to eat only vegetables and fruits for the duration of these treatments.

Talara and three other senior priestesses did most of the hands-on work, but it seemed to Kade that every other priestess and Pledged in the temple was also involved to some degree, fetching towels, hauling water, gathering ingredients, and mixing up the substances they kept smearing her with. Worst of all, the majority of the time, Kade was left nude, or scantily draped in sheets, and if she'd thought the others' curious stares were embarrassing before, they were downright intolerable now. Kade had become the unwilling center of attention for the entire temple, and she was starting to feel like her cheeks wore a permanent blush.

Even her thoughts during this elaborate process had been scripted for her. Qiturah had copied out prayers, hymns, and chants for her to recite during nearly every phase of the preparation. Kade did her very best to focus, as she was supposed to, on the worshipful intent of the words, but found some treatments more difficult than others to concentrate through. She could easily slip into a comfortable meditative state when she was asked to lie still, waiting for the latest poultice to dry or lotion to seep in, and in those quiet moments she was glad for the respite of the Goddess's presence. Strange hands briskly massaging various parts of her body were immensely distracting, however, and then she struggled to maintain that sense of serenity.

At last Kade was led into a small, windowless room at the heart of the Temple, with candles lining the walls and hanging in lamps from the ceiling. Talara dismissed the others and directed Kade to disrobe and lie down on the long, cloth-draped wooden table that took up nearly all the space in the room.

"What's this one for?" Kade asked, trying not to mind the fact that she was stretched out, completely naked, in front of someone else for what seemed like the hundredth time in the past few days. She eyed the small pot in Talara's hands, which contained some sort of thick, dark paste.

"This is the final step of consecration," Talara replied. "Silence, now, for I must apply the markings exactly."

She unfurled a scroll and smoothed it out on the table next to Kade's head, pinning the corners down. Kade got a brief glimpse before she set it down. It looked like a drawing of a woman's body, covered from head to toe in curling symbols. Talara picked up a small brush and dipped it in the pot of paste.

The tip of the brush tickled and left a cool sensation in its wake as Talara copied the designs from the drawing onto Kade's body. She worked slowly, beginning with Kade's left hand and working her way up to her shoulder, then moving to the other side of the table to apply matching paint to the right arm. Kade had no idea how long the process took, only that the candles that filled the room had burned down to half their height before Talara had finished her arms and started on her left foot.

As she had said this was the last step in their preparation, Kade was grateful that it was tedious. Over the past two days, she'd had an uncomfortable wealth of time in which to mull over every imagined answer to her many unanswered questions. The most optimistic scenario was that perhaps Ithyris had grown lonely after a millennium, and had chosen Kade to be her new Handmaiden because something made Her think Kade would make a desirable companion. Of course, that was also the most unlikely explanation. *Shaa'din* were called in times of war. Whatever the reason for her calling now, Kade could be certain it involved impending combat of some kind, though she didn't know if it would be a fight against man or god.

Kade had never been in a fight.

During the Battle of the Ranes, many of the temple priestesses had ridden out alongside the provincial guard to help Princess Shasta retake the royal palace from her traitorous cousin. However, Kade had been among the group that Qiturah asked to stay behind and care for the crowd of refugees sheltering under the Great Temple's roof. Kade had been glad for the assignment, regardless of the immensity of the workload. Even when the others had returned triumphant, regaling those who'd stayed behind with all the thrilling details—the true power of *shaa'ri*, an ancient martial art that turned out to possess more deadly impact than any of them had imagined, and the Goddess's unexpected gift of celestial fire, strange blue flames that devoured Her enemies and decided the battle in minutes once their use was discovered—Kade hadn't experienced the slightest twinge of envy.

She was not a confrontational person. She never had to be. As a child, Erinda had always been quick to fight her battles for her. But now an uncertain, imminent threat awaited, and Kade would face it alone.

Since she wasn't a fighter, Kade speculated glumly whether fighting was even a part of Ithyris's plans for her. Perhaps She intended for Kade to function as some sort of holy martyr instead. When word spread of Olsta's harrowing ordeal at the hands of Ulrike's men, it had kindled powerful public outrage. Followers of the Goddess flooded to the assistance of the Twelve, forming an army larger than any the land had yet seen. That army had made it possible for the Twelve to force Ulrike's people back into the northern mountains, where the border between Dangar and Ithyria remained today. Did Ithyris have a similar purpose in mind for Kade?

When she'd taken her vows, Kade had sworn lifelong commitment to the Goddess in body, mind, and spirit. She would not break those vows now, not even if it meant torture and defilement at the hands of barbarian followers of the Flesh God. She would see her calling through to the end. She just couldn't be sure she'd be able to do it with any semblance of courage.

"Are you cold, *Ostryn*?" Talara asked kindly, looking up from her work on Kade's belly. Kade looked down at her body, now covered with intricate, swirling patterns that unfurled from the tops of her feet and backs of her hands all the way to her torso, winding over her shoulders and hips, spiraling about her breasts and navel. She realized she was shaking and nodded, which was easier than trying to explain the dark path of her thoughts.

"I've only a few more strokes to go, if you can manage just a little longer?"

Kade forced herself to stare at the ceiling. She felt the light touch of the brush for several more moments.

"*Ostryn* Talara?"

"Hmm?"

Kade bit at her lower lip. "Have you ever read the Book of Verdred?"

"Of course."

"Then…you know what happened to Olsta of the Twelve."

The brush stopped moving, and Talara looked up at her with a slight frown. "Yes, *Ostryn*, I do. But it is not something that we speak of."

"Why?"

Talara hesitated, then dipped her brush in the paint again. "We honor Olsta's sacrifice with our silence."

Kade could find no sense in that. "But how can her sacrifice be honored when no one even knows about it? Without Olsta, the Division might never have succeeded. We shouldn't be hiding her story. We should be teaching it in every temple in Ithyria!"

"Teaching a story like that serves no purpose other than to titillate lurid imaginations," Talara snapped, so sharply that Kade jerked with surprise and caused the brush to skip across her hip at a haphazard angle.

Talara's frown deepened, and Kade felt remorseful. "I'm sorry, *Ostryn*, I didn't mean to—"

"Just lie still," the elder priestess sighed, reaching for a damp cloth to wipe the errant paint away. She traced carefully around the undamaged parts of the design, and Kade lay in guilty quiet while she repaired the pattern.

At last, Talara said, far more gently, "Think for a moment, *Ostryn*. If you were in Olsta's place, would you want your successors a thousand winters later to still be studying your darkest moments, keeping them fresh and alive with each new generation? Even if your tragedy was what ultimately saved the world, is that how you would wish to be remembered?"

With the ceremony that would thrust her into the shoes of the Twelve looming so close, it was all too easy to imagine herself in Olsta's place. The wisdom of Talara's questions filled Kade with shame. "No," she answered in a very small voice.

"We cannot praise Olsta's accomplishment without also memorializing her humiliation, *Ostryn*, and so it is out of our great respect for her that we speak of neither. Most of us only learn of it after a lifetime of study, when we have gained enough understanding of spirit to know this. I hope that you will take it to heart."

Her words were not chiding, only earnest. Still, Kade felt deeply contrite, and she nodded as Talara sat back and surveyed her handiwork. "Excellent. Once this dries, we can turn you over and do the other side."

"The other side?" Kade asked hopefully. It had been afternoon when they'd begun, so it had to be late evening now. Perhaps that meant she would get one more night of normalcy, or near-normalcy, at least, before the ceremony that promised to change her life forever.

Talara placed a lid on the pot of paint and unpinned her reference artwork from the table to roll it up again. "Yes. Forgive me, *Ostryn* Kadrian, but I'm afraid it will be another day before we'll be able to finish."

Inwardly, Kade gave a little cheer, which she did her best to keep from showing on her face. "That's all right."

Talara bent over and blew lightly on Kade's belly, then tested the paint there with her finger. "Dry," she pronounced, and handed Kade her robe. She averted her eyes politely while Kade redressed, never mind the fact that by now she had to be well acquainted with virtually every fraction of her.

"I know you must be tired. Why don't you go back to your chambers now, *Ostryn*? We shall bring food and water to you there. Mind you don't spill on yourself, as we don't want to have to start all over."

Wickedly, Kade allowed herself to entertain the possibility for just a moment. Would she gain another day of reprieve if such an... accident...were to occur? Of course she would never disrespect the Goddess or the work of her sister priestesses in such a way, but still the idea was mildly tempting.

Berating herself for even thinking such a thing, she made her way through the temple corridors to her room.

❖

Unfortunately, by the time Talara appeared at Kade's curtained chamber entrance the next morning, Kade was almost glad to see her. She'd lain awake most of the night, and the brief fits of sleep she'd managed had been filled with dark and terrifying dreams. Utterly exhausted, Kade followed Talara wordlessly back to the small candlelit chamber, stripped, and lay on the table as instructed, this time on her stomach with her face cradled on a small pillow.

Perhaps it was just the solace of Talara's presence after such a long, frightening night alone with her own thoughts, but ironically, as the elder priestess began painting a new set of swirls on Kade's back and shoulders, Kade was at last able to drift into relatively peaceful slumber.

She knew she was dreaming as Erinda's arms stole around her waist. Nonetheless, she welcomed the relief as she relaxed into the embrace, inhaling deeply as mousy brown curls tickled her cheek and Erinda's lips moved close to her ear. "Darling, stop worrying. I'm here."

"Rin." Kade closed her eyes. Though she knew dream-Erinda wasn't real, she still felt immensely comforted by the imagined presence of her childhood protector. Erinda had always been there to chase her scariest fears away with a sweetly dimpled grin. Kade couldn't remember ever having been this frightened in her life, and even if it was only a dream, right now she desperately needed the reassurance of Erinda's sheltering arms.

"Kadrian, I need you."

The bell-like voice surrounded her and Erinda with cool blue light that gradually concentrated before them in a shapely feminine silhouette. Though Kade couldn't make out the Goddess's face, a thrill ran through her. The shining figure extended an arm to her in supplication.

"Please, *Ostryn*, help me."

Kade took a step toward Her, but then stopped uncertainly. The pale fingers that beckoned to her were dripping with blood. Thick red liquid trickled ominously down Her forearm and pooled in Her outstretched palm. Somehow Kade knew that the blood was her own, and if she reached out and took that hand she would die. Still, everything inside her insisted that she had no choice. She loved this beautiful, featureless being more than her own life. She would willingly choose death if Ithyris asked it of her.

"Leave her alone," dream-Erinda demanded, positioning herself between Kade and the glowing figure. Long braids trailed behind her shoulders, tied with green ribbons.

"Kadrian is mine." Ithyris waved a brilliant hand, and Erinda no longer appeared quite...*solid*. Kade watched with horror as Erinda's body grew translucent and began fading away. Erinda turned to Kade, holding up her hands helplessly. Kade could see Erinda's apologetic expression right through them.

"No!" Kade said frantically, but it was no use. Erinda dissolved into nothingness, leaving Kade alone with the Goddess's radiant silhouette.

Again, She stretched out Her lovely, blood-covered fingers in invitation. "Awaken, Kadrian. It is time."

Kade felt herself reaching for the proffered hand, but something was jarring her uncomfortably. Talara's voice cut through her consciousness, wisping the blue light away like ringlets of candle smoke.

"Wake up, *Ostryn*."

Kade opened her eyes, realizing that she was still lying on her stomach on the table. Talara had finished her work and was shaking her gently. "We have finished, and all is prepared in the high sanctuary. It is time." She handed Kade a robe of wool, blue as a cloudless sky, and waited for her to dress.

❖

Verdred Temple's high sanctuary was laid out in a large square, the floor inlaid with white marble in a pattern of stars. Massive white columns rose to support the arched ceiling, which was painted with murals depicting the Goddess and Her various consorts: Love, Time, Faith, Peace, Hope, and many others. Twelve plaster-cast faces were set along the ceiling's perimeter, three to each of the four walls, representing the first Honored Mothers of Ithyria. The face at the head of the sanctuary was more prominent than the others, as it was the representation of Verdred, their temple's founder. Directly beneath Verdred's serene visage was a low dais upon which stood a marble statue of Ithyris, wreathed in flowers and surrounded by flickering candles and brass censers.

When Talara brought Kade to the sanctuary doors, Qiturah was waiting for them at the entrance. Kade looked past them to see that the sanctuary was packed with rows and rows of veiled women. Seated primly along the benches lining the walls were the unveiled Pledged, with matching sharp haircuts and white robes. Anticipation buzzed so thickly in the air that Kade could feel it prickling her skin.

Qiturah surveyed her and gave Talara a nod of approval. Then she touched her fingertips to her forehead and bowed to Kade.

"We are ready for you, Handmaiden." She handed her a long stick of incense set into a dainty silver handle, and Kade accepted it with a shaking hand.

Qiturah turned and entered the sanctuary, Talara behind her. Kade knew she was expected to follow, but she hesitated between the doors as hundreds of stares pressed her back. Eighty-four priestesses were in residence at Verdred Temple, but more than thrice that many filled the room now. Apparently, every priestess and Pledged within traveling distance had journeyed to the Great Temple for the chance to watch the initiation of a *shaa'din*.

For one harrowing moment, Kade's mind went entirely blank with terror. She closed her eyes. As she exhaled slowly, she visualized dream-Erinda's ribbon-trimmed braids going before her like a shield. Her imaginary champion led the way through the fearsome crowd, and with her courage bolstered, Kade stepped into the aisle.

The walk to the dais was not as bad as she had expected. The moment her foot touched the marble floor, a harpist at the front of the sanctuary began to play, so she did not have to cross the room in either awkward silence or a chorus of embarrassing whispers. Instead, the ethereal music led her dreamily down the aisle and made the pressure of all those eyes more bearable.

At the base of the statue, Kade lit the tip of her incense stick and used it to ignite the resin in the shining brass censers. When all of them were sending up steady columns of heady, perfumed smoke, she blew on the stick until it glowed and set its handle into the base of one of the censers.

That had been easy enough, but she had no idea what she was supposed to do next. She turned to Qiturah, who indicated that she should face the crowd. Talara stepped up behind her, gently unfastened the veil that covered the bottom half of Kade's face, and lowered it ceremoniously. Then she also drew back the one that covered Kade's head and drew it out from under the collar of her robe. Even though she had spent much of the last few days without her veils, it felt strange to stand before the entire temple without them. Kade had to suppress a shudder.

"Daughters of Ithyris, the Goddess has called our sister Kadrian to serve as Her Handmaiden." Qiturah addressed their audience calmly, and a rapt hush fell over the sanctuary. "From this day forth, Kadrian shall be a vessel through which our Divine Lady may touch us all with Her grace and glory. Her face shall no longer be hidden, her hair shall no longer be shorn, for the Handmaiden is a warrior consecrated unto Ithyris, a weapon wielded by Her hand."

Qiturah lifted a large silver goblet in her hands, and Kade recognized the Cup of Purification. The Cup was blessed by the Goddess, and every girl who wished to become a priestess drank from it the day she took her Pledge. Kade remembered its effect in vivid detail. It was like swallowing a mouthful of Ithyris's aura, bringing awareness of Her into brilliant focus. Kade trembled at the realization that she was about to be permitted a second drink. This privilege was usually reserved only for the elders in times of crisis, when they needed to enter deep meditation in order to seek guidance from Ithyris.

She accepted the Cup from Qiturah with reverence and raised it to her lips. The water inside tasted just as she remembered, rich and cool on her tongue. It coated her throat with liquid light, slid into her belly like a falling star, and spread into her blood until her vision began to blur at the edges. She could sense Her then, not quite directly over them but almost, hovering just at the edges of Kade's perception. Her pulse quickened.

Qiturah beckoned to their left, and two priestesses appeared, carrying a velvet-upholstered chaise. They moved past the Honored Mother and set their burden down directly behind Kade, who turned to squint at it blearily. The chaise had been placed facing the statue of Ithyris, with its high back toward the assembly. Two more women carried wooden poles draped with white fabric. In moments, they had assembled a curtain that obscured the onlookers' view. The candles at the statue's base allowed for just the silhouette of the chaise to be reflected onto the curtain.

Talara led Kade behind the partition. Then, she indicated that Kade should remove her robe. Kade stared at her in disbelief, but Talara was serious. Reluctantly, Kade shrugged out of the warm blue wool, the air raising bumps on her painted arms. She reminded herself that it could be worse. At least Qiturah had provided the curtain, instead of requiring her to stand naked before all those people. Talara emerged from the curtain with the robe and offered it to Qiturah, who handled it reverently.

"Please join me now, Daughters of Ithyris, in calling the Goddess to claim Her *shaa'din*." She held the robe aloft and began to chant. *"Y'kurakura nasiaa, y'vysashun lo siriaa…"*

A chorus of feminine voices took up the chant with her, filling the sanctuary until it reverberated with the ancient words of worship. In the background, the harpist continued to play her instrument. Even standing there uncertainly, naked except for the symbols staining her skin, Kade felt warmed by the collective passion the hymn evoked.

She was perplexed for several moments, but finally realized that she was probably supposed to lie on the chaise. She settled carefully on the soft velvet and brought her legs up to recline along its cushioned length. She discovered that the position put her at just the right angle to gaze up into Ithyris's beautiful marble face.

Behind her, the hymn went on, the atmosphere in the sanctuary growing increasingly ardent as the priestesses lost themselves in worship. According to the chronicles, the next step to becoming *shaa'din* was for Ithyris to arrive and touch her, whatever that meant. So what was she supposed to do to facilitate that? Should she chant with the others? Perhaps she ought to pray? Prayer was nearly always appropriate, so Kade looked up at the statue. The Goddess's benevolent features swam a little in her vision. Somewhere far above the temple, she could sense Ithyris's presence.

I am here, Lady, as You asked. What happens now? The statue gazed back unblinkingly. After a few more stanzas of verse, the chant ended, and the harpist began to play a different melody. Talara's voice rose in a song of praise. When she reached the chorus, the rest of the assembled women joined in. Though Kade could not see their faces, she could hear their expectancy infused in the music. They were all so eager to witness whatever marvelous thing was about to happen. But the Goddess remained just out of reach, on the periphery of Kade's consciousness.

Since nothing seemed to be happening at all, Kade had a terrible thought. What if all of this had been a mistake? What if Qiturah was wrong, and the Goddess had never intended to make Kade *shaa'din*? What if she lay here for hours…days…and Ithyris never came? As frightened as she was by the unknown perils she might face as a holy warrior, at this moment, the prospect of disappointing all those women out there was even more terrifying. Qiturah would probably have to disclose Kade's admission of impurity to explain the Goddess's rejection. Kade would be driven out of the temple after all. It was no more than she deserved, truly, but after all the effort that had gone into the past few days to prepare for this moment, Kade could not summon the dignity to accept such a fate.

Oh please, Lady, come for me, she begged the Goddess's impassive countenance, willing the prayer upward into the space above the sanctuary where She lingered. *I know I'm weak, and cowardly, and selfish, but I love You. I am Your humble servant always. Please don't send me away now. Come for me, Sweet Ithyris. Touch me and I will be Yours forever.*

Perhaps She had just been waiting for a personal invitation. A strange sensation began on the tops of Kade's bare feet, as if someone was tracing the delicate symbols with their fingertips. Kade gasped and looked down. As unseen fingers traveled over the markings, the painted lines started to glow with the pretty, pale blue light Kade remembered from her dream. The feeling began on the backs of her hands as well, a sensuous caress that followed the curling designs. Kade couldn't think of the right words to describe the effect. It didn't quite tingle, it didn't quite burn, but every nerve ending in her body was focused keenly on the shining, tactile path as if hovering eagerly on the edge of something greater to come.

Kade was bombarded with a jumble of emotion: relief, gratitude, fear, awe. Ithyris had not rejected her. Ithyris was coming for her. She, a junior priestess of only a few winters' service, was to experience the Goddess in a way few ever did. In fact, she already had the answer to the first question Qiturah had penned in her notes. *Touched by the Goddess: literal or symbolic?* This was a far more literal experience than Kade could have imagined. The sanctuary seemed to shrink as Her presence poured inside and enveloped Kade's naked form in layer upon layer of bliss. She was stunned as it occurred to her that she was the first mortal in a thousand winters to experience the Goddess like this.

The invisible sensation wrapped around her ankles and wrists, leaving the graceful designs luminous in its wake, and began to sweep languorously up her calves and forearms. Though Kade could not see Ithyris's hands moving on her, her heart beat faster and her breath came harder. Could it really be the Goddess, touching her so sweetly? Was it really possible that the Divine Lady Kade had worshipped all her life was not only here with her at this very moment, but was tenderly exploring every curve of Kade's body with Her own perfect hands? She could not deny the glorious spirit that surrounded her, and that spirit was growing stronger with each passing moment. Usually, many long hours of deep meditation was the only way to achieve an awareness of Her this intense.

No, this went far beyond even that. Kade had compared the Cup of Purification to a mouthful of Her aura, but now she realized how very diluted those sips of blessed water had been. They were merely the tiniest glimpse, a blind grasping for the vaguest impression of Her. But this was Ithyris incomprehensibly whole, so pure and absolute that She dominated Kade's every sense.

The sinuous paint swirled over Kade's knees and elbows, her thighs and shoulders, inviting the Goddess onward. Kade trembled as she felt Her on the back of her neck, the ridges of her collarbones, the blades of her shoulders. The patterns decorating her limbs glimmered like ice wherever the Goddess had touched them, though Kade couldn't distinguish whether the feeling was hot or cold. It was both. It was neither. It was something else entirely, a primitive fever channeled along the lines of paint like molten silver.

Even as Ithyris's touch progressed, somehow it never left where it had already been, as if She was over her, under her, around her all at once. Kade wouldn't have been surprised to find herself floating in midair above the chaise, because she could feel the Goddess brush along her spine, fan out over her hips and buttocks, curl softly around her breasts, take gentle possession of her ribs and belly, even descend purposefully over the swell of her femininity. When the light converged on its path front to back, top to bottom, every muscle in Kade's body grew taut with excitement.

A fine sheen of sweat broke out over her body and mingled with the radiance tattooing her limbs and torso. She was poised on the verge of something vital, something that was going to change everything, a precipice dangerous as a knife's edge. Suddenly, Kade sensed hesitation in Ithyris's aura, as if She were holding Herself back. Panting, Kade tilted her head back to look into the marble statue's face.

"Please," she said, though she wasn't even sure what she was pleading for. She didn't know what Ithyris had been pressing them both toward, but she might just burn to ash in the Goddess's hands if She chose not to see it through now.

"*Julias ailo, Makluran?*" The statue's lips did not move, but Her musical voice held the faintest hint of uncertainty. *Are you with me, Beloved?*

"Yes," Kade replied breathlessly.

The light contracted. Kade cried out as the gleaming patterns penetrated her skin sharply, though they drew no blood. She was aware of a foreign presence accessing places even deeper, places no physical sensation could reach. Just like that, Ithyris was no longer merely surrounding her. The Goddess had entered her, pulsing through her in elegant, undulating spirals, merging even the most fragmented pieces of Kade's spirit into one single, harmonious rhythm.

If it hurt, though, Kade did not remember the pain. The next moment, the light expanded and erased even the memory of any other sensation. It swelled against her bones, surged outward against her skin. Every other thought and emotion was pressed back with sweet, commanding urgency, as if the light was making room for itself inside her. Kade surrendered to Ithyris's will without a second thought. The Goddess filled her until pressure built to a dizzying crescendo. Kade's skin began to glow faintly with the effort it took to contain Her.

At last, it burst. Dazzling blue light exploded in every direction. For a moment, Kade blazed in the sanctuary like a miniature sun, and somewhere in the back of her mind she heard the astonished shrieks of the onlookers. She, however, had no voice to cry out with. Euphoria swept over her in an all-consuming wave, holding time captive for what felt like a small eternity.

Finally, the power that held her suspended began to recede. Ithyris was withdrawing now, having saturated every part of Kade until she'd overflowed. Kade knew she was not capable of holding any more, but spasms continued to shudder through her as the Goddess released her as gently and patiently as She'd begun.

Exhausted, Kade collapsed against the velvet chaise. She had barely the presence of mind to register that all the markings that had been so carefully painted on her body were gone. Awed silence filled the sanctuary.

Soft blue wool descended over her flushed skin, and Talara murmured quietly in her ear, asking if she could stand. Kade nodded, and though her bones felt like water, she managed to get to her feet with

Talara's help. She leaned on Talara heavily as they came around the curtain, into view of the assembled women.

No one seemed to know what to do at first. Then Qiturah touched her fingertips to her forehead and bowed deeply. "All hail the Handmaiden," she proclaimed loudly.

Every other priestess in the room followed suit. "Hail, hail!" a chorus of voices echoed. Even Talara, who could not bow and keep Kade upright at the same time, still inclined her head as deeply as she could.

Kade shook uncontrollably. They all knew. They'd been standing right there the entire time that the Goddess had touched her, entered her, moved inside her. They had witnessed it themselves. Surely they had to recognize that what Ithyris had just done with Kade was as close to mortal love as it could be.

Kade had expected to be the Goddess's warrior, her Handmaiden, her devoted servant. She had not expected to become Her…Her *lover*.

The priestesses would wrap it in far more sacrosanct language, of course. They would call it consecration, blessing, divine favor, a noble sacrifice of the feminine birthright to husband and children. But every woman here had witnessed the simple truth of it. Would they now be able to see the truth about her, too? Would they realize that for Kade, this had not been a sacrifice, but rather a manifestation of her most carefully guarded desires?

Is that why You chose me? Kade went numb at the thought. She could still feel the remnants of the Goddess's light pulsing gently within her, flowing through newly forged, silvery veins that tangled throughout her being like spider webs. Though Ithyris had withdrawn now, she still felt the current of Her presence under her skin. Those delicate, cool threads vibrated with Her spirit more powerfully than Kade had ever been able to access it before, even in her longest and deepest meditations. Love, they sang to her. Joy. Contentment. Passion.

Possession.

Sweet Ithyris, is that *why?*

Kade's ears rang, her cheeks flamed, and her vision grew dark and starry. Just before she lost consciousness, her rebellious conscience taunted her with one last, blasphemous memory of Erinda's dimpled smile.

CHAPTER SIX

The shortest route to Agar from the palace was still a journey of nearly a quarter moon, even for a fast horse and rider. For two battalions of soldiers laden with weapons and supplies, it would take almost a moon to get to the Monderan capital. Thankfully, the blistering heat of summer had not yet arrived in force, nor were the heavy rains of spring still deluging the roads, and though their progress was slow, it was not unpleasant.

Erinda was surprised to discover how much she genuinely enjoyed traveling with the soldiers. She liked everything about it; the long days spent in the fresh air and sunlight, the crisp nights spent under the stars, the simple, hearty food rations, and of course, the hundred or so beautiful, powerful war-horses that carried both soldiers and supplies with seemingly tireless strength. She had quickly made friends with Marlus, the lieutenant in charge of the horses' care, and he seemed all too happy to have an eager and knowledgeable assistant to share his work with. Erinda was allowed to help brush and feed the animals every night, inspecting for burrs in their coats and stones in their hooves that might prove troublesome the next day of their journey.

Today she had even been permitted to ride Oriel, one of the smaller bay mares who had strained her shoulder a few days earlier. Though she could not carry any of the men until her muscles had fully healed, she could manage Erinda's lighter weight without difficulty, and from her higher vantage point atop the mare, Erinda could keep a better eye on the other horses as well.

After scolding one young corporal who had failed to properly tighten the harness of the dappled gelding pulling his supply wagon, she looked up to see Talon riding a few paces ahead of her. Erinda sighed. Talon had not spoken more than two words to her since they'd set out from Ardrenn, no matter how hard Erinda tried to draw her into conversation. Talon seemed to resent her presence on their expedition, and Erinda wasn't certain why. She wasn't the type to let things fester for long, however, and so she urged Oriel into a canter until she'd brought them up next to Talon's big black mare.

"Are you angry with me?" she demanded. Talon didn't meet her eyes, but her lips tightened into a hard line. "Look, this is going to be a very long trip if you're not speaking to me."

"You shouldn't be here," came the clipped reply.

"I have just as much business here as you do, Captain." A trace of sarcasm edged her tone.

Talon flicked her reins. "You think I don't know why you're coming along? I don't need a nursemaid, no matter what Shasta might think. I'm perfectly capable of handling myself."

Erinda snorted. "For your information, Talon, I'm not here for you. I'm here for the Queen, whose heart you're trampling all over with this foolishness."

Pain eclipsed the androgynous features. "You think this is easy for me? I'm—" Talon broke off and closed her eyes. Erinda recognized the anguish that had usurped her composure, and sympathy twisted in her gut. In moments, though, Talon had regained control. "Shasta's not the only one who's hurting. But one of us has to leave, and I'm the only one who can."

"And just why, exactly, does either of you have to do any leaving? They're your family, Talon—the Queen and Princess Brita. You're running away from your family. It doesn't make any sense."

"Shasta and Brita will always have my heart. Always." Her hand went to her throat, and Erinda caught the glimmer of gold chain that disappeared into the collar of her uniform. That would be Shasta's precious blue feather necklace, Erinda was certain. Talon had worn it the last time she'd taken off like this, and it had become something of a symbol between the two of them. Of course Shasta would have given it to her again before she'd left.

"But no matter how much I care for them, I'm nothing but a stumbling block for them both. So long as I'm around, Shasta refuses to face her most difficult decisions. She won't even consider options that might not only affect her security and safety, and Brita's, but also determine the fate of the entire kingdom. Every day that I'm part of their lives, I put them both in danger." Talon gave her a hard look. "Go home, Erinda. I know you think you're helping Shasta by being here. But so long as you provide her with a connection to me, she won't ever let me go long enough to do what needs to be done."

"That is just the most…" Erinda shook her head. Ridiculous didn't even begin to cover it, but Talon was always so impeccably pragmatic that it was hard to find the words to argue with her. "Talon, maybe you're strong enough to set your emotions aside like that, but most of the rest of us aren't."

"That's why I'm the one who has to do this. I have to be strong for both of us, because she can't."

"You really think just because you can survive without her, she'll be able to go on without you?"

"She will," Talon said with a wistful smile. "She doesn't need me as much as she thinks she does."

"Goddess, you are so dense!" Erinda snapped. "You think once you're gone her feelings for you will fade away? That this will magically change her into a person you think she'd be happier being? Well, I've got news for you, love doesn't work that way." She knew even as she erupted that she was taking the whole conversation too personally, but she couldn't help the resentment that boiled over into every word. "Let me tell you what this is going to do. Shasta's going to spend every minute you're gone with a horrible, screaming void in her soul."

Talon appeared startled by Erinda's sudden vehemence, and her black eyes widened. "Erinda—"

"And it will never heal, Talon. Never, no matter how long you stay away." She struck her horse's flanks with her heels and veered off, back toward the rest of the marchers, taking deep breaths to calm herself.

Her friends were free to live their own lives, of course. But Shasta and Talon had a real opportunity for a life together, which was something Erinda would never have with the woman she loved. She would be damned if she was going to stand by silently while Talon threw that away in one of her fits of self-deprecation. Still, she had joined this venture with the express purpose of leaving all these dangerous personal feelings behind, and she couldn't afford to let them follow her out here as well. She needed to get herself under control before she could help her friends.

"Erinda."

She turned at the unexpected sound of another female voice, and blinked with surprise as she recognized the veiled priestess riding bareback alongside her.

"Lyris!"

Talon's younger sister, Lyris, had joined the temple a little over a winter ago. Erinda knew Lyris was serving in the palace temple, but had not heard that she would accompany the battalions to Mondera.

Remembering Lyris's station, she bowed her head respectfully. "I'm sorry, Your Grace, I just wasn't expecting to see you here."

"I wouldn't miss this for the world," Lyris replied with enthusiasm.

"Miss what, exactly?"

"There's a rumor. Well, most still believe it's a rumor, but I'm certain it's true. The Goddess has called a new *shaa'din*."

"A new what?"

The question seemed to give Lyris pause, and Erinda assumed this was something that she, as a Goddess-loving Ithyrian, ought to know. But Lyris elaborated politely. "A holy warrior. A Handmaiden. There hasn't been one since the Twelve, and now Ithyris has called a new *shaa'din* to Her service."

"Why?"

"That's what we all want to know." Lyris's eyes twinkled above her veils.

"And this *shaa*…this Handmaiden, she's in Mondera?"

"Not yet. At least, I don't think so. But she will be, and I must meet her there."

Erinda didn't bother to ask how she could be so certain. Priestesses often heard or sensed things from the Goddess that most others could not. Kade had always described the experience so rapturously. She had said that feeling the Goddess's presence in her mind was like being allowed a peek into eternity.

Erinda sternly shoved the thought down where it had come from. She was here to stop thinking about Kade. And it was working, mostly. At least, she hadn't had any of the crushing nightmares or panic attacks since they'd left the palace, and she was resolved to keep it that way.

"Talon says you're here to spy on her," Lyris said after a moment of silence.

"I'm here to keep the Queen from suffering," Erinda answered stiffly.

"I thought as much. I'm glad." The smile in Lyris's voice was genuine. "I do not believe Talon is making this journey for the right reasons."

Erinda had fully expected Lyris to take Talon's side and try to convince her to return to the palace, and this encouraging response caused her to return the smile, just a little. It very nearly disappeared at Lyris's next words, however.

"But nonetheless, I am certain that it's very important she go. Whatever's coming, she has a critical part in it."

"I suppose the Goddess told you that?" Erinda asked with more than a little irritation.

"Well, not directly, but…"

"And as we all know, whatever the Goddess wants, She gets."

Lyris's eyebrows rose. "Shouldn't She?"

"I don't know," Erinda muttered, then scowled. "No, you know what? I don't think She should. Not when it causes pain to the ones She's supposed to care so much about." She didn't care how heretical her assertion was. She didn't even care that she was declaring such thoughts so boldly to one of the Goddess's chosen Daughters. Ithyris seemed coldly determined to tear apart couplings She did not agree with. And Erinda could not care less for Ithyris's opinion of women who loved other women. If the Goddess truly was as loving and benevolent as She claimed, She would leave Talon and Shasta alone. They'd been through enough already.

She didn't realize she'd spoken those last thoughts aloud until Lyris responded gently. "Oh, Erinda, you're wrong. Ithyris celebrates love. She would never attempt to destroy it."

"You only say that because She's never done it to you."

Lyris reached out and laid a hand on Erinda's shoulder. When she spoke, her voice was full of concern. "Talon said you've been going through some kind of distress lately. I can see it too. There's so much darkness in you, Erinda. I don't know what's happened, but when you're ready to talk about it, please come find me."

Erinda shrugged her hand away, and after another long, compassionate gaze, Lyris urged her mount ahead, leaving Erinda alone with her bitterly impious thoughts.

❖

Kade's heart was fluttering so erratically in her throat that she thought she might choke. A hundred sets of expectant eyes watched her patiently, even as she was riveted to the courtyard flagstone, unable to move. She should have been more resolute in her refusal when the Honored Mother had asked her to lead the day's *shaa'ri* exercises. At the time, Kade could not see a way to turn the invitation down without hurting Qiturah's feelings. But now she could not even force her arms up into the opening pose. The pressure of such a large audience held her paralyzed.

Kade could imagine what they were all thinking. Five days had passed since the ceremony that had made her *shaa'din*, and though Kade could still feel the Goddess's power sluicing beneath her skin, she had received no special visions. No miracles had sprung from her fingertips, and she still knew nothing more about why she had been chosen. Many of the guests who had journeyed to Verdred Temple for the ceremony had stayed on afterward, eager to see what would happen now that a Handmaiden was in their midst. Thus far, Kade had nothing to show them, and some were getting restless.

Qiturah had been gracious and patient, of course, though Kade could tell she was disappointed that she didn't have more thrilling insights to dispense. The Honored Mother had interviewed her for hours, asking her to describe her experience during the ceremony in the most minute detail, and scribbling page after page of notes. Kade did her best to articulate what had happened, but there were certain parts of what she had been through that she didn't feel comfortable sharing. They seemed too intimate, and Kade was still reeling herself from their intensity.

Birds twittered in the courtyard trees, and a breeze ruffled the veils of the assembled women. Kade found herself longing for her own veils back, which might have offered some small protection from the merciless gawking. As it was, self-consciousness flamed her cheeks and the back of her neck. A few women shifted their weight as the awkward silence stretched on. Kade wondered if they would all really stand there for the rest of the day, waiting for her, if she couldn't summon the courage to move. She closed her eyes, panic threatening to suffocate her every breath.

Stop looking at me, stop looking at me, stop looking at me...

She opened one eye, just a tiny bit, but they were all still watching her. She quickly squeezed it shut again. The silvery veins of Ithyris's power pulsed through her with the headiness of a fine wine. *Please, Lady, get me out of this.*

She hadn't meant to address the silver current directly. Or maybe she had. Somehow, having the Goddess's spirit coursing through the deepest recesses of her being made it feel like Ithyris was listening to the inside of her soul. Instinct steered her plea toward those gently vibrating threads.

She felt them surge in response.

The entire crowd gave a sudden, collective gasp of wonder, and Kade's eyes snapped open. Everyone was still staring, and Kade looked down to see if there was something wrong with her robes. She didn't see anything out of the ordinary.

"Where is she?" she heard one priestess call out.

"What's happened?" cried another.

Frenzied exclamations broke out across the assembly, and Qiturah came hurrying to the front of the crowd. Kade stepped aside to give her room, but the Honored Mother didn't look at her.

"She's disappeared, Your Honor!"

"How can it be?"

"Has Ithyris taken her?"

Finally, the women quieted enough that Qiturah could address them. She appeared just as astonished as the rest. "Peace, Daughters of Ithyris. Peace. I do not know what has just happened any more than you do, but I am sure the Goddess will reveal Her hand in it in good time."

"But the Handmaiden is gone!"

Again, Kade looked down at herself, but everything seemed normal. She held a hand up in front of her eyes and waved it, and though she watched her fingers pass before her face not a single person turned to observe the movement. Confused, Kade waved again more emphatically. She wasn't sure whether to be alarmed or delighted that no one noticed.

"They cannot see you, Beloved."

Kade looked around for the source of the musical voice, but there was no one there.

"You wished they would stop looking, did you not?"

The tangled current under her skin throbbed with amusement, and Kade was amazed to realize that the sound she was hearing, as clearly as if someone was speaking right over her shoulder, was coming from within her. She backed away from the crowd of women, who had joined Qiturah in a hymn of awed praise, and slid around a supporting column of the walkway that ringed the courtyard. Even if no one could see her, she felt better hiding behind something solid.

"You did this, Lady?"

"You did it, Beloved, with my spirit in you. You called on me and I have answered."

"I'm invisible?" Kade felt silly to be talking to the empty air, but the awkwardness was far overshadowed by her awe at sharing a conversation with the Goddess, who so rarely spoke to any of her Daughters.

"Not exactly. You have willed them not to see you, and so they cannot."

"But how is that possible? And why now? You haven't come to me since—" To her consternation, Kade found herself blushing for what felt like the millionth time in the past few days. She certainly enjoyed this new awareness of the Goddess's spirit flowing inside her, but the sensation was somewhat vacant, as if it were merely the residue of Her occupancy of Kade's body. No matter how she had prayed and meditated over the past few days, Kade hadn't been able to regain that deeper, more satisfying connection. She had even wondered if she was being greedy. Before the ceremony, she had never even known it was possible to experience Her so powerfully. But now Kade couldn't quell the craving that emanated from the core of her soul. She wanted to feel Ithyris saturating her again, filling her with Her light. Even now, the sound of Her voice fanned that longing into nearly unbearable need. And Kade had to know, she was desperate to confirm that her suspicion was unfounded. That Ithyris had not chosen her just because she was...

She felt herself pressing the question, hard, into Ithyris's rippling current. She could not even bring herself to finish the visceral thought in its entirety.

The Goddess spoke again. "You have many questions, I know, and soon you will have the answers you seek. But right now, there is no time. You must go to Agar." Her voice was fading, as if She were receding already.

"Agar? In Mondera?"

"Yes." The reply was faint, and Kade strained to hear it. "Go to Agar, Beloved. I will come to you there."

The shimmering threads settled back into a soft hum as Ithyris withdrew. Kade was left panting for breath, already missing Her presence and ashamed of how selfishly she had tried to force the information that she wanted from Her. No wonder the Goddess had withdrawn so quickly. Kade would not allow herself disappointment; after all, she didn't deserve to hear Her voice at all. Cautiously, she peeked around the column again.

Qiturah was leading the priestesses in the morning *shaa'ri* practice, having evidently decided the Handmaiden was not going to return. Kade did not mind, as she had not wanted the role to begin with. For a few minutes, she watched the slow, graceful movements as the women swept their arms and shifted their weight from one fluid pose to the next. *Shaa'ri* looked like a form of dance, but in fact was an elegant martial art. The priestesses who had participated in the Battle of the Ranes said that *shaa'ri* channeled Ithyris's power like a weapon on the battlefield. Kade had a hard time picturing what that must have looked like.

The silver veins inside her swelled, a gentle reminder that she had a directive to fulfill. As quietly as she could, Kade entered the temple hall and headed toward her room. She shrank back against the wall and held her breath when a group of young Pledged came chattering toward her, but they passed without a single glance in her direction and she sighed with relief. She wasn't sure how long this odd phenomenon would last, but she was pleased. Would she now be able to conceal herself like this from anybody she wanted to? Perhaps being *shaa'din* wouldn't be so bad after all.

When Kade reached her small chamber, she ducked between the strands of beads that curtained the entrance. Agar. The Goddess wanted her to travel to the Monderan capital city. At least that was something. Maybe not the answers she wanted, but it was a place to start. Most importantly, Ithyris had promised to come to Kade in Agar. That alone was ample motivation to make the journey, as Kade would gladly travel to the farthest corner of the world to be close to Her again.

Kade pulled a satchel from beneath her cot. It was already loaded with most of her belongings, few though they were. The Honored Mother had asked her to pack in preparation to move to a new chamber of the temple, next to Qiturah's study. It was the room where the Ithyrian Princess had stayed last summer, and was much larger, with its own hearth, a huge bed, and an adjacent sitting room to host visitors. Kade had been prolonging the move as long as possible, reluctant to exchange her familiar quarters for such unnecessarily extravagant accommodations.

Now, however, she would not have to. She could slip away in secret, and no one would know until she was already gone. Everyone would probably continue to assume Ithyris had whisked her away, which was not that far from the truth, anyway.

She stripped the blanket from her cot and rolled it into a small bundle, tying it to the base of the satchel. On her way to the kitchens, she spied the little Pledged, Myka, coming down the hall with her arms full of clean linens. Kade stepped back against the wall and waited for her to pass.

When Myka spoke to her, she nearly jumped out of her skin. "Are you going somewhere?" She was eyeing the satchel slung over Kade's shoulder.

Startled, Kade drew back farther. "You can see me?"

Myka giggled. "Of course I can see you."

The effect must have worn off already. Kade closed her eyes and tried to remember how she had made it work the first time. *Stop looking at me, stop looking at me...* She prodded the resonating veins of spirit under her skin. *Please, Divine Lady, hide me again.* This time, however, no rush came. The current hummed on, deaf to her pleas.

Myka tilted her head. "What are you doing?"

"Nothing," Kade mumbled, pushing away from the wall and continuing down the corridor. So much for enjoying her new *shaa'din* abilities. She had no idea how to control them—if she even could. Perhaps the current would only respond at Ithyris's will, and Kade had offended Her with her arrogant press for answers. Perhaps the Goddess was no longer listening, had drifted too far away to hear. The thought made her heart ache with loneliness that was as disturbing as it was painful. She could hear the sound of Myka's slippers as she tagged behind.

"Don't follow me," Kade snapped over her shoulder. The footsteps stopped, but just for a second. Then Myka skittered after her again.

"Where are you going?"

"It doesn't concern you."

"Can I come?"

Kade grunted. "No." She entered the kitchens, which were empty during *shaa'ri* practice, and set her satchel down on the table. For the briefest moment, she was reminded of the last time she'd been alone in this room.

Erinda had appeared to help her wash dishes. She was so beautiful, so haunted, the somber ghost of a girl Kade had once loved more than her own life. Kade had wanted nothing more than to take that pain from her, absorb it into herself, and give back the smile she had stolen from those perfect lips. Then Erinda had kissed her, with lust that incinerated Kade's insides and tears that slit her conscience like razors...

A shiver ran down her spine.

She turned to see that Myka was busily stuffing a knapsack with food, the pile of linens she had been carrying left forgotten on the floor.

"You're not coming," Kade repeated.

"At least let me help." Myka wrapped a hunk of cheese in cloth and tucked it down with the other items. "I know how to pack for a journey. I used to go off with my father all the time." She threw open a cupboard and grabbed a packet of dried beef, then added a bag of seeds and a loaf of round bread. "You'll need a waterskin—there's one in that cabinet over there."

Kade retrieved it automatically, though it occurred to her as she was handing it over that Myka was a Pledged whom Kade well outranked. She was *shaa'din*; wasn't she supposed to be the one giving the orders? But following direction came as naturally to her as breathing, and it would be a difficult habit to break. She would have to be more conscious of herself.

Myka brought over a pitcher and filled the skin. "Do you have a flint, for making fire?" Kade shook her head. "How about a knife?" Again, Kade shook her head.

Myka stuffed a cork in the mouth of the skin. "Well, you'll need both. And this water will probably only last a couple of days before you'll need more. How far are you going?"

"I don't know. I've never been there before."

Myka gave her an exasperated look. "Been where?"

Though she didn't particularly want to divulge her destination, Kade had to admit she needed the help. With a sigh she responded, "Agar."

"Agar?" Myka repeated with wide eyes. At Kade's uncomfortable nod, she frowned. "Then I'm definitely coming with you."

"No, you're not. I have to do this alone."

"You won't even make it half way," Myka said firmly. "Agar's a good hundred and fifty leagues from here. That's a half-moon's journey, and unless you're strong enough to carry a very large pack, you're going to need to find food and water on the way. Do you have any money?"

She didn't. She supposed the Honored Mother would give her some if she asked, especially since she was acting at the Goddess's command. But Kade had relished the idea of sneaking away. If she revealed her plans to leave, it was likely that someone would want to make a ceremonial event out of it, which would only slow her down. Besides, in the past moon she'd had her fill of uninvited attention.

"Well, I'm sure that any of the temples along the way would be more than pleased to welcome a *shaa'din*—"

"No," Kade interrupted. Prancing into temples across the kingdom to be fawned over night after night was not what she wanted. She wanted to get to Agar as quickly as possible. She wanted—*needed*—to be with Ithyris again. She snatched the knapsack of food from the table and slung it over her shoulder with the satchel. "I'll be fine. Thank you for your help."

She left the kitchens and hurried down the hall. *Shaa'ri* would be ending soon, and now that her bout of invisibility had worn off, it was all the more important that she make her escape before anyone else saw her. She wouldn't worry about the technicalities of the journey. Sleep, shelter, food—they were trivial. What mattered was being where Ithyris was. The Goddess wanted her in Agar, and Kade didn't care if she slept a wink or ate a bite on the way there. She just wanted to get there, and be filled with Her again, and finally get resolution to the questions tormenting her every waking thought.

Kade reached the temple stables, stuffed her satchel and knapsack into a set of travel bags, and threw them over the back of the horse in the nearest stall. It nickered and eyed her with reproach, but she grabbed its lead rope anyway. Just as she was placing a stool by its side so she could climb onto its back, Myka appeared at the stable doors.

"You can't take that one. He's far too old. He'll be dead by the second day." Without waiting for a response, she tugged Kade's bags from the horse's rump and carried them past several stalls, tossing them over the flanks of a cream-colored mare. "This one will get you to Agar without any trouble."

She had another set of bags draped over her shoulder, which she settled over the back of the horse in the next stall. In seconds, she had fastened the straps of the travel bags securely beneath both horses' bellies, covered their backs with riding blankets, and led them from their stalls. She looked at Kade, who was still standing on the stool in a daze. How did this girl manage to keep ordering her around? She was just a kid.

"Well?" Myka demanded impatiently. "I thought you were in a hurry." She flipped over a crate with one foot, stepped on it, and mounted the second horse. Her white robes gathered up to her knees, revealing leather riding boots beneath. She held the mare's reins out to Kade. "Let's go."

Kade shook her head. "I told you, you're not coming."

A sly look entered her eyes. "Either I leave with you, or I go get the Honored Mother right now and tell her what you're up to. Your choice."

Huffing, Kade dragged the stool over to the mare and used it to climb onto the horse's back. "Why do you care so much?"

Myka grinned. "The first Handmaiden in a thousand winters is about to make Ithyrian history. No way I'm missing out on the chance to be a part of it." Then, for the first time, she gestured that Kade should take the lead. "After you, Your Grace."

Muttering under her breath, Kade urged the mare forward. Their pace quickly sped from a trot into a full gallop, and little by little, Verdred Temple disappeared behind their horses' pounding hooves.

CHAPTER SEVEN

*D*earest Erinda,
    I was overjoyed to receive your letter. I cannot tell you what a relief it is to know that you and Talon are well. How grateful I am that you are there with him! I shall never be able to thank you enough for your bravery and kindness.

    Yes, the girls of your staff are managing beautifully in your absence. Panna has been the model of good behavior, and I can assure you the Princess and I are in fine hands.

    Talon will probably be pleased to know that the provincial viceroys have redoubled their efforts to get me to entertain potential suitors. I have been invited to luncheons and conferences and balls, all with the covert intent of introducing me to one young nobleman or another. Just this afternoon, I was asked to tea with Lady Caldis, the wife of the viceroy of Aster, and naturally, she had neglected to mention that her bachelor nephew would also be in attendance.

    Of course, I had neglected to mention when I accepted her invitation that Princess Brita would accompany me to tea. Poor Lady Caldis—I'm afraid Her Highness was rather fussy most of the afternoon, and made quite a mess of the young man's tunic when he asked to hold her. We had to excuse ourselves so that the Princess could be put down for her nap. I do not believe the good lady's nephew will be seeking out my attentions any time in the near future.

    I miss Talon dreadfully, as I'm sure you can imagine. The mornings are the worst. It is difficult to fall asleep, but then for a few hours I dream, and forget. That first moment upon waking, when I remember that I'm alone, it feels like a great weight has just fallen from the ceiling to crush me all over again. Somehow, I make it through the days, but my heart is not fully here. I am in Mondera with the rest of you, and I pray to Ithyris daily for your swift return.

Please write again soon, as your letters are the salvation of my senses. I have enclosed a separate letter for Talon—will you see that he gets it?
Travel safely, my dear friend.

Shasta

Erinda folded the Queen's letter with a faint smile. She could well imagine Lady Caldis's disappointment when Shasta had arrived in her parlor with the baby Princess on her hip as a buffer against hopeful suitors. That was sure to be a topic of palace gossip for the next moon. She was also amused by Shasta's careful references to Talon's presumed gender, probably in the case that her letters to Erinda were intercepted by anyone else. Shasta was always so protective of Talon's secret, though she'd confessed to Erinda more than once that she wouldn't be opposed if Talon wanted to reveal the truth to the world. But it was Talon's secret to share, she insisted, and she would guard it fiercely for as long as Talon wished to keep it private.

The second letter that Shasta had enclosed was written on smaller sheets of parchment, but from the bulk, Erinda could tell it was many pages in length. She tucked her own letter into her bodice and looked around for Talon. It was difficult to spot her today, since Oriel had resumed her regular duties and Erinda was now on foot among the marchers. After several minutes of dropping back and then hurrying forward within the crowd, she finally caught sight of Talon's big black mare. She jostled her way through the trudging men until she caught up with her.

She tugged at Talon's boot cuff to get her attention and handed the letter up. "For you, from Her Majesty."

Talon gazed at the red wax seal, imprinted with the royal signet, with an inscrutable expression. Then she slid the letter wordlessly beneath her jacket.

Erinda scowled up at her. "You're not even going to read it?"

Talon kept her eyes focused ahead without answering.

"Will you at least send her a reply?"

"Something tells me you're going to, whether I do or not." Her deep voice held reproach.

Erinda stopped walking, letting Talon move ahead. "You're damned right I will!" she called after her angrily. She still couldn't understand how Talon could let the Queen suffer so much, when she knew perfectly well how deep Talon's love for her was. How hard was it to send a letter? "Stupid, stubborn woman," she muttered, and shivered as she drew her shawl closer around her shoulders.

Shortly after their battalions had crossed into Mondera, the sunny grasslands of Aster had given way to Mondera's thick, mountainous forests. Though it was late spring, the weather had grown progressively chilly the farther north they went, the canopy of trees overhead blocking much of the sun's rays as they competed for the nourishing sunlight. It was moist and cool here, and the air was scented with earth and decaying leaves. Here and there, Erinda could even see patches of snow remaining at the base of the trees, where the warmth of the season had yet to melt them away.

The men were marching in battle armor now, which meant their pace had slowed a bit. The moment they had set foot in Mondera, Talon and the captain of the Aster provincial guard ordered the soldiers to don their battle gear, which included a shirt of mail under their uniforms, molded shoulder, elbow, and knee guards, and breastplates laced to the front of their jackets. They were less adamant about the helmets and gloves that completed the ensemble, since those weren't practical for marching, but even without them, each man was carrying a good deal of extra weight now. Erinda imagined they were probably grateful for the cooler temperatures, though personally she preferred the sunshine.

The more distance they put between themselves and the palace, the better Erinda felt. This was a whole different world. Here there were no mops or dusting cloths, no laundry to fetch or bathing tubs to fill or furniture to polish. Here there was only the dirt road beneath their feet, the dense forest that hugged their path, the soft twitter of birds, and rustle of tiny creatures in the brush. She was surrounded by beautiful horses to groom and soldiers to flirt with as carelessly as she liked. Few things bolstered her self-confidence and lightened her mood like winning the attention of a few hundred men all at once. Men, in general, held little interest for her, but that didn't mean it wasn't nice to be so unabashedly admired. In this place, Erinda was at last beginning to feel like herself again.

She even liked being the only woman on this venture—well, aside from Talon, who didn't count because no one else *knew* she was female, and Lyris, who didn't count because she was a priestess and as celibate as they came—because it meant that while she might amuse herself in teasing the men all she wanted, she felt no inclination to seek out any serious entanglements. She had been wrong before. The last thing she needed was another lover. No, what she really needed was to rebuild her saucy, cheerful self entirely independent of anyone else. That was the only way she would be able to hold on to who she was, regardless of what relationships might drift in and out of her life. If she could just learn to be happy alone, she might find she did not need companionship as badly as she had always thought.

Erinda was startled out of her introspection when she very nearly ran into the young corporal marching in front of her. Their traveling party had stopped dead in its tracks in the middle of the forest.

"What's happening?" she asked the corporal, who had gallantly prevented her from tripping by clasping her arm. She rewarded him with a coquettish smile and flurry of eyelashes.

He shook his head, color rising in his cheeks. "Don't know, miss."

Erinda worked her way through the soldiers to the head of the group. There she found Talon in hushed conversation with the captain of the Aster battalion. Lyris caught her questioning look and dismounted, moving to her side.

"There's a village up ahead. The scouts are reporting it's being held by a faction of the barbarian army."

Erinda's heart lurched a little. She'd almost forgotten that they weren't making this trek across the kingdom just to enjoy the beauty of nature. These men were here to fight. "What's Talon going to do?"

"She's trying to work that out with Captain Farsh now. She thinks they should sound an attack, try to drive the barbarians out. Farsh says they're under orders from the Queen to join up with the Monderan provincial guard in Agar, and they shouldn't deviate from Her Majesty's directive."

"The Queen would want them to rescue those villagers," Erinda said.

"That's what Talon's trying to convince him of."

The captains debated for several minutes, but their argument was decided for them when screams echoed through the trees, presumably from the direction of the captive village. Talon and Farsh exchanged grim nods, and Talon whipped around to her lieutenants.

"Nolan, lead your unit east. Previst, Byler, take your men and flank them from the north. You're with me, Lieutenant May."

Farsh was barking similar orders to his men. A scuffle ensued as the soldiers rushed to don their helmets and gloves.

"Help me up?" Lyris asked, and Erinda made a stirrup with her hands so that Lyris could remount her horse. Talon turned and frowned.

"You two stay in the trees. Find a spot to hide, and I'll come for you when the battle's over."

"I most certainly will not," Lyris said. "Have you forgotten, big brother, who turned the tides at the Battle of the Ranes?" She wiggled her fingers to illustrate her point, and Erinda grinned. She had only seen Lyris's powers from a distance, but the ocean of blue fire dissolving their enemies by the hundreds was something she would never forget.

Talon glared, but apparently could not think of further argument, so she turned and urged her horse forward. Erinda stepped to the side of the road as the soldiers bustled past, and she followed behind to watch as they began to form ranks at the edge of the forest. She wondered if the barbarians were really so self-confident as to neglect to post sentries around their conquered outpost. Did they not fear reprisal from the provincial guard?

It took several long minutes for the units to move into position, and all the while the wailing from the village grew louder and more frantic. Smoke began to drift through the trees, stinging Erinda's nostrils. Just as Erinda was seriously contemplating charging the village herself, army or no army, to help those poor people, a shrill horn blasted through the air. The soldiers surged forward out of the trees.

The yelling escalated into a roar of metal on metal, horses shrieking and men yelling. Erinda knew she ought to obey Talon's instructions and find some place to hide, in case the barbarians chose to search the forest for stragglers. Halfheartedly, she looked around for a viable hiding spot, but curiosity got the better of her. She had promised Shasta a full report on Talon's well-being, and so she owed it to her to get a better look at what was going on. At least, that was what she told herself as she snuck through the dense underbrush and peeked out at the village, which lay not more than thirty paces from the edge of the trees.

As soon as she caught sight of the battle in progress, she rather wished she had listened to Talon and stayed back. Blood stained the trampled earth in grisly puddles. The huge, hairy monsters in leather and skins that she remembered from that terrible night at the palace were everywhere, wielding massive clubs and bloodied battle-axes, and they were striking down the Ithyrian guard as easily as if they were squashing pesky insects.

She watched one of the barbarians take a deadly sword swipe to the abdomen. He doubled over with a grunt, but a moment later had straightened and beheaded his attacker. He turned to his next victim and struck again, with no apparent thought to his injury. Erinda could see blood pouring from his stomach, drenching the belt of furs around his waist. Yet he fought on without seeming to notice.

And it was like that with all of them, Erinda realized as she crept along the forest border. She was hoping the battle might appear more promising from a different angle, but no matter how far she went, it all looked the same. The Ithyrian guard delivered killing blows that went largely ignored. The barbarians were fighting with mortal wounds—she even saw one with a sword planted through his back, sprouting grotesquely from his chest, and he was still swinging away with his spiked club as if it was of no consequence.

She stopped when she reached a large boulder jutting out from the trees and crouched close to its base. From here she had a direct line of sight into the village square, and she clapped a hand over her mouth and gagged.

Five or six pyres burned lazily in the middle of the square, and each had a stake at its center to which was affixed a charred corpse. An array of bodies littered the ground between them, most dressed in homespun linens stained with blood. Some of the bodies were so tiny... Erinda couldn't bear to think of it.

Something was wrong. Where was Lyris's pretty blue fire? The Goddess's brilliant flames should have made quick work of this battle. Had the priestess been killed? Talon would die before she'd allow Lyris to come to harm. Frantically, Erinda scanned the village, looking for her friends, but neither Talon nor Lyris was visible in the fray. This was bad. Erinda wondered what she would do if their battalions lost. What if they were all slaughtered out there, and she was left hiding in the forest alone? Would she be able to make it back to the palace on her own? And how, oh *how* would she ever be able to tell the Queen?

Erinda watched a few of the villagers diving for the doors of their huts. Most were probably hiding inside. Those who ran were struck down just like the attacking guard.

One woman in particular caught Erinda's attention. She was nearly prostrate at the base of one of the pyres, and despite the two sobbing children tugging earnestly at her skirts, she would not leave. She rocked back and forth on her knees, reaching for the scorched figure through the flames. Probably her husband, Erinda concluded. She could appreciate the poor woman's grief, but the children...they would be killed out there in the open, and their mother was doing nothing to protect them.

And then Erinda saw her. She came striding through the fires like a malevolent demon from a fairy tale, and for a moment Erinda thought her hair was a part of the flames; then she realized it was just a brilliant shade of red-orange that blended into the inferno around her. Bits of feathers and fur fluttered through that blazing hair, which was matted into dense cords. She wore heavy iron armor over her leathers. Her face and hands were spattered with blood. An enormous battle-axe was gripped in one hand, and a serrated short sword in the other.

She was also visibly pregnant.

Before Erinda had time to fully process this strange apparition, the barbarian woman had locked eyes on the distraught widow and children beneath the burning pyre.

Erinda did not think. She sprang from her hiding place and sprinted for the village. She got lucky, because at nearly the same moment, a large gray war-horse came trotting toward the trees, saddle vacant, its rider likely thrown or killed. Erinda seized its bridle in one hand, the pommel of its saddle in the other, and launched herself onto its back. With reins in hand, she veered it back toward the village.

She might not be a soldier, but she knew how to ride. She gave a sharp whistle to divert the barbarian woman's attention, then leaned low over the horse's neck, barreling straight for her.

The woman didn't flinch. She just stood there, amusement playing on her face as Erinda charged. To Erinda's utter astonishment, she also dropped both her weapons. When Erinda was nearly on top of her, the woman put up a hand.

The horse should have trampled her. Instead, the moment the barbarian woman's fingers connected with the horse's nose, it was like they had run directly into an unseen wall. Erinda was catapulted into the air as the war-horse collapsed beneath her.

This was not the first time she had been thrown while riding, and her body automatically tucked and twisted to brace for the impact. She exhaled sharply and hit the ground with her shoulder first, then her hip. Her muscles strained as she fought the instinct to roll with the momentum, because she'd landed a mere handbreadth from the smoldering pyre where the woman and her children cowered.

Erinda recovered her breath with a wheeze. The big war-horse lay on its side at the barbarian woman's feet, dead. The woman smirked at her, then bent and picked up her weapons from the ground.

Erinda scrambled around the pyre and threw herself in front of the weeping children. She threw her arms out and glared at the flame-haired barbarian, who stepped toward them purposefully and raised her axe.

❖

"Your Grace! Your Grace, we have to slow down!"

But Kade could not slow down. The Goddess's spirit throbbed painfully under her skin, urging her on. For nearly the past hour, the current had grown steadily insistent. She'd found herself nudging her mount into an impatient canter, then a full gallop, in spite of the discomfort of riding bareback. Myka was racing alongside her, shouting in protest. Kade could barely hear her.

She had no idea why her heart was pounding so hard, why she felt anxiety gripping her insides. She didn't even know where she was going. She only knew that she had to be there. Now.

"We're leagues away from the road!" Myka yelled.

Myka had been leading the way for the past quarter moon, and as obnoxious as Kade often found her overly chatty companion, Myka had nonetheless proved an excellent travel guide. They had traversed the lush farmland of Verdred and Olsta provinces, and just yesterday, the terrain had sharpened into the rocky hills of southern Mondera, which promised more dramatic mountains to the north.

As it turned out, Myka was quite a skilled little huntress, and had kept them well fed with the small game she was able to snare. Kade preferred camping at night to avoid unwanted attention, but they had stopped at a few small towns along the way for supplies. Travel was not unusual for priestesses, who regularly embarked on charitable crusades between rural villages. Though Kade was reluctant to announce herself to the temples in the towns they visited, the Daughters there were always willing to share with their migratory sisters. She had brought a set of veils to hide her stubbled scalp, and thankfully, everyone thus far had assumed she was just another priestess on a pilgrimage of mercy across the kingdom. No one seemed to suspect she was the *shaa'din* they were all babbling so excitedly about, even as she stood under their noses while they filled her waterskin and she accepted their gifts of food.

They had made very good time. Every day, Kade pressed onward at as fast a pace as the horses would allow, and Myka had assured her when they broke camp that morning that they would likely reach Agar in another day or so. Up until a few hours ago, she had followed Myka's confident lead without challenge.

But they were picking their way northeast, following a well-beaten path through the jagged topography, when Kade had felt something tugging her north. The farther they went, the stronger that pull became, until it sat like a sickness in the pit of her stomach.

Finally, she veered off the path, toward the source of the pull. Myka had followed along, confused, but willing to accept Kade's word that this was where they needed to go. Or at least, she had been until Kade pushed them both into an all-out run for no apparent reason.

"You're going to kill the horses!" Myka shrieked. "They can't keep running like this!"

"Look!" Kade cried, pointing to a column of smoke in the distance. "What is that?"

She didn't know, but felt certain it was where she was supposed to be. She clung to her horse's neck and tried not to let her teeth rattle as the mare's hooves pounded the ground, sweat glistening over its cream-colored withers. As they drew closer, she could see a small village nestled at the edge of a vast forest. The sounds of clanging metal and the screams of dying men reached her ears. From this distance, it appeared that a sizeable army of Ithyrian guard were being attacked by a pack of strange, hulking beasts. The scent of smoke and blood hung thick in the air, and from the looks of things, it wasn't going so well for the soldiers.

She couldn't slow down, even as fear shot through her. They hurtled toward the village over the rocky ground, and when they were within a stone's throw of the nearest huts, one of the enormous creatures turned toward them. It was not an animal at all, she realized, but a man, covered in so much matted hair, fur, bones, and horns that he was scarcely recognizable as human. He bellowed and lunged at them.

Kade's horse reared back, pawing the air. She felt herself falling, and landed with a *whumph* on the blood-soaked ground. The mare dashed for the safety of the forest trees, while the hairy man-beast thundered toward Kade.

Not knowing what else to do, Kade raised her arms and swept them in an arc. This was the opening pose of *shaa'ri* practice, but here it had none of the peaceful, meditative focus of their exercises. She felt energy course the length of her arms and explode from her palms. The barbarian's head snapped back and he stumbled as if something had just struck him in the face. When he straightened his head, his nose was decidedly more crooked than it had been before, and blood streamed from it to soak his beard. Still, he raised his club and resumed his charge.

Kade quickly brought her hands in front of her chest and stabbed them outward with pointed fingers. Again, the man paused in his attack as a red patch spread across his distended, fur-covered stomach. He grunted with irritation. Kade didn't have time to marvel at her first real look at *shaa'ri* in action. He was still running at her. She searched the man's face for the darkness that her sister priestesses had so enthusiastically described, the darkness they had said transformed *shaa'ri* into the blistering fury of Ithyris's celestial fire. But she could see nothing, and he was almost on her.

Kade did the only other thing she could think of. She closed her eyes and begged the silvery veins of the Goddess's current for help. She prayed they would heed her this time, because if they didn't, she was about to become the shortest-lived *shaa'din* in history. Triumph and relief filled her when she felt the current respond.

She curled and rolled sideways, out of the path of the barbarian's descending club. It struck the earth just a handbreadth from where she had lain. The man lifted the club again, but confusion filled his ugly face as his head swung back and forth, his gaze passing right over her without a hitch. Kade held her breath.

He howled and turned in a full circle, then spat blood on the ground at his feet.

"I'm coming, Your Grace!"

Myka was still on horseback, and though the barbarian warrior couldn't see Kade, it appeared Myka had no such difficulty. She galloped straight for her.

"Myka, no!" Kade yelled as the hairy man raised his weapon.

She stretched out an arm and felt the silver current surge once more. Myka's horse dodged the club, and the barbarian was left scanning the field in consternation as Myka darted past him and reached Kade's side. She put down a hand and pulled Kade up onto the horse behind her, but before she could kick the horse into motion again, Kade put a hand over her mouth and used her ankles to block Myka's heels.

"Shh. Wait."

The man was turning in another circle, his eyes passing over them sightlessly. Myka seemed to understand then, because she froze and, like Kade, held her breath. The horse beneath them shifted its weight, and Kade shot it a silent plea. *Don't move. Please don't move.* The horse stilled beneath them as if it were made of stone. All around them the battle raged on, the barbarians felling uniformed soldiers left and right, and after a moment, their attacker hefted his club and turned away, roaring as he reentered the chaos.

Kade took her hand from Myka's mouth then.

"What just happened?" Myka asked, though she kept her voice down.

"I think I've made us invisible." A strange thing to say, but there was no other explanation. They were right at the edge of the village, but no one else had noticed their presence. Indeed, though huge, furred men thrashed all around them like wild animals, bloodlust in their eyes, not one looked in the direction of Myka and Kade on their little horse.

Myka's face lit with delight. "Praise the Goddess! Your first miracle, and I was here to see it!"

Kade didn't bother to correct her. Turning oneself invisible to hide from enemies seemed scarcely less cowardly than doing so in order to hide from her own sister priestesses. It didn't seem at all like a heroic feat.

Myka's elation faded as she, too, took a good look around. "Your Grace, we can't just sit here. We have to help these people."

"I don't know how."

Myka gave her an incredulous look. "Isn't that what *shaa'ri* is for? And what about the celestial fire everyone's always talking about? You're *shaa'din*. You should have these monsters eating out of your hand by now."

"It's not working," Kade said in frustration. "Maybe I just don't know how to use it properly, but it's not working at all the way they said it would. I don't know what else to do."

Myka's reply was interrupted by a whistle, and they turned in unison toward the sound.

Kade's heart stopped. There, tearing into the village square, was a woman on a big gray horse. She was dressed in coarse split skirts and a brown, laced bodice, and her hair was plaited in two braids. From this distance, she looked so much like—

The rider flew through the air, over the head of a barbarian female in armor and leathers who appeared to have stopped the horse with a touch of the hand. Kade watched her fall, heart in her throat as the woman hit the ground and very nearly landed in a burning pile of— Goddess, was that a dead body tied to that post?

Kade flung a leg over the horse's back and dismounted.

"Where are you going?" she heard Myka call after her, but she was already running. She saw the fallen rider drag herself across the dirt and thrust two small children behind her as the barbarian approached. There was another woman on the ground too, gazing at their attacker with dull resignation. Kade could actually hear her thinking, *Go ahead. We have nothing left to live for.* But Kade didn't get the chance to ponder this strange phenomenon. She was focused on the woman with the braids, who flung out her arms to shield the others.

A split second before the barbarian woman's axe fell, Kade crashed into all four of them. Somehow she managed to wrap her arms around both women and both children at once. As she wrenched them all to the side, she reached for that cool silver current tangled in her mind, and she took hold of it with every ounce of determination she possessed. *Save us, Lady. Please, save us all.*

The spirit surged in response, so powerful that it took her breath away. For an instant, it felt like something burst from her skin, like she had to be glowing from the inside out with the force of it. Then Kade found herself lying on top of four very startled people as the heavy axe whistled past her ear to embed itself in the dirt beside them.

One of the children, a little boy, opened his mouth to let out a wail. Kade pressed a finger to her lips and he closed his mouth again, wide-eyed. She twisted over her shoulder to see the red-haired barbarian staring at the spot they had all been just a moment before. Her rounded stomach caught Kade's attention, and Kade's eyebrows flew up. She had the strangest feeling, like she was looking into a dark and very dangerous mirror. As if, somehow, the barbarian woman with her blood-spattered, pregnant belly was a distorted reflection of Kade herself. The impression made her cringe.

Disoriented cries went up all over the village, and the barbarian's head came up. Her eyes narrowed as she surveyed the battle that had abruptly come to a halt.

Kade followed her gaze and was amazed as she realized they were not the only ones the barbarian woman couldn't see. In fact, all of a sudden none of the barbarian forces seemed capable of seeing anyone except one another. She'd asked Ithyris to save them all, but she hadn't known the Goddess would take her so literally. The uniformed soldiers of the guard, the few remaining villagers, even the war-horses that trotted by without their riders...the marauders appeared blind to all of them. Like Kade's first attacker, they turned in confounded circles, seeking a glimpse of their mysteriously vanished foes. If she had not been so frightened, she might have even snickered at the bewilderment on their faces.

A few of the soldiers caught on quickly to this new development, however strange. They took advantage of the situation, hacking and slashing at their enemies from the safety of their invisibility. A few of the monsters fell at last, relieved of their hideously furred heads. But then someone blasted a horn and a cry of "Retreat!" echoed through the village.

The red-haired woman might not have been able to see the soldiers, but she certainly heard the horn. She looked back at the ground where her intended victims had been and hissed between her teeth. "It's a trick!" she bellowed and spun on her heel. "They're still here, all of them! Burn the village, you useless curs! Burn it to the ground!"

Kade shrank back as the woman seized a flaming log from the pyre and thrust it over their heads, into the straw thatching of the nearby hut. The straw caught quickly, and the barbarian snarled as her comrades began to follow her lead. Kade waited until she had moved a safe distance away, then turned back to the family she had just rescued.

The little boy squirmed out of Kade's embrace, tugging his sister with him. Their mother seemed too dazed to move, and Kade worried she might be crushing her. Awkwardly, she shifted her weight, trying to get off the poor woman so she could breathe, and only then did she find herself staring down into a pair of undeniably familiar gray eyes.

"Sweet Ithyris," she whispered.

It hadn't been her imagination after all.

Kade had no idea how long she lay there, carelessly draped over Erinda's panting form. Sparks from the burning hut rained down over their heads, singeing holes in Kade's robes. Beneath her, Erinda gasped for air, each breath pressing against Kade's ribs. Adrenaline had set her senses on edge, and every beat of Erinda's heart hammered against her until it seemed their breath and heartbeats had synchronized into a single frenetic rhythm. Erinda's eyes held hers with bottomless disbelief, and Kade found herself lost in them.

This was not possible. Erinda lived at the palace in Ardrenn, leagues away from this tiny woodland village in the depths of Mondera province. She could not be here. Surely she could not be here.

She was still so beautiful it made Kade's heart hurt.

The earth shuddered with pounding hooves. Instinct made Kade press herself over Erinda even harder, as if she could shield her from whatever was coming toward them. She dropped her head into the curve of Erinda's neck, Erinda's skin warm against her cheek, and closed her eyes.

"Your Grace! Come, Your Grace, we must go. Hurry!"

Numbly, Kade felt herself being dragged to her feet. Myka boosted her back onto the horse, then used an overturned barrel nearby as leverage to spring up behind her. Someone—another priestess— was lifting Erinda from the ground, herding her and the woman and children toward the forest until Kade lost sight of them in the smoke. Fire crackled everywhere, devouring the huts and longhouses on all sides, collapsing the flimsy structures in on themselves.

Myka struck the horse's flanks with her heels, and they fled.

CHAPTER EIGHT

They ran for what seemed like hours, scrambling through the underbrush and dodging trees. At some point, someone found the road again, and then the way was easier, but still they ran without stopping. If Erinda had been thinking clearly, she would have appropriated one of the many riderless horses that galloped past, and pulled the widow and her children up behind her. At the very least, she would have picked up the little girl, who was stumbling along as she gripped Erinda's hand and tried to keep up on short, chubby legs. Lyris hurried ahead of them with the boy clinging to her back, half dragging the children's mother by the arm.

But Erinda could only vaguely register the ground slapping against her feet, the sting of the cuts on her shoulder and scrapes on her arms, the little girl's fingers grasping hers. Everything felt dull around the edges, like none of the sensations her body was feeding her were real.

She had gone mad. That was the only possible explanation for such a strange hallucination. Or perhaps she was dead. Perhaps the barbarian woman had killed her back there in the village, cleaved her neatly in two with that enormous axe. Perhaps Erinda had passed into some strange hell, where she would continue to be tortured in death with the same cruel memories she had been so desperate to escape in life.

And only this morning she had been feeling light, optimistic... *normal*. She should have known it would not be that easy. Her heart was nowhere near ready to let go of the past, a fact that was evidenced by the way that, moments from death, her imagination had conjured a heartrending vision of her childhood sweetheart bursting through the fires to save her. What a pitiful mess she was. Would she ever escape this loneliness, this aching desperation that had turned her into such a pitiful fool? Despair blanketed all other thought, and she kept running because it was the only thing she could do to stay ahead of it.

The rocky forest road passed little by little beneath their feet, winding deeper into the trees. When they could not run anymore, their little group slowed to a walk. Eventually, they reached a cluster of men and horses gathered to the side of the road, the surviving remnants of the guard battalions. The little girl pulled her hand free of Erinda's and ran to her mother as they approached.

The battle hadn't quite decimated their small army, but it had come close. Makeshift tents were being strung between the trees, a few fires had been built, and countless wounded were being bandaged with the supplies that remained in the surviving horses' packs. Their campground for the night was tucked into the elbow of two sheer, rocky cliffs, just off the dirt road that cut through the forest. They would be able to see anyone coming from either direction in case they were being pursued, and their backs were protected by the walls of rock. It was as good a resting place as any for the men who had made it out of the battle alive, especially since the sun was going down. Few were in shape to be traveling at night.

Erinda wandered in a daze between the rows of tents. She fetched a roll of gauze from a nearby pack when one of the men asked her to, and handed it to him without comment. She passed a group of men who were holding a comrade down by the shoulders as another yanked his broken leg back into position. The man's wail echoed faintly in her ears. So much blood. So much pain. So much death. It was everywhere she looked, a garish nightmare she could not awake from.

At last, however, she heard a familiar voice, one that loosened the terrible knot in her chest and brought her back to her senses. Erinda skirted one of the tents, and relief flooded through her as she caught sight of Talon, whom she had not had so much as a glimpse of during the entire terrible battle. Talon looked disheveled and exhausted, her uniform stained and torn, the armor plate across her chest bearing several large dents. A blood-soaked bandage wrapped her left thigh, and a nasty bruise colored one side of her handsome face. But she was otherwise upright, and appeared to be in possession of all her major limbs. Despite her personal grievances with the Goddess, Erinda found herself breathing an earnest prayer of gratitude. Talon was still alive, and Erinda's next letter to the Queen would not be the one she had feared.

She was going to rush forward and fling her arms around Talon's neck, but caught sight of the woman Talon was talking with. Her stomach plummeted. With a gasp, Erinda darted back behind the tent and pressed a fist over her suddenly erratic heart.

No. This was not happening. Sure, Erinda had seen a marvelous apparition of Kadrian Crossis tear out of nowhere to save them. But she had been in a panic, and very close to death. Her mind was tormenting her as it always did, especially in those moments afterward when she lay there with Kade's vivid eyes hovering just a handbreadth above her face. But there was no possibility that Kade was here, out in the middle of nowhere. So how was it that Talon could be carrying on a conversation with a figment of Erinda's imagination?

But maybe it hadn't really been a hallucination, she amended after consideration. The woman might look a lot like Kade, but she was not wearing veils, and she had hair. Not much, just a fine coat of blond stubble, but even that would never be permitted of a priestess. She probably was the one who had saved them, and that was something of a comfort. At least the entire thing hadn't been a sick delusion. Erinda felt her pulse stabilize, reassured that she hadn't lost her mind after all.

"...never seen anything like that before," Talon was saying.

"Well, just you wait, 'cause you'll be seeing plenty more where that came from!"

Erinda could breathe a little easier. That was not Kade's voice.

"I don't know much about miracles, but none of us would have made it out of there alive today if it weren't for you," Talon said. "We owe you a great debt."

"Aw, that's just what a *shaa'din* does, Captain," came the answer, the tone of which was nowhere near as humble as the words themselves.

"It is an honor to be in your presence, Handmaiden," Erinda heard Lyris say.

So this was the special warrior Lyris had been so excited about? The one who was supposed to be the modern day equivalent of one of the Twelve? She had certainly played the heroine today, throwing herself over Erinda and those unfortunate villagers, though Erinda was not sure what Talon meant by "miracles." Still, this development seemed promising. If the *shaa'din* was really everything Lyris claimed, she would be able to quell the trouble in Mondera with little difficulty and, hopefully, a lot less bloodshed than what they had seen today.

Erinda stepped back a little as one of the soldiers passed by, leading a little cream-colored mare. The animal was limping noticeably on her right side. Erinda heard the man address the *shaa'din* hesitantly.

"Excuse me, Your Grace, but I was wondering if this here is your horse? She's too small to be one of ours."

"Oh, wow! We were so certain she was lost after she ran off into the forest! Where did you find her?"

"Wandering the road a couple leagues back. Figured she might be yours, being without a saddle and all. I know you ladies like to ride without them."

After a pause, a new speaker said quietly, "Thank you, sir."

Those three words made Erinda's stomach drop again, with dizzying force. Though she had not heard that gentle, bashful voice in seven winters, she would know it anywhere. But before she had time to accept what that meant, the soldier had come back around the tent and seized her wrist.

"Horse girl," he said, and tugged her into their midst. "Come take a look at this one, will you? I think she might be hurt."

Erinda could not look up, not even at her friends. She was not ready to confront the truth that awaited her at Talon's side. Instead, she directed her attention to the injured mare. She took the reins and stroked the animal's neck before running her hand over its right shoulder, then down the foreleg. She felt for the tendons that ran behind the knee joint, and gently manipulated the area between her thumb and forefinger so the horse would lift her foot. Sure enough, there was a large stone wedged into the hoof, between the prongs of her iron shoe. Erinda would need a pick to get it out, maybe even a pair of pliers if it was lodged as deeply as it looked.

"I'll take care of her," she said, straightening and patting the mare's nose. With as much dignity as she could muster, and keeping her eyes carefully averted to the ground, Erinda led the horse away to where several others were tethered at the far side of the camp. She only allowed herself to breathe once they were out of sight of Talon's group.

After securing the mare's reins to a sturdy tree branch and searching through every saddlebag she could find, Erinda collected a currycomb, stiff-bristled brush, and a coarse rag. Though she could not find a hoof pick, she did discover a pair of rusty pliers. She carried her prizes back over to where the little horse waited, and set to work. It took some doing, but at last she managed to dislodge the stone from the mare's hoof, and she carefully inspected the rest for damage. The animal might continue to limp for a few days, but Erinda could find no other cause for concern, so she released the hoof and picked up the currycomb.

"Since when did you become 'horse girl'?"

Kade's soft question sent a shiver down Erinda's spine. She froze for a moment, irrational joy sweeping her entire body at the sound of that voice. A thousand forbidden memories surged up with it, battering at her brittle defenses. Her head felt dangerously light.

So you're speaking to me now? Erinda bit back the sharp retort, but embraced the irritation that accompanied it. Irritation was an emotion she could trust, and hopefully it could keep her from doing something pathetic, like falling into a swoon or vomiting into the nearest bush. She began running the comb over the mare's glossy coat.

"It's been a while," she answered, concentrating on the feel of the horse's solid warmth under her hands. She let her agitation flow in brisk strokes across the cream-colored flanks. The beautiful animal's presence was soothing, and Erinda drew strength from it. "I needed something to occupy the time after—" A wave of grief threatened to choke her, but she swallowed it back and forced herself to finish the sentence. "After you left."

She felt Kade's eyes on her as she continued the rhythmic grooming. "So you don't work in the palace anymore?"

"I still serve the Queen. Right now I'm on a special assignment." Which was supposed to be my escape from you, she added mentally. The thought brought a humorless chuckle.

"Is something funny?"

"It's just...you're the last person I expected to run into out here." Erinda heard the bitterness in her words and winced, knowing Kade would notice as well. She did not dare lift her head as she heard Kade expel a breath. Kade had always been able to read her moods, sometimes to the point that she felt certain Kade knew what she was thinking. She suspected it would take her seconds to guess the real reason Erinda was so far from home.

And Kade's next words, saturated with guilt, indicated she had arrived at just that conclusion. "I owe you an apology for my behavior the last time we met."

Erinda lowered the comb. "You don't owe me anything." A dark feeling welled up in her, like the icy shadow of a storm cloud. "You didn't do anything wrong."

Suddenly, Kade was at her side, gripping her shoulders, turning Erinda to face her. With one hand, she lifted Erinda's chin to meet her eyes. "Neither did you."

The nearness of her should have been more than Erinda could stand. After so many winters apart, Kade's touch should have locked her insides like stone, sent her spiraling into dismal agony, or at the very least ignited an inferno of forbidden lust. But instead, her hands felt soothing, as if they were transmitting comfort directly into Erinda's soul. The sensation was such relief that it was very nearly irresistible. Erinda had to fight every desperate, greedy instinct she had to keep from getting lost in it. She wanted, more than anything, to wrap her arms around Kade's neck and claim her mouth with kisses. But she recalled all too well how poorly that had worked out the last time she had tried it. Her heart could not withstand another rejection.

With a snarl, she stumbled away, ducking under the mare's neck until she had positioned the horse safely between them. From the sanctuary of the creature's other side, where she could only just peer over the mare's back, she glowered at Kade. "You're right. I didn't." She threw the comb down. "And I'm *not* sorry. I won't apologize for the way that I feel about you, Kade. Not ever."

"Rin." Her name on Kade's lips was a plea. Erinda was taken aback by the emotion in her voice, but even more by her use of the childish nickname. She'd never expected to hear it again. She realized Kade's chin was trembling. "I've only ever wanted you to be happy, I swear. And I know I've only made things worse. I don't know what to…I can't…" Kade closed her eyes, and tears spilled down both cheeks. When she opened them again, her expression was despondent. "How do I make it better, Rin? Tell me what to do, please."

Kade cried more easily than anyone Erinda had ever met. When they were children, her fits of tears were never a surprise. She cried over everything, from a bruised elbow to a reprimand from her parents that she felt was undeserved. Still, Erinda had been certain that after so many winters in service of the Goddess, Kade had forgotten any feelings she might ever have held for her. The calm way she'd rebuffed her embrace in the Temple kitchens last spring—silently, as if they were strangers—had made that perfectly clear. Erinda stared at her. "I don't see why it would matter to you."

"Goddess, Rin, of course it matters!" Kade exclaimed, so loudly that she startled the little mare. The horse jerked her head up with a whinny, and stamped her hooves so that Erinda had to leap back to keep from getting her feet trampled. Before she had the chance to calm her, though, Kade had already laid a hand on the sleek neck.

"*Fen, fen, yi lo golna,*" she murmured in the Ithyrian tongue, and the mare stilled. Erinda lifted an eyebrow.

"She thought I was angry with her," Kade explained. "For throwing me earlier."

"And how would you know that?" Erinda asked incredulously.

Kade patted the little horse as she moved to join Erinda on the other side of the placated animal. "I think it has to do with being *shaa'din*. Ithyris sometimes lets me hear the things She hears."

"Like the thoughts of horses?"

"Sometimes."

Erinda narrowed her eyes as she considered another possibility. "What about the thoughts of other people?"

Kade paused as though she was only just remembering something important. "I think…sometimes that too."

Erinda took a step back.

"Not you, though," Kade was quick to add. "I've really got no idea what you…I mean, I can tell most of the time, but it's not because I'm listening, I've just always been able to…" Kade was clearly embarrassed as she trailed off awkwardly.

Erinda pressed her fingers to her temples. Without warning, the woman who had broken her heart had inexplicably shown up at the very place Erinda had fled to in the hopes of escaping her memory. What's more, Kade was no longer merely a priestess. Apparently, she was now the Goddess's new—what had Lyris called her? A Handmaiden. A living legend, destined to champion Ithyria. She even seemed to possess supernatural abilities to go along with that calling, miracles and mind reading and such. But the most staggering part of all was that after seven long winters spent in the belief that Kade had forgotten about her, it now seemed that was not the case. And if that were true, it would be all the more terrible. If Kade was unattainable before, she was a thousand times more so now.

Yet in spite of everything, Kade's shy admission that she could still sense Erinda's emotions as she had when they were young pierced Erinda beyond words. No one had ever known her as well as Kade. No one else had ever been able to tell when she was hiding her feelings, or decipher with such accuracy the reasons why. And oh, how she missed the intimate companionship of someone with whom she could always communicate, even when she could not find the words to speak.

Her throat closed up, and she bent to retrieve the brush from the muddy ground. She closed her fingers around it, and her hand felt very far away from the rest of her body. "It doesn't matter."

"Will you stop saying that?" Kade demanded. She snatched the brush from Erinda's hand, and even that brief contact brought another rush of bliss.

Defeated, Erinda turned to face her, her heart too heavy to keep up the battle of appearances anymore. "What do you want from me, Kade?"

The question hung between them, hungry and hopeless. Kade's eyes teared again. She moved to touch Erinda's face, but Erinda flinched away. "Don't." *You don't understand what it does to me.* But it was clear Kade did understand, because she looked at her own fingers for a moment as if they were ablaze.

"I don't know what to do, Rin," she admitted quietly, dropping her hand. "I can't stand it that you're hurting like this. I just…I want so much to give you peace."

"Peace," Erinda said, the word feeling ludicrous on her tongue. The only person she had ever loved was standing just an armlength away, and yet it might as well be a thousand leagues. She shook her head sadly. "There's no such thing, Kade, not for me." A long moment of silence passed, and she held her hand out. "Can I have the brush back, please?"

Kade dropped it into her palm, her eyes searching Erinda's face. Erinda could not look at her any longer. She was angry, grieved, sick to her stomach, and yet if she was going to be honest with herself, just having Kade within reach made her feel more complete than she had in a very long time. That, in and of itself, was terrifying. How could she have allowed herself to become so dependent on Kadrian Crossis? She had to put a stop to it now, or she would be enslaved to these feelings for the rest of her life. Determinedly, Erinda turned her back and resumed the grooming routine.

❖

Kade watched Erinda brush the mare down. She was at a loss for words. She sensed Erinda wanted to be left alone, but couldn't bring herself to walk away. There was so much more that needed to be said, though she could not think where to begin.

"Kadrian."

She jumped when the Goddess's voice bloomed in her head.

"Kadrian, Beloved, come to me."

Kade staggered a few steps away from Erinda, trying to make sense of Her odd request. There were no temples out here. Where was she supposed to go? The veins of spirit within her pulsed insistently, and she closed her eyes, seeking them out. *How do I find You, Lady?*

"Come."

Within that command, the silver current expanded, flooding Kade with a peculiar feeling. Light and spirit gushed through her consciousness, like wind or rushing water. The current swept around her, pulling at her, and it carried her along with it.

When Kade opened her eyes, she felt different. Less…corporeal. She still seemed to be inside her body. She had arms and legs, and could move them. But everything felt too light, improperly weightless.

And the place where she stood, wherever it was Ithyris had brought her, was something her brain could scarcely grasp. She was standing in a long white hall of glowing doorways. Or maybe it was a sphere? Perhaps it had spokes like a wagon wheel. She couldn't quite tell, since the form of her surroundings seemed to shift depending on where her eyes tried to focus. The floor was infinite. She couldn't determine where it ended and the walls began, as they were all composed of the same unbroken whiteness. Above her head, the sky rippled like the surface of an inverted lake, shifting hues of blue and silver dancing just beyond its glassy skin.

Where is this place? she asked of the Goddess, and to her surprise, she heard a tinkling laugh behind her. She spun and her mouth dropped open.

Ithyris floated not more than an armlength away, Her skin shining faintly, Her hair and clothes undulating like they were caught in a breeze. Kade had tried to picture Her a thousand times, but never would she have been able to imagine a beauty like this. Ithyris's face was the most splendid, faultless collection of feminine features that Kade had ever seen. Every line, every curve, every angle was precisely right, as if She were the original standard after which all other women had been less perfectly modeled. She was so blindingly flawless that Kade's eyes began to ache just from looking at Her.

Kade's entire being hummed with adoration. She was possessed by the need to touch Her, the desire to be made whole by that consummate perfection filling her once again. Nothing in the world could possibly be more important, more wonderful, than existing as a part of Her.

"Stand up, Beloved," the Goddess said. Kade realized she was kneeling, her head back and her arms reaching up of their own accord. She swallowed hard and rose to her feet, which was a strange experience because her weightless body moved without any effort on the part of her muscles. She simply thought about standing, and found that she was.

Ithyris swept a hand around them. "This place is called *Yura'shaana,* the spirit nexus. Through *Yura'shaana* all spirit passes in and out of the mortal world. That door"—she pointed to a glowing aperture over Kade's shoulder—"is yours."

"Mine?"

"It leads to the body you wear in the world."

Kade crinkled her brow and held up her hands, which looked perfectly solid even if she could barely feel them. "But..."

"Your spirit is choosing to view the nexus as if it were still within its flesh, as that is easier for you to comprehend. But your physical body lies beyond that door. It is your spirit alone that meets with me here."

"Is that why You're not speaking in the ancient tongue, Lady?" The question had been bothering Kade since her first conversation with the Goddess. She had always been taught that Ithyris spoke only in the language of their ancestors, yet from the moment the Goddess had first addressed her after the ceremony, Kade had understood Her clearly.

"Oh, but I am, Beloved. And so are you."

Before Kade could ask how that was possible, since she'd always been so dreadfully slow at translation, a man stepped out of one of the glowing doorways nearby. He didn't seem to see them. He walked out onto the floor of the nexus and looked around in confusion. His head tilted back to stare at the rippling lake above them, and to Kade's astonishment, he floated upward, his head breaking the glimmering surface, followed by his shoulders, hips, and legs, until he had disappeared within it.

"Who was that?"

Ithyris's smile was tender. "Marlus. He was a lieutenant in the Ithyrian royal guard. A good man. I'm afraid his body was too badly damaged to contain his spirit any longer."

"He died?"

"Far too many have died this day," the Goddess answered sadly. Kade experienced a flash of guilt, remembering how miserably her clumsy attempts at *shaa'ri* had failed, but Ithyris shook Her head. "No, Beloved, you mustn't blame yourself. This is my brother Ulrike's doing. It is why I need your help now." She leveled Her unfathomable gaze at Kade seriously. "Ulrike has invaded my lands with His own *shaa'din*."

"His own—" But with the question still poised on her lips, the image of the twisted mirror rose in her memory, and Kade found she already knew who Ithyris meant. "That pregnant barbarian woman."

"Yes. To create a *shaa'din* through whom we may channel our power, my brother and I may infuse a mortal with a part of ourselves. I am of spirit, and so I filled your spirit with mine and made a place for myself within you. But Ulrike is of flesh. He must access His *shaa'din* through her body."

Kade gaped as Her words registered. "You're saying Ulrike has possessed that woman's baby?"

"Not quite." Ithyris's tone was grave. "Ulrike has placed a child of His own within her."

While Kade tried to process this horrific statement, the Goddess's form flickered, like the flame of a candle threatened by the wind. "We do not have much time, Beloved. You are not yet strong enough to remain in the nexus for long. You must listen carefully. Ulrike has sent His *shaa'din* to recover a prophecy written by Mondera of the Twelve. You must find it before He does, and destroy it."

Ithyris flickered again, more violently this time. Kade felt herself being tugged backward, toward the glowing doorway that Ithyris had said was hers. She braced herself against its pull. She still had so many more questions.

"What does the prophecy say, Lady?"

But Ithyris did not answer, and Kade was being dragged backward. "Go to Agar, Beloved," the Goddess called after her. She was wavering in and out of sight, and Her voice was fading. "Find the staff of Fyn, which lies in the city library."

Kade strained to keep her footing on the frictionless floor, but it was no use. The doorway was drawing her back and she could not break free of its hold. "Please, don't go yet!" she cried, but the nexus shrank away as she was re-engulfed by the silver current, and Ithyris vanished.

As she felt the current sweeping her back into awareness of her own body, the Goddess's faint voice rang after her. "I will come to you in Agar, Beloved, as I promised."

Kade opened her eyes. The weightless feeling was gone, and her limbs had regained their normal heft and substance. The abrupt change left her feeling queasy. Erinda was still just a few paces away, brushing the horse down and distinctly radiating the message that she wanted Kade to leave her alone. The sight of her reminded Kade of the one question she had been so anxious to ask Ithyris, and she had not even brought it up this time. Her throat suddenly dry, Kade backed up a few more steps, and then turned away. She would leave Erinda to her work for now, and give them both the chance to absorb everything that had happened. There would be time for more words between them later, when Kade had collected her thoughts and figured out how she could best help Erinda without exacerbating her pain.

"I've been looking for you everywhere!" Myka exclaimed, running to her breathlessly. "*Ostryn* Lyris and Captain Talon have invited us to eat with them. Did you know they're siblings? Or were, anyway, before the *Ostryn* took her vows. Strangest thing. Anyway, I told them we would, and I hope that's all right. We can't travel any farther until the horses have rested anyway, so we're going to be here for the night as it is, and besides, they've been really very kind to us and the captain wants to know more about what happened on the battlefield today, and—"

"All right."

Myka broke off in the middle of her persuasive argument and beamed. "Really?"

"Yes." Kade cast one last glance in Erinda's direction, and then turned back to Myka. "Where is the captain now?"

"I'll take you to them." Myka skipped off with excitement, and Kade followed, butterflies fluttering in her stomach. She was not very good at making conversation with strangers, and she dreaded the interrogation she was sure to face from the curious captain. But she needed to get to Agar, and she was not ready to leave Erinda just yet. Surely the Goddess had brought her back into Kade's life for a reason. Perhaps this was Her way of granting Kade's earnest prayers on Erinda's behalf? If so, then She had given her a second chance to make things right, and Kade was determined she would not fail this time.

❖

Lyris leaned forward, her expression eager. "And Ithyris wants you to destroy this prophecy?"

Kade nodded, taking another sip of tea from the tin mug in her hands. "She's asked me to retrieve something called the staff of Fyn from the city library in Agar."

Lyris exhaled. "Of course."

"You know of it?"

"I've read much of the three sisters. They were the seers of the Twelve. According to the legends, Mondera could divine the future, Cibli could communicate with spirits of the dead, and Fyn could hear the thoughts of any mortal creature around her. It's said they had these abilities even before they were called to join the Twelve, but the Goddess's power made them stronger."

Kade was impressed. "Where did you learn all that? The Honored Mother let me read the Book of Verdred, but even that only said they possessed 'a sight beyond mortal understanding.' I could never figure out what Verdred meant."

"The Twelve have always been a particular fascination of mine," Lyris said, lowering her lashes shyly. "When I'd exhausted the archives in the palace temple, I asked the Honored Mother of Aster for access to the Ithyrian Treasury. You wouldn't believe the records kept there. All of the scribes' surviving work, dating back to the time of the Twelve."

"Really? Mother Qiturah told me that even she wouldn't be allowed access to those records. How did you manage it?"

"Truthfully, I'm not sure. I expected my request to be denied. Mother Nihla said I was the first she'd granted entrance to in all her winters as Treasuress, but when I asked why she wouldn't explain."

Talon interrupted. "This staff of Fyn, how is it related to the prophecy?"

Kade shook her head. "I don't know, Captain. Ithyris only said that I must find it."

"But the barbarian horde—you think it's this prophecy they're after?"

Lyris gave her brother an exasperated look. "She doesn't just think it, Talon. Ithyris told her so."

He rolled his eyes a little, and though Kade probably should have been appalled by his lack of faith, she couldn't help wanting to snicker. Talon reminded her so much of her own older brother. Jen didn't put much stock in the workings of Ithyris either.

"You're gonna help us, right?" Myka asked around a mouthful of bread.

Lyris lifted an eyebrow at the captain, who sighed. "If the barbarians really are after this prophecy, then destroying it is our best chance to get them out of Ithyria." He looked around them in the darkness. Moans of pain punctuated the evening quiet as the soldiers fed themselves and tended to their wounded brethren. "These men won't survive another battle like the one today. I'm not even sure many of them will make it the rest of the way to Agar, but we can't leave them here to be picked off by the barbarian army." Talon turned back to Kade. "We can escort you as far as Agar, Your Grace. Beyond that, I can't make any promises."

"Yeah!" Myka cheered, stabbing the air with the remainder of her bread.

Kade inclined her head gratefully. "Thank you, Captain."

"Talon, I've come to take a look at that leg wound."

Kade's head snapped up as Erinda appeared at the edge of their circle. Her pretty features were pale and drawn, the glow of the fire casting harsh shadows under her eyes and cheekbones. Kade had to sternly suppress the urge to jump up and wrap her in a hug. If anything, Erinda looked more haunted now than the last time they'd met. She was suffering so terribly, and it was all Kade's fault. Somehow, Kade had to find a way to comfort her that did not send them both tumbling back down the same aberrant path that had so nearly ensnared them in their youth.

Erinda had laid a hand on Talon's shoulder before she caught sight of Kade on the other side of the fire. Kade felt Erinda's jolt of surprise at the same instant that it registered on Erinda's face, and the misery that came with it roiled her stomach. Erinda quickly withdrew her fingers.

"Never mind, Captain. I'll find you again later." She disappeared from the ring of firelight.

Talon furrowed his brow and looked over at Kade. "Do you two know each other?"

Kade set her mug down. "We were…friends, once. It was a long time ago. If you'll excuse us, Captain, *Ostryn*, I think we're going to go get some sleep. Thank you very much for the meal."

Talon stood and bowed. "Sleep well, Your Grace."

She and Myka made their way to their own small tent, which Myka had erected in the midst of the camp. Strange—Kade could have sworn she felt the captain's dark eyes following her thoughtfully as they ducked inside.

CHAPTER NINE

General Urden of the Monderan provincial guard was an impressively large man, with a chest nearly as wide as two men standing side by side. His arms were the size of small trees, and his stomach lapped a good distance over his belt. In the center of the drafty stone-walled room that served as the general's private office, Urden towered over the heads of Talon and her group and scowled down at her and Farsh with disdain. "The Queen promises me reinforcements from her personal guard, and you show up in Agar with a half battalion of useless wounded?"

"As I explained, General, we were engaged by the horde before we reached you."

Erinda could hear the irritation in Talon's reply, though she kept her voice calm.

The general snorted. "You mean you barged into one of their occupied villages and wasted the lives of Ithyrian soldiers on a fool's errand."

"With all due respect, General, it is the provincial guard's duty to defend the villages under its jurisdiction." Talon was too diplomatic to add, *Where were you and your men while the barbarians murdered those people?* However, she didn't need to, because the implication echoed clearly through the room.

Urden bristled. "You listen to me, son. I've been holding the line in Mondera for more winters than you've had a heartbeat, and we've never seen anything like this before. First, it was the coal mines, at least a dozen all along the border, the miners butchered and their settlements wiped out. Seemed more organized than their usual burn-and-run scavenging, but I didn't think anything of it until Kordus, our largest northern city, was completely overrun. More Dangar animals in one place than the eye could count, and that redheaded witch by far the vilest of the lot. I lost nearly half my men in Kordus alone, and still they drove us out like marmots!"

He growled and spat on the floor by his feet. Erinda cringed and looked away, resisting the urge to find a mop and bucket. The cleanliness of the general's floor was none of her concern.

Urden was not finished with his tirade. "Now the brutes are advancing in packs, taking the forest towns one after another, and from what I've heard, those they kill in the taking are the lucky ones. Any fool can see they're headed straight for Agar. From here the witch and her army would have easy access to the entire eastern half of Ithyria, so right now, holding the capital is far more important than a few forest villages."

A muscle clenched in Talon's jaw. "I am certain Her Majesty would disagree."

"Well, Her Majesty's welcome to come down out of that fancy palace of hers and take a swipe at them herself, if she wants," the general retorted angrily. "You saw what happens out there. Something isn't natural about those animals. Won't go down, no matter how you injure them. Taking off their heads seems to be the only thing that works, and even then it's not always final." He tugged at his beard with frustration. "We're still trying to evacuate the citizens of Agar to cities in the south before the horde reaches us, and you've brought me more damned refugees and a bunch of broken soldiers. What am I supposed to do with them?"

Before either captain could reply, however, Urden waved a hand. "Never mind. We'll send them on to the Great Temple. Let the priestesses there tend them. Since those crazy holy women refuse to evacuate, they might as well make themselves useful."

"Mondera Temple is nearby?" Farsh asked.

"A league southwest," the general replied absently, shuffling through a stack of papers on his desk.

Talon and Farsh conferred quietly for a moment. Talon turned back to Urden. "We'll have a unit escort the surviving villagers and wounded to the temple in the morning. In the meantime—"

"In the meantime, gentlemen, I've got to go over these plans again. Figure out how to get the most out of the measly handful of viable men you've brought me when that she-demon shows up on Agar's doorstep, and it probably won't be long now. Even with the battalions from Fyn and Cibli provinces, we're still outmatched, and if it's true what Her Grace here says"—he jerked his head at Lyris—"then not even the

Goddess with all Her magical blue fire is able to stop these monsters on the battlefield. We can only hope we'll be able to do better with our swords, or we're all dead men."

Lyris's eyes widened with indignation, but the general just resumed his seat at the desk and bent over the maps in front of him, not even bothering with a formal dismissal.

Talon saluted sharply, though Erinda doubted there was much sincere esteem in the gesture. Farsh followed her example, and then the captains turned and left the room with Erinda, Lyris, and their lieutenants trailing in their wake. Erinda had tagged along without invitation when Talon was called to speak with the general; she'd insisted the Queen would want to know what was happening, though the truth was she just didn't want to be left alone where Kade might corner her for another chat. She wasn't sure why Talon hadn't made her stay behind, as it would have been easy enough to order one of the men to restrain her. But Talon had merely grunted and ignored her presence. Erinda wondered if perhaps Talon didn't mind, as much as she claimed, that Erinda was feeding Shasta news of their journey.

❖

Your Majesty,

I am relieved to report that we have arrived in Agar, though sadly not without incident. We encountered an occupied village to the north of the city and, in attempt to drive out the attackers, a good many of our men lost their lives.

It appears the stories being told at the palace are true; our enemy possesses a mysterious strength that makes them nearly impossible to defeat. Were it not for the fortuitous appearance of—

—Kadrian the Magnificent, Handmaiden of Ithyris, who saved us all with a prayer that made everyone invisible...Erinda's fingers stilled over the parchment. How was she going to explain this? How much was appropriate to share? She couldn't possibly write to Shasta without describing Kade's involvement in their rescue, but she didn't know how she'd ever get an explanation down on paper without her emotions coloring every sentence.

The night following their escape from the burning village, the remnants of the guard battalions had been granted a few hours' reprieve in which to rest while the barbarian army combed the forest in vain for their invisible foes. But no one knew how long the effect of the *shaa'din*'s miracle would last, and Talon and Farsh were unwilling to press their luck. Before dawn, they struck camp and prepared the injured as best they could for travel. Fewer horses than men had died in the disastrous battle, and so by riding two to a mount the remaining soldiers and handful of villagers they had managed to liberate were able to reach Agar ahead of the barbarians, who pursued on foot.

During this mad dash for the capital, Lyris had shared her horse with Erinda. Thrilled by their encounter with the Goddess's new *shaa'din*, Lyris was more than happy to fill Erinda in on the events of the battle that she had missed. She gave Erinda a glowing recount of Kade's version of what had happened, of how Kade said she had been pulled toward the village before she even knew it was under attack, and how she had rendered first herself, then her Pledged companion and their horse, and then every Ithyrian in that village invisible to their enemies purely via the power of prayer. Lyris chattered on, unaware that every word was a splinter pricking Erinda's heart.

Yet in spite of her discomfort, Erinda had absorbed these details with the relish of a starving woman offered a crust of bread. This was the true crux of her weakness, after all. For all the pain that accompanied thoughts of Kade, she still could not bring herself to rip this longing from her chest and walk away. And part of Erinda ached to write Shasta a full confession, to share her confusion and despair with someone she knew would sympathize with her dilemma.

But Erinda could not bear to worry her that way. It was going to be hard enough on Shasta to learn of the battle, of all the men who had died in her name, and how narrowly Talon and the rest had escaped death. Erinda would not add her own wretched problems to that burden.

With a hiss of frustration, she crumpled the paper and held it over the candle flame, watching the edges blacken. Though she'd relived the memory a thousand times in the past two days, it still felt like a surreal nightmare: the fires raging around them, the barbarian woman lifting her axe, and then Kade's arms around her, her weight pressing Erinda into the ground as she stared into her eyes. Their bodily rhythms had synced so naturally, so rapidly, as if they'd always been meant to function in tandem. As if they'd never been separated at all.

"Erinda! What the—Look out!"

Talon's warning pulled her from her thoughts, and she realized her sleeve had caught fire. She dropped the fragments of the letter in alarm. Talon stripped out of her uniform jacket and threw it over Erinda's arm to smother the flames. She patted it to be sure they were extinguished, and Erinda winced when the jacket was peeled back. The skin of her wrist was bright pink and promised a blister, and though the burn was no larger than her thumbnail, it still smarted.

Talon glared at her. "That does it. What in the name of the Goddess is going on with you?"

Erinda picked at the charred remains of her sleeve. "I was distracted."

"You've been distracted for more than a moon. You could have been seriously hurt just now. Talk to me." She shook out her jacket and slid her arms back into it, leaving it unbuttoned over her lightweight undershirt. The scarlet fabric was a bit scorched on one shoulder, but Talon paid it no attention.

"I—" Surely Talon had much bigger issues to deal with than Erinda's frivolous personal issues. But Talon was watching her with such concern that Erinda felt tears welling in her eyes. She looked down at the quill in her uninjured hand and willed herself to focus.

"I know who she is, Erinda." Talon's deep tones were gentle. Erinda's vision blurred until she could barely make out the shape of her own hand on the table. "At least, I think I do. Why didn't you tell me?" Talon pulled a chair from the table and turned it around, straddling it backward. She leaned over the chair's back and regarded Erinda seriously. "The Handmaiden is Kadrian, isn't she? She's the first girl you ever…"

Despite her best effort to hold them back, when she blinked, the tears spilled over.

"It is her, isn't it?"

She nodded, and a strangled sob escaped before she could stifle it. In an instant Talon was on her feet, pulling Erinda into her arms. Unable to fight her overwhelming anguish any longer, she collapsed against Talon's chest. She gripped the front of Talon's jacket until her knuckles turned white, and she cried helplessly.

Talon didn't say anything more for a long time. She just laid a cheek atop Erinda's hair and held her, rocking her side to side like she might comfort a distraught child. Her embrace was warm, strong, and safe, and though her touch no longer carried even a hint of sexual provocation, Erinda found she could still draw solace from it. When at last she was able to recover a bit of composure, she pulled back slowly, tucking an unruly curl behind her ear. Talon produced a handkerchief from her pocket, and Erinda used it to blot her eyes and wipe her nose. She eyed the damp spot on Talon's uniform, then held up the handkerchief with a teary grin.

"I bet you do this for all the girls."

"Even have a spare or two," Talon replied with a wink.

Erinda made a noise that came out half-snicker, half-sniffle. "Of course you do."

Talon helped her back into her seat and then draped herself over the back of her own chair once again. "Now, you're going to tell me everything." She took Erinda's hand and squeezed it. "Right?"

Erinda drew a shaky breath and nodded.

❖

Kade surveyed the iron pole that was set rather inelegantly into a rough block of wood in a remote corner of the library's musty basement.

"You're sure this is the staff of Fyn?" she asked the little man who had escorted her to the artifact. Kade was taller than most women, but she felt like a giant next to the librarian, whose head scarcely came to her shoulders.

"Of course it is. You can't read the sign?" He swept the lantern in his hand toward a small placard pasted to the wooden base. It read, *Iron Staff, circa the Great Division, belonging to Fyn of the Twelve.*

Myka was equally unimpressed. "It doesn't look like much, does it?"

The staff was as thick as Kade's thumb, and about a foot taller than she was. At the top was fixed a wrought finial with prongs curved into a hollow sphere, and underneath dangled four heavy rings that, as far as Kade could tell, had no purpose other than decoration. The entire thing was fashioned out of dull black iron, with rust spots marring its surface in several places.

Kade shrugged. "It's what Ithyris asked for, so..." She reached for it. The librarian rapped her on the knuckles, and she snatched her hand back. "What did you do that for?"

He huffed and used the lantern to illuminate another sign posted on the wall. *Do Not Touch.* "That staff's a thousand winters old, missy. You think it's survived that long because we let people run their hands all over it?" He looked her up and down. "I only let you and your friend down here because you're with the temple, even if you are the strangest priestess I've ever seen."

Kade resisted the urge to run a hand over her bristled hair. Myka, however, was not intimidated.

"We told you, *Ostryn* Kadrian is *shaa'din.* And she needs that staff. Ithyris Herself told us to get it from this library."

"Only the Twelve were *shaa'din*," the man sniffed, and he waved his light toward the foot of the stairs that led back to the library's main level. "I think you ladies had better leave now."

"Sir," Kade said in her most courteous manner, "I don't think you understand. I can't leave here without that staff. The Goddess has commanded me to retrieve it."

"And just how do I know that, hmm? You think we don't have people in here all the time trying to waltz off with our province's greatest treasures?"

"I should think that staff would be one of Fyn province's greatest treasures, not Mondera's," Myka said.

The little librarian puffed his chest in indignation. "For your information, young lady, this staff was a gift from Fyn to her sister Mondera, who entrusted it to the Agar library for safekeeping. We've preserved it for a thousand winters since, and we're not about to let a couple of insolent girls walk off with it. Now if you don't mind..." He indicated the stairs again.

Kade was at a loss. He clearly would not allow her to take the staff without a fight, and she wasn't going to resort to harming him in order to get it. The man was, after all, just doing his job. But the heavy oak doors that led to this basement were fixed with numerous locks, as were the main doors of the library itself. It wasn't likely that she could sneak in to take the staff later. Besides, Daughters of Ithyris did not steal.

"Make him believe you, Kadrian."

Kade started when the Goddess's voice sounded in her mind, though she was beginning to get accustomed to Her sudden interruptions. *How, Lady? He won't listen to me.*

"Will him to."

Will him to? Just how exactly was she supposed to do that? Feeling more than a little silly, Kade cleared her throat and stared hard at the librarian. "You will give us the staff," she said with as much authority as she could.

The man guffawed heartily. "You got mud in your ears, girl? I said you're not touching it and that's what I meant." He took her elbow. "Time for you to go."

The silver spirit beneath her skin pulsed. "You are my *shaa'din*, Kadrian. Will him to see you."

Kade took a deep breath and closed her eyes. She didn't understand what the Goddess meant, but so long as She asked it of her, she had to keep trying. Back at Verdred Temple, Ithyris had said the priestesses could not see her because Kade had willed them not to. Perhaps this was the same, only in reverse? Kade sought out the Goddess's current and concentrated on its shimmering threads, on the awareness of Her that it carried through the deepest parts of her being.

See me. She pushed the thought into the current and directed it outward, through her blood and muscle and skin and into the man's fingertips where he gripped her arm. She envisioned the demand flowing out of her with every beat of the silver veins, coursing into him, opening his mind to her resolve. *I am* shaa'din. *See me and know that this is true.* After a moment, she added, *And give us the staff, please?*

She could feel the current surging as she pressed her will into it, could feel its rippling vibrations streaming into him. But when she opened her eyes, he was still frowning up at her. Kade sighed. *Forgive me, Lady. I don't know how to—*

The little man's scowl melted into an expression of sheer reverence that was so at odds with his earlier pomposity Kade could hardly believe her eyes. "My sincerest apologies, Handmaiden." He released her arm. "Of course, the staff is yours. Please." He stepped past Myka and lifted Fyn's iron staff from its base, holding it out to Kade with his head bent low.

Myka's mouth dropped open. Her eyes went from the genuflecting librarian to Kade and back again. "No way," she breathed.

Kade rather echoed that sentiment herself. Tentatively, she took hold of the staff, which was heavy and cold in her hand. She half expected the man to snatch it back and crack her knuckles again, but he only stooped further as she took it from him.

"No way!" Myka exclaimed with greater excitement.

Kade shot her a warning glance. "Thank you, sir," she said, trying not to let her tone betray her immense relief, not to mention her astonishment that whatever she had done had worked. Gripping the staff in one hand, she followed him back up the stairs to the main floor of the library with Myka at her heels. He showed them to the entrance with formal deference, as if he were escorting the Queen herself across the threshold, and bowed again.

"You have honored us with your visit today, Handmaiden," he said as Kade and Myka descended the steps to the cobbled city street. "If there's ever anything else we can do for you, please let us know."

Kade had no idea how long his newfound compliance would last. Had he genuinely realized that she was *shaa'din*, or had the Goddess merely worked a spell over his mind and supplanted his suspicions with cooperation? She didn't plan on lingering around to find out. The staff was in her possession, and she wanted to get it someplace safe before the man could change his mind. As she hurried down the street away from the library, Myka trotted by her side, eyes wide with awe.

"How did you *do* that?" she said in a near squeal. "That was absolutely the most fantastic thing I've ever seen!" She lowered her voice into an imitation of the librarian. "'My sincerest apologies, Handmaiden.'"

As Myka dissolved into a fit of giggles, Kade shook her head. "Ithyris said I should will him to believe me. So I did, and he gave it to us."

"Just like that." Myka's hair swung around her ears as she skipped ahead. "You have no idea how much I envy you right now. What I wouldn't give to be able to make somebody do whatever I wanted them to!"

The iron staff was too heavy to carry for long, and Kade resorted to cracking its blunt end into the cobblestones every few steps like a walking stick. She could feel the reverberations all the way up its length, and its thick rings clanged with each impact. "I don't think it works like that," she said. "I think it has to be something the Goddess wants. She's the one requiring it of them. I just sort of push Her message along where others can hear it."

"Still, it's got to be incredible, being able to make something like that happen."

Kade shrugged uncomfortably. While the Goddess's power never ceased to amaze her, she wasn't sure she enjoyed the thought of having so much control over the minds of other people. It felt wrong, somehow, to rob others of their free will, even if it was in Ithyris's name. She banged the staff into the street a little harder and quickened her pace.

Agar was the largest city she had ever been in, larger even than the Ithyrian capital of Ardrenn where she had grown up. Agar was laid out in an enormous circle nearly two leagues across, with the viceroy's castle and keep at its heart. From there the streets spread out in concentric rings, connected at intervals by bisecting alleyways for faster access between blocks. Houses piled in haphazard fashion, one on top of the next. Though General Urden had said that the city was being evacuated, people filled the streets at every hour of the day and night, clattering down the cobbled stones with horses and wagons, shouting at one another. Agar was far too busy and noisy for her taste, and just walking from place to place set her nerves on edge and made her long for the peaceful solitude of Verdred Temple. She was beginning to feel a little homesick.

A massive stone wall, tall as ten men and nearly as thick, encircled the entire city. She could only imagine how long it must have taken to build such an enormous structure, but being so close to the Dangar border, she could easily comprehend the need for it. After the massacre she'd witnessed in the tiny forest village, she could understand why so many people chose to make Agar their home in spite of its cramped, crowded feel. Those thick walls and the safety to be found in numbers had to be very appealing incentives.

She and Myka reached the guard barracks near the city's center, where the Monderan general had grudgingly agreed the reinforcements from Ardrenn might stay upon their arrival. Agar boasted not just one, but four city temples, and the high priestesses of each had come in person to greet Kade the moment she'd set foot in their city. News of the *shaa'din*'s arrival had preceded them, it seemed, and all four high priestesses had eagerly offered her lodging within their respective temples. Kade had politely declined their invitations. In truth, she preferred the soldiers' company; most were practical men who harbored little fascination with her status as Handmaiden. They were content to give her plenty of respectful distance, and a few ignored her entirely. She found their disinterest much more comfortable than the prospect of being surrounded by grandstanding priestesses clamoring for her attention.

Myka stopped just outside the barracks gate. "If it's all right with you, Your Grace, I'm going to go get us some more tea. We need soap, too, since we used all of ours tending the injured on the way here."

Kade eyed the foot traffic that filled the street. "I don't think you should go into the markets alone. I'm sure we can find one of the guard who'd be willing to escort you."

Myka smirked. "Please. I've been running errands in far more dangerous cities since I was no taller than your kneecaps. I can take care of myself." To illustrate her point, she hiked up the hem of her white robe to a scandalous degree so Kade could glimpse the hilt of a knife tucked into the cuff of her boot. She dropped her robe again. "I'll be back in a flash." Before Kade could argue, she'd darted off down the street.

Kade rolled her eyes. In all her winters in the Goddess's service, Myka had to be the most irreverent, headstrong priestess-in-training she had ever met. She couldn't imagine how she fit in with the other Pledged, or how she'd ever obtained the Honored Mother's permission to Pledge at all with such cavalier manners. She breathed a quick prayer for her safety, then tapped the gate with the end of the staff. A little window, set behind an iron grate, slid aside for a moment. Then it shut again, and the gate creaked open.

"Your Grace," the guard acknowledged as she slipped inside. That was the extent of his greeting, and he shut the gate behind her without further comment or fanfare. Kade smiled to herself as she made her way over the hard-packed earth, wending between the buildings that marched in perfect, military symmetry across the barracks grounds. She passed a unit of Monderan guard in their burgundy uniforms running drills, and caught the barks of their captain.

The building at the far west corner of the barracks had been designated for the use of the new arrivals, and she stepped aside for one of the healers who was leaving. The front of his tunic was streaked with blood, and a bundle of dirty bandages was in his hands. He inclined his head as he went by. Kade pushed the door open and hastened down the narrow hall toward the chamber she and Myka had been assigned. She would feel better once she had deposited the staff with their other belongings.

As she passed one room in particular, however, she halted. The curtain was only partially drawn across the entrance, and she caught sight of Erinda inside, sitting at a rough-hewn table and speaking earnestly with the young captain of the royal guard. The captain was leaning over the back of his chair, one of Erinda's hands encased in his, and as Kade watched, he ran his thumb absently over the back of her hand while she talked. Kade could tell that Erinda had been crying. She'd only ever seen Erinda cry once before—that night in the temple kitchens, with her lips pressed to Kade's and her tears streaking both their faces.

Her back slammed against the stone wall next to the door. Her conscience pricked at her imperiously. This was none of her business, it insisted, and she should move on to her own chamber and leave them to their private conversation. But she found she could not move as Erinda's voice drifted through the doorway.

"You really can't see what madness this is? Talon, the Queen loves you desperately. She will never take someone else to her bed. Surely you have to know that."

"But I can't be the reason for it, Erinda. I can't be the reason that Ithyria doesn't have a strong heir, that Shasta doesn't have the support of her council. I can't be the reason that Princess Brita grows up surrounded by resentment and hatred. I won't do that to them."

"You already have, you idiot," Erinda said, but the fondness of her tone made the insult an endearment. "Like it or not, Talon, you are Queen Shasta's reason for *everything* now. Just like I know she is for you. Being away from her like this isn't protecting her or helping her. It's eating her alive."

"It's scarcely been a moon yet. It will get better. She'll…" Talon's voice sounded strained. "She'll learn to take comfort in someone else. We did, didn't we?"

"Yes, we did."

Kade sucked in a breath at the sensuality that infused Erinda's reply. The vision flooded her senses before she could quell it: Erinda, mousy curls sliding unbound over naked shoulders, moaning softly with pleasure as the captain's dark hands traveled her lush curves. Jealousy and arousal stabbed through her simultaneously, and her mouth went dry. Oh, Goddess, she'd been with him. Kade knew this with absolute certainty. He'd seen her, touched her, tasted her in all the ways Kade had forbidden herself to think about. Her ears started to ring, and she scarcely made out the rest of Erinda's words.

"But that was different, Talon. That was when you believed she would never be able to accept you for who you are, that you could never tell her the truth. And anyway, you gave me up the moment she asked you to, now didn't you?"

Kade heard no rebuke in Erinda's voice, but she stiffened anyway. Talon had rejected Erinda's attentions for someone else? How could any man possibly choose another woman over her? As miserable as it was to picture Erinda in anyone else's arms, she had always prayed that one day Erinda would find an adoring husband and build the family she deserved. She'd hoped that someday Erinda would enjoy the normal, happy life she would surely have had if it hadn't been for Kade's selfish, misleading influence.

She could still remember the exact day she'd crossed the line from innocent infatuation to utterly self-centered exploitation of Erinda's feelings. They'd had only a few days left before Kade was to take her vows, and they'd agreed to spend every possible remaining minute together. Kade would slip out of the palace temple right after morning prayers, and find Erinda waiting outside the temple doors. Hand in hand, they'd head for the moors, smuggling themselves out of the palace gates behind a cart bound for market or a visiting dignitary's carriage. And then they would run together, laughing, until they found a spot in the grass that was soft and welcoming. They flopped down side by side and stared at the sky, pointing out the shapes of animals in the clouds, trying to see who could string the longest chain of wildflowers, counting the birds that winged through their field of vision. They stayed out there, hidden in the tall grass, until the sun began to dip westward and they knew they had no choice but to go back.

After one such perfect morning, when Erinda at last propped herself on one elbow and suggested reluctantly that they'd better return to the palace before they were missed, Kade burst into tears. They only had a few more precious days together like this one. Then, everything would change. The thought was unbearable.

"Oh, darling, don't cry. Please don't cry," Erinda murmured, pressing kisses into Kade's cropped hair.

"But I don't know how I'm going to live without you, Rin. My heart's being cut right down the middle." It was more than that. With every day that passed, she was less certain she could do this. Leaving felt like dying.

"You want to be a priestess, though. It's what you've always said you wanted, more than anything."

"I know, but I don't want to leave you. I'm so scared."

"Shh. It will be all right, you'll see."

"But, Rin." Kade rubbed her cheek against the soft skin of Erinda's throat. "I love you."

Erinda's fingers wove into Kade's hair, and tugged gently at her scalp. "I love you, too. Always, no matter what." She used her grip in Kade's hair to lift her face, and touched her lips to Kade's forehead.

Kade was not ready for their time together to end. She wasn't ready to go back to the palace, to bid farewell to yet another sunset that pulled her closer to the moment she'd be parted from her dearest friend forever. She tilted her head back and kissed her. She needed the comforting warmth of Erinda's arms and softness of her body molded against her. She needed to hold on to Erinda while she still could, so she captured Erinda's face in her hands and laid her down into the grass without breaking the kiss. She covered Erinda's torso with hers, felt their legs tangle together. She moved her mouth on her until just the dance of lips wasn't enough, and she had to use her tongue as well. Erinda opened to her willingly, let her push inside. The taste of her was warm and delicious, bursting in her mouth like ripe berries.

She stroked her tongue tenderly against Erinda's, explored the slippery inner surfaces of her mouth. Her hands moved restlessly over Erinda's ribs, her hips, her thighs, grasping and tugging, trying to pull every part of her closer at once. They rocked against one another, their bodies instinctively seeking deeper connection. Kade left Erinda's mouth to press kisses along her jaw, down the silken column of her neck. Her sun-bronzed skin was warm and salted, and Kade grazed it with her teeth, lapped with her tongue, caressed with her mouth until she reached the neckline of her shift, which denied her access to anything further. No matter. Kade traveled back up the way she'd come, and when she reached the earlobe again she switched sides.

She'd never tried anything like this before, with anyone. This wasn't what she had intended. But she couldn't stop. Erinda was making soft sounds, half-strangled whimpers and moans that Kade had never heard her utter before. And she was making her sound like that. Those little noises of wonder, of pleasure, those were for her. They made blood rush to her head in a frenzy.

"Goddess, Rin, I need you. I need you so much."

One of her hands found its way beneath the edge of Erinda's laced bodice. Erinda gasped and arched beneath her when her fingers brushed the sensitive peak of a nipple. She fumbled with the leather thongs of Erinda's bodice until she'd managed to get them free of their eyelets, and caressed Erinda's breast through the linen of her shift. Erinda made that noise again, the one that set off explosions deep in Kade's gut, and Kade slid her hand beneath the fabric to cup her naked flesh without hindrance. Erinda was indescribably soft in her palm, full and sweet. She pressed her lips to Erinda's throat, felt the pulse against her tongue, kneaded her with her fingers and plucked softly at the pebbled nipple hardening between her fingertips. She gloried in the ecstasy pouring off Erinda's skin, her silent plea for more.

Kade tugged the shift down Erinda's lightly freckled shoulder, until the curves of her breast were bared. Goddess, she was so beautiful. So perfect. Kade bent to kiss her there, and when her mouth closed over the rigid apex of her nipple, Erinda cried out. Kade explored its rippled texture with the same languorous care that she'd spent learning Erinda's mouth. She brushed her tongue lightly across the turgid tip, swirled circles over the puckered surface, felt the flesh slide against her tongue as she sucked and drew it deeper. Beneath her, Erinda writhed in pleasure. Expectant wetness built between Kade's thighs, flooding her with a kind of desire she hadn't known she was capable of.

Slowly, breathing hard, she drew herself back up Erinda's torso until she could look into her eyes. Her heart thundered. She wanted Erinda's bare skin against hers, all of it. She longed to bury herself inside Erinda's body, to claim her, to fuse together with her so that no one would ever, ever be able to separate them. She could feel, too, that Erinda's wishes were the same as hers. The pulse that pounded in the hollow of Erinda's throat matched Kade's riotous heart beat for beat; their chests rose and fell against each other as if trading the air back and forth between them in perfect duet. In that moment, she knew Erinda would allow her anything she wanted. Anything at all.

And gradually, it occurred to her that this was probably not something either of them ought to be feeling. Girls didn't want other girls this way. Pledged weren't supposed to want *anyone* this way. As she gazed down at Erinda's lovely, enraptured face, her petal-pink lips parted and swollen from the violence of their kisses, eyes shining with exhilaration, guilt knifed through her. What was she doing? In just a few days, she would join the temple. She would go on to lead a chaste, sanctified existence in the service of the Goddess. But Erinda was supposed to find a handsome husband who would give her a comfortable home and a healthy handful of boisterous children with their mother's brown curls and secret dimples. That was who she should be granting this precious gift of herself to. Kade didn't deserve it.

"Kade," Erinda said breathlessly, "what is it?"

When she related her thoughts, Erinda shook her head. "It doesn't have to be that way."

"We don't really have a choice, do we?"

"Of course we do!" Erinda rolled onto her side, her shift draping off one shoulder in a way that made Kade's mouth water with the longing to taste her again. "Kade, no one will force you to take vows if you don't want to. No one can force me to marry against my will. There's always a choice."

Kade shook her head. "I shouldn't be doing this to you, Rin. In a few days, I'll be gone, and this isn't fair. I just..." She reached for Erinda's hand and interlaced their fingers. "I feel like I need to be closer to you. Like a part of me is lost inside you, and I have to say good-bye, and I don't know how, and it hurts."

Tears started falling again. She was going about this all wrong, and she knew it, but what else could she do? Erinda was everything. Soon, the Goddess would replace her in Kade's life, and that was supposed to be even better. It would be better, wouldn't it? She loved Ithyris, too. And Erinda had her own life to live. She shouldn't have to worry about taking care of Kade for the rest of their lives. This was meant to happen. They had to give each other up, move on. Grow up.

Kade choked on a sob.

"Kade, darling, come here. Shh." Erinda lay back on the grass and drew Kade over her, and Kade curled her body around Erinda's so that her head was resting on her shoulder. "Don't think about it. Okay? I'm here. You're here. That's all that matters. Just be with me now, today, and let tomorrow take care of itself."

Kade sniffled, and Erinda hugged her closer. She closed her eyes and let herself be lulled by the steady rhythm of Erinda's breathing. But in spite of Erinda's brave words, she was perfectly aware of the truth.

Erinda was every bit as terrified as she was.

Kade opened her eyes and inhaled deeply. When she pushed away from the wall, a liquid rush between her legs made her eyes widen in surprise, then embarrassment. Goddess, what was she doing, indulging in such lecherous memories? She was *shaa'din*. Pure. Holy. Beloved of Ithyris Herself. The spirit current beneath her skin was humming softly, and it filled her with shame. Kade stumbled down the hall toward her chamber, one hand clutching at the staff's iron rings to prevent them from clanging together and alerting Erinda and Talon to her childish eavesdropping.

When she reached the little room, she propped the staff in a corner and fell to her knees. *Forgive me, Lady*, she pleaded. *I have failed You before, I know, but I am Yours now. I swear I am Yours.*

She gasped when the silver current swelled, and she felt the Goddess descend on her as purposefully as She had at the ceremony when She'd claimed Kade the first time. The Goddess enveloped Kade in bliss inside and out, caressing her flushed skin, pouring into her consciousness and pressing outward, filling Kade with Her perfection and light until Kade could not help the groan of longing that tore from her throat. Ithyris held her suspended, carefully, in that exquisite state for what felt like a lifetime. Then, just as before, She burst from her in a dazzling eruption of light and euphoria, leaving Kade boneless and spent on the cool stone floor of the barracks. Her spirit continued to throb deliberately, possessively through Kade's body.

"Yes, Beloved. You are."

CHAPTER TEN

*L*ike the thunder preceding a great storm, the Daughters of *Ithyris could sense the ominous threat gathering over our lands from the mountainous north. In Verdred, the Handmaiden had vanished from our midst, but already we were hearing reports that she was working miracles in Mondera, under the very nose of that mounting unease. Even more disturbing, we were hearing rumors that Ulrike had raised His own* shaa'din, *and that this unholy warrior and her armies were somehow impervious to our Lady's celestial fire.*

None of us wanted to believe it, but it made more sense than I wanted to admit. After Her intervention at the Battle of the Ranes, the Dangar armies, with all their overwhelming numbers, had turned back without even setting foot in Ithyria. We had assumed they feared Her power. Now it seemed clear their dark God had been devising a way to render His forces immune to it.

My thoughts turned to the Handmaiden often. I wondered how she must be feeling, the things she must be thinking as she began to encounter the brutality of Ulrike and His followers. I envied Kadrian's connection to the Goddess even as I worried for the integrity of her gentle soul in the face of such violence. With no way to assist except in prayer, I and the rest of the temple spent every available moment in commune with Ithyris. We offered up praise and invocations of protection, trusting the Goddess's infinite wisdom to guide our people through whatever tempest now threatened to break over our heads.

The spirit nexus was no less strange on her second visit than it had been the first time Ithyris had brought her here. Overhead, the inverted lake shimmered, indistinguishable shadows passing in its depths. The glowing doorways interrupted infinite whiteness in a neat row for only a moment before shifting into new positions; bordering a rectangle, narrowing into a hall, curving into a semi-circle around her with disconcerting inconsistency.

In the aftermath of the Goddess's touch, Kade's entire being was pulsing. Even her mind seemed to be dancing with the cadence of Her spirit, every thought curling like a wisp of poetry through her consciousness.

"You have done well, Kadrian."

The musical notes of Her voice would likely have buckled her knees, if she had knees in this place. As it was, Kade felt herself crumbling into a nebulous mass of emotion as Ithyris appeared before her, smiling down at her with impossible perfection.

"Oh, Sweet Lady, I am so unworthy. I am so ashamed. I am—"

"You are mine, Beloved. That is all that matters. You have obtained the staff of Fyn as I asked. I am pleased."

"You…You are?"

She laughed, a gorgeous sound. "I am. But there are greater tasks ahead. Three items are needed to retrieve the prophecy: the staff of Fyn, the stone of Cibli, and Mondera's sepulchre. You already have the staff. The sepulchre is not far; it rests in the cemetery at Mondera Temple. And the stone…The stone is on its way to you now."

Kade furrowed her brow. "These things belonged to the three sisters?"

Ithyris inclined Her head.

"And they're going to help me find the prophecy that Ulrike wants?"

"The staff, stone, and sepulchre are the work of my Daughter Marin of the Twelve. Think of them as keys, if you will. Marin designed them to work in harmony, to unlock Mondera's final resting place at precisely the right moment." Pride resounded in Her words, and Kade almost felt jealous of her long-deceased predecessor.

"When is the right moment?"

"Mondera predicted your arrival on the first night of the Fifthmoon, one thousand winters after the Division. Marin's keys will work on that night alone, and as it is less than a moon away, you must hurry."

"Mondera predicted my arrival?" Kade's head was swimming. "Lady, are You saying that Mondera of the Twelve knew about *me*?"

The Goddess's smile brightened. "My Mondera knew a great many things, Kadrian. She saw you nearly a thousand winters before your birth, just as clearly as you see me now. She described the color of your eyes, your hair, your height, the shape of your face. She asked

Marin to help her prepare for your arrival, and here you are, just as she said you would be."

But if Mondera knew a millennium ago that all of this was going to happen, why had she gone to all the trouble to lock her prophecy away, only for it to be destroyed a thousand winters in the future? Wouldn't it have been far more efficient to leave her predictions unwritten, and never give Ulrike a reason to invade Ithyria? She didn't ask the question aloud, but Ithyris seemed to hear it anyway.

"Everything must happen as it is meant to, Beloved. Mondera said that this would be the beginning of the end."

That made no sense, but now Kade's brain was grasping hopefully at a new line of thought. "Lady, is that why You chose me for Your Handmaiden? Because of Mondera's prophecy?" *And not because I'm...*

"Oh, Kadrian." The Goddess reached out and touched Kade's cheek with a cool hand. Kade felt a shiver run all the way to her toes, and she struggled to remind herself that she had neither a cheek nor toes in the nexus. Any physical sensations she experienced here were conjurations of her mind in an attempt to make sense of her bodiless state. Still, the love that filled the Goddess's shining eyes reduced every other conscious thought into a swirling vortex of yearning, and Kade trembled at Her next words. "You were always meant for me, Beloved. Mondera didn't create that truth; she just knew it before anyone else did."

"You loved her." Kade couldn't keep the jealousy from her voice.

"I love all my Daughters, all my children. But *shaa'din* are mine like no other mortals can be. I speak with you, know you, infuse myself within you. For that reason, every one of my *shaa'din* has a special place in my heart."

"And did You..." Kade blushed, but she made herself blurt the question out. "Did You touch the Twelve, too? Like You do with me?"

"Of course."

"So we're Your...Your lovers." She nearly whispered the last word.

"Do you love me?"

The question took her off guard. "Oh, Lady, yes. Yes, of course."

"And do you enjoy how it feels when I touch you? When I enter your body, fill your spirit with mine, create rivers of myself within you and burst from your skin when it cannot hold any more?"

She could barely get the reply past her imaginary lips. "Yes."

"Then believe me when I tell you, Kadrian, that it is just as wonderful an experience for me. There is nothing quite so joyful, so fulfilling, as connecting with those I love in that way. Being heard, seen, felt by the mortal creatures who are my most precious treasures, yet are so rarely able to perceive me at all. It has been such a long time since I have shared this with one of my Daughters, and you bring me great pleasure." The Goddess tilted Her head. "But even so, I am not quite enough for you, am I?"

Horror shot through Kade. "Oh, You are! Of course You are!" She felt an unwelcome pull at her heels and found herself being tugged backward. "Wait, Lady, please, don't send me away yet!"

"I am not sending you away, Beloved. Your flesh cannot endure for long without your spirit. It calls you back."

"No, please, I'm not ready!" Kade called after Her, even as the current gushed around her, and she felt her arms and legs growing heavy, the cold press of stone against her shoulder and hip. Gradually, she came back to herself, still prostrate on the barracks floor. The room was dark, and the small opening that served as a window showed a black sky broken by a few faint pinpricks of starlight. Kade didn't know how long she'd been lying there. She didn't care. She squeezed her eyes shut and let hot tears leak from her eyelids to strike the stone floor. The Goddess's astute question had bruised deeply. What a miserable failure she was, Handmaiden or no. Even Ithyris knew it. Selfish, ungrateful, weak…

Candlelight bobbed into view as the curtain was shoved aside and Myka entered. She stopped when she caught sight of Kade huddled on the floor.

"Your Grace? What are you doing down there?"

"Nothing," Kade mumbled, drawing the sleeve of her robe over her eyes as she sat up.

Myka plunked a bulging sack down on the little wooden table beside their bunks. "Well, I got the tea and soap. A few other things too, since I figure if we're going to see more battles we could both use better clothes. You should have seen me haggle with those merchants! Didn't even spend half of what Captain Talon gave us. I am *that* good…"

Kade tuned out the rest of her babble and pulled herself into the lower bunk. She tugged the blanket over her head so Myka would not see the tears that kept falling, and rolled to face the wall.

Divine Lady, please, You have to know how much I—

"Sleep, Beloved," Ithyris commanded, once again from within her mind.

I'm sorry. I'm so sorry. You are more than enough for me, of course You are, far more than I deserve. I will serve and obey You always.

"Sleep." Kade felt Her descend again, but this time Her presence held only reassurance and comfort. Ithyris settled in and around Kade softly. The veins of Her spirit beat with love and peace, absorbing Kade's protests into their calm, resonating flow.

Somewhere behind her she heard Myka say testily, "Well, good night to you too, Handmaiden." The bunk above her creaked as Myka settled into her own bed.

Though Kade was so sleepy she could not open her eyes, or even lift the blanket from her head, somehow she managed to reply. "Good night, Myka." Then Ithyris's gentle insistence won out, and Kade drifted off.

❖

The sound of boots pounding the floor and men shouting woke her in the early hours of the morning. Myka's head popped upside-down over the edge of her bunk.

"Wake up, wake up! Something big's happening. Come on!"

Apparently, Myka had forgotten her irritation with Kade the night before. She somersaulted from her bunk and landed, catlike, on the floor. Kade sat up, rubbing the sleep from her eyes, and was startled when a man's voice came from beyond the curtained door of their chamber.

"Forgive the disturbance, Your Grace, but Captain Talon's asking for you as soon as possible."

"We'll be right out!" Myka called and tossed a bundle of fabric at Kade. "Here, put those on." She was already hopping around on one foot as she shoved the other into a pair of leggings.

"What are these?" Kade asked.

"Clothes. Better ones. Hurry up and get dressed. We're going to miss all the excitement!"

Kade held up the articles of clothing Myka had selected for her. They were snowy white, like the robes of her priesthood, but that was where the similarity ended. A pair of thick, snug leggings dangled from one hand, while a short-sleeved tunic and belt were in the other. Boys' clothes. "Myka, we can't wear these."

Myka had already shoved her arms into her own tunic and was reaching for her belt. "Sure we can. You're *shaa'din*. You can wear whatever you want. You think the Twelve went traipsing around Ithyria in formal robes? We'll actually be able to move in these." She sat on Kade's bunk to tug her riding boots on over her leggings. When Kade continued to stand there, she huffed. "Fine. Don't wear them. Go out there dressed like that if you want."

Kade looked down at her robes, which had taken on a brownish tint from the dirt of their travels. The sleeves and hem were stained and frayed, sagging thanks to so many nights of sleeping on the ground and days astride a sweating horse. "We could ask one of the temples for replacements."

"And still be running around with drooping sleeves and skirts tangling our ankles." Myka grabbed her knife from the table and slid it back inside her boot. She patted the hidden weapon with satisfaction. "It's getting hotter every day. Summer's about to arrive in all its glory. You want to swelter through it in stuffy robes, go ahead. But I'm going to be comfortable. And mobile."

She stood and twirled, demonstrating her freedom of movement. Kade sighed and looked down at the clothes in her hands. In her mind's eye she recalled the redheaded barbarian looming over Erinda and those unlucky villagers. What if Kade hadn't been able to reach them in time? A second more, one little stumble, and she might have been too late. Myka had a point; in clothes like these she wouldn't have to worry about tripping over her own feet.

"Oh, all right." She sat and pulled the leggings on, then turned her back and shrugged out of her dirty robes and into the tunic. When she twisted back around, Myka was ready with her sash and a triumphant grin. Kade sighed as she knotted the sash around her waist and accepted the pair of boots Myka held out to her, made of soft white leather that matched the rest of the ensemble. She had to admit, as she stood, that the new clothes felt much lighter. She took a couple of long strides, all that their tiny chamber would allow, to test the feel of her legs unencumbered by layers of heavy fabric.

"Nice, huh?" Myka crowed.

A corner of Kade's mouth tweaked upward as she grabbed the iron staff from its spot in the corner. Ithyris had said it was one of the keys she needed to fulfill her mission, and she wasn't about to leave it unattended.

Myka swept her arm toward the door with a flourishing bow. "After you, Your Grace."

❖

Fear iced through Kade as she surveyed the ocean of hairy, snarling creatures that seethed beneath them, pressing toward the city walls. She had never imagined the barbarian army could be so vast. She gripped the iron shaft of Fyn's staff so tightly that her knuckles ached.

"How many, do you think?" she asked quietly of Talon, who stood at her shoulder. They were atop Agar's walls, directly over the main gates of the city, with General Urden on one side and Farsh on the other. There were two other captains there as well, one in a turquoise military jacket and the other in brown. Kade knew they were from the Cibli and Fyn contingents, respectively, but she had been too nervous at their introduction to remember their names.

"Hard to say," Talon replied. "The first group arrived a few days ago, shortly after we did. After that, there were more every day. This looks like a couple thousand, maybe more."

Two thousand of those unkillable monsters? Just a handful had proven nearly impossible to escape, much less defeat. How could they hope to survive against so many? Talon pointed down at the lone woman sitting on a huge black horse several paces in front of the rest of the horde. The scarlet ropes of her hair hung beneath a horned and saw-toothed helmet. Her naked belly bulged under a curved breastplate, and it was painted gaily with a red substance that was most likely blood. "She's been asking for you all morning."

"Handmaiden," the woman called up to her, a guttural accent sharpening her consonants. "We meet again. A shame I did not recognize you the first time, or I would have introduced myself properly. My name is Mardyth." She bared her teeth in a smile that was not at all friendly, and laid a hand on her swollen stomach. "You know why I have come?"

"The prophecy belongs to Ithyris." Kade was impressed at the conviction in her voice, which thankfully did not shake with the terror she was fighting so hard to control. "She will never allow you to have it."

"I see you've found the staff," Mardyth said, ignoring Kade's challenge. "So now we're at a bit of an impasse, aren't we? You see," she tugged a pendant from beneath her metal breastplate, "I have the stone."

She dangled it where Kade could get a good look. The stone of Cibli was about the size of a bird's egg; blue, translucent, and roughly spherical. Kade felt a bit dizzy and realized she'd forgotten to breathe.

The stone is on its way to you now, Ithyris had said. But She had failed to mention that it was in the possession of Ulrike's *shaa'din.* How had Mardyth gotten her hands on it? More importantly, how did the Goddess expect Kade to get it from her now?

"If you want it," Mardyth swung the pendant between her fingers, "you're going to have to come out here and take it." The men behind her chuckled as she dropped the stone between her breasts. After a dramatic pause, she called up to Kade again. "Don't make us wait too long, Handmaiden. Otherwise we might get bored and decide to come in there ourselves to find you."

Kade backed away from the edge of the wall, more than a little overwhelmed. If she went out there, she would surely die. But there was no doubting that Mardyth would happily butcher every last living creature within Agar's walls to get to her. The soldiers, the innocent residents of the city, the priestesses. Myka. Erinda. She couldn't be responsible for their deaths. It was unthinkable.

"Are you all right, Your Grace?" Talon asked.

"I think I just need to sit down for a minute."

"Of course. Byler?" One of the lieutenants, in a red jacket that matched Talon's, stepped forward with a smart salute. "Escort the Handmaiden back to her quarters."

"Yes, sir." He offered Kade his elbow. "Your Grace."

As she allowed the lieutenant to lead her down the steep stone steps, she could hear Talon, Farsh, Urden, and the other two captains arguing over their next course of action. She wanted to shake her head, knowing that no matter what plan they came up with, it could never be good enough. Not when their enemy was two thousand strong, nearly impossible to kill, and under the command of a *shaa'din*.

Myka, who had been denied access to the top of the wall with the commanding officers, was waiting at the foot of the steps for her. "Well? What are we going to do?"

"Just leave me alone," Kade snapped.

Myka stopped in her tracks as a look of hurt spread over her face. Kade and Byler passed by her, and then Kade touched a hand to her escort's arm and held back. "Please, Myka," she said more gently over her shoulder. "I need some time to myself to think."

"Fine!" Myka yelled as they walked away. "You don't need my help, that's fine. I don't need you either!"

Kade winced, but she did not turn around. She already knew what she was going to have to do, and it was probably better for Myka to be angry with her when it happened. Maybe anger would make her death a little easier for Myka to accept. Swallowing hard, Kade kept her eyes on the street and concentrated on putting one foot in front of the next until they reached the barracks gate.

❖

When Erinda rounded the corner of the stables after finishing her nightly rounds, she caught sight of Kade sitting on a bench a few paces away. She very nearly turned around and slunk behind the building again, but something about Kade's expression gave her pause. She looked so grim, staring at the bonfires flickering in the soldiers' exercise yard without even seeming to see them. A heavy metal staff was in her hand, and she rolled it absently between her fingers. She was wearing such a strange outfit, a boy's leggings, tunic, and boots, all in white like her priestess's robes. In the firelight, her delicate skin glowed orange and yellow, tipping her bristly hair with gold, shadows sharpening her distinctive vulpine features.

Erinda knew that look. It was the one Kade wore when she was terrified. The one that always made Erinda's most fiercely protective instincts rage to life. Up to now, she had avoided Kade as much as possible, and she knew she ought to be more concerned with protecting her own fragile state of mind. Nonetheless, Kade's distress beckoned to her, and she could not help but answer it. She walked over and laid a hand on her shoulder. "What is it?"

Kade looked up. "Rin?" Relief filled her eyes, and she put a hand up to Erinda's, almost as if to reassure herself that Erinda was really there. Her thin fingers were cold to the touch, in spite of the warmth of the early summer evening.

Erinda sat next to Kade on the wooden bench, nudging her amiably with one hip to make room. "Something's wrong. Tell me."

"It's no use. You can't save me this time, Rin."

She sounded so hopeless that Erinda gritted her teeth to hold back a surge of irrational anger. Already she was poised to lash out at whatever or whoever had made Kade so upset. She wanted to gather Kade in her arms and kiss her cheeks, as she would have when they were children. Instead she dug her nails into her palms. "Just tell me what's going on."

Kade twirled the staff in her hand. "I have to go out there."

"Out there? You mean, outside the city walls?"

Kade nodded. "It's a long story, but...well, you remember the barbarian woman from a few days ago?"

"The pregnant one who nearly chopped my skull in half with a giant axe?" *Until you came along, and*...Her skin goose-bumped as the memory of Kade's body covering hers overtook her. "How could I forget?"

"Her name is Mardyth, and it turns out she's Ulrike's *shaa'din*."

"Ulrike? As in, evil God of the Flesh, Ulrike?"

Kade nodded again. "Mardyth is here to get her hands on a prophecy written by Mondera of the Twelve. This staff is one of the keys that unlocks it, and Mardyth has the second key. If I don't go out there and try to take it from her, she's going to come in here and take the staff from me. And she'll kill every person in Agar in order to do it." Kade's fist tightened around the staff. "I can't let all these people die because of me."

Though this was a lot of information to process at once, Erinda brushed nearly all of it aside in favor of what was most important. "That's crazy, Kade. You're not going out there. Besides, just look at how thick the city walls are. The barbarians will never get in here."

"They'll get in," Kade said with glum certainty. "You've seen them fight. *Shaa'ri* barely touches them, and somehow they've blocked the Goddess's celestial fire. You think arrows, boiling oil, rocks, fire, or anything else we can throw at them is going to stop them from climbing the walls? From breaking down the city gates? And what am I going to do about it? Invisibility's not going to help this time."

"But you can't go out there. They'll kill you in a heartbeat."

"I know." The reply was soft and frightened. Erinda felt her blood heat furiously.

"Kade, no. Ithyris has no right to ask this of you. It's not fair. What would be the point? How is the Goddess's precious Handmaiden supposed to save Ithyria if she's dead?" She could hear the hysterical edge in her voice as the determined look in Kade's eyes never wavered.

"Stop, Rin." Kade squeezed Erinda's hand. "I swore when I took my vows to obey Ithyris in all things."

"I don't care! This is taking it too far. She can't expect you to just—"

"Lay down my life for Her?" Kade finished with a wry smile. "But I will, Rin, gladly. And not just for Her. For all of them." She indicated the grounds, where soldiers clustered around the bonfires and jabbed at one another cheerfully. "For her." Kade pointed across the yard to where her young traveling companion was sparring back and forth with Talon. One of Erinda's eyebrows went up at the unusual sight of a Pledged in boys' clothes darting around with a short sword, but she was quickly distracted when she felt Kade's lips press against her fingers. Her stomach clenched as she met Kade's steady gaze. "For you."

Her breath caught in her throat. "Kade…" Goddess, those vibrant eyes pierced her soul. Held in their spell, Erinda found she could not remember what she'd been arguing with her about. The heat of Kade's mouth lingered on her fingers, sending shivers of longing up her arm until her own lips began to tingle. Without warning, her stomach dipped and desire spread like liquid gold into her muscles, contracting her sex painfully. Ah, there it was, the rush of lust she'd been waiting for. She'd known she would not escape it indefinitely. No one but Kade had ever made her feel like this, a need so intense that every nerve ending in her body cried out for the relief that could only be found in Kade's touch. Her skin burned, her insides cramped, and she was suddenly wet and hot. Though she managed to stifle the groan that filled her mouth, she knew the instant her affliction showed in her eyes, because Kade's gaze turned wary and she shifted on the bench.

Kade's fingers brushed the burn on her wrist, and Erinda flinched. "Ow."

"What's this?" Kade asked, turning her hand toward the firelight. "You're hurt."

Erinda tried to pull away, embarrassed. "It's nothing." But she hissed between her teeth when the movement scraped her blister against Kade's palm. The pain dragged the heavy pulsing from between her legs to pound angrily in her injured wrist instead, and for that, she was grateful.

Kade grasped her forearm. "Just hold still a second, will you?" she asked with a hint of amusement. "I think I might be able to help." She closed her eyes.

To Erinda's amazement, a faint blue glow began to emanate from Kade's hand. Cool relief replaced the pain, until Erinda could no longer feel the burn. She was surprised when Kade released her wrist and the blister was still there, red and puffy as ever. "It doesn't hurt anymore," she said in astonishment, prodding the blister a little with her fingertip.

Kade smiled. "Good."

"That's so strange. It looks just the same, but now it feels like it isn't burned at all. What did you do?"

"The Goddess has been teaching me a few things…how to use Her power to change people's perceptions. I can't heal your skin any faster, but I can take the pain away."

"That's amazing. Thank you." She began to lean forward, and then clamped down hard on the instinct to plant a kiss on Kade's cheek. Winters ago, she would have done so without a second thought, a gesture of affection that came as naturally as breathing. She drew back slowly. Kade's eyes widened, and Erinda knew she'd read the impulse in her face. Awkward silence ensued.

Erinda was about to divert the subject back to Kade's ridiculous plan to take on the barbarian army alone, which seemed a far safer topic than the hazardous territory they were stumbling headfirst into, but she was interrupted by an enormous bouquet of flowers that dropped onto Kade's lap.

"Handmaiden." A veiled priestess knelt at Kade's feet, her long golden earrings swinging as she touched her fingers to her forehead. "A tribute, from your sisters of the western temple of Agar."

Kade's cheeks flushed, but before she could say anything, a second veiled woman had deposited a basket of fruit on her knees, nearly crushing the flowers. "As do we of the eastern temple. We honor you, *Ostryn* Kadrian, Beloved of Ithyris."

Erinda had to lean back as two more gifts were thrust at Kade from either side.

"We are from the north…"

"…and from the south…"

For a moment, the two women exchanged dirty looks before the first continued, "…and we, too, have come to bless your name and praise Ithyris for the gift of your exalted presence among us."

"May the Goddess heed your voice, Handmaiden."

"Remember us in your prayers, holy one."

"We are your most humble servants."

"Praise the Goddess!"

"Hail the Handmaiden!"

Kade held up her hands. "*Ostryn*, please, I…thank you, but this really isn't necessary."

Erinda's eyes widened when she realized that other veiled women were now entering the light of the bonfires, approaching Kade like they might a skittish colt. She wasn't sure how so many of them had managed to talk their way past the barracks gates, but they were converging on Kade rapidly. "Don't look now," she murmured in Kade's ear, "but I think your admirers brought a few friends."

A loud clang sounded from across the yard, and a dozen veiled faces turned toward it. Talon had just disarmed her overeager opponent, and she picked up Myka's short sword from the dirt and handed it back to her. In slow motion, she repeated the stroke she'd just used, exaggerating Myka's mistake. Myka nodded and adopted a defensive stance, ready to try the move again.

"Sweet Ithyris, what is that girl doing?" gasped one of the women indignantly.

"What is she *wearing*?" cried another.

"This is an affront to the Goddess!"

The first priestess, the one who had handed Kade the flowers, rose to her feet. "We must put a stop to this."

Kade reached out and caught the sleeve of her robe. "Leave them be," she commanded, and when the priestess turned to look at her she added a bit more shyly, "Please."

"But, Handmaiden," the woman stammered. "A Pledged cannot be allowed to, to…"

"Learn to defend herself?" Kade suggested mildly.

"Well, certainly, but that is done via the study of *shaa'ri,* not flailing around gracelessly with one of those crude weapons."

"Was not Zarneth of the Twelve a master of many such 'crude weapons'?" Kade asked.

The woman's eyebrows went up. "Well…"

"And this," Kade continued, lifting the heavy staff in her hand and bringing it down so that its rings clanked together. "Fyn of the Twelve carried this very staff into battle. Even after she was blinded by a head injury, it didn't stop her from fighting alongside her sisters, however 'gracelessly.'"

The priestess sank slowly to her knees again, her attention suddenly rapt on Kade's face. Kade seemed oblivious, watching Myka struggle to block Talon's assault. When she spoke, it was almost to herself. "Besides, I do not think temple service is to be Myka's path as it is ours. Ithyris says she is destined for another purpose."

"The Goddess told you that?" one of the women asked.

Some of Kade's self-consciousness seemed to return when she looked down to see the group of women settling themselves on the ground before her, clearly captivated by her every word. She turned to Erinda in bewilderment. Erinda jerked her head slightly toward the waiting audience. *Go on,* she projected with an impish smile, knowing Kade could read the encouragement in her eyes. *They want to hear anything you have to say.* Kade drew a breath.

"Ithyris speaks to all of us," she answered hesitantly. "But not every mortal has the same ability to hear Her. She is a being of divine spirit, and some are born with greater sensitivity to Her presence than others. Often, those of us who are lucky enough to possess this gift choose to enter Her service in the temple."

Heads nodded in assent throughout the group, and confidence built in Kade's voice. "But even with heightened awareness, we all know it's not always easy to break through the boundaries of our physical world so we can connect with Her. Meditation helps strip some of those distractions away, and drinking from the Cup of Purification allows us a few minutes of clarity during which She can reach us, but the truth is that we've become so attached to our mortal flesh that it takes many winters of discipline to learn how to make ourselves fully accessible to Her."

Erinda watched the women scoot closer, entranced. Kade's timidity seemed to dissolve as she kept talking, and even Erinda found herself listening in wonder as Kade began to relate her personal encounters with Ithyris, the way Her voice sounded like music and Her feet never seemed to touch the ground. She spoke of a place she called *Yura'shaana*, the spirit nexus, a mysterious passageway through which she claimed all mortal souls entered and left the world.

After a while, Erinda noticed a handful of soldiers lurking at the fringes of the group, edging nearer until a few finally just sat down next to the veiled women and stared at the *shaa'din* with a fascination as spellbound as the priestesses'.

Sitting there next to Kade, the source of so many sleepless nights of loneliness and grief, Erinda realized that for the first time in a long while she felt truly complete. Almost happy, though nothing had changed, really. Kade was still a priestess, still untouchable. She belonged to the Goddess, and never had that been more evident than it was now, her features ethereal in the firelight as she spoke of Ithyris's beauty and love. Yet Erinda found it didn't matter. Kade was where she belonged. She had become everything she had always been meant for. While Erinda's heart still ached for the things that would never be between them, she was, in that moment, unspeakably proud to have called this magnificent woman her friend.

A while later, Erinda slipped from the bench and crept quietly away from the others. Kade was so absorbed in her audience at that point that she never even looked up, and Erinda smiled to herself as she went in search of a quill and parchment. It was high time she finished that long overdue letter to the Queen, and at last she knew what she was going to say. A new *shaa'din* had arrived in Ithyria. She was courageous and powerful, and she had saved them from death at the hands of the barbarian army.

Also, Erinda resolved, no matter how determined Kade was to fulfill her quest of ancient keys and hidden prophecies, when morning dawned, Erinda was going to see to it that the Goddess's Handmaiden was not facing that barbarian horde alone.

CHAPTER ELEVEN

K ade gawked open-mouthed at the crowd of veiled women gathered at the city gates. The four high priestesses appeared to have brought the entire residency of their respective temples; there had to be at least two hundred priestesses barring her path to the gates, about half of whom were mounted on horseback. She recognized Lyris among them, with Myka on foot at her side. Myka was still refusing to speak to Kade after Kade's brusque dismissal the previous morning, but nonetheless she was there, with a short sword clanking at her side and the hilt of her knife peeking from her boot cuff.

Next to the priestesses stood Captain Talon and about thirty of his remaining guard, those who had been lucky enough to escape the village battle with relatively minor wounds. Among them, she could also see a few jackets of turquoise and brown, which had to be men from the Cibli and Fyn regiments. And beside the shoulder of Talon's big black mare, Erinda regarded Kade with her arms folded across her chest. A faint breeze tousled the tips of her braids.

"We're going with you," she announced.

Kade had no doubt that Erinda had orchestrated this. Of course she had, and Kade cursed herself for not having seen it coming. She should have kept her mouth shut last night, sent Erinda away instead of spilling her fears so recklessly. Erinda had always assumed personal responsibility for solving Kade's problems. But they weren't children anymore, and this was no adolescent bully they were dealing with.

Kade had spent most of the night tormented by the same dream she'd had just before the *shaa'din* ceremony; Ithyris, beautiful and brilliant, reaching out for her with hands stained with Kade's own blood. Kade understood what it meant. Her life belonged to the Goddess. If Ithyris asked her to die in Her name, Kade would do so without complaint. Thousands of barbarian warriors waited for her on the other side of that wall. Once again, Erinda was assuming the role of her protector, but Kade could not allow it. Not this time.

"No." Kade's gaze moved from one person's face to the next. So many people, and every one would be slaughtered if they set foot outside the city walls. "You can't. It's too dangerous."

"We have faith in the Goddess," one of the high priestesses said. "She has sent you to us, Handmaiden, and it is our privilege to fight Her enemies at your side."

"But you can't," Kade said. "*Shaa'ri* has scarcely any impact, and the barbarians are somehow masking the darkness that creates celestial fire." She turned to Lyris. "Tell them, *Ostryn*. You've seen it."

Lyris dipped her head. "Yes, Handmaiden, I have. But Talon has learned from General Urden that the barbarians may yet be killed. S*haa'ri* should be effective if used in the right manner."

"You gotta cut their heads off!" Myka interjected. When Kade frowned, she seemed to recall their quarrel and clamped her mouth shut with a scowl.

Lyris continued. "It is imperative that Ithyris's command be carried out, Handmaiden. We do not have to defeat the barbarian army today, but we will endeavor to hold them back so that you may acquire the stone of Cibli and convey the stone and staff to Mondera Temple."

The women behind her nodded, as did several of the men in Talon's group. Kade had to fight back tears at the incredible selflessness of their offer. Every one of those soldiers had lost friends in their last encounter with the barbarian army. They had only barely escaped with their own lives and limbs, and yet they were ready to march out there and face those monsters again. But courageous though these men and women might be, they would still be outnumbered ten to one, and those were not odds she was comfortable with.

"*Ostryn*, Captain, I appreciate your support, truly. But the army we face is far too great. I cannot allow you to risk your lives this way."

"You don't have a choice," Erinda declared. Her expression said clearly that she had every intention of strolling out there at Kade's side as well, even though she had no more experience with a sword than Kade did. "You can't stop us from coming."

"I can stop *you*," Kade said quietly and turned to Talon. The very sight of him knotted her stomach with animosity. With broad, high cheekbones and androgynous elfin features, the captain of the royal guard was strikingly handsome. Grudgingly, Kade might see how Erinda would be drawn to Talon's dark good looks and understated confidence, but Talon had been intimate with Erinda only to cast her away at the behest of another woman. Kade would never forgive him for that. She hated asking for his help, but she was hoping he still cared enough for Erinda to want to keep her safe. "She's a civilian, Captain, not a soldier."

Talon held Kade's gaze before his eyes slid to Erinda. "I agree."

"Oh no, you don't," Erinda said, looking from one to the other. "Neither of you gets to dictate what I do. This is my choice."

"You're staying here, Rin."

"You can't make me."

"I can," Talon said, and motioned for one of the guard behind him to step forward and take Erinda's arms. "Take her back to the barracks, Corporal."

"No!" Erinda shouted, struggling in the man's grasp. "Talon, please, you have to let me go with you. The Queen—"

"The Queen would have my head if I let you do this, Erinda, and you know it."

"Oh, she would not! Let me go, you oaf!" Erinda stomped hard on the corporal's booted toes, and he released her with a bark of surprise.

Talon dismounted in one fluid motion and took Erinda's arm himself. "Don't make me lock you up," he growled.

Kade's attention fixated on Talon's hand where he gripped Erinda's arm. He was holding her close, their bodies nearly touching, and Kade's imagination began to taunt her with visions of Talon's olive skin pressed to Erinda's, the two of them rocking in one another's arms, as Erinda made those feral sounds that Kade so readily remembered. Before she realized it, she'd reached out and taken Erinda's other arm.

"Captain, may I speak with her alone for a moment?"

Talon regarded her with mild surprise, and then strangely, understanding. "Of course, Your Grace." He let go of Erinda, and Kade almost sighed with relief.

She drew Erinda aside, turning away from the crowd for privacy. She kept her voice low. "Rin, please. I need you to stay here."

"I'm not letting you go out there alone!"

"I won't be alone. You've brought me an army." Kade grinned and Erinda's glower faded, just a little. "You are amazing, Rin. And I'm more grateful than you could ever know, but I need you to stay inside the city. If anything ever happened to you, I—" Her fingers trembled, and she withdrew her touch from Erinda's forearm. "I have to know you're safe. I can't do this otherwise."

Erinda rubbed her skin where Kade had been holding her. "What are you doing?" she asked suspiciously.

"What do you mean?"

"I felt that. Whatever it was you were pushing into me just then." Her eyes narrowed. "Kadrian Crossis, if you're using your *shaa'din* magic on me..."

"I'm not!" Her fingers were tingling a little, however, and she looked down at them. "At least, I don't think so. I wasn't trying to."

Erinda made a disbelieving noise.

"Honestly, I wasn't. Though I'm not above attempting it if you won't listen." When Erinda's brows began to draw together, Kade sighed. "Look, I will ask the captain to lock you up if that's what it's going to take. But I really wish you'd just give in on this one."

"And why would I do that?"

"Because I'm asking you to. For me."

Desperation flickered behind the indignation in her eyes, and Kade's breath caught. This was no petty power struggle. Erinda was on the verge of panic.

"Do you have any idea what you're asking? How can I just sit behind these walls doing nothing, while you and the others fight your way through that horde? I heard what Lyris said. Once you've got the stone they're taking you on to Mondera Temple. I may never see you again." Her voice broke, and it broke Kade's heart right along with it. "I only just found you again, Kade, I can't...It's been so long, and I just can't..."

I'd rather die out there than lose you again.

Kade heard that bleak thought as clearly as Ithyris's voice in her mind. Propriety forgotten, she pulled Erinda into her arms. "I'll come back," she found herself saying. She would have said anything to assuage the anguish that was rolling off Erinda with torrential force. She could barely breathe, it was so strong. Kade buried her nose in Erinda's soft curls, inhaling deeply of her clean, earthy scent, like soap suds and sun-dried laundry. Even after all these winters, Erinda still smelled like the very essence of home. Kade pressed her lips against Erinda's ear. "You hear me? I promise you, I will come back. I won't leave without saying good-bye."

She felt it then, the flood of silvery spirit gushing out of her. She wasn't doing it on purpose, not at all, but she couldn't seem to hold it back either. The current was acting of its own accord, surging more swollen and mighty than she'd ever felt it before, and it flowed from her hands, her arms, her torso, engulfing Erinda with tenderness and reassurance that felt like it originated from the very core of Kade's being.

Erinda shuddered against her. "I want to go with you."

"I know you do. I know." She held her for a few moments more, letting the current flow freely between them, then pulled back. "But I wouldn't be able to live with myself if something happened to you out there. So just please say you'll stay. I swear to you, I will come back."

Gradually, Erinda's body relaxed as the current continued to course from Kade's hands. "I'll stay," she said weakly. Kade wasn't sure whether her acquiescence was a genuine surrender or whether it was the effect of Ithyris's spirit, but either way the response was what she needed.

"Thank you." She turned back around again. "Myka." She beckoned her over. Myka narrowed her eyes as she approached, but before she could begin to argue Kade held up a hand. "I need your help."

Myka rocked back on her heels and rested a hand on the pommel of her short sword. "I'm listening."

"I need you to look after Erinda for me. If we fail, if the barbarians breach the city, I need you to promise me you'll protect her." She was relatively certain Myka could see right through her request. After all, she was just seventeen, and despite the rakish knife in her boot and a few hurried lessons in swordplay, she was hardly a seasoned soldier. Kade couldn't allow her to be part of this mad venture, not when it was very likely a suicidal mission.

Myka pursed her lips and eyed Erinda. "Why her?"

"She's important to me. I need someone I can trust for this."

She could practically see the wheels turning in Myka's head. The girl was definitely flattered, which had been Kade's intention, but she wasn't stupid.

To Kade's very great surprise, however, she nodded. "I'll do it."

Kade laid a hand on her shoulder and squeezed gratefully. "Thank you, Myka."

"You'll owe me."

"I will," Kade said with a smile. At last, she turned back to the priestesses and soldiers who were waiting for her.

"You're all very sure you want to do this?"

"Hail the Handmaiden!" came the response from the women's side, and while the men were somewhat less vocal, not one seemed inclined to change his mind either.

Squaring her shoulders, Kade moved forward, and the priestesses parted to let her through. Agar's walls were so thick that they had to pass through a wide, tunnel-like vestibule to reach the enormous gates. She was followed by several of the guard, who prepared to lift the heavy oak bar from its iron clamps. Kade held her breath and gripped Fyn's staff in her hand. *Sweet Ithyris, protect us—*

"Hold," boomed a severe male voice. General Urden approached on horseback, flanked by uniformed provincial guard.

"Come to join us, General?" Talon asked acerbically.

The giant man glared at them. "You want to get your people slaughtered, Outlander, it's no concern of mine. I and my men will defend Agar from within, where we belong. But you're not opening the gates of my city to that pack of barbarians. You want to make it easy for them? Invite them in for tea, perhaps, before they overrun us?"

"General," Kade said, stepping toward him, "you heard what their leader said. If I don't go out there they will attack the city. I'm…We're trying to defend Agar just as much as you are."

Urden gave her a contemptuous sneer. "As far as I'm concerned, Your Grace, you're welcome to throw yourself to the wolves any time you want. Just find a way to do it that doesn't put my city at risk."

The spirit current prodded Kade, and she looked up at the mouth of the vestibule. "Is that a portcullis, General?" she asked. He grunted in assent. "If I remember correctly, there's another one outside the city gates, so the solution is simple. Let us out, and the moment we're all past the gates, drop both grates behind us."

He snorted. "You're either very brave or very stupid. You do realize once I drop those grilles I'm not lifting them again. It will be hard enough killing off any of the enemy who get caught between them, not to mention closing the gates again afterward. You and your friends will have nowhere to retreat, so if I let you out there, you won't be getting back into Agar unless you finish off that entire horde yourselves."

Kade looked questioningly at Talon and the high priestesses, but every one of them nodded. "We understand."

The general stared at her. "You're crazy, the lot of you." But finally, he shrugged. "Very well. It's you that barbarian witch wants. I won't stop you from handing yourself over to her if that's what you want to do."

He turned to his men. "Man the portcullises, and by all means," he met Kade's eyes with an expression that said she was out of her mind, "open the gates for the lady."

❖

Agar's gates swung open with an ear-splitting screech that echoed the dread shrieking through Erinda's insides. The comforting blanket of

Kade's aura still enveloped her, but terror was swiftly burning the effect off as the priestesses and soldiers ran for the city exit. Her confused brain knew only that Kade was leaving, that she should be going with her, that she'd given her word not to follow. A roar went up beyond the city walls, and a wave of nausea gripped her.

"You gonna just stand there?"

The strawberry-haired Pledged, Kade's seemingly ever-present shadow, had drawn her sword, and with the other, she seized Erinda's hand. "Come on. They're closing the portcullis already."

Erinda let Myka tug her toward the vestibule in the wake of Kade's volunteer army. "We promised her we'd stay behind." But her feet kept moving anyway.

"Oh, please. I'm not missing this. Duck!" Myka shoved her beneath the descending iron grate.

Erinda tucked her head and shoulders and darted through, with Myka right behind. Ahead, Erinda glimpsed flashes of white robes and mottled furs, heard the crash of metal and guttural battle cries. Men were already working to swing the massive gates closed again, and the outer portcullis was coming down as the barbarians charged forward. "No time to argue," Myka shouted. "Go, go!"

Together, they squeezed between the narrowing gap and plunged beneath the second grille. Erinda felt the sharp points graze her shoulders as she scrambled beneath it. Myka had to drop to the ground and skid on her back, narrowly escaping impalement as the tips of the heavy portcullis struck the earth. Howls went up behind them, and she realized that as they'd been running to get out, a few of the barbarian warriors had managed to slip in. They were now trapped in the vestibule, between the portcullis grates, and the Monderan guard were pouring hot oil over their enemies through slots in the roof of the tunnel. The enormous gates boomed shut, blocking her view. Myka yanked her down by the hand.

"Quick, over here!"

They dove into a thicket of brush alongside the city's entrance. The plants were dense and thorned, and tore at Erinda's clothes as she ducked next to Myka.

"What have we done?" she panted. General Urden had made it very clear he would not open the gates again unless the barbarians were defeated. Now she and Myka were trapped outside the city walls along with the others.

Between the needle-like leaves of their hiding place she could see the tiny Ithyrian army swallowed up by the barbarian masses. Blood sprayed the air at random intervals, and the ground was scattered with disembodied heads as the priestesses and guard went immediately for decapitation, not bothering with any other type of offense. The barbarians were much bigger and stronger, but they were not particularly light on their feet. The priestesses whirled and dodged, slicing their arms in the direction of one enemy after another. The soldiers, too, were fighting with carefully targeted strikes to the barbarians' necks. Furred heads fell from enemy shoulders on every side, rolling gruesomely across the rocky ground. Erinda found it quite disturbing when she realized that most of the headless bodies continued to swing their weapons, though admittedly with less accuracy once they'd lost their governing senses. After a minute or two, a good hard shove to the body usually made it fall, and after that, it remained down.

Though the Ithyrian army was holding its own far better than anyone might have expected, they were nonetheless overwhelmed by sheer numbers. She watched one priestess behead three barbarian warriors in rapid succession, only to be caught from behind by the stroke of a heavy axe. A mounted lieutenant whose blade moved faster than Erinda could track was yanked from his horse, and both the animal and man disappeared under a flurry of leathered arms and falling clubs. The horse shrieked with fury as it went down, and Erinda cringed.

Flashes of blue light drew her attention, and she spotted Kade, who was wielding the staff of Fyn as a weapon. Though Kade's movements lacked the polish of the soldiers' swordsmanship, in her hands, the iron staff was glowing a brilliant cerulean hue from end to end. Whenever it connected with an enemy warrior, he burst into the extraordinary blue flames that Erinda remembered from the Battle of the Ranes. Though Kade's celestial fire did not spread from man to man as it had then, the sight of it still filled Erinda with hope. At least Kade's powers were protecting her.

Crouched at her side, Myka gripped her sword with one hand and a little knife in the other. Uncertainty had replaced her swaggering bravado, however, as she took in the chaos. She had gone very pale. Erinda resisted the unhelpful impulse to remind her that sneaking onto the battlefield had been her idea.

"I should be out there," Myka said shakily.

"Neither of us should be out here," Erinda replied. She dropped her eyes after watching a broadsword cleave through the outstretched arm of one of the veiled women. "Oh, Goddess." The priestess's wail of pain was heart wrenching, and Erinda fought the need to gag.

And then something crashed through the thicket and landed wetly in Erinda's lap. A barbarian head, covered with grizzled beard and matted hair, stared up at her with wild eyes. Blood gushed from his severed neck, soaking her skirts and bodice. To Erinda's horror, the head seemed to *see* her...and drew back its lips in a grotesque grin, exposing teeth that had been filed into cruel points.

Erinda could not help herself. She sprang to her feet with a shriek, heedless of the thorns that ripped at her skin and hair, and pitched the head as far as she could throw it.

She never saw it land.

A vise clamped about her neck and lifted her out of the bushes. She was swung around, choking, until she was face-to-face with another of the barbarians who held her by the throat in an iron grip. Erinda scrabbled with her nails at his hand and kicked her feet frantically. Spangled darkness shrank her vision as he lifted his sword. She felt the point of the blade against her sternum. Instead of running her through, however, the barbarian seemed to take pleasure in drawing the metal slowly through her ample cleavage, her breasts wiping the blood from his weapon. He leered at her. His fingers loosened a little, just enough that Erinda could suck some air into her lungs. She wheezed, the trickle of oxygen scorching her chest like threads of fire, and she understood the evil intent in his face—he would not kill her yet.

But then a little blade snaked around his neck and opened a bloody geyser beneath his chin. Erinda dropped to the ground, her ankle wrenching beneath her as she fell, and she gasped for breath as the man's head flew off to join his comrade's in the dirt.

Myka planted a foot in the barbarian's back and kicked him over. She brandished her dripping sword with a crow of victory. "Yeah!"

Erinda didn't get the chance to thank her. Myka's head snapped forward with a terrible cracking sound, and her eyes rolled back in her head as she collapsed. The barbarian who had hit her raised his club over her fallen form, preparing to crush her skull.

With a cry, Erinda snatched up the first man's sword where it lay beside her. She swept it at Myka's attacker with all her strength, severing his leg just above the knee. He wobbled long enough for Erinda to scramble to her feet, ignoring the fiery protest from her ankle. Before he had regained his balance, she struck again. The sword's heavy blade cut through his neck and spine with a meaty crunch. Erinda lost her grip on the heavy weapon while it was still lodged halfway through his neck. The barbarian's head lolled garishly off to the side, dangling from his body by a flap of skin and tissue.

Even so, the injury proved sufficient to fell him, and he tumbled over backward with flailing arms.

Erinda dropped to her knees at Myka's side. "Myka!"

Blood soaked her hair, though Erinda couldn't tell where she had been wounded or how bad it was. She was unconscious, though, one hand still wrapped stubbornly around the hilt of her sword. Erinda moaned inwardly. She should never have allowed Myka to drag them both out here. She'd broken her word to Kade, and now Myka might very well have paid for it with her life.

Erinda was not the praying type, but the plea tore from her lips anyway. "Goddess, please…oh, please, Lady, don't let her be dead…"

She was lifted from the ground again, this time by one of her braids. Her captor flung her away from Myka's body, and Erinda cried out as she collided with another of the stinking barbarian monsters. His foul breath assaulted her nostrils as he sniffed at her neck, then ran a gooey tongue up the side of her face. His arms clamped around her and he ground himself obscenely against her back.

Meanwhile, his companion advanced on her with a nasty smile.

❖

Kade had at last spotted Mardyth's flaming head of hair. Ulrike's *shaa'din* was strolling through the fray, unaffected by either sword or *shaa'ri*. She reached out and touched priestesses and soldiers as she passed, and anyone she laid her hand on collapsed to the ground.

"To your left," Ithyris's warning sounded in her head, and Kade swung the shining staff. The Goddess's silver current flowed from her hands through the metal, and when the end of the staff struck the chest of her would-be attacker, sapphire flames burst from his skin and consumed him in seconds. Kade had discovered that, though she could not target the dark aura that drew celestial fire, Fyn's staff was able to channel *shaa'ri* directly into the bodies of her enemies, destroying them from the inside. Her confidence built with every swing; for all her inexperience, she wasn't doing too badly in battle after all.

But they were losing. Even though more barbarian dead littered the ground than priestesses and soldiers, their enemy was just too numerous. Kade had to get the stone of Cibli away from Mardyth so that the others could make a run for it. Otherwise, the horde would kill them all.

Kade thrashed toward the barbarian leader, cutting a blazing passage through the hairy men blocking her way. She charged, bringing the staff down toward Mardyth's head. Mardyth sneered and caught it with one hand. She clamped Kade's forearm with the other. Kade's skin luminesced beneath Mardyth's fingers, as if the silver current was sheathing her arm.

"Careful, Beloved," Ithyris said in her ear. "Her touch kills. Use my fire."

Kade pressed the spirit current outward, sending it coursing through the staff toward Mardyth's hand. Though Mardyth did not go up in flames like her men, she hissed as Ithyris's celestial fire scorched up her arm. She let go of both Kade's wrist and the staff and stepped backward.

"Ulrike's child is the source of her strength," the Goddess said. "Strike her womb and she will fall."

Kade grimaced. Enemy or not, the idea of hitting a pregnant woman in the belly was revolting. Ithyris's veins sizzled under her skin. "Now, Kadrian. You must do it now!"

Kade thrust the staff out. Its ringed finial dug into Mardyth's protruding stomach, and she roared as blue light crackled beneath her skin, illuminating the bloody designs that decorated her belly. Mardyth dropped to her knees.

"The stone, Beloved."

Cibli's pendant had fallen from Mardyth's breasts, dangling by its leather cord as she bent over her swollen belly. Kade reached out and grabbed the stone, pulling until the cord broke from Mardyth's neck. A thrill of triumph fluttered through her as she fisted it in her palm.

"Run!" Kade shouted to the others, lifting her head so her words would carry over the noise of the fighting. "I have the stone! Everybody run!" She heard other voices echoing her command. Three more of the enemy lunged at her and she reduced them to columns of blue flame, but as she surveyed the battlefield, she realized the horde was too thick for the Ithyrian army to break free. They could not run.

"Kill her," Ithyris commanded. "You must kill Ulrike's *shaa'din* to break her hold on her men. Strike her again."

Kade hesitated. Mardyth was still hunched on the ground, her arms wrapped around her middle, shuddering as Ithyris's spirit racked her body. Kade tried to lift the staff, but found her arms reluctant to respond. The woman was pregnant, and even if the child she carried was the spawn of the Flesh God, murdering her in cold blood felt unconscionable. "I can't," Kade gritted through her teeth. As she tried to convince her insubordinate arms to move, an unwelcome male voice invaded her mind.

We'll have fun with this one. The thought was accompanied by an image of Erinda's blood-spattered face. Erinda was screaming under the man's swarthy hands as he tore at her skirts and penetrated her with both his body and his sword at once. Her blood spurted over his hands in a scarlet fountain as she convulsed around him in the throes of death.

The world fell away. The battle faded from her awareness. Kade's heart became molten lava in her chest and she spun around, bellowing Erinda's name.

Twenty paces away, one of the barbarians held Erinda by the arms while another stalked toward her. Erinda's clothes were soaked in blood, curly strands of hair plastered to her face, but Kade saw her bosom rise and fall and knew she was still alive. It was the second man's thoughts she had heard, Kade realized; somehow, she'd glimpsed the perverse fantasy filling his head, but he hadn't yet had the chance to carry it out. Kade launched forward, slamming Fyn's staff into every enemy in her path and leaving a trail of cerulean fires behind her. In moments, she was on him, and before he could lay a hand on Erinda, Kade thrust the blunt end of the staff all the way through his breast. She felt it puncture his skin, and with a strength she didn't know she possessed, she kept shoving until it erupted from his back. His ugly features contorted in shock as the Goddess's celestial flame engulfed him.

Kade jerked the staff back and lashed out at the man holding Erinda, catching him on the side of the head. He, too, dissolved into blue fire, and dropped Erinda to the ground. Kade took a step toward her before the Goddess's voice resounded inside her skull with such force that it rattled her teeth.

"Fit the stone to the staff, Kadrian," She ordered. "Quickly."

The stone of Cibli was still clenched in her left palm. "How do I—"

Ithyris flooded her mind with images and Kade obeyed them. She pulled and twisted two of the iron rings in opposite directions, then repeated with the other two. The curved prongs of the finial separated, and she pushed the stone of Cibli down between them, clamping the prongs shut around it. Once encapsulated within the staff's finial, the stone brightened until its light was nearly blinding. The glowing iron vibrated in her hand.

"Now lift the staff and put them to sleep."

"Put them to sleep?"

"Will it, Beloved. Hurry."

Kade raised the staff over her head and squeezed her eyes shut so she could concentrate. *Sleep*, she demanded, pressing the word into the spirit current. She pictured the command sliding up her arm into the shaft of the staff, coursing to the stone in its tip. *Sleep, all of you. Drop your weapons. Close your eyes. Sleep.*

Together, the stone and staff suctioned the spirit's flow eagerly from her palm, and her arm started to shake. She began to feel dizzy and grasped the staff with her other hand as well to keep hold of it. Gradually, the sounds of battle began to quiet, and Kade opened her eyes.

The battlefield was bathed in eerie blue light that radiated in all directions from Cibli's blazing stone. All around her, members of the barbarian army were staggering, unable to lift their swords and clubs, unable to keep their balance under Ithyris's powerful influence. They blinked heavily, tumbled to their knees, collapsed into snoring heaps on the ground at the feet of the astonished Ithyrian fighters.

Captain Talon appeared at Kade's side. He was no longer on horseback, his uniform filthy and blood-soaked, a wicked gash over one brow bleeding into his eye. He looked around with an incredulous face. "How have you done this?"

The staff was still drawing power from her, and Kade could not lower it. "Rin," she gasped, tilting her head toward Erinda's crumpled form on the ground. "I think she's hurt. Help her, please."

Talon cursed and scooped Erinda into his arms. "I knew I should have locked her up, damn it. What is she doing out here?"

"Is she all right?"

"She's breathing."

"We have to get our people out of here, Captain. I don't know how long Ithyris's control of the horde will hold out." She didn't know how long she would hold out, either. A headache thundered against the inside of her skull like an avalanche of stones striking bone. Her shoulders were cramping with the effort of holding up the staff.

"Understood." He gave a sharp whistle, and his black mare galloped toward them. He pulled Erinda up into the saddle with him, cradling her limp form against his chest.

"Your Grace!" Lyris rode up next to Kade and put down a hand. "Climb up, come on."

Kade dropped one hand from the staff so she could scramble up behind Lyris. She kept the staff aloft as they circled the battlefield, rounding up whatever horses they could find, getting as many of their surviving army mounted as possible, gathering up their wounded. In spite of the pain that battered behind her eyes, she managed to keep the Goddess's current flowing, passing the staff from one hand to the other as each arm tired. Her muscles shook with exhaustion, but she forced herself to keep her grip; she had to hold their enemy in Her thrall for as long as possible to give the others time to escape. Her heart caught in her throat as she recognized Myka, slung over the withers of one of the priestesses' horses. The priestess gave Kade a tense nod before she urged them into a gallop, headed for the Great Temple to the southwest.

"Handmaiden!" Mardyth marched toward them, kicking the slumbering forms of her men with disgust as she passed. She alone seemed unaffected by the Goddess's sleeping spell. Kade hefted Fyn's glowing staff in warning, and Mardyth halted a few paces away, her hands moving to her belly. "This isn't over," she growled, though she made no move to come closer. "Ulrike wants that prophecy. I will take it from you by any means necessary."

"I have no doubt that you will try," Kade responded. She tilted the staff toward the battlefield, and at the movement, Mardyth shrank back a little. Kade smirked. "But as you can see, Ithyris does not intend to make it easy for you." She fixed Mardyth with a baleful glare. "Neither do I."

Talon rode up to them, with Erinda still curled against him. "That's the last of them, Your Grace." He nodded in the direction of the horses galloping off after the others, most with two or even three riders clinging to their backs.

"Let's go, then." Kade tightened her grip at Lyris's waist as she nudged their mount in the direction of the temple as well. Talon kept pace alongside them. As they rode away, Kade twisted over her shoulder.

Mardyth stood alone on the bloodied field among the prostrate bodies of her dead and sleeping men. Her hands were on her hips, the matted cords of her hair dancing in the breeze. Her thoughts unfurled menacingly in Kade's mind.

You haven't won yet, Handmaiden. I'll be coming for you.

CHAPTER TWELVE

Shards of golden light slashed beneath her eyelids, urging them open. Erinda groaned, and her hand was enfolded by someone else's. She felt lips against her fingers, and struggled to get her bleary eyes to focus. "Kade?"

"How do you feel?"

She reached out with her awareness, testing the sensations she was getting from the rest of her body. The response surprised her, and she propped herself on her elbows. "I feel pretty fantastic, actually."

She was lying on a cot along the wall of a large, open room, with Kade seated on a stool next to her. The entire space was filled with neat rows of cots, separated here and there by modest curtained screens. The room was almost uncomfortably hot. Early summer sunshine poured through the thick stained glass of the windows, painting the beds and floors with discordant rainbows. Priestesses in gleaming white robes walked between the rows of cots, tending to the injured. The musky scent of incense mingled with the faint tang of blood in the air.

"Mondera Temple," Erinda said in amazement. "I can't believe we made it. How long was I asleep?"

"Just through the night. It's nearly midmorning now."

She tried to swing her legs over the side of her cot, but Kade laid a hand on her knee.

"Don't. You wrenched your ankle pretty hard. The temple healer says it's not broken, but you should stay off of it for a while."

Erinda looked down at her foot. "But it doesn't hurt."

"I know."

It was then that she noticed the faint blue halo beneath Kade's hand where it rested on her leg. "You're doing it again, aren't you? Taking the pain away." Deep shadows ringed Kade's eyes, vivid against her pale skin. "You look exhausted. Have you even slept?"

"I'm fine. Channeling so much of the Goddess's power just took a bit of a toll, that's all. I've never used so much before."

"Then stop," she insisted, swatting Kade's touch away. "I can deal with a little pain. You need to rest."

"No, what I need is to be sure you're all right. Goddess, Rin, what were you doing out there? When I saw you in the arms of that monster, I…You can't imagine what he was thinking. I saw what was in his head, the things he planned to do to you. If I hadn't gotten to you in time…" She screwed her eyes shut, and her throat worked as if she was trying not to throw up. Her fingers tightened over Erinda's until her hand shook. "You said you'd stay behind."

"I know. I'm sorry. I wasn't thinking. You were leaving, and before I knew it, your friend Myka had grabbed my hand, and—" A bolt of fear brought her erect. "Oh Goddess, Myka!"

"She's alive."

The statement wasn't nearly as reassuring as it should have been. "But?"

"But she hasn't woken up yet." Kade's chin trembled as she gazed across the room, and Erinda caught sight of familiar strawberry blond hair resting on one of the cots a few rows away. "Myka took a terrible blow to the head. The healer's not sure she will ever wake up again."

"No," Erinda breathed, craning her neck to get a better look, but from this distance she could see only a sliver of Myka's profile. "Sweet Ithyris, no. Oh, Kade, this is all my fault. I should have stopped her."

"Don't blame yourself. Believe me, Myka would have done whatever she wanted no matter what you tried to do." Still, Kade's eyes spilled over to streak her cheeks. "If anyone's to blame it's me. We made it to the temple with thirty-seven survivors. Thirty-seven, out of more than two hundred. Lieutenant Byler lost an arm. One of the Agar high priestesses will probably never walk again, and the other three are dead. Myka might never wake up. You were almost—" Kade made a small choking sound and folded over, burying her forehead in Erinda's lap. "All because of me. I knew the odds were too great. I let them come anyway. Now they're all dead because of me."

She hadn't mentioned Talon, and Erinda knotted one fist in the blanket in fear. "Kade, what about Captain Talon?"

Kade went very still before she answered. "The captain's all right. Had a nasty gash over one eye that the healer stitched up, and I hear he might have a few broken ribs, but you don't have to worry. He's going to be fine."

Puzzled by the bitterness that had entered Kade's voice, Erinda stroked her spiky golden hair. Kade was quiet for so long that Erinda thought she might have fallen asleep. When Kade did finally speak again, she kept her face hidden in the blanket that covered Erinda's lap. Her question was so painfully shy that Erinda could not miss its meaning. "Why did you let him go, Rin?"

Erinda inhaled, sharp and quick. Her fingers froze against Kade's scalp, and it took a long time to summon her voice. "How did you know?"

Kade gave a clipped laugh. "Come on, it's you. Of course I know."

To her consternation, she felt her cheeks burning. "It was never serious, I swear. Talon and I, we just…We had an understanding for a while. We were lonely, and we needed each other."

"I'm not judging, Rin. Talon's exactly the kind of man you should be with—strong, capable, kind. And I know he cares for you." Her words were still half muffled by the blanket. "So why did you let him go?"

"Talon's always been in love with someone else." She bit her tongue, debating the wisdom of her next words. She wasn't sure this was an argument she had the strength for right now. But finally, she just closed her eyes and let them come. "As have I."

Kade stiffened and raised her head. She stared into Erinda's face with a mixture of guilt and sadness, and Erinda watched the protests play behind her eyes, like she was trying to decide whether she might be able to feign incomprehension of her meaning. She raised the inner corners of her eyebrows in challenge. Kade could pretend if she wanted, but Erinda knew she'd been perfectly understood. At last, Kade's shoulders slumped. "Rin, you know it was never supposed to be that way. You and I, we could never be…You were supposed to move on, find someone else."

"Oh, I tried. Many times, with many other someones." She traced Kade's jaw with her fingers, and Kade's mouth began to tremble. She knew she was taking this too far, but she ran her thumb lightly over Kade's lower lip. She couldn't resist; the touch was as close as she would ever get to kissing her again. "But it's always only ever been you, Kade."

"No," Kade moaned, closing her eyes. "Oh, Rin, no, you have to let me go." Yet even as she said the words, she turned her face into Erinda's touch, her lips brushing her palm. "This isn't right. It's not even natural. Surely there have to be any number of men at the palace who could give you far more than I ever could."

"No man will ever be right for me." She placed just enough emphasis on the words that she knew Kade would get her point.

Kade's elegant brows contracted. "But you just said that you'd tried, with—"

Erinda locked eyes with her pointedly and held her breath. There was no turning back now. This was a conversation they had needed to have for many winters. She watched realization dawn slowly as Kade scanned her face. "They weren't men," she murmured.

"Not a one."

Kade sat back on the stool in shock. "Sweet Ithyris, what have I done?"

"Now you listen to me, Kadrian Crossis, I happen to like who I am. I would be attracted to women even if you and I had never met, so don't you dare go trying to take credit for it."

The confused wrinkles returned to Kade's forehead. "But wait. What about Captain Talon? I know you were with him, and he's a man…isn't he?"

Erinda was so startled that she cursed, making Kade jump in her seat. Before she could mask her expression, she knew it was too late. Kade had read the truth in her face. As shock spread over Kade's features, dismay welled up inside Erinda, eclipsing the bittersweet fervor of their conversation. In four winters of guarding Talon's secret, she had never slipped, not once. Yet now in her desire to make sure Kade heard the truth, she'd also managed to betray the trust of one of her dearest friends.

Kade picked up on her sudden plunge into guilt just as quickly. "It's all right, Rin. I won't tell anyone."

"It's not all right," Erinda snapped. "I can't believe I just…" At a loss for words, she cursed again. Several of the priestesses wending through the room looked up at her, *tsk*ing in disapproval.

Kade, however, had a tiny smile toying at the corner of her lips. "Wow. I can't help but think of what your mother had to say the last time she heard those words coming out of your mouth."

That brought Erinda around a little, and she snickered. "She made sure that I couldn't sit down for a quarter moon."

"And I had to sneak supper to you for at least that long."

"I remember." When she and her older sister had misbehaved, their mother sent them to bed without supper—sometimes for days at a time. Yet no matter the season or how cold it might be outside, whenever Erinda was being punished Kade would always appear at her bedroom window after dark. She kept Erinda distracted from her growling stomach with idle chatter, even when her teeth were chattering so hard she could barely form words, until Erinda's parents went to sleep and it was safe for her to climb through the window into Erinda's room. Erinda wrapped Kade in blankets to warm her frozen limbs, then dug into the packet of contraband that Kade had brought her. Once she'd eaten her fill, she and Kade would snuggle down into bed together and she would rub the circulation back into Kade's hands and feet. They cuddled and talked for hours in whispers and stifled giggles, until the early rays of dawn forced Kade to sneak out and run for home before they were discovered.

"I was supposed to be punished, but you always made it so much fun."

Kade grinned at her, and sadness twisted in Erinda's chest. She sternly wrenched the topic back to the present. "I've made such an awful mistake, Kade. Talon is my friend, and she counts on me to preserve her secret. You can't tell anyone else what you know. Promise me."

"Of course I promise. I'm just not sure what this means. I've heard the rumors like everyone else. Are they true, then? Are Queen Shasta and the captain really…"

"They love each other. A fact I have been trying to remind Talon of ever since she volunteered for this insane mission." At Kade's questioning look, Erinda pursed her lips. "It's a long story. Suffice to say that Talon is one of the most pigheaded people I have ever known."

She watched as Kade tried to absorb this, and wondered how much further she might push her luck with this exchange. There were things Kade needed to hear, things Erinda had spent seven winters wishing she might someday have the chance to say, though she wasn't sure Kade was ready to hear them. Erinda took a deep breath.

"Kade," she said softly, "there are so many people, men and women both, who fall in love with someone of their own gender. Too few are willing to speak of it openly, but it's far more common than you think. Sometimes, the lucky ones even get the chance to make it work, and it's beautiful to watch. So I don't want to hear another word about how our feelings for each other aren't natural. You can deny it all you want—I know being a priestess probably makes that easier—but you know it as well as I do. We're the same, Kade, you and I. We always have been."

Kade's features contracted and she stood up quickly. "I should go." Emotion thickened her voice, though Erinda couldn't tell if it was sadness, anger, embarrassment, or something else. But she recognized the brightness that had sprung up in Kade's eyes.

Erinda did her best to keep disappointment from her face as she nodded. "Get some rest, Your Grace."

Kade walked away. Though her back was turned, Erinda saw her lift a hand to her face as she went, and she knew Kade was crying again.

❖

Kade spent the next few days avoiding Erinda as much as possible. She had plenty to occupy her time, as the Monderan priestesses begged her to participate in their prayers and services. She was entreated to bless various items of worship, to conduct temple meditation, and at one point, she even found herself standing before the Great Temple leading the daily *shaa'ri* practice—the irony of which was certainly not lost on her.

Though not even two moons had passed since she had left Verdred Temple, somehow it felt like a lifetime ago. She didn't have the luxury of bashfulness anymore. Kade was beginning to understand that for the Ithyrian people, her voice was Ithyris's voice, her hands Ithyris's hands. Just by being *shaa'din*, she brought the people closer to their Goddess than they had been in a thousand winters, and for that, they would follow her into battle no matter how hopeless, even suffer and die for her, whether or not she asked it of them. The responsibility of such absolute devotion was daunting, and Kade knew she wasn't worthy of it. She threw herself into service because it was the only way she could think of to honor their faith in her.

When she wasn't busy with temple practices, Kade sought Ithyris's company. The Goddess spoke to her with increasing frequency, and Kade had learned how to rouse Her current so that it would carry her to the spirit nexus at her will. Sometimes Ithyris was there, and they would talk together until Kade's body called her back. Sometimes Kade would roam the shifting halls alone. Occasionally, she would see other souls step out of their glowing doorways and into the nexus; most rose to the shimmering overhead lake and disappeared, but every now and then one was pulled back into their portal before they could reach the lake's surface. Once, she even thought she glimpsed Myka peeking from one of the apertures, but the figure was tugged away too quickly for Kade to be sure of what she'd seen.

At night, however, long after the rest of the temple was asleep, Kade lay awake for hours while Erinda's words replayed in her mind—*we're the same, you and I*. She wasn't sure what had disconcerted her more, learning that Erinda had exclusively pursued female company after they'd separated, or Erinda's assertion that such things were not entirely unusual. That the Queen of Ithyria herself had taken a female lover.

Kade had always lived under the impression that her feelings for Erinda were unnatural. She could even remember how sharply her parents had rebuked the intimacy of her friendship with Erinda when they were young.

"Honestly, Kadrian, it's just not healthy how you two cling to one another," her mother had said one night. "You're going to corrupt that poor girl with all your overreaching attentions, and then she'll be ruined for any match her parents might make for her; I've seen it happen before. It's just as well you're entering the temple. I'd never allow such a thing to happen to my own daughter."

Kade had never given it much thought until now, but her mother's offhand remark that she'd "seen it happen before" took on a whole new meaning in light of what Erinda had said. Was it true? Were there other women out there who felt for each other the things she felt for Erinda—the hot stirring in her blood, the echoes of longing in her stomach? Certainly nothing had ever felt so instinctual. Even now, her body's response to Erinda came almost entirely as a reflex she had no control of.

But Kade was a priestess, dedicated to the Goddess. She was sacred and celibate. So did it really matter? She belonged to Ithyris and was Hers alone.

Part of her longed to ask the Goddess Her opinion, but she was far too ashamed to broach the subject. Thankfully, Ithyris had made no mention of Kade's deviance from Her commands on the battlefield, even though Kade had failed to kill Mardyth as She had asked. Nor had She chastised Kade for putting Erinda's welfare above Her orders, and Kade had fully expected at least some measure of reprimand for that. So Kade couldn't possibly bring the matter up, not without the risk that she would also have to answer for her disobedience. She didn't think she could bear the shame of Ithyris's gentle rebukes again.

For obvious reasons, she couldn't talk to Erinda about it either. Every time Erinda was near, Kade's heart beat a little harder, her muscles tensed deliciously, and—she was ashamed to admit it—she often found her sex growing wet and heavy with desire. She craved Erinda's touch, the sunshine scent of her skin, the beauty of her dimpled smile, and these forbidden feelings were only becoming more stringent with every day she spent in Erinda's presence. Whatever hold Erinda had over her, it was nearly as powerful as the Goddess's, even without vows binding them or a current of Erinda's spirit running under her skin. Erinda pulled Kade away from her calling at Ithyris's side. No matter how Kade tried to tell herself that her role was to encourage

Erinda to move past their shared history and find happiness in someone else, she could not seem to stifle her own weaknesses long enough to be of any help. In fact, the more time she spent near her, the more difficult it became for Kade to maintain focus.

As the Fifthmoon approached, the barbarian army set up camp outside the temple walls. Oddly, they made no attempt to attack, and issued no challenges or demands. Kade wasn't sure what Mardyth was waiting for, though she wasn't foolish enough to think that she would be content to sit quietly for long. Their presence made the temple residents nervous, however, and the Honored Mother summoned Kade to her study one afternoon to discuss how they might prepare for whatever Ulrike's army was planning.

Before reporting to the Honored Mother, Kade went in search of Talon. Though the Honored Mother had not included Talon in her invitation, any discussion of strategy ought to include the ranking military officer amongst them, even if Kade did not particularly relish the idea of working with the man—the *woman*, she corrected herself— who had used and discarded Erinda as it suited her purposes.

One of the priestesses told her she'd find Talon in the temple infirmary with the wounded soldiers, so Kade headed there with apprehension. Her own visits to the infirmary had been carefully timed to coincide with Erinda's work in the temple stables, because when Erinda wasn't tending the horses, she was at Myka's bedside. Kade needed to stay away from Erinda, at least long enough to make some sense of the emotions roiling her equilibrium.

When she entered the infirmary she glanced quickly in the direction of Myka's cot. The sight of Myka's pale, waxen face immobile on the straw-stuffed pillow filled Kade with sadness, but she was relieved not to find Erinda there. She scanned the room for Talon, finally sighting her dark hair and worn scarlet uniform among the rows of beds. As she approached, she could see a sheaf of papers in Talon's hand, which quivered as she read from them. Her other hand was busy fingering a small blue feather that she wore by a chain around her neck. Talon was so engrossed that she did not seem to hear Kade approach, and suddenly Talon's voice was reading the words directly into Kade's consciousness.

Brita has been so ill the past few days, feverish and cross, and I can't for the life of me get her to eat. Nurse says it isn't serious, but I'm at my wits' end with worry. I think our little girl misses her father almost as much as I do.

Oh, my love, how I wish you would come home to us. Our bed is so cold and empty without you, my heart so heavy. I long for you so fiercely that at times it seems I might conjure your presence through sheer force of will. I dream every night of your touch, your kiss, the warmth of your arms around me and your skin pressed sweetly against mine...

Kade felt her cheeks flame. It was awkward enough to find herself privy to the thoughts that flashed through others' minds, but this was an even more intimate intrusion. Why would Ithyris want her to know any of this? Since she didn't know how to block Talon's voice from her head, Kade cleared her throat to interrupt the reading before it went any further.

Talon looked up, folding the letter in her hand. "Your Grace," she said, and Kade thought she heard the words catch a bit in her throat. "What can I do for you?"

"Mother Hirrow has asked to meet with me about the barbarian threat. I thought you might want to come along."

Talon rose to her feet, tucking the letters back inside the front of her jacket. When she moved to Kade's side, Kade was struck by the realization that Talon was one of the few women she'd ever met who was taller than she was. With her broad shoulders and slim, angular build, no wonder it was so easy for Talon to convince everyone she was male. She lifted a dark brow, and Kade realized she was staring.

"This way, please," she stammered, and led them out of the infirmary.

They walked the temple halls shoulder to shoulder, and Kade summoned her courage. "May I ask you something, Captain?" When Talon nodded, she said, "I want to know about you and Erinda."

Talon stopped, and turned toward her. "What has Erinda told you?" The question was cautious.

"Nothing, really. I overheard the two of you talking and sort of pieced things together from there. I know the two of you used to be... involved."

"You should be asking Erinda about this, not me."

"I tried, but Erinda and I have a very complicated relationship."

Talon shook her head. "Erinda is my friend, Your Grace. If she doesn't want to talk to you about it, I won't betray her confidence."

"I'm not asking you to," Kade said. "Let me ask it a different way. Do you love the Queen, Captain?"

Talon's hand went to the feather pendant at her neck, and she began walking again. Kade scurried to catch up. "I'm not trying to be nosy. It's just that I don't really understand why you're here instead of at the palace if—"

"I am captain of Her Majesty's royal guard," Talon interrupted, her voice brusque. "Mondera requested our assistance with the barbarian attacks, and we responded."

"But it didn't have to be you, did it? Surely the royal guard have plenty of commanding officers that could have led the units out here. I heard you say something to Erinda about an heir?"

"Oh, for the love of the Goddess," Talon huffed and stopped again. She crossed her arms and eyed Kade suspiciously. "Did Erinda put you up to this?"

"No, not at all." Kade realized she would need to put all her cards on the table if she hoped to get the answers she was looking for. She lowered her voice. "But I know, Captain Talon. I know you're a…" She mouthed the last word silently. *Woman*.

Talon took her elbow and drew her back toward the wall, her eyes scanning the hall for potential eavesdroppers. "Erinda told you?" She didn't sound angry, but her expression was deadly serious.

"No, she didn't. Not on purpose. But…well, as I said, we've always had a complicated relationship. I've always just seemed to understand the things she's thinking, what she's feeling, without her saying a word. Often they're things she doesn't want me knowing at all. But it's not her fault. She can't help it."

To her surprise, Talon gave a bemused smile. "Neither can you, I'd wager." Kade was flustered by the knowing look that entered the captain's eyes as she said, "Tell you what, Your Grace. I'll answer your question if you answer one of mine."

"And what's that?"

Talon leaned back against the wall and crossed her arms again. "Do you love Erinda?"

It was Kade's turn to drop her eyes. "I…We were very close, growing up. I still care for her very much."

"Then why are you here, instead of at the palace?" Talon threw Kade's own question back at her with a gentle, mocking tone.

"Because I have a duty," Kade said in frustration. "My life belongs to the Goddess. And besides, Erinda and I could never be…I can never be…"

"Hers?" Kade felt pinpricks behind her eyes as she nodded. "Fair enough, Handmaiden. To answer your question: yes, I love the Queen. But I cannot be what she needs. I cannot change the color of my skin, the circumstances of my birth. In the eyes of her court, I will never be an acceptable mate for her. And I cannot give her a child. I am here for the same reason you are, to give the woman I love a chance at all the things I cannot offer."

"But, Captain, at least you have the ability to be with her." Kade could not believe that Talon couldn't see what a gift she was throwing away. "So the court doesn't approve of your Outlander blood, and Queen Shasta's adopted daughter is the only heir to the royal house. But look at you." She swept a hand, indicating Talon's male attire. Everything about her, from the casual confidence of her posture, to the way she walked and the unusually deep timbre of her voice was carefully masculine. "At the end of the day, you're still just the man who won the heart of the Queen. Living as you do, there'd be nothing to stop you from marrying her if you wanted, and raising the Princess together as a family. The court might be disgruntled, but no one would ever be the wiser. You can't imagine how I envy you that. If I'd had that opportunity seven winters ago, I would have taken it."

Kade froze as that assertion washed over her with stunning veracity. She exhaled. The possibility had never occurred to her before, but she knew it was true. "I would have taken it." Had she possessed the benefit of Talon's male disguise, she and Erinda might have had a viable option for survival together in the world. If the idea had presented itself back then, Kade would have given in to Erinda's pleas to run away with her. *I would have chosen Erinda over the temple.*

The Goddess's threaded current might have stung her with reproach, but Kade was too floored by this revelation to pay mind to anything else. For so long, she had told herself that she'd entered temple service because it was her calling, her birthright as her parents' eldest daughter. This was the only path that had ever been laid out for her, and it had even been a very appealing one. Kade had always delighted in the Goddess's presence in her life. Leaving Erinda had been the most difficult thing she had ever done, but she had done it because she'd believed it her only choice. Ithyris, Kade could have. Erinda, she could not. Simple. Except that this enigmatic woman-dressed-as-a-man presented an alternative that Kade had never thought of. And it had come seven winters too late to be of any use.

Talon seemed equally lost in her own dark thoughts, and so for a minute the two of them just stood together in the temple hall, contemplating their respective dilemmas. Finally, Talon pushed away from the wall. "The Honored Mother is waiting, is she not?"

They walked the rest of the way to Mother Hirrow's study in diplomatic silence.

CHAPTER THIRTEEN

Erinda paused with uncertainty at the entrance to the temple infirmary. Inside she could see Kade at Myka's bedside, holding her hand, apparently lost in prayer.

She knew Kade had been avoiding her for the past few days, and Erinda had done her best to grant her the distance she seemed to need, no matter how difficult it was. More than anything, Erinda longed to sit with Kade and talk again. She knew how much she had rattled her with their last conversation, and her state of mind vacillated between certainty that she'd done the right thing and equal certainty that she'd made a terrible mistake. She desperately needed to know what Kade was thinking and feeling, but Kade had given her no opportunity to ask. This, however, did not seem to be an appropriate time. Kade was worried for Myka, and it would be selfish of Erinda to add to her burdens right now.

Erinda steeled her resolve and approached. She reached out to touch Kade's shoulder, then thought better of it and cleared her throat to herald her presence. "How's she doing?"

Kade started, then looked up at her warily. "The same, I'm afraid."

"May I?" Erinda gestured to the stool next to Kade's and held her breath as Kade seemed to consider the question. She looked so uncomfortable that Erinda didn't wait for an answer. "You know, never mind. I'll come back later."

"No, it's all right." Kade stood. "I was just leaving anyway."

"You were here first. Stay. I'll go."

Kade began to protest, but broke off when Myka arched off the cot beside them. Her eyelids fluttered and she began to convulse.

Erinda cried out in alarm. Kade dropped back to Myka's side, calling for the temple healer. Every priestess in the room rushed over to them, and the healer had to elbow her way through. As Myka continued to spasm, the healer shooed everyone back. She whipped a handkerchief from her sleeve, and in seconds had rolled it and slid it between Myka's chattering teeth.

"Help me get her on her side," she said, and together they managed to roll Myka over until she was facing them.

Helpless, Erinda could only watch as the girl kept shaking. Her skin was turning a chilling shade of gray, and Erinda's heart clenched at the terror on Kade's face. The healer tucked pillows around Myka's head to be sure she didn't injure herself on the cot's wooden frame. She called for her bag of herbs and soaked a cloth in cold water and pungent oils, then applied the compress to Myka's forehead and held it there as best she could while she seized. Kade held Myka's hand in an iron grip, her lips moving in soundless prayer.

They waited tensely. Erinda forgot to breathe for so long that her ears started ringing.

At last, Myka gave one final, great tremor, and then she was still. Gently, the healer moved her onto her back again. She checked beneath Myka's eyelids, felt at her wrist for a pulse, and then tried her neck. She put an ear to Myka's lips and a light hand on her sternum. Then the healer shook her head woefully, and a collective sigh of sadness went up from the onlookers.

Erinda felt sick. "Oh, no…Kade, I am so sorry."

Kade's eyes were vacant. Her expression had gone alarmingly lifeless. She was staring down at Myka without even seeming to see her, her pupils constricted to tiny points within the brilliant viridian of her irises. Erinda turned to the healer anxiously. "Is the Handmaiden all right?"

The healer turned to Kade and laid a hand on her shoulder. When she did not respond, she waved a hand before Kade's eyes, then felt her forehead. A frown crinkled her nose.

"I think perhaps Her Grace is in shock." When she tried to extricate Kade's hands from Myka's, however, Kade's white-knuckled hold refused to loosen.

"Wait, Madam Healer."

Erinda looked up to see the priestesses parting respectfully for the Monderan Honored Mother, who knelt at Kade's side. "The Handmaiden is with the Goddess. We must not disturb her." She, too, looked sorrowfully at Myka's limp form on the cot. "Come, *Ostryn*, we must bless this brave young woman who has given her life in the service of our Lady." Mother Hirrow tilted her head back and began chanting in the Ithyrian tongue, and the other women joined in.

Erinda could not take her eyes from Kade's empty face. The Kade Erinda knew would have dissolved into tears, great heaving sobs of grief lasting for many hours. But this Kade was inanimate, as if her soul had retreated somewhere far, far away. Erinda had never seen her react this way to anything so terrible before, and it was frightening. As the priestesses chanted over Myka's body, Erinda offered up a little prayer of her own.

❖

The Goddess's current had swept Kade into the spirit nexus faster than ever before. The moment Kade opened her eyes, Ithyris was regarding her gravely. "You must hurry, Beloved. There isn't much time."

Kade shook her head in a panic. "I can't be here right now, Lady, please! Send me back! Myka—"

"Myka is here." The Goddess stepped back so that Kade could see Myka emerging from a nearby doorway. Though in the infirmary Myka had been draped only in a light shift, here in the nexus she was wearing her white tunic and leggings, and Kade even thought she saw a knife hilt peeking from her riding boots.

"She has been lurking about the nexus for days now as her injuries have been healing," Ithyris said. "The longer she's gone without waking up, the weaker her spirit's connection to her body has become. This time her flesh will not be able to call her spirit back. She will be lost."

"No," Kade breathed. Myka had taken several steps into the hall, looking around in confusion. Kade knew what would happen next, and sure enough, Myka tilted her head back and gazed at the shimmering lake overhead. A beatific smile crossed her face, and her feet left the unbroken whiteness of the floor as she floated upward.

"If you want to save your friend, Beloved, you must do it now. Catch her."

The Goddess's instructions were unneeded, as Kade was already running. She reached the spot where Myka had been and grabbed for her ankle, but Myka was already out of reach, ascending toward the glittering surface of the lake.

"No!" Kade cried in frustration. She jumped, swiping for her, but Myka was too high up.

"You will have to go after her, Kadrian."

Myka's head broke the surface of the lake and disappeared, followed by her shoulders. "How?" Kade demanded frantically.

"Jump."

"I'm trying!" Kade leapt again, even though Myka was hopelessly beyond her grasp. As her feet thudded to the ground, she growled.

"You have no body here, Beloved, remember? The weight you feel is only your mind perpetuating the rules of your world here in the nexus. You must forget the rules. Forget your body. Just jump."

Myka's legs were vanishing now. Kade took a deep breath, and with every ounce of determination she possessed, opened herself to the disconcerting sensation of weightlessness that she usually tried so hard to ignore when she was here. She reminded herself firmly that here in the nexus she was pure spirit, unfettered by physical limitations. There was nothing holding her to the floor but her own presumption. Embracing that awareness and gathering herself once more, Kade jumped.

Her feet left the floor and propelled her upward. She put her arms up as the rippling lake swallowed Myka's ankles and closed over the soles of her boots. Kade rose after her. Her fingers broke the cool surface of the lake; her hands and arms followed.

The water, if it was in fact water at all, felt very strange. It prickled and tingled, and Kade had the discomfiting impression that the lake *wanted* her, wanted to take her apart in the tiniest fragments imaginable and scatter her across its infinite depths. Worse, she found herself nearly enjoying the feeling. How delightful to be welcomed into the vastness of spirit itself! Her head entered the lake as well, but she still could not see Myka, or even her own arms above her. The water showed her only shifting shadows in a thousand shades of gray and blue and green. She could not breathe, but then again, she was only spirit here; she did not need to.

"Myka!" she shouted, and though she had no breath to shout with, the prickling shadows still flitted away from her as if she'd frightened them. There! Not an armlength away she glimpsed a hard shape, its tawny color starkly out of place among the drifting penumbrae. Kade shot a hand toward it, and her fingers closed around something solid. She found, however, that it was a struggle to keep her hold. Both her hand and the thing she was holding felt spongy, like their structures were already softening.

"Quickly, Beloved," she heard Ithyris say in her mind, "or the lake will take you both."

Kade kicked her feet, hard. She was still only half submerged, but the water was drawing her into itself now. She tugged at the thing in her hand, which she was hoping was Myka's ankle, and used her other arm to paddle backward, fighting the lake's pull. She struggled and thrashed, but her body felt too malleable to exert the force she needed.

She was dissolving into the spirit lake right along with Myka, and it was sapping her strength with each passing minute.

Just as Kade was beginning to think she would never be able to get them out of there, a familiar yanking sensation at her heels told her that beyond the nexus, her body was calling her back. This time, she welcomed its insistent bidding. She swung her free arm up to reinforce her disintegrating grip with both hands, and relaxed into the demanding tow of her Flesh as it hauled her downward. The prickling feeling subsided as she emerged from the lake, and as she watched, her hands appeared overhead clasping a well-worn leather riding boot. Kade nearly cried in relief when Myka's leg followed, and then her hips and torso. The lake finally released them with a slurping sound like a sigh, and they fell from the lake's inverted surface to the floor of the hall. Kade caught Myka against her own body as they struck down. Their landing wasn't painful since they had no actual weight here, but Kade didn't have time to marvel because her glowing doorway was already dragging her backward across the floor.

She couldn't leave the nexus until she'd put Myka back into her own portal. She could tell which one was Myka's, too, because its light was sputtering ominously. Fortunately, her own door was going to pull them both right past it. Kade wrapped her arms tightly around Myka, who now seemed free of the lake's hypnotic spell.

Myka blinked at her slowly in recognition. "Handmaiden?" She tried to twist around in Kade's arms as they skidded across the unbroken whiteness of the nexus floor. "Where are we?"

Myka's flickering doorway was coming up on their left. Kade kept her eyes on it, but still gave Myka a tense smile. "Just hang on, Myka. I'm getting you out of here."

"Out of…Sweet Ithyris, is that who I think it is?"

Kade couldn't answer, because they were passing Myka's aperture. She rolled, shoving Myka at the opening with all her might. Myka slid backward and vanished into it, staring off over Kade's head with a look of sheer awe on her face. The portal's glow brightened as it engulfed her.

Kade was still gliding on her back toward her own doorway. Myka's appeared stable enough now, but she couldn't see Myka within it. Had she made it back in time? Kade was dragged past Ithyris's hovering feet, and looked up to see the Goddess smiling. "Did it work, Lady?" Kade begged. "Please, did I save her?"

The silver current sluiced around her, drowning out the Goddess's reply.

❖

Erinda grabbed at the Honored Mother's shoulder, interrupting the priestesses' hymn of mourning. "Please, Your Honor, there's something wrong with Kade!"

Though her eyes were still open and unblinking, Kade's complexion was becoming as gray as Myka's, her lips bluing a bit around the edges. The Honored Mother broke off in the middle of their song, and worried mutters filled the room as the priestesses got a good look at Kade's face.

Heedless of decorum, Erinda stepped around the Honored Mother and squeezed between her and Kade. She crouched down at Kade's side, on the verge of hysteria. The healer was feeling for Kade's pulse. "Is she breathing? What's wrong with her?"

The healer looked as confounded as Erinda felt. "I don't know, dear. I can't tell." Erinda spun to Mother Hirrow.

"Do something!"

The Honored Mother reached around Erinda, placed one hand on Kade's back, and lifted the other to the ceiling. She tilted her head back and began yet another chant. Erinda had to swallow the screech that threatened to shred its way out of her throat. Chanting was not going to help. She turned back to Kade and shook her shoulders hard. "Kade, wake up! Damn it, breathe!"

The healer waved an acrid-smelling vial beneath Kade's nose, and the odor was so strong it made Erinda's own nostrils recoil. But Kade did not respond. She continued to stare down at Myka's body, Myka's hand knotted woodenly in hers.

Myka suddenly gasped awake. Her eyes snapped open, and she sprang straight up on the cot with a deep, sucking inhale. A few of the priestesses shrieked, and Erinda nearly fell over backward in shock.

A second later, Kade's lungs inflated abruptly, color rushing back to her cheeks as a renewed flow of blood reclaimed her graying skin. Her pupils expanded back to their normal size. Erinda threw her arms around her, trembling, and pressed her cheek to Kade's chest.

"Oh, thank the Goddess!"

The astonished onlookers were railing in a cacophony of exclamations and chatter, but for Erinda the noise faded into the background the moment Kade's heart slammed back to life against her ear. One of Kade's hands came up to caress Erinda's hair, while the other moved lightly to her ribs. "Rin?"

Erinda squeezed tighter. "I'm here, darling."

"Child," came Mother Hirrow's disapproving voice through the din, "release the Handmaiden, please, so that the healer may examine her."

Reluctantly, Erinda dropped the embrace, and the healer was quick to edge her out of the way as she set about checking Kade's pulse and the dilation of her eyes.

Myka was nearly buried by curious priestesses, all demanding to know what had just happened. This was a miracle of the most wondrous proportions. They had all watched the girl die with their own eyes. How was it that she was now alive? Did she remember any of what she had seen? Had the Handmaiden resurrected her? Had she seen the Goddess?

And for someone who had recently been deceased, Myka seemed scarcely the worse for wear. In fact, from what Erinda could tell Myka was positively glowing under all the attention, and she was rattling off answers to their questions so fast that Erinda could barely make sense of them. Something about a lake and doors of light, and yes, she had seen Ithyris with her own eyes, but the Handmaiden had dragged her away before she could get a really good look at Her.

Kade, on the other hand, was murmuring as the Honored Mother and several others hammered eager questions at her. But unlike Myka, she did not appear to be enjoying the experience, and at last the healer rose to her feet, placed two fingers in her mouth, and gave an earsplitting whistle that quieted the room.

"*Ostryn*, we have surely witnessed something miraculous here today, but there will be time later for these interrogations. The Handmaiden is tired, and our young Pledged has just been returned to us from an unimaginable journey. I must ask you to leave them in peace for now. Out with you all." She began to shoo them toward the infirmary exit.

Erinda tried to linger behind, wanting to reassure herself that Kade was really all right, but the Honored Mother took her elbow and steered her away. "Come, child," was all that Hirrow said, but Erinda could hear the reprimand in both clipped syllables. The Honored Mother clearly did not approve of the liberties that Erinda, a mere serving girl, took with the Goddess's *shaa'din*. Upon their entry into temple service, priestesses were no longer considered friends or even family to those they had left behind. They were certainly not to be embraced with such presumptuous familiarity. And Kade was no ordinary priestess, which made Erinda's behavior all the more inappropriate.

But Erinda was beyond caring what the Honored Mother might think of her. It was only out of respect for Kade that she bowed her head and allowed herself to be led away.

CHAPTER FOURTEEN

Temple life, Erinda discovered, was not all that different from life at the palace. Because the priestesses kept no maids or servants, they observed the day-to-day duties of cleaning, cooking, gardening, laundry, and so on themselves in addition to their ritual prayers and ceremonies. Like Erinda, the priestesses' mornings began before dawn, so she always passed several groups of them as she made her way to the stables in the early morning.

Erinda had assigned herself the task of looking after the dozen or so surviving war-horses that the soldiers had brought with them from Agar. The women tasked with care of the temple horses had no idea how to properly tend to the needs of the much larger breeds ridden by soldiers; Erinda was appalled to find that the temple stables offered very little in the way of an exercise arena. Perhaps the dainty temple palfreys were content to make lap after lap around the tiny stable yard, but the huge war-horses required a much larger space in which to stretch their legs. Since the barbarian army was camped outside the temple walls, excursions into the surrounding terrain were impossible, and so Erinda had arranged to ride the larger horses around the circumference of the temple grounds to ensure they were getting adequate exercise.

This morning she began with Brindle, a bulky chestnut mare whose shoulder towered a good two handbreadths above Erinda's head. She had to drag a set of wooden steps over to the massive animal's side just to get her saddled. Brindle was a dignified creature, and every muscle in her mighty body bunched and flexed in harmony, even when her gait was restrained to a walk. Erinda would have loved to take Brindle out for a real run and unleash that power in earnest, but within the temple walls, the most either of them could hope for was a brisk canter.

They trotted past the pitiful little stable yard and followed the outer temple wall around the dormitories, the temple library, and the kitchens and dining hall. Of the three Great Temples Erinda had visited in her life, Mondera Temple was the only one that had a gigantic wall enclosing the entire temple grounds. It was similar to the one that also surrounded Agar, and a sharp reminder of the dangers that plagued this province; even priestesses here were not exempt from attack by their violent northern neighbors.

All her life, Erinda had heard of the horrors experienced by the residents of Mondera, who were mostly miners, tradesfolk, or loggers, and ill-equipped to fend off the barbarian raiders. Even so, seeing this place for herself was an eye-opening experience. The Monderan people lived under a cloud of fear so ever-present that it had become ingrained in them, something they seemed to have accepted as a matter of course. Erinda had resolved to sit down with Queen Shasta upon their return and give her a long, frank account of what she had seen. The Queen might have all sorts of insight as to the political situation in Mondera, but Erinda was willing to bet she had no idea just how difficult even the most basic elements of life were for the people who lived here every day.

When they passed the temple gardens, Erinda had to guide Brindle in a wide berth around the enticing vegetable plants, most of which were in midsummer bloom. The horse snorted with disappointment, and Erinda patted her neck.

"Let's finish our ride and then you'll have a treat, girl." Brindle tossed her head with displeasure, but she was too well trained to disobey. Her smooth gait never faltered, even as they left the succulent vegetables behind. They passed behind the high sanctuary, and when they reached the other side, they entered the temple cemetery.

This was Erinda's favorite part of the ride. The cemetery grounds were by far the most beautiful place within the temple walls. There were thirty-two grave markers here, each one a unique memorial to the Honored Mother interred beneath it. As a general rule, Ithyrians burned their dead, with just two exceptions: members of the royal family and Honored Mothers. These were returned to the earth intact in the belief that the land would be blessed by their nobility and wisdom. In the burial grounds of the Great Temples, the graves dated back a thousand winters, to the time of the Twelve.

The cemetery was carefully tended. The grass was neatly shorn, the marble grave markers were meticulously polished, and their engravings painstakingly preserved generation after generation. Small cones of incense burned in brass censers beneath each carved name, filling the tree branches overhead with rich fragrance.

And beyond the neat rows of headstones, an ornate mausoleum presided over them all with a watchful maternal air—the supposed resting place of Mondera herself. A squat, rectangular building made entirely of white marble, Mondera's sepulchre was a self-contained work of art. As usual, Erinda's attention was drawn to the face carved into the stone above the heavy oak doors. Time and weather had softened the woman's features, but she could still see that the sculptor had depicted Mondera with her eyes closed. Her two normal eyes, at least. There was also a third eye in the middle of her forehead, and that one was very much open, gazing out over the cemetery grounds at the high sanctuary beyond. The carving always gave Erinda chills, especially at this time of morning. The early rays of dawn made the pale marble take on an otherworldly glow.

This morning something was different, and Erinda drew Brindle to a stop. The mausoleum doors were cracked open, and soft blue light radiated from their seams. Erinda glanced around, but she and Brindle were alone. The groundskeeper was probably taking care of some routine maintenance within the mausoleum, she decided, and urged Brindle on again.

Yet after a few more steps, the curious light had grown brighter, and again she reined Brindle to a halt as a woman's cry reached her ears. Kade's voice, though Erinda couldn't tell whether it was a sound of joy or pain. She dropped from Brindle's back to the ground and tossed the reins over a nearby tree branch.

By the time she reached the doors the light had intensified. Erinda pulled at the open door until it was wide enough to see inside. She shielded her eyes with one hand and squinted into the brilliant interior of the mausoleum. It took several moments for her brain to grasp what she was seeing.

Kade was suspended in midair. It was definitely Kade, in her boy's tunic and leggings, floating on her back above the ornately carved sarcophagus that lay in the center of the sepulchre. But her skin and clothes were shining blue, like the hottest part of a metalsmith's flame, and Erinda couldn't look directly at her for very long. The light grew brighter and brighter, and Kade's back arched.

Erinda was beginning to get used to seeing strange things when Kade was around, but this concerned her. This was the Goddess's power, of that Erinda was sure, and it looked like Kade was completely overpowered within it. Erinda ran forward, determined to yank Kade out of whatever strange spell this was, but before she could reach her, the light swelled into whiteness and shoved her back. Erinda squeezed her eyes shut and threw an arm over her face, and Kade let out an exclamation that brought Erinda to her knees.

She knew that sound. She'd replayed that same ragged cry only in her most decadent and torturous memories. Occasionally, she heard it in her imagination while in the arms of some extemporaneous lover, and it always meant the relationship would not endure for long. Erinda had cherished that sound, had at times craved it to the point of agony. But this time, it was not for her.

The realization struck like a hammer on glass. She fractured and fell, shattering on the cool marble floor, and when she could finally open her eyes again, Kade was descending onto the lid of the sarcophagus. Her ribs and chest expanded and contracted rapidly.

Erinda stumbled to her feet. She wasn't supposed to have seen this, she reminded herself. She shouldn't be here, and she had to get out. With one hand clutched against her churning stomach, Erinda turned and fled. As her hand struck the heavy wood barring her exit, Kade called her name. A sob caught between Erinda's teeth, and she shoved at the door.

Kade's hand grasped her wrist, pulling her back. "Rin, wait. Let me explain."

"Let go of me." Erinda tried to wrest herself from Kade's grip. But at her touch, soothing waves of comfort lapped up her arm and sabotaged her will.

"Don't go, Rin, please. Talk to me."

"About what?" Erinda struggled as Kade tried to draw her into an embrace. Tears of frustration welled up in her eyes. "How happy you are with Her? How wonderfully fulfilling your life is? Or maybe you just want to point out what an utter fool I've been making of myself? Well, don't worry, Your Grace, I won't trouble you any more with my pathetic mooning and pining. She's won. I get that. So just let me go."

"No." Kade pulled her in so hard that Erinda had to stop fighting or risk hurting her. A fine sheen of moisture still coated Kade's flushed throat, and her skin was hot against Erinda's cheek. "No, Rin, I need you to understand. This was never a contest between you and Ithyris."

"You think I don't know that? She's a Goddess. I'm well aware I can never compare with that." Erinda was shaking so hard that Kade's arms were the only thing keeping her upright. *I just always thought at least there was one part of you that would only ever belong to me. How atrociously stupid.*

She felt Kade's aura escalate in intensity, washing over her with such tenderness that it hurt to breathe.

"Oh, Rin, you're not stupid. Not at all."

Erinda pushed away, anger helping her find balance again. "Stop that! Stay the hell out of my head, Kadrian. You may be *shaa'din*, but that still doesn't give you the right."

Her blissful energy recoiled in response, but still Kade did not let go.

"I'm sorry." She sounded genuinely contrite. "I can't help it. Ithyris decides what I hear and I can't block it out."

"That figures," Erinda muttered.

"Rin, what you just saw—this is how Ithyris connects with me as Her *shaa'din*. It's how she keeps a channel open between us, so that Her spirit can flow through me."

The heightened points of color in Kade's cheeks, however, belied the innocuous explanation, and Erinda was in no mood to be coy. "She makes love to you."

Those points of color expanded until Kade's entire face was the color of an overripe tomato. "That's not it."

"Isn't it? You're still glowing." The initial shock was passing, and in its place came the stabilizing safety of reason. Erinda embraced its grounding influence with relief, and before Kade could protest she continued. "And you know what? It's really none of my business. Goddess knows I've had plenty of lovers myself." Kade flinched, but Erinda ignored it. "I'm happy for you, Your Grace. Truly I am. And I'm sorry to have intruded. It won't happen again."

Rather proud that she'd managed to recover her dignity so quickly, Erinda tried to step away. But Kade's arms only tightened around her. Kade's breath was still coming hard as she lowered her lips to Erinda's ear.

"She's not you."

The whisper was so strained that Erinda wasn't sure she'd heard correctly, but in the next moment, she gasped. Kade's aura, or whatever it was, had unleashed itself in full force, and this was no calming tide of benevolence. Unadulterated desire sluiced over Erinda's skin like needles of fire, and her stomach dropped. Erinda found herself clinging to the front of Kade's tunic to keep from losing her feet again.

"Goddess, Kade, what are you—"

Kade's hand moved to cup her jaw. Her eyes glittered, sharp as emeralds. And then, before Erinda could finish the question, Kade kissed her.

❖

The east tower suite had long been vacant. At this time of night, the King was snoring away in his chambers many doors down the hall, and the royal twins, Prince Daric and Princess Shasta, were fast asleep in their own suites on the far side of the palace. Aside from the occasional guest of the royal family, no one had used the east tower rooms in a decade or two, and only the royal chambermaids ever ventured this far down the hall anymore. They would be alone here.

Erinda unlocked the door and Kade dragged her through it by the hand. No sooner had the door swung shut behind them than Kade had her pressed up against it, raining haphazard kisses over her face and neck. Erinda sighed and threaded her fingers into the silky blond hair, drawing Kade's mouth up to hers. Their lips met feverishly, tongues tangling in excitement. The weight of Kade's body pinned her to the door, and Kade was already fumbling with the laces of her bodice. Erinda captured her wrists.

"Wait, my darling, not here. Come on."

She slid out from beneath Kade's arms and darted through the dark parlor. "Mind the furniture," she said as she skirted the hulking sideboard that stood in the center of the room. The bedchamber doors creaked open on leather hinges, and she ran to the huge four-poster bed. "Mother and I put clean sheets on just this morning, so…Mmph."

She'd turned, and Kade was right at her heels, stopping her words with another deep, frenetic kiss. They tumbled onto the brocade coverlet, sinking into its downy softness. Kade had her bodice open in moments, one hand roving over Erinda's breast while the other went after the ties of her split skirts and her mouth worked greedily against Erinda's throat.

Erinda moaned again, her blood streaking like lightning beneath her skin. She knew why Kade didn't want to talk, and she certainly wasn't going to press her into it. Tomorrow morning, Kade would stand before the palace temple, the high priestess would shave her head, and she would take her vows as a priestess of Ithyris. Just like that, their lifelong friendship would come to an end. But Erinda had always known that there was another possibility. She'd tried to tell Kade countless times, but it wasn't until this, their last night together, that Kade had finally worked up the courage to act on her feelings without backing out at the last moment.

Ultimately, the choice would be Kade's, of course. Erinda would never try to manipulate Kade down a path that she didn't want, no matter how absolutely it would destroy her to let Kade go. In the deepest part of her soul she knew that Kade was as much a part of her as her own beating heart, and if she did choose to leave tomorrow, Erinda would be forever missing a vital piece of herself. She would never love this way again. It was even probable that she would never find happiness again. And though that knowledge terrified her, she had resolved not to breathe a word of it to Kade. If Kade was really meant to be a priestess, she should be able to move into her new life without guilt.

But tonight was Erinda's chance to show Kade just what they could have together, to try to help her see past her fears and self-doubts and understand the simple *rightness* of their feelings. Tonight, Erinda wasn't going to give Kade the chance to entertain second thoughts.

While Kade struggled with the ties of her skirts, Erinda reached around her and deftly undid Kade's sash. She'd helped Kade don her white Pledged robes so many times that the familiar knot came apart easily under her fingers. When she slid the robe down, baring Kade's slender shoulders, Kade seemed to regain some self-consciousness. Uncertainty entered her eyes, and she hesitated.

Erinda was not going to let Kade call this off. Emotions raged wildly through her body, along with the knowledge that this was their last chance. If Kade ended this now, Erinda might just lose her mind. She sat up and tugged her shift up and over her head, tossing it aside. She arched her back, just a little, and grinned when Kade's entire body went rigid.

They'd seen one another naked, of course. As children they'd spent many a hot summer afternoon swimming in the palace duck pond in their undergarments. Their mothers had bathed them together to conserve bathwater. Even now, she and Kade often washed up and changed clothes side by side after a romp in the moors or a long day of lugging scrub buckets up and down the palace or temple stairs. But lately there had been something different in the air between them, a fizz of fascination that grew especially sharp when they looked upon each other unclothed.

Erinda used that to her advantage now, gliding a hand under Kade's robe and brushing her fingertips over the sensitive swell of flesh beneath. Kade's eyelids fluttered and she gave a soft moan.

"Please, Kade, I want to feel you."

She tugged at the robe again, and this time Kade allowed her to remove it. It joined Erinda's shift on the carpet. Erinda rolled on top of her, sliding their bare skin together in glorious friction that sent shock waves of pleasure plunging deep into her belly. She seized Kade's narrow ribcage in both hands, trailing her lips and tongue across the silken skin of Kade's collarbone, down between her breasts, and then traced the curves back up to one small, rosy nipple. This she kissed as sweetly as she could, remembering how good it felt when Kade had touched her this way a few days ago. She wanted Kade to experience it for herself, to feel how right it was. For Erinda, nothing had ever felt so perfect, so natural as this. If she could only get Kade to realize it too.

She straddled Kade's hips with her knees. Beneath her, Kade's body was surging upward with the need to get closer. Erinda sat up a bit and Kade whimpered so anxiously that Erinda had to smile. She finished untying her skirts, tugging them away from her hips so that, like Kade, she was clad in only linen undergarments. Then she let Kade pull her back down, and their mouths melded hotly once more.

Erinda lost all sense of time as they moved against one another, taking turns exploring tastes and textures and the overwhelming loveliness of skin pressed against skin. She caressed Kade's back, the delicate planes of her shoulders, her thighs and hips, first with featherlight strokes and then with more expectant pressure. Kade could not seem to decide which angle was best; she was under her one moment, over her the next, lying between Erinda's legs, and then encasing Erinda's hips with her thighs. Eventually, she somehow maneuvered herself against Erinda's back, with one arm wrapped possessively around Erinda's stomach while her lips and fingers burned nonsensical paths across her shoulder blades.

At last, Kade's hand found its way beneath Erinda's underclothes, and Erinda cried out when those questing fingers reached the aching folds of her sex. Pleasure like Erinda had never known blossomed between her legs and swept into her thighs. Her hips pushed back against Kade's, and Kade's already labored breathing increased even more as she ran her fingertips through the delicate, desire-soaked flesh. It didn't take her long to find the spot where Erinda most needed her, and with her other hand she kneaded Erinda's breast while her fingers danced and pressed and tugged.

A golden crescendo built powerfully in her bones, and Erinda could not help the stream of inarticulate cries that tore from her throat, each one only seeming to fuel Kade's determination to drive her over the edge. But she wasn't ready for that, not just yet. She managed to turn over, panting, and pulled at Kade's underclothes.

"Together," she insisted hoarsely. "I need to share this with you."

Kade complied, wriggling out of the linen garment as Erinda did the same with her own. They came together again, one of Erinda's thighs sliding between Kade's legs to push against her slick, swollen center. A sharp noise erupted from deep in Kade's chest, and she caught her lower lip between her teeth.

"Did I hurt you?" Erinda asked.

Kade shook her head and buried a hand in Erinda's unbound hair. She bent and pressed her mouth to Erinda's neck, just beneath her ear, and flicked the skin lightly with her tongue. "You feel so good," she breathed into Erinda's ear. "So good. I can't…I want…Goddess, Rin, I have to touch you again, please."

The candid plea set off an unbearable ache in Erinda's lower abdomen, and she guided Kade's hand back down. Kade groaned as her fingers slid between Erinda's legs, and Erinda shifted a little so she could slip her own hand between her thigh and Kade's sex. At first she just cupped her tenderly, but Kade was so wet, so warm and silky to the touch, that she quickly found herself addicted to the feel of her. Erinda began to match Kade stroke for stroke as they thrust against one another. And then, at the same moment, they entered each other completely, muffling their simultaneous cries of wonder against each other's skin.

The pleasure built again, amplified a hundred times over. Erinda had wanted Kade to experience this along with her, but she hadn't known just how much higher the ascension would be for the sharing of it. They were mirrors, reflecting every magical sensation and emotion back at the other, only to be magnified and returned. They were joined entirely—one breath, one pulse, one perfect and indestructible bond. As they soared toward climax together, Erinda was overcome with joy. *No matter what happens tomorrow, no one—not even the Goddess— can ever take this away from us. This moment will belong only to you and me, forever.*

When the explosion took them at last, Kade let out a roar that liquefied Erinda's very core.

Kade broke the kiss with a gasp, as Erinda's body convulsed against her and her own crested right along with it. For a long moment, they stood, clinging to one another and shaking in the aftermath of that…that…whatever that had been. A vision, perhaps? But Kade had never experienced anything like this before. For a few minutes, she had been eighteen winters old again, lost in blissful union with the girl she had loved since childhood. But somehow she'd relived the experience from within Erinda's awareness, not her own, and what she had learned there burned like sour ash in her stomach.

Erinda was the first to recover her senses, and though she was still trembling, she pulled out of Kade's arms, breaking the silvery connection that still hummed riotously between them. Kade felt the loss of contact as sharply as if it had been severed with a blade, and she wrapped her arms around her midsection as if to keep her insides from spilling out onto the floor in pursuit.

Panting, Erinda brushed a wayward curl out of her eyes. "What did you just do?"

"I don't...I didn't mean to..."

"You were there too, weren't you?"

Kade understood what she meant, and nodded. Erinda shuddered, pressing a hand hard to her chest. "Why are you doing this to us, Kade? I don't understand."

"You knew." Kade managed to force a complete sentence past her lips, though her voice felt like razors in her throat. "You knew and you never told me."

"Knew what?"

"What we were to each other. What would happen to you when I left." Even in the midst of her own terror, even knowing the misery that was to come, Erinda had remained Kade's protector to the very end. "You knew it would...that you would never find anyone else." She shook her head so hard it sent tears flying. "You should have told me, Rin. If I'd known I never would have...I thought I was doing the right thing for both of us."

"What are you saying?"

Kade opened her eyes. Tiny beads of sweat glistened on Erinda's forehead, her features flushed and altogether crushing in their beauty. Kade's heart locked up in her chest. "I'm saying..." She struggled for air. "I'm saying that maybe I made the wrong choice."

Erinda's wide gray eyes suddenly got even wider. Kade took a step toward her, but she moved away, and Kade watched her shock transform into fury.

"Don't you dare say that to me now, after all this time. It's not fair."

"I know," Kade said, reaching out to her, "but it's the truth."

Erinda slapped her hand away and backed up against the heavy mausoleum door. "I don't want to hear it! It doesn't matter!"

She nearly screeched the last words. Erinda was fighting to hang on to her anger, and Kade could glimpse the reason for it. Anger was a fragile lifeline, the only thing keeping Erinda suspended over a chasm of utter despair.

"How can you say that?"

"You tell me, Your Grace. I've a good horse waiting right outside. Will you really leave Her, now that you've had this epiphany? Are you ready to ride away with me now, far from all of this, and start life over again at my side?"

Guilt and frustration knifed through Kade as she grasped Erinda's meaning. "You know I can't."

"Can't. Won't. It's all the same. Call it divine duty or just plain cowardice, in the end all that matters is the choice you make. And I can't do this anymore. I can't keep playing these games with you. I survived losing you once, but I can't go through that again." She shoved at the door, and harsh sunlight shafted into the mausoleum. Kade lost sight of her in the glare.

"If you ever do figure out what you want, Kadrian, you know how to find me."

Footsteps pounded across the grass, and then came a distant whinny. Kade assumed Erinda had retrieved the horse she'd spoken of. She heard hoofbeats thud away and slumped to the mausoleum floor, her back against the marble of Mondera's sarcophagus.

"Oh, Lady, what have I done?"

There was no response from the spirit current. It had gone so quiet that Kade had to probe for it to be sure it was still there. It was, but trickled so weakly she could barely sense its presence. Kade wasn't sure whether to feel dismayed or relieved. Was Ithyris angry with her? She certainly had every right to be. The Goddess had called Kade out to the sepulchre that morning to prepare for tonight's ceremony. She had gifted Kade with Her touch and Her spirit anew, readying her for the things to come, and Kade had run straight from Her arms into Erinda's. She had given herself over to selfish and heretical desires. She had even gone so far as to assert that perhaps her calling as a priestess had been the wrong one, as if the Goddess had made a mistake in choosing her to begin with. If Ithyris were to end Kade's entire pathetic mortal life at this very moment, to snatch her into the nexus forever as punishment for her sins, Kade wouldn't blame Her in the slightest.

But right now, the pit of Kade's stomach boiled with guilt that had nothing to do with the Goddess. She needed Erinda, needed her in a way she didn't understand, and time after time, Kade reached out to her in love only to wind up tearing her apart. She had inflicted so much pain that she couldn't comprehend how Erinda couldn't hate her by now. It didn't matter anymore what the rest of the world thought; Kade would gladly spend the rest of her life trying to make that up to her—if only she wasn't destined to save the kingdom as a holy vessel of the Goddess instead.

Kade was on the verge of dissolving into sobs when Lyris appeared through the sepulchre doors. Lyris drew up short when she caught sight of her, and bowed.

"Forgive the interruption, Your Grace, but I've been sent to fetch you. The barbarian *shaa'din* is at the gates, and she's asking to speak with you."

Kade scrubbed the back of her hand against her eyes and stood. "Thank you, *Ostryn*."

Lyris inclined her head as Kade passed, but Kade still caught the concern in her eyes and knew she must look a mess. She squared her shoulders as best she could and took up Fyn's staff as she marched from the mausoleum. As she went, she tugged at the hem of her tunic and swept her knuckles beneath her eyes. It would never do for the Goddess's *shaa'din* to appear before Mardyth disheveled and teary, no matter how wretched a failure she might be.

❖

Mardyth's scarlet hair was piled festively atop her head, garish bits of feathers and fur poking out here and there as if she'd strangled some unfortunate woodland creature within its ropes. The minute she caught sight of Kade on the temple wall she grinned and yanked a wizened old man forward by the arm. She gestured at him with a finger across her throat, and before Kade had time to think, the man raised a knife to his own neck and slashed it open. His fragile form crumpled into the dirt at Mardyth's feet in a pool of blood.

At Kade's side, Mother Hirrow bellowed in anger—or perhaps fear—and though Talon didn't make a sound, Kade watched the tendons strain in her hand as she gripped her sword hilt. Kade was still too overwhelmed with the morning's emotion to sort out her own response, but she felt some clarity begin to return as two of the barbarian men slung the dead man's body onto a pile of others before the temple gates. Yet another needless, innocent death. While Kade was preoccupied with her own petty interests, the Goddess's people were suffering and dying at the hands of Her enemies, and she was doing nothing to stop it. Her guts heaved and she swayed on her feet, steadied only by Talon's surreptitious hand at her elbow.

"We thought you might like to have your people back, Handmaiden." Mardyth wiped the blade of her knife on the bare skin of her protruding belly.

"What do you want, Mardyth?" Kade was grateful that the challenge came out sounding much more stalwart than she felt.

"You know what I want. When you retrieve that prophecy tonight, you will bring it directly to me. If not..." She gestured behind her, and one of the hulking barbarian warriors dragged two limp, dirty children forward. Neither could have been more than ten or eleven winters in age, and they whimpered as Mardyth patted their hair. "If not, I'll add these two little brats to the pile there. But not before their cries of agony bring down the very wall you stand upon. Am I understood?"

Kade ground her teeth. "I cannot give you the prophecy. It belongs to Ithyris."

Mardyth shrugged. "It's your choice. Just remember that their fate"—she pinched one of the children's cheeks—"rests with you." She flicked her wrist to have them taken away. "See you tonight, Handmaiden."

Mardyth turned and sauntered back into her camp. Kade stared after her, wishing with all her might that she could figure out how to channel the Goddess's power across all that empty space and make Mardyth go up in flames right then and there, pregnant or not. She should have obeyed the Goddess the first time. She should have killed Ulrike's *shaa'din* without hesitation when she'd had the chance. If those poor children were tortured to death tonight because of her...

Bile rose in her mouth and Kade gagged. Captain Talon produced a handkerchief from her sleeve and slipped it into her hand. "Here, Your Grace."

Kade gave her a grateful look and pressed it to her lips, spitting out the vile taste as politely as she could manage. Talon pretended not to notice, and instead pointed down at the bodies piled against the gates. "We can't leave them like that."

Kade nodded, recovering some of her composure. "No, we certainly can't."

"You're not suggesting we open the gates?" Hirrow asked.

"We must, Your Honor. Those are Ithyrian dead. We cannot abandon them."

The Honored Mother appeared very much like that was exactly what she wanted to do, but Kade fixed her with the most imperious, Handmaidenly expression she could muster. She brought Fyn's staff down so that its iron rings clanked together with authority, and turned to Talon. "Go, Captain. I will make sure you get them inside safely."

Talon nodded and descended the ladder to the ground, shouting orders to the few soldiers who were not confined to the infirmary with the others. The temple gates groaned as they were opened.

Kade held her breath, scanning the fringes of the enemy camp for any sign of attack, but luckily, not a single barbarian rogue attempted to storm the open gates or accost the soldiers as they worked. Talon and her men moved quickly, gathering up the bodies and laying them out one at a time before the high sanctuary steps.

There were nine bodies in all, including three children. The sight of them made Kade sick to her stomach all over again. All this time she'd been promenading about the temple like a pampered dignitary, utterly absorbed in her own concerns while these poor people were being captured, starved, beaten, and murdered right outside the doors of her safe little sanctuary. She'd done nothing to help them. Nearly two hundred deaths were already on her head, and what had happened to these people was her fault as well. The Twelve would never have allowed such a thing to happen. She had to be the worst *shaa'din* in the history of Ithyria.

Kade heard the gates creak shut again. The heavy iron bar slid back into place with a bang that loudly underscored her morose thoughts.

"Sweet Ithyris!" one of Talon's men exclaimed. "Captain, this one's still alive!"

Talon hurried to the side of a red-jacketed soldier, the only man in uniform among the bodies. Talon bent over the man's bloodied head, putting her ear close to his lips. She listened a moment and then called out, "Someone fetch the healer, quickly!"

Kade hurried down the ladder, but by the time her feet reached the ground, the unlikely survivor was being carted away to the infirmary, flanked on all sides by his astonished comrades. Kade moved to follow, but was stopped by Hirrow.

"Handmaiden," the Honored Mother said with an obsequious bow, "there are still many preparations to be made for tonight's events. Might I ask that you join the elder *Ostryn* and myself in the sanctuary? We would appreciate your guidance."

Kade hardly felt like she was in any condition to be guiding others in the Goddess's matters at the moment, especially when the silver thread of Ithyris's spirit was barely detectable. Her reassurance to Talon had been something of a bluff, in fact; right now, she wasn't sure she could draw enough of the Goddess's power to light Cibli's stone within the staff, let alone hold back an attack from the barbarians if they'd decided to press their luck against the temple while the gates were open. What if she'd angered Her so terribly that She would not return by the time the sepulchre was to be opened? After what had happened with Erinda that morning, compounded by the guilt of all those murdered captives and two children whose lives now hung on a demand she couldn't possibly fulfill, Kade wanted nothing more than to find a dark hole somewhere to crawl into and disappear until this whole dreadful day was over. But of course, she could hardly share any of this with Hirrow. As she stammered for a plausible excuse, Lyris interjected from beside her.

"Your Honor, pardon my impertinence, but would it not better serve tonight's purpose to allow the Handmaiden a period of private commune with our Lady?"

Hirrow pursed her lips unhappily, but Kade was quick to seize the opening.

"*Ostryn* Lyris is right, Mother Hirrow. I must withdraw and prepare myself for the task ahead. But I have every faith that in your capable hands, tonight's ceremony will be a fine tribute to the Goddess." She touched her fingertips to her forehead, and before Hirrow could protest, she turned and headed for the dormitories, looking forward very much to being alone with her misery.

CHAPTER FIFTEEN

There is a story in the Book of Verdred that I have returned to many times in my life, especially at moments when the future is feeling dark and uncertain.

The day the Twelve were introduced to one another for the first time, they met on a small stretch of beach to the south that today is part of Daiban province. There, the Goddess appeared to give Her newly created army their first mission: to march on the great city of Bellsund, which was in those days so overrun with Ulrike's hateful influence that even the mention of Ithyris's name within Bellsund walls was a crime punishable by death. Ithyris charged the Twelve with driving out the wicked priests and warlords who had enslaved Her people there, and reclaiming the city in Her name.

All of them were filled with fear at this request, and Aster asked of Her, "How are we to do this impossible thing, Lady? Bellsund is a dark place, and we are but farm girls and scullery maids, not soldiers."

"Do you not know why I have chosen you?" the Goddess asked. "Each of you has a heart rich with love, and love is the lifeblood of divine spirit; it protects, heals, binds, creates, and endures always. So when darkness lies in your path, do not be afraid. Carry love in your hearts, my Daughters, and you carry my light with you into even the darkest of nights."

Centuries later, we scribes still proudly tell the story of how twelve young girls from the countryside marched alone against a city of thousands that day—and triumphed.

Blessed Kadrian, Handmaiden of Ithyris, on this Fifthmoon eve, I and the rest of the kingdom share in this prayer for you: that you may hold fast in love, so the darkness invading our lands shall be once again made subject to Her light.

Erinda had ridden every one of the Ithyrian war-horses in their usual circuits around the temple grounds, and when she finished she put them all through their paces a second time. She brushed and curried the big animals' coats until they gleamed as sleekly as the horses of the royal stables, then she groomed each of the smaller temple palfreys as well. She mucked out the stalls, polished every bit, bridle, and saddle she could find, and by the time Myka tracked Erinda down in the temple stables, Erinda had a mallet in one hand and a bunch of nails clenched between her teeth, and was driving hooks into the stable walls to organize the grooming and cleaning tools.

Myka surveyed the militantly tidy stalls and whistled. "Wow. You sure do like things clean."

Erinda stepped down from the footstool she was using, eyed her handiwork, and grunted. She spit the remaining nails into her hand. "Myka. Shouldn't you be in the infirmary?"

"Not anymore, thanks to you," she replied. "I've been trying to tell everyone for the last two days that I'm perfectly well since the Handmaiden brought me back. And of course I am. You don't think the Goddess would go to all that trouble to bring me back from the dead just to leave me injured, do you? But no one would listen, until they brought in that other man today who's in much worse shape than me, and I finally talked them into letting me out so I could bring you this." When she at last stopped to take a breath, she held out a folded piece of parchment.

Erinda wiped her hands on her apron and reached for it. "What other man?"

"Soldier. Red uniform just like the captain's so he must be royal guard, and we think he's probably a courier since he had that on him. It's addressed to you. Captain Talon seemed to think it's important."

Erinda turned the paper in her hand and recognized the royal seal. "It's from the Queen! How in the world did a courier manage to get past that army outside?"

"He almost didn't," Myka said. "You should see the knot on his head. It's the size of my knee and all kinds of disgusting colors. I guess the barbarians thought they'd killed him, but he's not all the way dead yet. Pretty amazing that he's still breathing though, considering, even if it's not as amazing as being brought back from the dead—which is still the greatest thing that *I've* ever heard of, don't you think? So, aren't you going to read it?"

Myka chattered so fast and in such impossibly long sentences that Erinda could barely follow what she was saying, but when she paused and tapped her foot impatiently, Erinda took the cue and tore the wax seal.

> *Dearest Erinda,*
> *How it breaks my heart to be writing you this letter, but oh, my dear friend, I need you now more than ever. Princess Brita is dead.*

Erinda gasped, her knees giving way, and she sat down on the wooden footstool. "Oh Goddess, no…" She'd spent all morning trying in vain to scrub away her troubles, yet all self-pitying thoughts vanished in the face of those four terrible words.

"What is it?" Myka asked, but Erinda was too busy reading the rest to answer.

> *The healer says the Princess's illness was too much for her; she went peacefully, in her sleep, and for that, I am grateful. But I do not know how I shall ever bear this grief.*
> *Please, you must not tell anyone what has happened. Just come home as quickly as you can. There is no one else I can share this with, and I feel so dreadfully alone.*
>
> *Shasta*

Erinda scanned the letter for a date, but there wasn't one. Slowly, she crushed the parchment in her hand. It would have taken the courier at least a quarter moon to get this deep into Mondera, and who knew how long the barbarians had held him before dumping him with the other dead. How long had Shasta been anguishing over the loss of her baby girl alone? The palace healer would know of Brita's death, of course, and Nurse as well, but clearly, the Queen hadn't announced the news to her court yet, or it would have been all over Ithyria by now.

Erinda knew exactly why Shasta wanted to keep it quiet. Talon would torture herself senseless over this, agonizing over whether her greater duty now was to Shasta or to her mission with the guard, blaming herself for leaving Shasta to face their daughter's death alone, blaming herself if the battle that was sure to come by morning went awry without her, and ultimately blaming herself for having left Shasta and Brita in the first place. Such distraction could easily be a death sentence on the battlefield. So long as Mardyth was in Ithyria it was better that Talon remain ignorant of this.

But Shasta needed Erinda at the palace now, far more than she needed her here. Too much time had passed already, and the thought of

Shasta grieving her child's death all alone was too much to bear. Shasta wouldn't be able to keep Brita's death a secret forever, especially not once the royal chambermaids got wind of it; Clio and Oralie in particular were terrible gossips. If word got out before Shasta had someone at her side to lean on, Erinda could only imagine how much more terrible the public backlash would be for her. No one should have to go through that alone.

"You okay?" Myka was asking, kneeling at her side and looking at her with concern. "You've gone white as milk. I can fetch the healer—"

"No." Erinda balled her fist around the letter in her hand as her mind began to work. "Listen, Myka, something awful has happened, and I have to return to the palace right away."

Her eyes widened. "You mean, now?"

"Now," Erinda said. "I just have to gather a few things together, and then I'll slip out through the south gate and keep riding south long enough that I'm out of sight of the temple. The barbarians will never even see me leave." At least, she had to hope they wouldn't. Mardyth's army was camped on the northern side of the temple, in front of the main gates. With any luck, they would be so preoccupied waiting for Kade's mystical ceremony tonight that they wouldn't notice a lone horse and rider escaping in the opposite direction. And if they did spot her, well... Erinda would just have to make sure she was on a very fast horse.

"I could go with you," Myka offered.

Erinda suspected Myka was eager to avoid any more forced confinement in the temple infirmary, and in truth, she wouldn't have minded the company in her present state of mind. But she shook her head. "Once I'm through the gate I can't bar it again myself, and the temple has to be kept secure from that army outside. I need you here, Myka. Will you help me?"

Myka nodded, and Erinda squeezed her hand. "Good. And one more thing. It's very important that you don't tell anyone about this, you understand? Not even the Handmaiden."

Myka nodded again even more solemnly, though she looked somewhat pleased at having been entrusted with such an elite secret. "I promise."

❖

Kade had no idea how long she'd been kneeling there, eyelids swollen from crying, swaying back and forth as she chanted every prayer and sang every desperate hymn she could think of. But Ithyris wouldn't come. Kade couldn't feel Her. There were even paralyzing moments when she couldn't sense the vibration of Her spirit current either, and Kade would hold her breath and rake through her awareness until she found it again. As she prayed, a thousand images raged together in her mind: A neat row of corpses in the dirt. Her lips trailing hungrily over Erinda's soft skin. A dirty child cringing under Mardyth's hand. Captain Farsh with his bandaged stump of an arm. The Goddess, holding out Her beautiful, blood-covered fingers. Myka's feet disappearing into the spirit lake. Talon lifting Erinda's limp body from the battlefield. The memories hammered her with guilt, and Kade would not attempt to hide from them. She *should* feel guilty. Some legendary heroine she'd turned out to be.

Exhausted, Kade finally pulled herself up from her prayer cushion and curled into her borrowed bed. She threw the blanket over her head in spite of the summer heat, and gave herself over to despair. She should stay like this forever. Fall asleep and never wake up, let everyone just go on their way without her. Ithyris could choose a new *shaa'din*, someone stronger and wiser who wouldn't make such a mess of things. The world would be much better off if she stopped being part of it, if she just vanished into nothingness where she couldn't do any further harm.

Gradually, her agitated thoughts slowed to a disgruntled mumble, and her consciousness drifted. Her breathing relaxed and deepened, interrupted by the occasional residual sob. Peace crept over her, wrapping her in the cool, desensitizing mist of oblivion.

"Kadrian. Beloved, can you hear me?"

"Lady?" Kade was certain she was dreaming, because her own voice was echoing in her head just like Ithyris's always did.

"I'm here, Beloved."

Relief washed over her. "Oh, Sweet Ithyris, You came back! I was so afraid You wouldn't, after everything I've done. I'm sorry, Lady, so very sorry. Please forgive me."

"My Daughter, there is nothing to forgive. Don't you understand? I never left you. I have been here all along—you are the one who is blocking me out. Talk to me, Kadrian. You must let me in, or soon this guilt you are piling upon yourself will cut you off from me completely."

"I can't!" Kade cried. "I'm too ashamed. I'm trying so hard to be faithful, Lady, but I'll never be as strong as the Twelve were. My heart is weak and selfish. Everything I touch turns out wrong!"

"Kadrian." Her name on the Goddess's lips was like music, and Kade felt Her love sweep over her, stunning and absolute in its purity.

"Open your mind, my Daughter, and hear me. This standard you are punishing yourself with is one I have never asked of you, or indeed of any of my children."

"What do you mean?"

"Love, Beloved. Love is the lifeblood—"

"—of divine spirit," Kade finished automatically. She knew the proverb by heart; it reappeared often in temple hymns.

"And what am I?"

"You are the Goddess of Spirit, Divine Lady."

"Ask yourself then: how could I, as a being of spirit, ever forbid love?"

Kade tried to piece this together, but she couldn't figure out what Ithyris was trying to tell her. "I'm sorry, Lady, but I don't understand."

"I have never asked you for celibacy, Kadrian. I have never asked that of any of my Daughters."

Kade was so shocked she could not even feel the embarrassment that would normally accompany such frankness. "But...I've read the Book of Verdred. The Twelve were virgins. All Your priestesses are supposed to be."

She heard the Goddess sigh.

"Ah, Beloved, you cannot imagine how weary I am of all the needless rules and rituals attributed to my name. Yes, it is true that I selected my first *shaa'din* based in part upon the fact that they were all free of intimate involvements. I knew the magnitude of what I was going to ask of them, and had any of the Twelve been lovers, wives, mothers, the trials they endured would have placed more than their own interests in harm's way. And the Twelve understood this. It was their choice to remain celibate after the war, to take up roles as spiritual leaders for my people and guide other young women who wished to dedicate their lives to my service. Over the centuries, the choice they made has somehow evolved into a dictate.

"But it is one that I never issued myself, just like so many of your practices now. I will never understand why mortals feel such need to regulate each other's behavior! Shaved heads and veils are superficial silliness, but withdrawing from your families and friends in order to serve me—this serves no worthwhile purpose and causes only suffering. I have never wanted nor asked for such a sacrifice, and it has been a very long time since I've been able to speak directly to one of you long enough to set the record straight again."

As She spoke, some of the mist that surrounded Kade began to clear.

"That being said, Beloved, there are times when love can overwhelm a mortal's spirit to the exclusion of everything but the object of that love—and that includes me. You have discovered this for yourself. Your own love is so strong that even with my spirit flowing inside you, there is a barrier forming through which I cannot reach. Left unchecked, that barrier will become permanent. When the Twelve realized this, they each chose to remain free of mortal relationships so as to never diminish their connection with me. I did not ask it of them, though I will always be deeply honored by their devotion."

Kade could see Her now, just the faintest outline of Her face and floating hair, and Ithyris reached out to lay a translucent hand against Kade's cheek. She was smiling. "But you, Kadrian...you were meant for me from the beginning, yet I have always known that I would never have you completely to myself."

"Lady, I—"

"I will never hold you against your will, Beloved. Your heart is wonderful, and it is nothing to be ashamed of. You have but to ask, and I shall release you from your vows."

Kade didn't know whether the Goddess's words horrified her or filled her with hope. "But I can't leave You. I haven't even found Mondera's prophecy yet."

"I care more for you, Beloved, than I do about the prophecy. My service brings you suffering. That suffering cuts you off from my spirit, and in such a state your life and the lives of many others could be in great danger."

Kade looked into Her brilliant eyes and understood what She meant. "I have to choose, don't I?"

Ithyris shook Her head. "Your heart has already chosen, Kadrian. What you have to decide now is whether it is able to wait any longer."

Vaguely, Kade realized that they were in the nexus. She recognized the unbroken whiteness of the floor and the shifting walls and doorways surrounding them. But her mind was echoing the Goddess's words: *Your heart has already chosen.* Erinda's face materialized in her thoughts, and her breath caught with longing. Ithyris was right. No matter how Kade might try to override her feelings with guilt, with duty, with sheer force of will, the choice of her heart had been made a very long time ago.

"I love You, Lady, truly I do, and I love being Your *shaa'din* more than I know how to say. But I need Rin. I've always needed her, and I...I don't think I can be apart from her anymore."

The Goddess inclined Her head in understanding. Then Kade recalled the children Mardyth was holding captive. What would happen to them if she walked away now? And all the men and women who had been killed in the battle at Agar, and the peasants who had died in that forest village, and the bodies laid out so neatly before the high sanctuary...it was her responsibility to make sure every one of those deaths counted for something. Could she really abandon Ithyria to Mardyth's hands in pursuit of her own desires? She would never be able to forgive herself.

Kade took a deep breath, certain of what she had to do. "There will come a day, Lady, when I will ask You to release me. But Mondera said I was the one to do this. I still have no idea why, but so many people are depending on me to see this through. I have to find that prophecy and destroy it."

Ithyris was quiet for a moment, and Kade got the uneasy feeling that perhaps She knew the assignment would not be quite that simple. But then She held out a hand. "Are you sure?"

Ithyris's shining fingers weren't dripping this time, though Kade was reminded, uncannily, of the vision of her blood pooling in the Goddess's outstretched palm. Still, she nodded and reached for Her. "I'm sure."

Ithyris pulled her into an embrace, enveloping her with spirit that sparkled wondrously against every one of Kade's senses. The veins of Her current swelled beneath Kade's skin, drawing from Her until they were rushing so fast that Kade started to get lightheaded. The Goddess lifted Kade's chin in one hand.

"Kiss me," She commanded.

Kade closed her eyes and leaned forward. Ithyris's lips brushed past hers like a million tiny stars, and then She was within her. The Goddess's spirit filled Kade with light, with life, with the very essence of love itself, until every remote corner of Kade's being strained to contain Her. Kade heard Her gentle, musical voice again, this time from within the depths of her own soul.

You honor me, Kadrian. Thank you.

❖

On this side of the Great Temple, the ground sloped away from the temple wall in a hazardous array of fallen rocks and crumbling cliffs, with bits of grass and wild chicory springing up wherever they could find root between. The path leading from the temple wound in snakelike switchbacks down the steep hill, and Erinda gripped Brindle's reins tightly, leaning back to help the big horse balance as she sought footing among the gravel.

"Easy," she said, feeling Brindle's hooves scuffle beneath her. It would take a good deal more than a few loose rocks to bring the war-horse down, but she was in a hurry and knew Brindle could sense it. When she thought about what Shasta must be going through, she wished there was some way she could sprout wings and get to her faster. Her own heart was broken, thinking of the little Princess's sweet, chubby face and bright eyes, her precious baby giggles. How much more awful must Shasta feel right now?

She didn't see them until they were almost on top of her. The path curved around an enormous boulder, and as they rounded it three burly, leather-clad barbarians moved to flank her. Standing behind them, in the middle of the path, was the redheaded *shaa'din*, Mardyth.

"You must be Erinda, then," she said with a triumphant smile.

Erinda drew up on the reins and looked from Mardyth to her men in shock. What were they doing out here? Their army was supposed to be concentrating on the temple's front gates. "How do you know my name? What do you want with me?"

Mardyth peeled her lips back from her teeth in a sneer. "With you? Nothing. But your friend the Handmaiden has something I very much want, and you're going to help me get it." She gestured upward, and too late, Erinda realized one of the men had clambered up on a rock behind her head. He swung his club, and everything went black.

At the head of Mondera's ornate sarcophagus, the marble had been shaped into a thick column, which was topped with a large orb of polished silver. Following the Goddess's instructions, Kade tugged and twisted at the silver globe until it came loose, revealing a deep, narrow hole. The iron shaft of Fyn's staff fit easily into this channel, sliding down an armlength into the stone.

When the staff struck bottom, Kade felt a vibration along the iron that spread into the marble floor under her feet, and beneath her skin, the Goddess's current sang with contentment. In amazement, she recognized that the emotion was not her own. Each of these items— Fyn's staff, Cibli's stone, and Mondera's sepulchre—still held an echo of the three sisters' spirits, and they had been waiting a very long time for this moment. Kade stepped back as the crowd of onlookers jostled for a better view.

She had placed the staff just as Ithyris asked, and now it rose from the head of Mondera's resting place as if it had always belonged there. Candlelight danced within the small space inside the mausoleum, as every priestess in attendance carried her own small light. There was only enough room inside the mausoleum itself for a handful of the women, so the rest spilled out the doors and into the cemetery grounds beyond in a parade of twinkling candle flames. The sky had gone dark hours ago, its velvety depths sugared with stars and the heavy, luminous sphere of Fifthmoon ascending in the east.

"What happens now?" Lyris asked.

Kade was rather wondering that herself. Ithyris had described the staff and stone as keys, so Kade had assumed that once she put them in the proper place in the sepulchre something would happen. A hidden compartment would open, perhaps, or the prophecy would appear in glittering letters on the mausoleum wall, or Mondera's voice would ring out from beyond the realm of the dead and recite the words they were all waiting to hear. But there the staff stood, stiff and regal at the head of Mondera's sarcophagus, and nothing whatsoever had come of it. Maybe she hadn't done it quite right? Perhaps if she jiggled it a little…Kade almost reached out to try it, but Ithyris spoke to her instead.

"Just wait, Beloved. It is nearly time."

Kade turned to Lyris. "She says we wait."

For several awkward minutes, they stood in silence. Kade could feel everyone's eyes shifting from the staff to her and back again. Lacking anything else to do, Kade began reciting a prayer of worship. She spoke under her breath at first, but Lyris quickly joined in, indicating to the others that they should do the same.

Beautiful Goddess, blessed are we who stand in the glory of Your light. You are infinite in wisdom, perfect in compassion, boundless in love. Divine Lady of Spirit, I praise You, I praise You, I praise You…

For Kade, the words were infused with so much gratitude she could barely contain the feeling. Ithyris had given her more than she could have ever imagined. The Goddess had chosen her, filled her with Her spirit, worked miracles through her hands. She had given Kade the opportunity to know Her in ways few ever would. She had shown Kade wonders the likes of which the world had not seen in a thousand winters. She had allowed Kade to bring Myka back from the nexus. She loved Kade without condition, through her weakest and lowest moments. And now, Ithyris had even offered to set her free.

Kade could hardly wait to find Erinda and tell her. Once the prophecy was destroyed and Mardyth banished back to her own lands, Kade would ask to be released from her vows. After everything she'd been through in the past moon, the uncertain future that used to worry her so much seemed unimportant now. So long as they had the Goddess's blessing, everything else would work itself out. After all, if the Queen of Ithyria could make a life with the woman she loved right under the noses of the entire kingdom, surely a priestess—or former priestess, rather—and chambermaid could do the same. She just hoped Erinda would be willing to wait for her a while longer.

A shaft of light shot through the darkness of the mausoleum. Everyone, including Kade, gasped in surprise. A tiny opening in the sepulchre's roof was drilled at exactly the right angle, and the staff was held in the sarcophagus at precisely the right depth so that a single brilliant moonbeam had lanced from the ceiling to strike Cibli's stone. The ray was needle-thin, captured at precisely the moment when the Fifthmoon rose over the cemetery.

Kade realized what Ithyris had meant when She'd said that hiding the prophecy had been Marin's work. Only Marin of the Twelve could have calculated a phenomenon like this so perfectly, a millennium before its time. No wonder no one could have retrieved the prophecy except on this very night, for the moon was not likely to be in this exact position again for another thousand winters. Whatever Mondera's message was, it had to be unimaginably important, for this was the most well-guarded secret Kade had ever heard of.

A soft hum filled the mausoleum as Cibli's stone began to vibrate, and then the staff was quivering as well. Kade watched in fascination as within the stone the thread of moonlight appeared to thicken, rather like honey. It flowed down the iron staff in a cascade of syrupy blue, until it struck the marble of the sarcophagus. Then it ran into the swirling channels of the elaborate scrollwork, and when it had filled every possible crevice on the sarcophagus's surface, it dripped onto the marble floor and continued spreading outward toward the walls. Kade stepped aside as the liquid light swept past the toes of her boots.

In a matter of minutes, honeyed moonlight decorated every surface inside the mausoleum, the swirling designs on the sarcophagus, the seams of the floor, the intricately carved murals on the walls, and the arched lines of the ceiling overhead. Surely nothing had ever been quite so beautiful. Ribbons of light formed patterns and pictures all around them in the darkness, setting the priestesses' white veils and robes awash with a silver-blue glow. Kade turned to take in the full effect. It was like being suspended inside a star.

"Praise Ithyris!" she heard Mother Hirrow exclaim next to her. Several of the other women raised their arms in prayer.

"Do you like it?" Ithyris asked in Kade's head. Kade could hear the smile in Her voice.

"Oh, Lady, it's so beautiful."

Outside, the moon rose higher, and the moonbeam dropped away. Yet the light that surrounded them remained, and gradually, the staff seemed to draw it back into itself. The gleaming ribbons receded in the same way they had spread, and as they gathered, the staff began to shine so brightly that it hurt Kade's eyes.

At last, Cibli's stone gave a great flash. Everyone in the mausoleum had to cover their eyes. When Kade was able to blink away the effects, the sepulchre was dark again save for the dancing points of the priestesses' candles.

"Handmaiden, look," Lyris said, holding her candle up. Fyn's staff glinted in the candlelight, its surface now glimmering like polished silver. Kade could glimpse the shapes of strange-looking runes etched into its shining surface.

"Is that it?" Lyris asked, leaning closer. "Is that the prophecy?"

Hirrow stepped forward and ran her own candle up and down the length of the shaft. She made a harrumphing noise. "If it is, it's not written in any language I've ever seen before."

Kade took hold of the staff, lifting it from the sarcophagus to get a better look. The entire thing glittered as if a jeweler had plated the dull, rusty iron with precious metal, and the runes ran down its full length, from the base of the ringed finials to its blunted end. She couldn't make any sense of the odd symbols either, however.

"It is not necessary that you be able to read them, Beloved."

Kade turned the staff slowly in her hand. "But this *is* Mondera's prophecy?" she asked the Goddess under her breath.

"Yes. You have done well."

Triumph surged through her as she held the staff up, and her hand shook with excitement. Just one task remained, then. "So how do I destroy it?"

"Not just yet, Beloved. The staff has been returned to its full power now, and it is meant for one last purpose. Have you forgotten my brother's *shaa'din*?"

"Mardyth," Kade said slowly.

"She still holds two of my children captive. The staff can help you to save them, and drive Mardyth and her army out of Ithyria. Once Ulrike's *shaa'din* is no longer a threat to my people, we shall destroy the prophecy together, and this will truly be ended."

Kade was taken aback. She had expected to destroy the prophecy upon finding it. That way Mardyth would limp home, licking her wounds, and by the time dawn broke Kade would be a free woman with Erinda in her arms and a whole new life of possibilities stretching out before them. But even as she fought to quell her disappointment, she knew Ithyris was right. It was naïve to think that Ulrike's *shaa'din* would give up. Even if Kade did destroy the prophecy here and now, Mardyth would certainly kill her two captives out of spite, and might very well go on another murderous rampage through the kingdom in revenge.

And there was no doubting the power that the staff held now. It thrummed against Kade's palm like a living thing, in sync with the rhythm of the spirit current. The blue stone was even glowing faintly of its own accord. Kade could sense its eagerness and knew that it, too, had a mission to fulfill.

Reluctantly, Kade nodded. "It will be as You command, Lady."

Hirrow, Lyris, and the other priestesses were watching her with great interest. They could only hear Kade's side of the conversation, of course, but waited to see if she would share Ithyris's words with them. Since it had already been a night of ceremony, Kade decided to maintain that formality as best she could while she addressed them.

"Daughters of Ithyris, tonight we have recovered a legacy left to us by the Twelve, orchestrated by our predecessors one thousand winters ago in anticipation of this very moment in our history. A warrior of the Flesh God waits outside these temple gates, and our Lady has provided us the weapon we need to defeat her." The women cheered, and Kade waited until their excitement had died down before saying, "Come, my sisters, and let us send our enemies back to the darkness from which they came."

The crowd parted as Kade moved through them, stepping down out of the mausoleum and onto the cemetery grass. She passed Captain Talon, Captain Farsh, and a few other uniformed men on the fringe of the group and exchanged a quick nod with Talon as she went by. Though Kade did not look back, it seemed every single person in the temple was following on her heels as she marched for the gates.

CHAPTER SIXTEEN

A nasty odor assailed Erinda's senses. Consciousness returned in a surge of nausea and terror as she became aware of the gag invading her mouth, the rope binding her wrists and ankles, the sharp dig of a tent pole against her spine. The first thing she saw when she got her eyes to open was a pile of stinking furs lying in the dirt nearby. A dim oil lamp hung over a rough-hewn table, and within its sickly yellow light flies buzzed over the remains of a half-finished meal, something bloody and disgusting that Erinda didn't even want to identify. She could just make out the texture of animal skins and burlap all around her, supported by wooden poles, and a small opening overhead which did little to freshen the stagnant air. A large black beetle was creeping over the fabric of her split skirts, but Erinda couldn't brush it away. Her arms were bound tightly behind her back, around one of the tent poles.

Goddess, what have I done?

Her first instinct was to panic. Her head throbbed where the barbarian had struck her, sending pinpoints of pain jabbing through her neck and shoulders. How had this happened? Why had the barbarian *shaa'din* been out there, on the wrong side of the temple? Wasn't she supposed to be watching for Kade's miracle tonight, the one everyone was so excited about? And, even more disturbing, Mardyth had called Erinda by name.

She knew I would be out there. Somehow, she knew! How does she even know who I am? And now she's going to try to use me against Kade. Sweet Ithyris, how could I have been so stupid?

No one even knew she'd left the temple except for Myka, and she'd sworn Myka to secrecy. No one would go looking for her any time soon. And Shasta…Goddess, what about Shasta, waiting day after day in lonely grief for a friend who would never come?

Erinda realized she was beginning to hyperventilate, and forced herself to breathe more slowly, filling her lungs, holding the breath for a moment, then blowing it out in a measured *whoosh*. The noise it made was a comfort, and after a few breaths, she became aware of another sound in the tent with her, a soft whimpering. Erinda turned her head as far as she could over her shoulder.

A wooden cage, just a couple of armlengths high and scarcely any deeper, stood in the far corner. Pressed between its bars were two small, pale faces, smudged with dirt and framed by stringy hair. Two pairs of dark eyes watched her warily, and Erinda tried to straighten up a little against the tent pole.

"Hello," she tried to say, but she'd forgotten the gag. The word came out an unintelligible mumble.

The children shifted, never taking their eyes from her. Then their little hands disappeared from around the bars and they shrank into the shadows as the tent flap lifted.

A hulking, bearded man entered, bits of bone and teeth swinging from a leather thong around his neck. He glanced at Erinda and grinned. "Awake, are you? That's good. But the Mistress doesn't want you just yet."

He shuffled over to the cage and slid its wooden bolt aside. One of the children, a boy, quickly popped up as if he were trying to run, but the barbarian grabbed him by the scruff of the neck. He lifted the kicking child out of the cage as easily as one might lift a wayward puppy. He reached back in and grabbed the second boy by the arm, hauling him out as well, and their thrashing fingernails and snapping teeth had no effect on him as he dragged them both toward the entrance.

Erinda struggled against her bonds, protesting as loudly as she could through the gag. The barbarian turned to her, chuckling. "You'll get your turn soon enough, miss." He swept the tent flap aside and left, one screeching child trapped in each hand.

Erinda exclaimed again in frustration. She wriggled down as far as she could get against the tent pole, and peered out through the gap where the tent flap had not quite fallen completely back into place. She didn't have much of a view, but it was enough that she could see the edge of another tent just a few paces away, and beyond that, the ground sloped up toward the temple. She could see the barbarian man towing his two charges up the hill.

From this angle, she had a very narrow view of the temple gates. A line of priestesses stood before them, bearing torches and dressed in white like an army of ghosts. They were too far away for Erinda to make out much detail, but she thought she saw a flash of scarlet amongst them, which had to be Talon or one of her men. Near the center of the line there was a point of light far brighter than the torches, and as it tilted forward it illuminated the edges of a figure standing before them. From this distance, the silhouette was no taller than her thumbnail, but Erinda recognized the flame-colored hair.

Faintly, she heard a voice call out, "We have come to demand your surrender, Mardyth."

Kade. Erinda tugged against the ropes even harder, mindless of the way they bit into her skin. Try as she might, though, she couldn't make out Kade's face in the line of holy women, because the details were obscured by the brilliant light. She called Kade's name as loudly as she could, but the gag in her mouth absorbed most of the sound.

"What a coincidence," Mardyth replied. "I have come to demand *your* surrender, Handmaiden, and I think you will find that I have far more leverage."

Erinda heard a shriek from one of the children, and cringed.

The grounds lit in a blue flash, and another cry came, this time from Mardyth. A roar went up from the barbarians, and then chaos erupted. More blue light pulsed against the translucent skins of the tent. In Erinda's limited range of vision, the shadowy edges of the barbarian line boiled over into the glowing white of the priestesses. For several minutes, darkness tangled with light, punctuated by sapphire columns of flame. Streaks of blue fire arced away from the primary brilliance that was Kade and struck the seething blackness, outlining clumps of barbarian warriors for only an instant before igniting and dissolving them into nothingness. Metal clanged and men shouted.

And then the noise and commotion quieted as abruptly as it had began, and the darkness fell away to reveal Mardyth crouching on the ground at Kade's feet.

The staff sang in Kade's hand, its stone blazing down on the red-orange head of the woman cowering before her.

"My baby," Mardyth moaned. "Please, don't hurt my baby."

Kade called over her shoulder. "Do we have the children?"

"Yes, Handmaiden," Hirrow replied from behind her. "I'm taking them inside now."

The temple gates creaked as the Honored Mother ushered two small forms between them, but Kade kept her attention focused on Mardyth.

"It appears your leverage is gone," she said, "and as you can see, you and your men are no longer quite so immune to the Goddess's celestial fire. Mardyth of Dangar, you have invaded Ithyris's lands without provocation. You have butchered innocent people, destroyed their homes, stolen their goods and livestock, tortured and murdered their families. You have dared to attack the Goddess's Daughters before Her own Great Temple. By all rights, I should destroy every last one of you tonight."

Indeed, the staff was trembling in her hand as if it longed to do that very thing, and Kade squeezed it a little tighter in agreement.

"Please, Handmaiden, I don't want to die. My baby—"

"Your child is spawn of the Flesh God," Kade snapped.

Mardyth lifted her head. Maybe it was just a trick of the light, but her eyes, Kade noticed with a start, were the same dove gray as Erinda's. She wrapped her arms around her blood-spattered belly. "A child cannot choose its father," she said in a whimper, "even as a woman cannot always choose the one who gets her with child."

Kade hesitated. "You're saying this wasn't your decision, becoming *shaa'din*?"

Mardyth cast her gaze aside. "One does not say no to a God, Handmaiden. But surely you know this. Were you not called as I was?"

Ithyris had chosen her, it was true, even though Kade still didn't know why. And perhaps at the time Kade hadn't known Her well enough to realize she had more say in the matter than she'd imagined. But if she'd refused Her—even if she refused Her now—Kade was certain that the Goddess would not retaliate as Ulrike surely did to anyone who refused Him. Kade drew the staff back a little.

What should I do, Lady? she asked of the silver current.

Ithyris's voice was gentle in her thoughts. "What does your heart tell you, Beloved?"

She's hurt so many people. Shouldn't she have to pay for that?

"Do you want to kill her?"

I never wanted to kill anyone. She recalled the barbarian she'd impaled with Fyn's staff, the one who had been about to violate Erinda so horribly. She couldn't bring herself to feel sorry over his death. And she wouldn't feel sorry over Mardyth's either, she realized. The woman was a monster. But what if Mardyth was telling the truth, and she hadn't wanted this any more than Kade had? *Please, Lady, just tell me what You want me to do.*

"Not this time, Kadrian. This is your decision."

Kade huffed in frustration. *I don't understand. You've been guiding me this entire time. At Agar, You commanded me to kill her, and I failed.*

Yet now, all of a sudden, at the most important moment of all, You're making me decide this on my own?

To her annoyance, she heard the Goddess laugh. "I have faith in you, my Daughter."

Kade pressed her lips together and lifted the staff. Spirit surged along its length, and she braced herself, staring down hard at the barbarian *shaa'din*. Those gray eyes met hers, resigned to their fate.

Kade set the staff back down.

"I will ask you one last time, Mardyth. Surrender. Give me your word that you and your army will leave Ithyria and never come back... and I will let you live."

She saw a shudder of relief pass over her shoulders, but still Mardyth hesitated. "The prophecy. Please, if I return without it Ulrike will kill me."

Kade shook her head. "I'm sorry, but this is the most I can offer. The prophecy remains with me. You will leave, or you will die."

Mardyth hung her head. "You leave me little choice, then. Give us two days to pack up our camp, and—"

"You have two hours." Kade raised a hand, beckoning the other priestesses to return to the temple. "And if you or your men harm even one more creature in Ithyria on your way home—I don't care if it's so much as a horsefly—I will come after you, and I will kill you. Do we have an understanding?"

Mardyth rose to her feet, still bent forward, and backed away several steps. "Yes, Handmaiden."

As she watched Mardyth and her men retreat down the hillside, Talon came to stand at her shoulder.

"You're letting them go," she said. If the deep tones held reproach, Kade couldn't detect it.

"There's no sense in any more death. We've defeated them."

"Are you sure?"

Kade turned to her in concern. "You're not?"

Talon's dark eyes followed the barbarians back into their camp. Already, they were pulling up tent pegs and gathering up supplies, seemingly taking Kade's threat seriously. "I don't know. The Dangar barbarians have always been little more than bullies. Quick to attack when they believe they have the advantage, and just as quick to flee when things don't go their way. Cowards, the lot of them, but this seems too easy. They haven't spent the last three moons tearing through Mondera after this prophecy just to turn and go home now."

"So you think I should have killed her?"

Talon was quiet for a moment before she answered. "Perhaps. But that decision is not mine to make. I do think it's a mistake to let them leave without an escort, however. Three of my men are still well enough to travel. As soon as the barbarians leave, we'll follow them. Make sure they cross the border without incident."

"Four soldiers aren't enough to take them on, Captain," Kade said.

"We'll follow far enough behind that they won't know we're there. If they keep their word and leave, we'll return to the temple. If they start trouble again, we'll send for help." Talon nodded at the staff, still shimmering under Kade's fingertips. "I've seen what that thing is capable of. You might have need of it, if things go wrong."

Kade drew the staff toward her. "All right. I won't destroy it until after you and your men have returned." Inwardly, though, she sighed. It would be that much longer before she and Erinda could be—*Erinda*. She hadn't even told her yet!

Behind them, the priestesses were filing back into the temple. "Excuse me, Captain," she said, and turned. The women parted to let her past, and she entered the temple with her heart pounding. She had to find Erinda. There was so much they needed to talk about.

❖

Erinda shrank back against the tent pole as Mardyth swept the flap aside, followed by the burly man who had come earlier to take the children away. Mardyth paid no attention to her, striding over to the table and lowering herself weightily into a chair. Her self-satisfied grin seemed rather at odds with the sniveling she'd demonstrated for Kade outside.

"I don't understand, Mistress," the big man said, though he kept well out of arm's reach of her as he spoke. "What did we go to all the trouble of taking her for," he pointed at Erinda, "if you weren't going to bring her out? I thought you said she was our best weapon against the Handmaiden."

"Patience, Haggett." Mardyth flicked the flies away from the plate before her with a disgusted look. She pushed the plate back and picked up a mug, bringing it to her lips.

"But, Mistress," he said, "we *surrendered*. We're really going to leave without the prophecy? Almighty Ulrike will strike us all dead the moment we set foot in Dangar without it."

"I've already told you, Haggett, we can't defeat the Handmaiden here on her own lands. The Goddess's power is too great. We have to

get her into Dangar, where I shall be the one with all the strength."
Mardyth fixed her mean eyes on Erinda. "And our new friend here is
going to bring her right to us."

"How?"

She raised an eyebrow and he clamped his mouth shut, apparently
remembering that it was not a good idea to question her. But she didn't
seem to mind too much, because she answered. "Remember our last
run in with her? She'd gotten the best of me, the little bitch, but instead
of finishing things she ran off to save this one. Never mind how many
of her other starry-eyed acolytes we'd killed, for some reason this one
is special to her." She returned her attention to Erinda, tilted her head
with curiosity. "So what are you two to each other? Sisters? You don't
look much alike."

Erinda shook her head violently and cursed, though the words were
indistinguishable through the gag. This seemed to amuse the *shaa'din*.

"I don't suppose it matters. Whatever it is, it will be enough. I
hope you didn't tell anyone where you were headed, my dear," she said,
taking another sip from her mug. "Though I suppose that even if you
did, anyone who goes looking for you will be headed for the palace,
won't they? But don't worry. Once we reach the border we'll send word
back to the Handmaiden so she can come to rescue you. Of course, by
the time she makes it to the border we'll all be safely tucked away in
Rok Garshluk, waiting for her.

"I should thank you, by the way. I'm so glad you got my letter and
decided to go running off to the Queen's aid. I wasn't sure you would."

"Your letter?" Erinda mumbled around the gag. *Then the Princess
isn't—*

Mardyth must have read the question in her face, because she
laughed. "Sadly, the Ithyrian Princess is alive and well as far as I know.
Perhaps one day I'll come back for her, and wipe out the Goddess's
precious Rane bloodline once and for all. But it *was* a good story, no?
At least, it was convincing enough for you to dart right into my hands."

Erinda cursed at her again, but Mardyth had turned to Haggett.
"Don't just stand there, idiot. We're packing up. Strike the tent and
see to the wagons. And find something for our guest to wear. Wouldn't
want anyone recognizing her until we're ready for them to know we
have her."

He bowed and scuttled off, and Mardyth sat back in her chair. She
sipped at her mug.

"You're wrong about Kade," Erinda said, not caring that Mardyth
would not be able to understand her. "She's not going to come for

me." She looked down at her lap, where the beetle had found her again and resumed its journey over the landscape of her skirts. Kade's tear-streaked face rose in her memory. *You knew and you never told me… Maybe I made the wrong choice…You know I can't.*

I can't.

I can't.

The words echoed in her head, and Erinda squeezed her eyes shut. Once again, Kade would be forced to choose between Erinda and the Goddess. And Erinda already knew what that choice would be. She didn't blame her; it was the right thing for Kade to do. Too many lives depended on Kade holding fast to the Goddess's commands, so She could protect Her people from the evil woman who was sitting in this tent, watching Erinda with such calculating eyes.

But even so, it was just one more way in which Ithyris had bested her when it came to Kadrian Crossis. And it hurt.

Kade was so tired. Other than the sentries Talon had posted above the gates, everyone else in the temple had gone right to bed after the night's climactic events. Dawn would not come for a few hours yet, and the priestesses had wandered off to their chambers with excited chatter and languid yawns. They were already discussing the feast that Hirrow had declared for the next evening, a celebration of Ithyris's glorious victory. Kade had been curtsied to and saluted and congratulated and thanked more than she knew how to respond to, and so she'd been rather grateful when the commotion died down and the temple fell quiet.

She knew she should get some sleep herself, but first she had to find Erinda. Their encounter that morning had ended so awfully, but what Kade had to tell her now would more than make up for it, she was sure. She entered the dormitories first and checked the room she knew Erinda shared with Talon, but found no one there. She checked the temple stables next, then the infirmary, but without any luck. She tried the gardens, the kitchens, the laundry, the common hall where most of the refugees from Agar were sleeping. She tiptoed among their cots and sleeping mats, but did not find Erinda among them.

Worried now, she walked back across the temple grounds to Mondera's sepulchre, thinking perhaps Erinda might have returned there. The sepulchre was empty. Kade tried the high sanctuary and the library beneath it, walking every one of the marble benches and tall shelves of books. At last, she went back to the dormitories and began peeking into each and every room, drawing back the curtain and holding a candle before the sleeping faces of the inhabitants. A few awakened, peering at her, and Kade apologized for disturbing them and moved on. On the second floor, at the end of the hall, she reached her own guest chamber. As she reached for the curtain she imagined discovering Erinda inside, sitting on her cot, waiting for her…the idea sent a little thrill through her and she pulled the curtain aside.

Someone *was* there, and she sat up when Kade's candlelight swept the room, but the sleepy voice did not belong to Erinda. "Your Grace?"

"I'm sorry, Myka. I didn't mean to wake you."

Myka leapt up. "I know I shouldn't have taken your bed. I just didn't know where else to go. I didn't want to spend another night in the infirmary, and you weren't here so I just thought I'd—"

"It's all right. I won't be needing it tonight. Go back to sleep."

Myka looked her over. "Is everything all right?"

"It's fine. I'm just…I'm looking for someone."

"Oh."

An odd note entered Myka's voice, and Kade narrowed her eyes. "You haven't by any chance seen Erinda tonight, have you?"

"Not since sunset," she said.

But Kade caught the evasiveness in her tone. "Where is she, Myka?"

Once they'd taken a drink from the Cup of Purification, the Pledged could not lie. Myka sputtered and stammered before finally just crossing her arms in front of her. "I won't tell. I promised."

"Promised who? Erinda?"

Myka pinched her lips together. Kade stepped toward her. "I've been looking for her all night. Please, Myka, it's important."

Myka shook her head again.

"Fine. I'll find her myself," Kade said angrily and turned to go.

"You're wasting your time," said Myka from behind her. "She's gone."

"Gone?" Kade spun back around. "What do you mean, gone? Gone where?" When Myka didn't answer, she took two steps forward and shook her by the shoulders. "Answer me, Pledged. Gone where?" She realized as she said it that the demand was coming out in the ancient Ithyrian tongue.

Myka's eyes widened. "The palace," she blurted out. "I brought her a letter from the royal courier, the one Captain Talon brought to the infirmary, you know? She read it and said she had to leave."

"What did the letter say?"

"I don't know. She didn't tell me. Just said something bad had happened and she had to go to the Queen. I helped her out the back gate and barred it behind her. That's all I know, I swear."

"She left?" Stunned, Kade dropped her hands from Myka's shoulders and sat on the cot, speaking mostly to herself. "She didn't even say good-bye." Erinda must have been more hurt by their encounter that morning than Kade had realized. But Myka had said she'd left because of a letter from the Queen, so maybe she wasn't running away from her. Kade hoped that was the case, because the thought that she might have driven Erinda away was unendurable.

"She asked me not to tell anyone, not even you." Myka sat next to her, watching her face anxiously. "I'm sorry, Your Grace. It's just that she made it seem so important."

"It's all right, Myka. Thank you for telling me."

So Erinda had returned to the palace. Kade couldn't go after her until after her business with the prophecy was complete, but it should only take a few days, no more than a quarter moon at most, for the barbarian army to reach the border. As soon as Talon's group returned, Kade would destroy the staff, and then it would be over. Less than a moon's time, for certain. Then she would take her leave of Mondera Temple and return to the palace in Ardrenn. She hadn't been back there in seven winters, but it seemed only fitting that she be reunited with the woman she loved in the same place where Erinda had first stolen her heart, so long ago.

That was, of course, if Erinda would still have her.

Kade stood. "You should go back to sleep. Tomorrow's going to be a big day."

"But what about you?"

As tired as she was, Kade knew she would never be able to fall asleep now. "I'll be all right. It will be morning soon. I think I'm going to go for a ride around the temple grounds." As she moved for the door, she realized she was still carrying Fyn's staff in one hand, and she stopped to prop it against the wall in the corner. "Watch over this for me?"

Myka's eyes lit and she hopped back onto the cot, snuggling under the blanket. "You bet!"

"Sweet dreams." Kade swept the curtain aside and strode away down the hall. Just one more moon. She could make it one more moon, couldn't she?

CHAPTER SEVENTEEN

The road through the northern mountains was steep in many places, at times so narrow that the wagons were veering over it with one set of wheels dangling over empty space. The barbarian horde clambered over the debris of rockslides, slogged through the icy snowmelt that dribbled across their path, and waited while the strongest among them cleared fallen trees that were blocking their way.

Erinda's feet burned like they were on fire. This was their third day of walking, and blisters had long since given way to a ring of raw flesh around her ankles where her shoes had rubbed away the skin. The soles of her feet were so swollen she could feel them squishing against the ground with every step. Erinda had planned on riding to the palace, not walking, and the thick socks she'd packed in Brindle's saddlebags were long gone now. The summer sun beat down on the smelly fur hood that Haggett had plopped around her shoulders, its sweltering pelt drooping down her back. She was so hot and thirsty that, if she had control of her own body, she would have fainted away long ago.

But she did not have control, and she remained mercilessly conscious as one foot plugged after the other. She wished she could ask one of the men trudging next to her for a sip of water, but knew she would be unable to even open her mouth to form the words.

The barbarian *shaa'din* rode ahead, mounted on a sturdy chestnut charger. Even in the summer heat, she wore leggings and leather gloves, and a large helmet with curling horns that Erinda suspected was more for visual impact than for function.

When they were ready to leave the temple, Mardyth had taken great pleasure in informing Erinda that she'd "gifted" her with her blood while she was unconcious, just as she had her men. The thought that she'd been forced to drink the *shaa'din*'s blood was revolting, but its effects were far more frightening. While it masked the barbarians' aura from the Goddess's celestial fire, kept them alive and moving even with mortal wounds, it also meant that Mardyth could now dictate every movement of Erinda's body—which she had helpfully demonstrated by making Erinda slap herself in the face a few times. If she chose, she could also desensitize her to pain, but of course she had not granted her that. Erinda could feel every fiery step as her feet plodded on against her will.

The first day, Mardyth had seemed much entertained by Erinda's helpless state. She'd forced her to walk next to her horse, and spent the day regaling Erinda with all sorts of things Erinda did not care to know. Apparently, Mardyth belonged to a mighty tribe from Kizgrik, the second largest kingdom in the Dangar Empire. She killed her first Ithyrian at the tender age of seven, when she'd joined her father's war party in a raid on a migratory Outlander village. She was the oldest of five siblings, all the rest boys, but by the time she was eighteen she'd killed two of her brothers and the other two had willingly conceded her superiority. She was her father's favorite and the greatest warrior in her tribe, with more kills to her credit than even their tribemaster.

Erinda learned that Mardyth had been selected, among three hundred other young women in Dangar, for the honor of becoming the Flesh God's *shaa'din*. The priests of Ulrike had brought them to a great arena, and for two moons, she and the other women had been pitted against one another in battle after battle, each one a contest to the death. In the end, Mardyth was the undefeated champion, and this was her prize—the God's child in her belly and blood that could make any living creature her personal puppet. It was the greatest power any mortal in Dangar had ever held.

"And yet your sweet Handmaiden was so very taken in when I told her how Ulrike had forced Himself on me," Mardyth chortled, snapping the reins against her poor horse's neck. "You Ithyrians are so eager to believe any evil that tickles your ears."

Of course, Mardyth lamented, her powers within Ithyria were significantly diminished. Here she could only obtain control of a person if they had consumed her blood, and the effect wore off after a while. But in Dangar, she had only to look at someone and their flesh was hers to command.

Erinda had listened to this dissertation only because it kept her mind off the suffering of her feet. Today, she was almost wishing Mardyth would talk to her again, just for the distraction.

She berated her own stupidity for days. The letter she'd received had been a ruse, and while she was infinitely relieved to know that the Princess was all right, she was angry with herself for having fallen into Mardyth's trap so easily. She should have brought the letter to one of the priestesses. They had the ability to detect lies and would have recognized the message right away as a fake. Or she could have taken it straight to Kade who, if the letter had been genuine, would certainly have kept the Queen's secret, and would have helped her figure out what to do.

But none of it mattered now, because the fact was that Erinda had believed it, and she had left the temple like an idiot, and now she was going to die. The only question was how badly Mardyth would torture her, once she realized Kade wasn't coming. Erinda doubted Mardyth would be in any mood to show mercy when she discovered her plan had failed.

When her legs stilled beneath her, Erinda could have cried with relief. They had reached a broad plateau on the mountainside, and an enormous stone tower rose out of the rock above it. Erinda knew it was a border tower, though this was far bigger than any of the ones she'd seen at the provincial borders. It appeared to be unoccupied, and Erinda wondered if its guardians had been killed, or if they had merely fled when the horde approached. The barbarians gathered onto the plateau, and Mardyth twisted in her saddle to address them.

"Well, here we are, boys. Home, sweet home."

Erinda heard nervous muttering. She wondered if these men feared the same thing Haggett had mentioned, that setting foot in Dangar would be an instant death sentence, courtesy of their angry God. But Mardyth gave a whistle that quieted them, and waved an arm. "Bring him here, Haggett."

The barbarians parted, and if she still had mastery of her lungs, Erinda would have cried out. Haggett came forward, shoving the point of a broadsword into the back of a captive.

Talon! Her name rose to Erinda's tongue, but her lips would not move, and she watched as Haggett forced Talon, uniform torn and her handsome features swollen and bruised, up to where Mardyth waited. Talon was limping so heavily on one side that she stumbled over several steps, but she held her head high and glared at Mardyth.

"The others are dead, I presume?" Mardyth demanded of her second-in-command.

"Yes, Mistress."

"Excellent." She beckoned to Erinda.

Erinda's feet carried her forward until she was standing at Talon's side. She felt her arms moving, and her hands came up to draw the hood back from her face.

"Erinda?" Talon asked incredulously. Up close, Erinda could see that one of Talon's eyes was blackening, blood dripping down the side of her face. Whatever blow the barbarians had struck, it had reopened the gash from the battle at Agar. Erinda could not reply, but she tried to put as much welcome into her eyes as she could; they seemed to be the only part of her body she had any governance of.

Mardyth slid down from her horse and looked from one to the other. "You two know each other? Well, that's even better. Now, I'm counting on you to watch this carefully, Captain."

She produced a small dagger from between her breasts, then snatched up one of Erinda's long braids and yanked. Erinda blinked at the pain, and she felt the blade of the dagger hovering behind her ear. She closed her eyes, waiting for the strike that would cut her throat. Instead she felt a strange release of pressure, and then her head was free of Mardyth's grasp. She opened her eyes to see Mardyth holding the severed end of her hair. Her eyes widened in shock, but her body remained unmoving as a statue as Mardyth moved to hack off her other braid as well.

Mardyth tugged a leather thong from somewhere on her belt and used it to bind the braids together, then held them before Talon's eyes. They were still curling at the bottom, with bits of green ribbon securing their neat plaits. Talon stood stiffly as Mardyth wound the braids around her fist, undid the first two buttons of Talon's uniform jacket, and tucked Erinda's hair inside. Talon was watching Erinda with a mixture of sympathy and horror.

"Now, soldier, you are going to carry these back to the Handmaiden just as quick as this horse will carry you. You are going to tell her that she has three days to bring the prophecy to me in Rok Garshluk. Here. I've made her a map, so she won't get lost." She flicked her gloved fingers toward Haggett, who handed her a bit of folded paper. Mardyth tucked it into Talon's jacket with Erinda's hair, and refastened the buttons. "And you be sure to tell her that if she's not there on time, the next thing I chop off of her pretty friend here will be far more permanent. Got that?"

Mardyth turned to Erinda. "Anything you want to add? Go on. Now's your chance."

Erinda felt the invisible grip on her jaw fall away. "Don't let her come," she rasped, her voice grating through her dry throat. "You hear me, Talon? Don't you let her—"

Mardyth snapped her fingers, and Erinda's mouth locked shut again. "Ithyrians are such martyrs. You. Get on the horse." She held the reins of the chestnut courser out, and Haggett prodded Talon to indicate she'd better take them.

Talon leaned forward and touched Erinda's arm. "We'll get you out of this, Erinda," she said. "You have my word." Then she swung onto the horse's back, favoring her injured leg. She wheeled the courser around, and with one last earnest look into Erinda's eyes, she kicked the horse into motion and raced back the way they'd come.

Mardyth shook her finger at Erinda as if reprimanding a naughty child, then strode out in front of her men. "Come on, then, you cowardly curs. Let's get ourselves home before the Handmaiden comes looking for us, shall we?"

Erinda's legs carried her behind, but the men hung back until Mardyth was well down the road ahead of them. She paused, almost imperceptibly, at the edge of the shadow cast by the border tower. Her confident gait resumed. Only after her men saw that Mardyth had passed the tower without falling dead to the ground did they begin to follow.

❖

"Your Grace?" Myka tapped Kade on the shoulder, jolting her out of her meditation. Or what was supposed to be meditation, anyway; Kade's mind kept drifting to thoughts of Erinda and what she was going to say when she saw her again at the palace. Maybe she wouldn't say anything at all at first. Perhaps she would just run to her and take her in her arms, and kiss her until she had no breath left.

"Your Grace, I'm sorry to disturb you, but you said you wanted to know as soon as the captain returned."

Kade shot up from her prayer cushion. "He's back already?"

"Yes, but—"

Kade darted past her and down the center aisle of the sanctuary. What perfect timing. That very morning she'd received a messenger from Agar who had confirmed there was a blacksmith in the city with a forge large enough to destroy the staff. Now Talon had returned, which meant her wait was almost over. Beaming, Kade pushed out the sanctuary doors and ran for the gates, which were just closing behind a sweating chestnut horse. Kade skidded to a stop when she caught sight of Talon, and the giddy smile vanished from her face. Her stomach wrenched. Something was very wrong.

"Someone fetch the healer!" she cried out as Talon slid off the back of the horse and into the waiting arms of several priestesses. A few of them ran for the infirmary. Kade dashed to Talon's side. Talon was battered and bruised, one side of her face a mess of blue and purple, blood crusted across her forehead and down her neck.

"Sweet Ithyris, what happened?"

"No time," Talon wheezed, reaching into her jacket. "We have to go. They have her, and we have to get her back. I gave her my word."

"Captain, slow down. What are you talking about?"

Talon pressed something into Kade's chest. Kade held it out, and two long, mousy braids unspooled from her fist. Kade felt her legs go numb.

"Rin."

"They have her, Your Grace. They've done something to her—I'm sorry, I didn't even recognize her until they captured me at the border."

The healer arrived, puffing, and she shooed Kade back. She tilted Talon's face into the light, then bent to check her leg. Talon grunted as the woman probed her ankle. "We have to go back as quickly as possible. I promised her we'd get her out of there."

"You are going nowhere, Captain," the healer said. "That ankle's broken, and I'm going to have to cast it."

"It can wait," Talon insisted.

"It most certainly cannot. Not if you want to be able to walk without a cane for the rest of your life."

Kade was still staring at the braids in her hand when she realized something else was also crinkled in her fist, and she unfolded a piece of paper that bore a diagram, clearly scrawled by hand. "What's this?"

"A map to Rok Garshluk."

"That's one of Ulrike's temples," Lyris said, stepping up behind them and looking over Kade's shoulder. "Talon, are you all right?"

"I'm fine," Talon replied, fanning the healer's fingers away from her face. "Your Grace, Mardyth said you have three days to bring the prophecy to Rok Garshluk. There's no time to waste. We have to get to Agar and ask Urden for a contingent of their guard."

"I'm going alone."

Everyone stared at her.

"Alone?" Lyris asked. "I've read dreadful stories about that place. Forgive me, Handmaiden, but I don't think even you should be traveling into Dangar by yourself, and especially not to one of the Flesh God's temples."

"Erinda wouldn't even have been in Mondera if it wasn't for me. I'm coming with you," Talon said.

"An army will only slow me down," Kade replied, "and I mean no disrespect, Captain, but so will you in your condition. You said yourself that Rin doesn't have that kind of time. Besides, I won't ask any more Ithyrian soldiers to risk their lives for me. This is between me and Mardyth now."

"She'll kill you," Myka said. "We couldn't even get *shaa'ri* and celestial fire to work against her here in Ithyria."

"I'm not leaving Rin to die. Mardyth wants the prophecy; I'll bring it to her. No one can even read the thing anyway." She heard the recklessness in her own words, but didn't care. Mondera and her unintelligible, trouble-causing prophecy could be damned. This was Rin. *Her* Rin.

"Your Grace," Talon said, "I thought that all of this, your whole calling to become *shaa'din*, has been about keeping that prophecy out of Dangar's hands."

"If there's one thing Ithyris has taught me in the past moons, Captain, it's that love is more important than any other calling. Even mine." She held Talon's eyes for a long moment, until Talon inclined her head.

"Safe travels, Your Grace."

Lyris laid a hand on Kade's arm, her gaze just as somber as Talon's. "May the Goddess heed your voice, Handmaiden."

She understood what they weren't saying. Neither expected to see her again. Kade swallowed hard around the lump in her throat and turned before her eyes could spill over. She couldn't bring herself to say good-bye to Myka too, and so she brushed past her and ran for the dormitories, where Fyn's staff was waiting.

She took it up from its resting place against the wall, and it vibrated in response to her touch. Ithyris's spirit current was muted beneath her skin, as it often was when thoughts of Erinda were strong in her mind.

Reverently, she laid Erinda's shorn braids across her cot, and she untied the green ribbons at their ends. As she retied them around the staff's gleaming silver rings, Kade breathed a quick prayer. She wasn't sure if it was to the current, the Goddess, the spirits of the three sisters, or the staff itself.

"If I die, so be it. Just, please, let me save her. Please."

❖

The horse's hooves pounded the ground beneath her, and Kade leaned low over its neck, urging it faster. As she rode, she concentrated on clearing her mind, on the feel of the spirit veins beneath her skin. It wasn't easy, but the hypnotic rhythm of the animal's gallop lulled her raging emotions until they were a murmur inside her head instead of a roar.

Are you there, Lady?

"I am here, Beloved, always."

You said You care more for me than for the prophecy. I hope that's still true.

"That will always be true."

I don't understand, Lady. How could You not tell me they'd taken Rin? You must have known.

"I wish that I had. But Ulrike's power is great. Sometimes He has ways of blocking my children from my sight."

Kade had never heard the Goddess's voice catch like that, so painfully, a dissonant chord within an otherwise perfect piece of music. *He's done this before?*

"Yes."

And that single word was so sorrowful that Kade guessed what She was referring to. *Olsta. He did this when they took Olsta, didn't He?*

"Yes. He did."

Tell me. Kade tried not to make it sound like a demand, but she desperately needed to know.

"I knew where she was. I even had some sense of what was happening to her, the despicable things my brother's followers were doing." There it was again, that dissonance, jarring the Goddess's words like sobs. "But I couldn't reach her. Her cries rang in my ears because I was within her, yet I couldn't reach her. Couldn't help her, or even transport her to the nexus where her spirit might find some respite from the horrors being wrought against her flesh.

"At the time, the rest of the Twelve were spread out all over the countryside, working to liberate villages from Ulrike's influence and gather support from my people. When Olsta was taken, I called to every one of them and sent them after her. Tabin got there first, being the fastest, but Ulrike's forces were too numerous and she was badly wounded. Zarneth and Fyn arrived shortly after that, then the others. It took all of them to get to her, to get her away from there. And by that time she was…" Ithyris did sob then, a heartrending sound.

"Her spirit was mortally wounded. Changed. She was still my Olsta, but broken so that even I could not fully repair the damage that had been done. I comforted her the best I could. I promised I would never let her be taken from me again, never, and I held her close to my heart until the day her spirit rose to *Yura'shaana* on its own."

Tears splashed onto Kade's fists, knotted in the horse's mane.

"That day I swore I would never create another *shaa'din*. I would never again put one of my precious Daughters in that kind of danger. But Mondera assured me there would be more. 'In a thousand winters, Lady,' she told me, 'You will find another who is meant to follow in our footsteps. She alone will begin the end that must be.'"

You don't know what she meant by that?

"I know she meant you, Beloved. Beyond that, I am not sure. Mondera's gift for divining the future was within her since birth. I believe it was part of her flesh as well as her spirit, and for that reason it exceeded even my own abilities."

For the longest time, Lady, I thought that Olsta's fate was something You had intended for me.

"Oh, Kadrian, no. Never. I would gladly go back and prevent it if I could. But time, like love, life, and faith, are all forces over which I have no sway."

You don't think that...Please, tell me this isn't what's happening to Rin. Kade's concentration wavered as this thought swept over her, and she had to strain to hear the Goddess's reply.

"If I knew, Beloved, I would tell you. But I was able to maintain connection with Olsta only because she was *shaa'din*. I am afraid I cannot see Erinda at all."

Kade rode until night fell, and kept going through the darkness, using moonlight and the staff to light her way. She was forced to slow their pace, however, once they'd entered the treacherous mountain road. She brushed past the grasping branches of trees and ignored the biting insects that nipped at her arms and face. Once, she thought she saw the glowing eyes of a wild creature standing in the path, but she waved the staff over her head and it darted into the underbrush.

For hours, they kept moving, and when her stomach began to feel queasy, Kade pulled some dried meat from the pouch at her belt and chewed it without tasting. She didn't feel much like eating, but she would need strength if she was going to have any hope of facing Mardyth when she arrived. On and on they went, around cliffs and up steep, rocky inclines. They splashed through creeks and skirted boulders, and the darkness around them felt endless and ominous. When the mountain air turned chilly, Kade wrapped herself in her woolen cloak and slumped forward over her horse's neck, resting her cheek in its mane.

When the steady gait beneath her finally slowed and stopped, Kade sat up and rubbed her eyes, dismayed to realize that she'd fallen asleep. She blinked and looked around her. They had reached a large, flat plateau, and the sky overhead was a pearly color that meant the sun would rise soon. To the west, an enormous tower erupted from the rocks, a monstrous shadow against the lightening sky.

The Goddess's voice resounded in her ears. "Dangar. Once you cross the border, Beloved, I will not be able to reach you."

"Why, Lady? I've never understood that."

"When the Twelve pressed Ulrike's disciples back into these mountains, my brother realized that not even the mountain range would stop them—me—from progressing ever further into his territory. With every league we gained, more mortals, weary of his tyranny, turned to me for freedom. I wanted to liberate every last person who cried out to me, and we would have kept advancing had he not erected a wall against me here."

"A wall, Lady?" Kade glanced at the tower, which for all its imposing dignity, appeared to be a singular construction.

"Not a wall of stone and mortar, Beloved, but a Division of far greater magnitude. A curtain of hatred, madness, fury, and fear, every gruesome disease that warps and destroys spirit. Mortals may pass through it and scarcely notice the difference, but it holds me here, on this side, and I have not been able to breach it for a thousand winters.

"What Ulrike did not consider, of course, is that the same sicknesses that cripple spirit also waste away the flesh. His blockade had effectively shut Him out of my lands as well. How He raged when He discovered it! But His mistake has kept my people safe for all this time, though there are so many more…so many, Beloved…who are held on his side, out of my reach."

Kade thought of the barbarian warriors, with their inhuman strength and unnatural ability to survive deadly wounds. If what Ithyris said was true, how had Mardyth endowed them with so much of Ulrike's power within Ithyria, leagues away from Ulrike's domain? But before she could even voice the question, the answer scorched onto her tongue behind it, and she went rigid with shock.

"Now you begin to understand," Ithyris said, not unkindly.

"You and Ulrike can't venture into one another's lands. But *shaa'din* are mortal. We can cross the wall. And when we do, we take You with us, don't we?"

"Mardyth's flesh is infused with Ulrike's, just as your spirit is infused with mine. As *shaa'din*, you can carry a portion of our power across the Division. However, the moment you cross the wall, our direct connection is severed, so you are able to take with you only that remnant of us which your bodies can hold."

Would it be enough to save Erinda's life? Anxiety tangled her guts like fishing nets. She could not live with the alternative.

"My brother has been jealous of my lands for a thousand winters. He has schemed for centuries, trying to find a way to take Ithyria from me. His most recent attempt very nearly succeeded, until my Daughters discovered how to call celestial fire."

"The Battle of the Ranes," Kade said.

"He is growing desperate, I think. When Ulrike created His *shaa'din*, I felt it—felt the drop of spirit He stole from *Yura'shaana* to inhabit His offspring, planted in a mortal womb. *Yura'shaana* is a dangerous place for Him, and He has not tried such a thing in a very long time. I knew that what Mondera had foreseen was upon us, and it was time to give myself to you."

Something brushed Kade's cheek, and she knew it was the Goddess's touch on her face. She could feel Her embrace like a shawl of starlight settling over her, glittering and warm. But the Goddess did not enter her. She just held her for several long minutes, and the silver veins of Her spirit pulsed so urgently that Kade found herself wondering if Ithyris was afraid for her. Or did She fear it was a mistake, letting Kade go?

Guiltily, Kade became aware of the staff in her hand, a beautiful shining thing of graceful rings and ethereal light. Mondera had gone to great lengths to hide it away from the world. Now Kade was about to do the very thing that would make all Mondera had planned, every one of Marin's ingenious machinations to keep the prophecy from falling into the wrong hands, worthless. She was going to hand it over to the enemy to save the life of the woman she loved.

"Why are You letting me do this?"

The starry embrace shifted and shimmered, lifting from her shoulders. Still, the love in Her words was undiluted as She replied, "Faith, Beloved."

Kade wondered if She meant faith in her, or faith in Mondera's predictions. Ithyris didn't seem to know the specific details of her supposed destiny any more than Kade did. Yet She was willing to allow Kade to hand-deliver the prophecy to Her brother, all because Mondera had said that Kade was the one to—how had She put it—*begin the end that must be*. Whatever that meant. Right now Kade was sure it couldn't mean anything good.

The Goddess had drifted away again. Kade tugged at her waterskin and brought it to her lips. A rustle behind her, however, made her turn.

"Who's there?"

The challenge was met with silence at first, but then came a snuffle and the sound of hooves pawing the earth. Kade directed the staff's light back along the path. If she was going to encounter an attacker, it might as well be on this side of the border, where she still had full access to Ithyris's spirit.

"I know you're there. Show yourself."

The hoof beats came closer, and then Myka entered the circle of light cast by Cibli's stone. Myka was leading a little gray palfrey, and she gave a sheepish grin. "Guess I should have stayed back a little farther. Didn't realize you'd stopped until we were almost on you."

"You should have stayed at the temple," Kade replied irritably. "What a troublesome little fox you've turned out to be."

Myka seemed unbothered by the scolding. "You followed me into the arms of death, and I intend to return the favor."

"It's far more likely that you'll end up right back in death's cozy arms. And I might not be able to bring you back a second time."

Myka shrugged. "I'm going with you. You may be the Handmaiden, but I can handle a sword far better. I'm better at tracking, and hunting, and making a fire, and—"

"Go home, Myka."

"I don't have one." The sun crested the eastern slope, turning Myka's ruddy hair to gold. "I've been a lot of places in my life, but the only place I ever really feel at home is traveling the in-betweens. Besides, you're my friend. I'm coming whether you want me to or not."

"This isn't going to make you famous. It's probably going to make you dead. And I don't want to see you get hurt."

"That makes two of us." Myka grinned and mounted her horse, riding up until she was shoulder to shoulder with Kade. "But I'm still going."

The sun was gilding the clouds in pink and gold, pressing back the shadows of night with rosy palms. Kade pushed her cloak behind her shoulders.

"You still have the chance to change your mind." She urged her horse forward, past the foreboding border tower.

Faintly, she heard the Goddess whisper a farewell. For a moment, Her spirit current glowed, like one last, loving caress. Then a profound chill swept in behind, the light in Cibli's stone winked out, and Kade shivered to the depths of her soul. She had crossed the Division. She reached back for Her, using all her senses, but it was just as She had said, as if an invisible wall had sprung up behind her. Prod as she might, it was as if she had passed through a sheet of glass that blocked contact from the other side. Kade could sense Her, lingering just beyond it, but their connection was gone.

She was alone.

Tears rushed up behind her eyelids, and Kade scrubbed them away. She was always crying at inappropriate moments. Now was not the time for such frivolity. Somewhere here, behind Ulrike's wall, Erinda was also alone. And who knew what Mardyth and her brutes might be doing to her, with every passing hour that it took for Kade to arrive?

She pressed her mount into a canter and heard Myka's little palfrey clip-clopping determinedly behind. Kade ground her teeth, but she didn't have any more time to waste arguing with her. Erinda only had one day left.

CHAPTER EIGHTEEN

The temple of Rok Garshluk was a flamboyant display of power, carved into the face of a vertical granite cliff that had to be a half-league high. Eight gargantuan columns, chiseled out of the rock, towered fifty paces above the ground. At first, Erinda thought they were sculpted to resemble a macabre display of dead body parts, larger than life and perhaps impaled on a massive pike, but when they drew closer, she realized the carvings were clearly a tribute to life, not death. She could see arms and legs, hands and necks, chests, stomachs, and even—she might have quirked an eyebrow if she could—well-formed buttocks, all rendered in painstaking detail. They were finely muscled, powerfully veined, each a celebration of strength and carnality.

Behind these great columns there were a few paces of empty space, just enough room to allow a glimpse of the temple's façade as they approached. This was decorated with more etchings, of beasts as well as men. Or maybe they were men with the bodies of beasts? Exhaustion and pain had her mind processing things in a haze, and she didn't have the chance to study the murals in detail because her feet carried her into the temple's gaping maw. Here she found herself in a long corridor of stone, with torches set low along the walls and a ceiling so high that it was lost in the blackness above, out of reach of the torchlight.

Once they had crossed the border into Dangar, Mardyth forced them to walk ceaselessly, night and day, so that now it had been nearly three full days since Erinda had last slept. Her ankles had stopped bleeding yesterday, not because they had scabbed over, but because it seemed her body had decided it was wasteful to keep sending blood to them. Her feet were dull blocks of agony, skinned raw and bruised to the bone, and they felt very far away from the rest of her, as if her mind was trying to forget she even owned them.

Like the limbs of a marionette, her legs kept moving beneath her, following the beacon of Mardyth's hair down the corridor. The deeper they went, the cooler the air became. The temple was musty, but the smell was rich and unexpectedly welcoming, earth and rock and ash so ancient that it remained untainted by the stench that clung to the barbarians like a pestilence.

The stone walls reverberated with the cadence of the horde's footfalls as they bottlenecked into the corridor behind their leader. They passed openings that branched into other halls on both sides, but Mardyth did not stop until their own corridor terminated in a set of enormous doors. These she shoved open, and strode into the cathedral beyond with all the arrogance of a war hero returning to her clan in victory.

The room was cavernous, with row after row of granite pillars supporting a ceiling so high it was indistinguishable in the shadows. Yellow-robed priests sat about the floor in clusters. Most were engaged in rituals and meditations which apparently involved mortars, pestles, sharp knives, and a number of foul-smelling herbs. Mice and snakes squeaked and slithered in tiny cages, and Erinda caught glimpses of fur and blood in the priests' bowls, snakeskin spread glistening on wooden trays before their knees.

The priests were swift to push their things aside and bow their foreheads to the floor as the *shaa'din* passed by them. A sort of raised dais had been carved into the stone in the center of the cavernous room, and Mardyth left Erinda and her army standing at its base as she climbed its steps. She waited for the priests and warriors to surround her, and raised her arms in triumph.

Then she fell to her knees and screamed.

Abruptly, the invisible puppeteer's grip on Erinda's body went slack, and Erinda, too, dropped to her knees, her exhausted body unable to support her. Darkness surged forward, promising a respite from the pain, but she fought it back and looked up at the dais. She wanted to see what was happening as Mardyth convulsed over her burgeoning belly.

She continued screaming. Behind them, Erinda heard grunts and footfalls as many of the horde fled back down the corridor in fear. Those who remained edged toward the exit in case it seemed wise to follow their comrades. Every priest lay prostrate and trembling on the floor, not even daring to look up.

At last, whatever gripped Mardyth seemed to withdraw enough that she could raise her head. Blood streamed from her eyes, staining her cheeks like garish tears. "My Lord, please," she croaked, "I have not failed You."

Another wave racked her body, but this time her screech was half-swallowed, as if she was fighting the pain. "She will come, my Lord, I promise You. Ithyris's Handmaiden will deliver the prophecy to You with her own hands."

"She will not," Erinda choked out, her voice razing her throat like shards of glass.

Mardyth managed to turn her head, even through her own obvious pain. She narrowed her eyes, and Erinda's hands came up of their own accord, her fingers wrapping around her neck and squeezing. She felt her thumbs wrap around her vocal cords with a strength she didn't possess, pressing so sharply she could almost feel them touching through the layers of flesh. She couldn't breathe, and she wheezed as her hands tugged outward. Her eyes bulged as she comprehended Mardyth's intent. Just a little more pressure, and her thumbs would tear through the skin. Just a little more force, and Mardyth could make her rip out her own throat.

Mardyth released her, though, struck by a fresh onslaught of her master's wrath. Erinda pulled her traitorous hands from her neck and trapped them protectively between her thighs, gasping and coughing against the smooth stone floor.

Mardyth was in little better straits herself, curled into a moaning ball as blood flowed down her face. "She will come, my Lord. She will come. I swear it. Please…"

For a moment, it seemed as if her unseen God was unconvinced, but then Mardyth's body relaxed and Erinda felt an odd sort of lifting, as if a weight she hadn't even known was there had retreated into the fathomless blackness of the cathedral ceiling. Everyone seemed to take in a deep breath simultaneously. The priests lifted their heads.

Mardyth straightened. She held out a hand, and one of her men hurried up the dais steps to her side, helping her up. Then she turned her lurid, blood-streaked countenance on Erinda.

"Stand up."

Erinda's body obeyed in an instant, though it felt like her bones were creaking with the effort.

"Hold out your hand."

Erinda's left hand came up. Then her right followed, and it took hold of her left index finger. Erinda had just enough time to register Mardyth's cruel smirk, more grimace than smile, and she shook her head. "No, please!"

"You'd better start hoping that little bitch comes for you. Otherwise…"

Erinda's right wrist wrenched back, and Erinda felt a sickening, splintering crunch. The pain followed a second later, and it was Erinda's turn to shriek helplessly. The men still lingering by the door cheered, and began calling out sundry suggestions as to what Mardyth might do to her next. The priests merely returned to their pounding and cutting as if the torture of captives was a common occurrence in their midst.

Mardyth wasn't done with her yet, however. She stalked down the dais steps and wiped a bit of the blood from her own face with a gloved finger, smearing it along the length of Erinda's broken one.

Erinda cried out again as the tiny muscles in her finger clenched and fired. Laboriously, they contracted until they'd ground the bones back into place. She felt a calescent fusion of bone to bone, like smelt metal being poured into the break. Her flesh rearranged itself around the welded bones, and Erinda screamed until her voice was gone.

Then the pain ended, leaving behind only a deep, throbbing ache. Mardyth flicked her own index finger up and down, causing Erinda's to mimic the movement as perfectly as a reflection in a mirror.

"Good as new," she said. "Want to try it again?"

Erinda sobbed as her right hand took hold of her newly repaired finger. "No! Oh, Goddess, please don't!"

Mardyth arched an eyebrow. "I think now we understand each other, yes? If I feel like it, I can crush every bone in that delectable body of yours, then put you back together again and start all over. So you'd better start praying that your simpering Handmaiden comes for you. Because the longer it takes for her to arrive, the thinner my patience becomes. And you won't like me when I'm impatient."

The pressure against Erinda's finger increased, and she whimpered. Hunger and exhaustion had already driven her body to its limits, and torture was more than it could withstand. Her eyes rolled back in her head, and even with Mardyth's control holding her erect, she swayed out of balance.

Mardyth paused. She seemed to realize she was dangerously close to pushing her over the edge because she said, "Then again, I can't have you dying on me before the Handmaiden gets here."

Erinda's hands dropped to her sides, and she was pirouetted around. Mardyth marched her to an iron cage beneath one of the great pillars. Erinda's legs stepped into it one at a time, then bent until she was sitting, and her shoulders and head slouched down until they were fully inside. Mardyth flipped the top of the cage down and slid its deadbolt into place.

"And in case our little bird gets any ideas about trying to escape…" Mardyth gestured to one of her men, and he began to crank a wheel set into the wall by the door. Chains clanking, the cage lifted off the floor, carrying Erinda with it. She lurched from side to side as her little prison rose higher and higher. When she was a good twenty paces in the air, the man stopped cranking and set the wheel. Erinda kept swinging back and forth in gentle, nauseating passes.

But she was free. Mardyth had relinquished control. The cage was so tight that Erinda could barely move, but after being imprisoned within her own skin for the last three days, this new arrangement felt like a precious gift. She curled her legs beneath her, slumped against the cold iron bars, and immediately lost consciousness.

❖

"Well, that certainly looks like an unholy temple of flesh to me," Myka said, stepping so close to the edge of the cliff that Kade put out a hand to steady her. "Just look at those columns, all carved up like body parts. Yech."

Mardyth's scrawled map confirmed they were in the right place, but Kade didn't need to be told. Here the road clung to the side of the mountain like a snake, dropping into a sheer cliff along its outer edge. They had rounded the pass to find that below them, the cliff plunged into a jagged canyon, and at the base of the canyon floor a massive temple had been sculpted into the opposite cliff face. Eight grotesquely wrought columns rose halfway up the canyon wall, shadowing the entrance behind.

Erinda was somewhere inside that mountain. Kade felt that knowledge pulsing inside her with every heartbeat. Staring down at the monstrosity of Rok Garshluk, she felt very small and insignificant. She was not at all the force of daring rescue that Erinda needed. Yet she was all Erinda had, and so she could not fail.

"What do we do now?" Myka asked.

Kade thunked the end of Fyn's staff into the dirt. "I give Mardyth what she wants."

Myka's eyebrows did a funny dance. "*That's* your plan? You're going to just walk in there?"

"You have a better idea?"

"Yes!" Myka exclaimed. When Kade looked at her expectantly, however, she faltered. "We could at least, I don't know…Sneak?"

"We're in Dangar now. I really don't think it's going to matter if they see me coming."

"But you can't trust Mardyth to keep her word, even if you do give her the staff. She'll probably kill your friend Erinda anyway, just to be cruel. And we don't know where they're keeping Erinda in there, or even if she's still—"

"Don't," Kade snapped.

Myka broke off under Kade's hostile glare and sighed. "All I mean is, shouldn't we try to find her first, see if we can maybe get her out of there without having to stand nose to nose with Mardyth again?"

"How?"

"Can't you make us invisible, like you did before?"

"No, Myka, I can't. That's what I've been trying to get you to understand. I'm cut off from the Goddess here. I'm alone."

"But have you even tried?"

Kade would not even dignify that with an answer. She was beyond trying to reason with the silly girl, who had trailed her all the way out here and was, more than likely, going to get herself killed. Another innocent death on her conscience. Kade returned to her horse, tucking Mardyth's map back into her pack.

Myka caught her arm. "Look, I know you're angry with me for following you. But I'm trying to help. Why won't you let me help?"

"You want to help? Boost me up."

"Not until you listen." Myka punched her fists into her hips. "You're not alone here. I'm not leaving you, no matter how much you glare and snip at me. And I believe Ithyris is with you too, even if you're being too bullheaded to listen to Her either."

Kade scowled. "I am not."

"Are too. If Mardyth could still use Ulrike's power in Ithyria, then you should be able to use at least some of Ithyris's here. But you won't even try. Like I said: bullheaded."

Kade's irritation magnified. "You want me to try? Fine." She closed her eyes and felt for the spirit current, still running cold under her skin like an echo. But her annoyance warmed it with new urgency, and she pushed into it, urging it outward and around her like a misty silver veil. The spirit felt thick and sluggish, but with some coaxing, she did get it to move.

Myka crowed. "See, I told you so!"

Kade opened her eyes to see Myka looking at her, but her gaze was just slightly off center, as if she was staring at some point just past Kade's right ear. Myka was grinning as she reached out and felt for the front of Kade's tunic. She patted her hands blindly along Kade's shoulders and then her cheeks, and her eyes skimmed after her fingers without recovering their target. "I mean, it's not quite the same. I can't see you, but I can see something. Like the edges of the space where you ought to be."

"I don't think I can..." The silver haze was wavering, and Kade had to keep constant pressure on the current in order to hold it in place. "This is a lot harder than before."

"Try this." Myka tugged the staff from the ties that held it to the horse's pack, and thrust it out.

Kade's fingers closed around the cool metal, and she felt suction against her skin. She fed the current into it and the staff hummed. After a moment, Cibli's blue stone began to glow, faintly, and the hazy veil thickened around her. She still had to keep pressure on the current's flow, but the staff did much of the heavy work.

Myka cheered again. "It's almost perfect now. You can sneak into their creepy temple and look for Erinda before anyone finds out you're there."

Kade held on to the current for a few moments longer before letting the veil drop back into its cool flow. Myka's eyes refocused on her face. "The staff helps, but even so, I can barely hold it. There's no way I'll be able to cover the both of us."

"That's all right." Myka dropped to one knee and made a stirrup with her hands, apparently ready to give Kade the requested boost now that she'd made her point. "I can take care of myself."

Kade regarded her for a moment with a mixture of exasperation and gratitude. She bent and drew her to her feet. "You were right, Myka. And I'm sorry for being so short with you. You're a good friend." She hugged her, then took her horse's reins and pressed them into Myka's hand. "I've changed my mind. I'm going on from here by foot. If I asked you to stay behind, would you do it?"

"Probably not. But at least I don't plan on doing anything so stupid as strolling inside in plain sight."

Kade rolled her eyes, then squeezed Myka's shoulders. "Please, Myka. I know arguing with you is pointless. But whatever you do, be careful."

Myka pressed her fingertips to her own forehead with a bow. "May the Goddess be with you, Handmaiden."

❖

Erinda dozed in fitful spurts of misery. The cage was so small that she could not straighten her legs, or lie down, or even find a comfortable place to rest her head. Her finger ached and her feet burned, and the discomfort dragged her into consciousness long before her body finished getting the rest it needed. Erinda wriggled into a new position, cradling her head against her arm. The movement set the cage swinging, gently, and she was able to drift off again for a while.

The next time she woke, her arm had fallen asleep, and it hung from her shoulder like a dead thing while her circulation returned in sparkling needles. She reached down and fumbled for the laces of her shoes, gasping between her teeth as she freed her blistered feet. The cathedral was too dark to make out the damage, but without the shoes the awful burning was somewhat alleviated. She tucked the shoes carefully into her lap, curled up, and slept some more.

A while later, she woke again, this time because her feet had grown cold. She found herself missing the smelly fur cloak, as she could barely keep her teeth from chattering in the dank underground air. She twisted and thrashed until she managed to get the hem of her split skirts tucked over her frozen toes, and then leaned forward, resting her forehead on her knees and wrapping her arms around her thighs for warmth. She sighed and tried to send herself back to sleep.

The enormity of her situation was sinking in. She was going to die, and as Mardyth had so pointedly demonstrated earlier, it was going to be a slow and horrific experience. She was already so cold, exhausted, and weak. She raised her head and looked up at the cage bolt. It wouldn't be too difficult to slip her hand between the bars and pull it aside. Of course, if she did the cage would open and drop her twenty paces onto the stone floor. Probably not enough to kill her. Definitely enough to break some bones, and she was not at all eager to experience Mardyth's twisted healing powers any time soon.

Beneath her, mice skittered and squeaked in their own little cages. Erinda sighed and lowered her head. Two moons ago when she'd left the palace, she never could have imagined she'd end up here, of all places. Kidnapped, tortured, held captive by the Flesh God's *shaa'din* in an underground temple in Dangar, all because the barbarians believed her to be their ultimate pawn against the Goddess. Little did they how utterly, tragically preposterous that was. Ithyris hated her.

And Kade…Kade was probably praying herself into a sickness over this. And crying, too, of course. But in the end, she would do the right thing, as she always did, and for the first time, Erinda was grateful for it. Kade didn't belong here, among all this violence and death. The Goddess needed Her Handmaiden. Ithyria needed their champion. And in a few more hours, when Mardyth finished with her, Erinda wouldn't be in need of anyone ever again.

One of the cathedral doors opened, sending a dim slice of torchlight slanting across the floor. Snakes hissed at the intrusion. Erinda grabbed the bars of the cage and peered down. The cathedral had been empty for hours, the priests having abandoned their work to see to Mardyth's needs. The door closed, and she thought she saw a hint of movement below, a whisper of space that was lost in the wavering shadows cast by the torches along the walls. But everything went silent again, and all she could hear was the sound of her own breath and the scritching and slithering of her fellow captives.

"Is someone there?" she called out. She was not quite sure why she was asking. What if Mardyth had returned? But the quiet was unsettling, and she pressed her face between the cage bars. "Hello?"

"Rin!"

Something shimmered, white and gold against the dark. Suddenly, Kade was standing there, looking up at her. Her face and tunic were smudged with dirt, dark shadows ringing her eyes. The shining silver staff in her hand clattered to the floor.

Erinda covered her mouth with both hands.

"Oh, sweet Ithyris." Kade's voice broke as she took in the cage, and her eyes followed the chain that suspended it until she spotted the wheel set into the wall. "Hold on, Rin. I'm going to get you down."

She ran to the wheel and pulled back the pin that held it, grunting as the weight of both Erinda and the iron cage lurched into her hands. She braced herself against the wall. The cage creaked and swung, lowering almost halfway, but Kade was not strong enough to keep hold of it. The wheel spun out of her fingers.

Erinda felt herself go into free-fall, and instinctively she curled sideways, the same protective position she assumed when being thrown from a horse. The chain above her rattled and clanked. The cage hit the floor with enough force to drive the air out of her body. Her shoulder and hip took the worst of the blow, though her left knee jerked forward and struck one of the iron bars. Her head would have cracked against the bars as well if she hadn't curled one arm underneath it as a cushion. She lay there stunned, trying to remember how to get air back into her lungs.

Above, the bolt slid back, and the top of the cage was flung open.

"Rin, oh Goddess, Rin…"

Hands tugged at her gently, as if Kade was afraid of hurting her. Erinda stumbled to her feet, mindless of her bruises, and let herself be drawn into Kade's arms. Kade's linen tunic was warm under her fingers, her shoulder real and solid against her cheek.

"You came for me," she mumbled in disbelief. She felt Kade's hand in her shorn hair. Kade's aura swept over her, soothing and blissful as ever. The burning in her feet receded. The pain in her muscles melted away. Erinda clung to her in shock, in joy, and Kade pressed kisses against her temple and forehead.

"I will never leave you again, Rin. Never. I'm so sorry."

Erinda held on to her with every last bit of strength that she possessed. Kade was here. Which meant that she had chosen Erinda over her duty to the Goddess. Such a thing was unthinkable. Amazing. So wonderfully, incredibly...

Wrong.

Erinda's eyes snapped open. Over Kade's shoulder, she saw the cathedral door open. She moaned and tilted her mouth to Kade's ear.

"Run."

"What?" Kade mumbled against her hair.

Mardyth entered the room, her eyes locking with Erinda's. Erinda planted her hands against Kade's chest and pushed her back.

"Run!"

It was too late. Mardyth's control clamped down over her, and she could only watch in horror as her arm drew back and her fist clenched. With the *shaa'din*'s inhuman strength possessing her body, Erinda punched Kade squarely across the face.

CHAPTER NINETEEN

"Welcome to Rok Garshluk, Handmaiden."
Kade lifted onto her elbows. The force of Erinda's blow had sent her sprawling, nearly on top of the silver staff where it lay on the floor. Confused, she raised a hand to her lip, and her fingers came away with blood. "Rin, what…?"

Erinda stepped woodenly out of the cage and moved to Mardyth's side, and Mardyth wrapped an arm around her waist.

"Ah, I see it now," Mardyth said, looking between them with delight. "Of course. This is going to be so much more entertaining than I thought." With her free hand, she pulled Erinda's curls back, baring her neck. Erinda tilted her head to the side, and Mardyth made a great show of exhaling on the pulse point just beneath Erinda's jaw, her teeth a hairbreadth from the skin. She ran gloved fingertips over the swell of Erinda's breasts.

Erinda's face was blank, but her eyes told Kade everything she needed to know. Whatever Mardyth might be trying to imply, Erinda was not a willing participant in this. Kade rose to her feet, taking up the staff as she went.

"Let her go."

"What makes you think your little bird even wants to fly away with you, hmm? She seems perfectly content to me."

Kade hardened her voice. "If you want the prophecy, you'll let her go."

Scoffing, Mardyth said, "You think this is a negotiation? You're in my world, Handmaiden. I make the rules here. You have the prophecy, I presume?"

"Yes. But you're not getting it until—"

"Let me guess. Until I let her go?" Mardyth grinned. "I have a counter offer." She threw a wink in Kade's direction as Erinda's fingers dipped between her fur-clad breasts.

A growl built in Kade's chest, and she stepped forward.

"Careful, now," Mardyth said, but the warning was not for Kade. She had directed it at Erinda.

Kade's heart began to pound as she remembered. *Her touch kills.* She froze, the breath caught in her throat.

Carefully, without contacting Mardyth's deadly skin, Erinda withdrew a small knife from Mardyth's bodice. The weapon twirled in her fingers, a flourish that never would have come naturally to Erinda. She began walking toward Kade, the knife in one hand and frantic apology filling her eyes. Kade took an uncertain step back.

Erinda lunged. Kade dodged, the blade catching the edge of her cloak. She recovered her footing just as Erinda swiped at her again. She hopped backward, but the tip of the knife slit the linen of her tunic like soft butter and sliced across her ribs. Kade stumbled and whirled away, clutching at her abdomen. She felt wetness beneath her fingers, but there was no time to even register pain. Erinda came at her a third time. She would have sunk the blade into Kade's shoulder, but Kade brought the staff up instinctively. It cracked against Erinda's wrist, hard. Remorse swept over her, and she drew back. Had she hurt her?

But if Erinda was hurt, she showed no sign of it. She ducked underneath the staff so fast that Kade barely had time to track the movement. And then the knife was pressed to Kade's throat.

But it was trembling.

"Interesting," Mardyth said, sounding impressed. "She's fighting me. No one's ever managed it quite so well, at least not on this side of the border. Tougher than she looks, isn't she? I don't think she wants to kill you."

"Stop this," Kade panted, backing away. She pressed a hand against the stinging cut across her ribs. "Let her go."

"Give me the prophecy."

"You and I both know the prophecy is the only leverage I have right now."

"And your little bird is the only leverage I have. I'll release her after I have the prophecy."

"I'll give it to you after you release her."

Mardyth sighed. "Oh, this is going nowhere." She turned to Erinda and flicked her hand.

Erinda twirled the knife, and Kade braced for another attack. But this time, Erinda took the hilt in both hands, and drove the blade into her own stomach.

"No!" Kade roared. She lunged forward, but Mardyth put up a hand.

"One more step, Handmaiden, and I'll let her die."

Kade stopped in midstride. Erinda had not made a sound, but blood coated her hands and splattered onto the floor at her feet. The blade was buried to the hilt in her stomach. It was a mortal wound. No one could survive an injury like that. Kade felt her throat closing up in terror.

"If she dies, I'll kill you."

"Oh, don't be so dramatic. I plan to heal her. But there's something you should understand." Mardyth yanked the knife from Erinda's body. Erinda still made no noise, though her pupils constricted with pain. "Healing hurts, Handmaiden. Most of the time it's far more painful than the injury itself, and I can keep it up indefinitely. So I'm going to heal your pretty bird, and you can listen to her sing while I do it. Pay close attention, because we're about to play a game. Every time I ask for the prophecy and you refuse, I'm going to hurt her—and then heal her again. As many times as it takes, until you give me what I want."

Mardyth slashed her forearm, and a deep scarlet line formed against her pale skin. She held a gloved hand beneath for a moment or two. Then she turned, and pressed her fistful of blood into Erinda's wound.

Erinda screamed.

Kade leapt forward, shoving Mardyth aside. Mardyth stepped back with a laugh. Kade fell to her knees as she pulled Erinda into her arms. Released from Mardyth's control, Erinda sobbed and shrieked. She grabbed white-knuckled at the front of Kade's tunic as her flesh repaired itself with excruciating speed.

The silver current responded in fury, rising to the surface of Kade's skin. If they'd been in Ithyria, it would have surrounded them explosively in an instant. Here, it beaded on her arms and chest like sweat. Kade locked Erinda in the circle of her arms and took hold of Fyn's staff in both hands. The Goddess's spirit had once been an infinite river, but this was more like working with water from a bucket. Frustrated, she forced what she could into the staff, where it was magnified and returned again. She kept straining until Erinda was completely enveloped in it.

Erinda's cries subsided as the spirit worked, drawing her pain into the space between them. She shuddered violently instead, and in spite of her own smarting wound, Kade pulled her closer, whispering comfort in the Ithyrian tongue. When the current was saturated and could hold no more, Kade took the excess into herself. Her insides cramped and burned as if the mending flesh was her own. She pressed her face to Erinda's neck and rocked her.

No sooner was the healing complete than Kade found herself sprawling on the floor again. Her vision went starry as pain burst across her left cheekbone. Stunned, it took her a moment to realize that Erinda had just punched her across the face again. Kade blinked at her. Erinda's jaw was once again set so that she could not speak, but her eyes sought Kade's desperately as Mardyth forced her back to her feet.

A soft *shing*, and Mardyth had drawn her sword.

"The prophecy, Handmaiden. Or I'll cut off her arm next. And believe me, not even your Goddess's magic will spare her the pain of regrowing it."

"Stop." Kade stood, clutching at her throbbing eye. With the other hand, she held the staff out, and the torchlight glittered along its length. "It's yours."

When Mardyth tilted her head, Kade gave the staff an impatient shake, its rings tinkling. "Take it."

"The prophecy is inside?"

"Look closer."

Mardyth stepped forward, and when she caught sight of the runes etched into the staff's surface, her face lit. "Of course," she breathed, snatching the staff from Kade's hands and sliding her palm along the etchings. "Clever girls, you Handmaidens are." She used her teeth to tug one of her gloves off so she could trace the symbols with her fingertips. "Do you know what it says?"

"No," Kade said flatly, crossing her arms.

Mardyth flicked her gaze up, and Kade's smugness dissipated. "Would you like to?"

"You can read it?"

"It's a very old dialect, of course, but these"—she swept the runes with her fingers—"are Kizgrish. The language of my tribe. I'm surprised your Goddess never told you. Mondera and her sisters? Long before they belonged to Her, they belonged to us."

Kade gaped after her as she went to the cathedral doors and threw them open. The movement startled the group of priests who were clustered just beyond, eavesdropping. Mardyth waved them into the cathedral.

"Come on, all of you. You'll want to hear this."

They crowded inside in a flurry of yellow hoods and shuffling sandals. Mardyth gestured for one of them to seize Kade's arms. The priest was shorter than she was, but he dug his fingers into her wrists and wrestled her after Mardyth.

Mardyth strode to the center of the room and mounted the dais, with Erinda right behind her.

"Almighty Ulrike," she shouted, her voice echoing off the cavern walls. "As You have commanded, I have obeyed! I bring You the prophecy of Mondera!"

She held the staff up and read from it. Her native tongue was harsh and guttural, and when she was done, she caught Kade's eyes and grinned, translating. *"When the Avatar of Flesh rises, the house of Rane shall fall, and darkness will no longer stand divided from the light."*

Kade listened to this proclamation with a quiver of anger. Mondera and her riddles. How many people had suffered and died for that single nonsensical sentence?

"You have what you want," she shouted. "Let Rin go."

Mardyth sneered. "As you wish."

When Kade realized what was about to happen, she howled. The priest let go of her arms. She charged the dais, but Mardyth had already taken hold of Erinda's wrist.

With her bare hand.

Erinda stiffened. Kade saw her eyes roll back. Mardyth shoved her down the steps, and Erinda tumbled, lifeless, into Kade's arms.

Her touch kills.

Kade gave an inarticulate cry. She lowered Erinda to the floor, her head cradled in her lap. "No! Sweet Ithyris, no…Rin!" The silver current feathered over Erinda's body, plucking at her face and arms. But Erinda lay without heartbeat, without breath.

Kade glared wildly at Mardyth. "Give her back!"

"Now why would I want to do that?"

Kade's ears were ringing. Her mind worked frantically. Here, she was cut off from the Goddess's voice. She had a mere bucketful of Her spirit to work with. But Ithyris had said She could hear Olsta, even when She had been separated from her. Kade threw her head back, reached her arms up, and with tears pouring down her face, she prayed as she had never prayed before. *I can't lose her. Lady, please. I can't lose her, not like this.*

Tendrils of the spirit current were still grasping at Erinda as if confused. Kade pulled them back and into herself. She knew exactly where Erinda had gone, and if she was going to follow, she had to do it now. The paltry trickle she could access here was insufficient to get her to the nexus. So Kade began to feed it with the only other thing she had. From every corner of her being, Kade gathered up her own spirit and pressed it into Ithyris's residual current.

The response was sluggish. Where the current would normally have swept her away like rushing water, instead it felt like kneading bread dough. She shoved and prodded. The more of her own spirit she was able to blend into the Goddess's, the easier it moved. When she had thinned it as much as she could, it flowed a little better, more like the consistency of cake batter. That would have to do, and she plunged into it.

Usually, the journey to the nexus took no longer than a breath. But this time the current would not whisk her there. She was going to have to force her way through it. She strained and thrashed, every handbreadth of progress a hard-fought victory. A bright spot waited far ahead, the arched doorway that opened onto the whiteness of *Yura'shaana*. At this very moment, Erinda was probably emerging from her door, crossing the endless floor of the nexus, looking up at the lake…

She felt the Division as soon as she began to cross it. All around her, the current splintered into what felt like millions of tiny mirrored shards. They flayed into her eagerly. Bits of her spirit shredded away in ribbons, devoured by the wall's insatiable appetite for destruction. Hatred, the Goddess had said it was. Fear. Anger. The pain was terrible, and she understood what Ithyris meant. The Division wanted to tear her apart.

With every piece the wall took from her, she weakened. The current became thicker, more viscous, and she had to push that much harder. Everything hurt, yet even the pain in all its magnitude could not outstrip her grief. It kept her clawing forward with single-minded will.

Funny, she had never been very strong-willed. Kade had spent her entire life trying to make others happy: her parents, the other priestesses, the Honored Mother, the Goddess. Somehow, she'd gotten it into her head that anything she wanted for herself must be wickedness. If what made her happy differed from what was expected of her, was it not her duty to give it up? But when she had been too timid to stand at Erinda's side and fight for their love, Erinda had not stopped her from leaving. Fierce and fearless, Erinda had suffered on alone for seven winters rather than let their love go.

If Kade did not go on, she would lose Erinda forever. So let the Division destroy her, if it could. This time she would not be meek. She would not be gentle. The nexus was just a few paces away now, and this time, Kade was going to fight like she should have winters ago. If there was nothing left of her by the time she reached the other side, so be it. She would die here or in Erinda's arms, but either way, she would see this through.

The instant she breached the other side, a silver flood engulfed her. Power surged through the current's straining veins, and she was swept at once from the barbed clutches of the Division into the dazzling brightness of the spirit nexus. Kade lay gasping on the pristine floor. She couldn't be sure, but it felt like parts of her were missing. An arm, or a leg maybe. The Division had torn away too much, and it was irreversible. She would never be whole again. Blood began to puddle beneath her, glistening crimson against the white floor. Kade could not help but remember the vision, all those moons ago, of her blood dripping from the Goddess's fingers. This wasn't quite how she had imagined it would turn out, but it seemed fitting that it would end like this, dying in a pool of her own blood after failing spectacularly at the one thing the Goddess had charged her with. Holy warrior, indeed.

But after a moment, it occurred to her that she didn't have a body here, or blood either. Injured as she was, it was easier than usual to embrace the idea. As some clarity cut through the blinding pain, the puddles beneath her vanished. She remembered why she had come.

She found Erinda, rising overhead, already caught in the lake's tow. Kade didn't bother rolling over or standing up. She just thought about being beside her, and the next moment she was. With a deep sigh, she twined the rags of her spirit around Erinda and held on. The lake drew them both inside.

"Kade…is that you?"

"I'm here, Rin."

"You came for me?"

"I told you. I'm never leaving you again."

"You're hurt." Erinda touched her, and shreds of Kade's spirit drifted away into the lake. "Oh, my darling, you're really hurt!"

The water closed around them, prickling in welcome. Kade couldn't summon the energy to resist it. "I'm sorry. I'm not strong enough to get you out of here, not anymore."

"Oh, Kade, you shouldn't have done this. You shouldn't have come. Ithyria needs you."

The lake tingled, drawing them deeper. Curious shadows drifted near, then darted off into the murky depths. So much of her was gone already, and Kade felt herself dissolving much faster this time. Erinda was softening, too, even as Kade kept hold of her. "I need you more."

Soon the lake would take them apart. They would return to the infinite state of oneness they'd been drawn from at birth, and nothing would ever separate them again. She might have lost the chance to share a life with Erinda, but at the very least she could die with her. That was something.

Kade noted that a few of the flitting shadows had begun to form a ring around them. Most were as tall as she was, and of decidedly human shape. One, two, three, four, five…

"You do not belong here, *Ostryn*." The figure directly in front of her darkened and pulsed with each word.

"Who are you?" Erinda demanded.

A second shadow pulsed. "We were once Twelve."

Another added, "Now we are all, just as you were once and one day shall be again."

"But today is not that day," said a fourth, with a deeper voice. "You must return, Kadrian."

Kade pulled Erinda closer. "I won't leave her. I may have failed at everything else, but I won't in this."

"What makes you think you have failed?"

"If you really are the Twelve then you know already. Ulrike has Mondera's prophecy. After all the work you put into hiding it away, I handed it over to Him. And," Kade mustered some defiance in spite of her exhaustion, "I'd do it again."

A chorus of laughter swept through the throbbing shadows. One of them moved forward, and its voice was deliciously textured, like gravel and honey. "But of course you would, *Ostryn*, and that is exactly as it should be. You have not failed. You have done everything just as I saw that you would."

Kade tried to focus on the undulating shape. "Mondera?"

"Why do you think I went to all the trouble to write down what I saw? To hide it away with such care?"

"And genius!" This bright interjection came from the other side of the circle.

"Don't you see? The prophecy was never meant for Ithyrian ears. It was meant for Ulrike all along. And because He believes He's stolen the knowledge from us, He's certain to follow the thread we've spun for Him. As for your part, you have played it perfectly. But this is not yet finished. Do you not know what you have done?"

Another interrupted. "You brought Ithyris's pure spirit through the Division, *Ostryn* Kadrian. Even we were unable to accomplish such a thing."

"Without your flesh it should not have been possible," added someone else.

"Indeed," Mondera said, "it would not have been possible, but for your gift."

"My gift?" Kade repeated weakly.

"When the Goddess calls a *shaa'din*, Her spirit enhances their natural talents. In my case, precognition."

"And in my case, brilliant intellect," the bright voice piped in.

The deep-voiced shadow muttered, "But unfortunately not humility, hm, Marin?"

Tired as she was, Kade still almost chuckled. Myka and Marin were most definitely kindred spirits.

Marin gave an audible huff. "The point is, *Ostryn* Kadrian's gift is more powerful than any of ours."

"I don't care how powerful it is," Erinda interjected. "Look at her. She's been torn to pieces! She doesn't have anything left for any of you. Why can't you just leave her alone?"

"Peace, child." This speaker was calm, yet her words were delivered with resounding authority. "What we are trying to say is that Kadrian's gift is *you*."

Both Kade and Erinda exclaimed in unison. "What?"

Mondera's voice came again. "It's difficult to explain. Handmaidens are the only mortals who can visit *Yura'shaana* while their flesh still lives. Ithyris's spirit creates a foothold in both places, a path along which the *shaa'din*'s spirit may travel. The Goddess's spirit can only cross the Division if it is contained within flesh, which is why a Handmaiden can bring only a small part of Her into Dangar. But when Kadrian followed you here from within Dangar, she had to bring the spirit of the Goddess across the Division without the protection of her flesh. She should have been destroyed."

"Except that she loves you. And just as importantly, you love her."

"Love is the lifeblood of spirit. It is stronger than hate, stronger than fear."

"Kadrian's love created a path through the Division, even when the Goddess could not."

"Love is her gift. Love protected her."

"You protected her."

"And you can heal her again."

"You must, for her work is not yet done."

The voices melded into and over one another and the shadows blinked in dizzying succession. Kade was too far gone to make sense of what they were saying. She was scarcely more than a shadow herself now, and her hold on Erinda was slipping.

Erinda seemed to feel it too, and she asked frantically, "How?"

"We will help you."

The shadows closed in, and they were pushed downward through the prickling lake. The shadows swirled and blackened, and more of them appeared. Kade felt them pressing into her.

Gradually, she realized she felt firmer, as though the lake's dissolution was operating in reverse. She congealed slowly, felt the bits of her spirit that had drifted into the lake returning a little at a time. Still, there was so much of her that had been lost to the Division. Even if the lake returned everything that it had taken, she would be just a sliver of herself.

"It's not enough," she heard one of the shadows say. "Lady, we cannot do it alone."

After a moment, a tiny silver bubble floated up through the darkness and merged with her. Strange—it was a different pattern, something definitely not hers. Yet it adapted, shifted in rhythm and shape until it was indistinguishable from the rest of her. Another bubble came, and then another, until she was surrounded. A thousand drops of spirit, each unique and not one her own, packed into the missing places. Each adapted to her as it converged. *Yura'shaana* was re-creating her from itself.

Erinda, too, felt more solid against her. As Kade's senses sharpened, she could hear Erinda's voice guiding the others, recalling Kade's features in perfect detail. A gaping space on her right side was restored. Shreds were smoothed down, fused together, made whole. As she was reconstructed, her mind began to translate the sensations into bodily awareness, which was a more comfortable way to perceive herself, even if she didn't really have a body here. New weight hung from her hip and shoulder, and she felt it sculpted into familiar shapes. After a moment, she could wiggle fingers and toes—figuratively, anyway—that had not been there before. Erinda even directed a small constellation of freckles to reappear where they had been on her left forearm, and the shadows complied without argument.

Kade's feet emerged from the lake, then her legs and torso. She drifted down until she was standing sure-footed on the floor of the nexus, with Erinda tucked safely in her arms. Where moments ago she had felt like a mere tenuous fragment of herself, she now felt whole like never before.

What was more, Ithyris was beside them.

"Lady," Kade breathed. The Goddess was beautiful as ever, though Her face was drawn. If Kade hadn't known better she would have said Ithyris looked tired.

When Erinda caught sight of the Goddess, she erupted in a startled curse. Kade half expected the walls and floor of the nexus to crack wide at such irreverence, but Ithyris only tilted back Her head and laughed.

"Oh, Erinda, I am so pleased to finally meet you."

Kade felt Erinda's fingers dig into her shoulders. "What do You want?"

"You do not need to fear me, Child. I will not take Kadrian against your will."

"You already have," Erinda said, her voice catching. Kade tightened her arms around her in reassurance.

"I have borrowed her for a time, yes. And well do I know the sacrifice it has required. But it is because Kadrian's heart belongs so completely to you that she was able to do what no one else could. Thanks to you, Kadrian has pierced the wall that keeps me from my brother's lands. Now, if you will permit it, she can return and finish the task she has always been meant for. The love between you will bring my power to Rok Garshluk. Kadrian can bring Ulrike's temple, and His *shaa'din,* down."

Kade interrupted before Erinda had the chance to answer. "No."

The Goddess turned the liquid light of Her gaze on Kade. Kade could scarcely believe her own nerve. She would never have thought she could deny Her anything, but in this she could not concede. "I'm sorry, Lady, but I won't leave Rin again."

"Once you've returned Erinda's flesh to Ithyria, Beloved, I will be able to send her spirit to you. You have my word."

"It's too dangerous. Her body might not last that long."

"Wait." Erinda squeezed Kade's shoulders gently, then turned to study the Goddess. "If Kade returns now, You can protect her?"

Ithyris inclined her head. "If you remain with me, love will connect you to Kadrian across the Division. You can give her full access to my power, even within Dangar."

A look of determination, one Kade was well acquainted with, filled Erinda's eyes. "And You'll see to it that she stops Mardyth?"

The Goddess nodded again.

"Rin, no," Kade protested. "It's not worth—"

Erinda laid a finger to her lips, then rose on tiptoe and kissed her. Even in the nexus, without their physical forms, Erinda's kiss was everything Kade remembered. Soft. Redolent with fire and promise. It set her trembling.

"A long time ago," Erinda murmured against her mouth, "you told me you were born for this. You were right." She drew away. "Go, my darling. Save the world, so there will be a place for us together in it."

"But I—"

"Go." Erinda gave her a gentle shove, and Kade tumbled backward into her glowing doorway. The Division snapped her up with razored teeth, but she barely felt it. All she could see was Erinda, silhouetted at the Goddess's side, watching her go with adoration and pride in her face.

Such breathtaking love welled up in Kade that it coated her being like perfumed oil. In a sweet, silvery rush, she slid through the Division without so much as a scratch.

CHAPTER TWENTY

*T*he fifth day of Fifthmoon had never been a remarkable date for the Ithyrian people. The day brought no holidays or feasts, commemorated no historical events. But on this fifth of the Fifth, the Daughters of Ithyris would experience something that had never happened before, and may well never happen again. Those of us who were present for it will certainly never forget that day for as long as we live.

Some of us were working in the kitchens, peeling potatoes for the evening meal. Some were sitting with groups of Pledged, guiding afternoon meditation. Still more were scrubbing floors, mediating disputes among local villagers, pulling weeds in the gardens, mending robes, blessing childbirth, or fetching water. All across the kingdom, priestesses in every temple, in every province, were tending to daily chores of service and worship. I myself was perched on a ladder in the basement of Verdred Temple's library, looking for a text that had been requested by one of the elder priestesses, when Ithyris spoke.

"Help her, my Daughters."

We all heard Her at once, the old and the young, those who had encountered Her voice before and those who had not. And we listened—how could we not? For She was showing to us the broken and tattered spirit of one of our sisters.

I recognized her. I think perhaps we all did, even those who had never met the Handmaiden. We did not know what had happened to her, or how she had been brought to such a state. But we gave what Ithyris asked without hesitation. From across the distance, we joined together, a thousand priestesses from every corner of Her lands, from the western desert to the eastern Outlands. From each of us She took a small piece, no more than a drop, and we watched as She used those *tiny flecks of our spirits to heal our sister. We felt the Handmaiden's regeneration echo within each of us.*

It could not last, of course. Each of us was returned to our work within a breath, as suddenly as we had been taken from it. For my part, it was such a startling transition that I lost my footing on the library ladder and had to clutch at the rungs to keep from a fall. There had never been record of something like this. We could not imagine what it must have cost Her, to bring us together in such a way.

But that, dear readers, is the reason why every fifth of the Fifth thereafter, the Daughters of Ithyris in every part of the kingdom have paused in their work and joined hands. We remember the day when our Divine Lady worked a miracle, and brought us together to save one of our own.

When Kade's eyes snapped open, her cheeks were wet and cold with tears. Erinda's body lay in her lap, and she reached down to touch her face in wonder. The real Erinda was still in *Yura'shaana*, on the other side of the Division. Yet Kade could feel her there. Longing, sharp and bright, was strung between them like a wire, and even the blight of the Division could not sever it. Ithyris's spirit flowed surely along that connection, and Kade was drenched with silver and light.

She heard Mardyth speak to one of the priests. "You."

His head came up, face obscured by the yellow hood of his robe. She tossed her weapon to him.

"Kill her."

He caught the sword, and after a moment's hesitation, took several steps toward Kade. Fisting the hilt with both hands, he raised the weapon over his head. Kade raised an arm, feeling the spirit current surge to her fingers. Then she glimpsed the face hidden beneath the hood, and drew up short.

It was Myka, winking down at her. Kade gasped and Myka spun, plunging the blade into Mardyth's shoulder instead.

An indignant cry went up from the other priests, who immediately surrounded the traitor. But their assistance was unnecessary, since Mardyth gestured at Myka and she went stiff, like a statue, while Mardyth examined her injury.

The blade had gone all the way through. It was protruding from her back, forcing her shoulder blade into an awkward angle, but she didn't seem to be in pain. She looked between Kade and Myka. "What sort of magic is this?" she asked as she pulled the sword out. A gush of blood followed, but did not last long.

Kade just twitched her lips to the side in amusement. Mardyth narrowed her eyes. "You have no power here." She stalked over to Myka and yanked her hood back.

"You will tell me what—" she broke off as red-gold hair fanned from the yellow hood. She seemed genuinely startled to find a teenaged girl beneath, glowering at her.

"No magic, you horrible cow. Just a good old-fashioned sword through the heart!"

Mardyth eyed Myka with no small measure of mirth. "Well, my dear, I'm afraid you need a great deal more practice, if that was your intent. You missed my heart entirely."

"Hah! That's if you even have one. If the sword had been longer I would have gone for your head."

"You are one of the Goddess's recruits, yes? I assume you serve the Handmaiden, then. What's your name?"

"I'm Myka. And I serve no one."

"A shame, young Myka, that Ithyrians find their women of no better use than in their kitchens and temples. In another time and place, perhaps, you would have made a fine warrior." She beckoned to the priests, and they raised their blades. Myka did not so much as flinch as they came down, but her eyes looked to Kade as if to say, *what now?*

The exchange was no longer humorous, and Myka was in trouble. Kade flung out her arms with a roar. Torrents of blue fire streaked from her hands, swallowing the priests surrounding Myka. They disappeared, their knives and swords clattering to the floor. Kade rose, gently transferring Erinda's body out of her lap. When another group of priests charged, she dispatched them just as quickly. Facing Mardyth, she brought her palms up. Torrents of celestial fire licked at her fingers. All around them, the priests began to yell and run for the cathedral doors.

Mardyth took a step back. "That's…that's not possible. Ithyris can't reach you here!"

"Looks like She can now!" Myka exulted.

"The staff, Mardyth. I want it back." When Mardyth tightened her grip on it, Kade thrust one of her palms out. Spirit whisked down her arm and burst from her hand, clubbing Mardyth's wrist. She let go, and before the staff could hit the ground Myka had snatched it up.

Mardyth flailed in the direction of the doors, and every one of the fleeing priests stopped in his tracks. They turned, unnaturally, and marched back toward her. Mardyth positioned herself behind them. "I don't know how you've done this, but it doesn't matter. You'll never get out of here alive, Handmaiden. This is Ulrike's temple."

"So it is." Kade thrust out a palm again, but this time the energy was directed at one of the giant pillars that supported the ceiling. *Shaa'ri* smashed into it with the force of a lightning bolt, and the pillar crumbled with a sound like thunderclaps. Kade repeated the motion again, and again. One by one, the enormous columns disintegrated into gravel.

Mardyth sent a few of the priests running forward, and Kade sliced a hand toward them. Every one collapsed to their knees, their heads rolling across the floor. Mardyth followed up with a second group, and these, too, lost their heads. Kade continued alternately smashing pillars and warding off the unwilling priests until above them the cathedral ceiling began to groan and quake.

Myka was busy whipping the staff into every yellow robe within range. She bludgeoned her way through the line of priests until she reached Kade's side.

"Here," she said, pressing the staff into Kade's hand. Large chunks of the cavern ceiling crashed around them. "What do we do now?"

"Take Erinda," Kade ordered. "Get her out of here."

"But Your Grace, she's—"

Kade swung a hand, and blasted a falling rock before it could crush Erinda's body. It rained in powder over Erinda's face and clothes. "Now, Myka!"

Myka stopped arguing and hefted Erinda over one shoulder. Kade poured spirit into the staff. It drew from her eagerly, but now there was an endless spring to replenish it.

Ithyris had been right. Kade was acutely aware of Erinda's spirit in the nexus. As the Goddess's current rushed beneath her skin, Kade realized that Erinda was there too, an earthy undertone to Ithyris's delicate shimmer. Her lungs filled and her heart swelled. Love and spirit burst from her skin, until Kade was shining in Ulrike's cavernous cathedral like a ferocious star.

She waved the staff, and the remaining priests went up in flames. Mardyth dodged a falling rock and gaped at Kade in terror.

"How are you doing this?"

"Rin was all I wanted. You could have let us walk away, and we would have left you in peace. But you took her from me." Kade raised the staff, and it hummed with anticipation. "I want her back."

Cerulean flames shot from Cibli's stone. They struck Mardyth's swollen belly and she screamed, dropping to her knees and curling over her stomach as she had on the Agar battlefield. Kade looked up at the crumbling ceiling. The staff quivered, and she understood. She let it go.

The staff shot upward like a silver arrow. Somewhere far overhead, it collided with the rock in a deafening explosion. Kade threw an arm over her eyes as light seared through the cathedral.

Erinda's voice sounded in her head. "Run, my darling. Run!"

Kade ran. She dove through the cathedral doors just before they crumbled into debris behind her. She tore down the corridor, the tunnel collapsing on her heels as she went. Pebbles stung her back. Once or twice, a larger rock bounced away from her at an improbable angle, and Kade was dimly aware of a faint blue haze surrounding her, like a protective shield. She burst from the temple entrance in a flying leap, stumbled as she hit the ground, and staggered a few more paces.

Someone grabbed the back of her tunic and hauled her upward, until she was dangling across horse-scented haunches. She looked up to see Erinda's limp form draped just as haphazardly over the back of the gray palfrey. In front of her, Myka kicked the horse into motion, keeping tight hold of the palfrey's reins.

This was hardly a dignified escape, but while they galloped away, Kade was able to watch as the eight mighty columns of Rok Garshluk toppled to the canyon floor.

❖

They stopped only once so that Kade could mount her horse properly, with Erinda's body tucked against her. Myka resumed her place on the palfrey, and together they navigated the steep, winding curves of the mountain road that would lead them home.

They rode mostly in silence, Kade preoccupied by a strange dichotomy of sensation. Erinda's weight lay lifeless against her, but at the same time a warm thread of Erinda's spirit still coursed under her skin, pulsing with a different cadence than the Goddess's silvery veins. The feeling was sweetly intimate. Under other circumstances, Kade might have gloried in it, but right now she was too anxious.

The Goddess had promised to send Erinda back once Kade had returned her body to Ithyria. But they were hours from the border, and league after league, Erinda's skin grew colder, her limbs heavy and stiff. The color in her cheeks and lips faded. Fearfully, Kade kept glancing down and muttering prayers under her breath. *Stay with me. I'll get you there, just stay with me. Please, Lady...*

What if they didn't make it to the border in time? What if Erinda's body was uninhabitable by the time the Goddess could send her spirit back? Or, what if Erinda did come back, but her body suffered permanent damage? What if she had to spend the rest of her life unable to walk, or speak? These thoughts created such a knot of panic in Kade's throat that she could barely breathe.

She switched the horse's reins to one hand and pressed the other to Erinda's chest. The spirit current, both Ithyris's and Erinda's, funneled from her palm into Erinda's body. She couldn't tell if it made a difference. The color did not return to Erinda's face, and her body continued to stiffen. But Kade kept channeling, because it was the only thing she could think of to do. Maybe if she could keep even a little spirit running through Erinda's body, it would help.

To the west, the sun had reached the horizon. The tips of the mountains captured it gently, gilding themselves in its fire, until the sky was striated with pink and orange. Kade pressed her horse faster, tears burning behind her eyelids. They had to get back in time. After everything that they had lost, all the winters they had spent apart, Kade could not see how she could go on living if Erinda could not come back.

Darkness fell. The night birds began to call to one another from the treetops. Crickets chirruped in the underbrush, and the air grew cooler. Ahead, the Ithyrian border tower loomed like a vast sentinel above the cliff face. Kade urged her horse faster, and Myka wisely did not say a word as she kept up.

Kade crossed the Division like a drowning woman spluttering to the surface. On the other side, her senses expanded, as if she were taking a full breath for the first time in days. Her connection to Erinda's spirit flared and shortened, and Kade reined her horse to a stop, clutching Erinda to her chest.

"We're here, Rin. We're safe. Come back to me."

Myka pulled up next to her and regarded her sadly. "Your Grace, Erinda is gone. You know she's gone."

Kade pressed a kiss to Erinda's forehead. "I can feel her. I've felt her every moment since I came back from *Yura'shaana*. She's the one who helped me channel the Goddess's power across the Division. Ithyris said She'd send her back once we got back to Ithyria. You promised," she reminded the Goddess, closing her eyes. "Please, Lady. You promised."

Now that the spirit current was no longer directly tied to her connection with Erinda, Kade was able to decipher them separately. The silver veins thrummed back to life beneath her skin, and Erinda's unique, primal vibration grew stronger. That, at least, was reassuring. But it was dark, and the mountain air had taken on a chill, which was sure to sharpen as the night went on. This was no place for Erinda to wake up.

"We have to get her inside, lay her down somewhere. Come on."

They rode for the border tower. The cylindrical turret soared high above their heads, but widened into a rectangular structure at its base. When they drew close, they could see that the iron grate guarding the entrance had been left ajar. Whoever had been stationed here had departed carelessly.

Inside, the air was damp and only slightly warmer. Everything was dark, save for the rectangle of moonlight that fell through an unshuttered window. The horses headed for several bales of hay stacked in a corner. Myka dismounted, and Kade lowered Erinda's rigid body into Myka's arms. She dropped from the horse herself, and Myka gestured toward the stone steps that led to the next level.

"Let's get you someplace to rest. Then I'll find some kindling and start a fire."

In the gloom of the tower's interior, Kade could just make out that the next level of the structure was set up as a kitchen. Deep shadows indicated a large hearth on each end, and a heavy table set down the middle. Barrels, boxes, and the pale outlines of canvas sacks lined the walls. She heard the squeak and scurry of mice as they continued up to the next floor.

Here the stone steps ended, and a set of wooden stairs spiraled around the wall, up through an opening in the floorboards of the level above. This room had more windows, long and narrow and set high in the wall, which probably served as slits for archers in times of battle. There was a hearth here too, but more important to Kade was the row of rough-hewn bunks, stacked military style with nailed planks serving as ladders to the upper beds. The flimsy straw mattresses were moth-eaten and appeared to have been unoccupied for quite some time. Kade selected the one that looked cleanest, and Myka helped her ease Erinda onto it. The task was difficult, as Erinda's body had grown stiff and she had to be laid on her side.

Kade knelt beside her and folded one of Erinda's rigid hands into hers. She scarcely noticed when Myka went back down the stairs, all her attention on Erinda's ashen face. She closed her eyes, her lips moving in silent prayer, and felt for the warmth of Erinda's spirit running alongside the Goddess's. She gripped Erinda's hand, trying desperately to will that current back into her inanimate body.

*Come back to me, Rin. Come back. You promised, Lady...*She prayed to them both at once, and interchangeably, prodding the different currents with agitation. She didn't care which answered, so long as at least one of them did.

Something passed through her. Where the Goddess's spirit-veins were usually cool and tingling, they abruptly filled with fire. Her insides felt incandescent, and heat shot through her shoulders and arms and seared from her palms. There was no discomfort, but when it was over she was left with a disturbing sense of emptiness. The Goddess's current was now the only one she could feel. Erinda's was gone.

Kade whimpered in terror. "Oh, Rin, where are you?"

"Here." Against the dingy mattress, Erinda shifted. She couldn't seem to open her eyes, and she appeared to have trouble moving her lips and tongue. But her head turned very slightly toward Kade's voice. "I'm here, Kade."

Kade groaned in relief, tears scorching her cheeks. "Oh, thank Ithyris. How are you feeling? Are you all right? Can you move?" Erinda's fingertips twitched against her palm, and she gave a pained whimper. "No, wait, don't try. Save your strength." She pressed her lips to Erinda's hand, then to her forehead. "Just rest, all right? You're back. That's all that matters."

By the time Myka returned, Kade had stretched out next to Erinda on the cot. Her arms were wrapped around Erinda, emanating a soft blue glow in the darkness.

She heard Myka ask uncertainly, "Your Grace?"

"She's back, Myka. Ithyris gave her back."

"Wow!" Myka bounded over, the candle in her hand casting shadows over her features. She leaned over, nearly singeing the ends of her hair in the flame as she held a finger beneath Erinda's nose. "She's breathing! You really did it! You've brought two people back from the dead. You are the best *shaa'din* ever."

Kade chuckled softly. "I didn't do much. But, Myka?"

"Yeah?"

"Do you think you could get her some water?"

Myka pounded down the stairs and returned, panting, with a water skin in hand. She helped Kade roll Erinda onto her back, and tilted her head in order to help her swallow. Kade tried to be gentle, but Erinda's hips and knees remained contorted at unyielding angles. Her tiny mewls of suffering broke Kade's heart.

"What's wrong with her? Why's she still so crooked?"

"Her spirit's been gone a long time. I'm going to help her. Can you start a fire?"

"Sure."

"And keep the water coming." Carefully, Kade settled Erinda back onto her side. She put one hand on Erinda's hip and the other on her knee, and the blue glow resumed beneath her fingers. Erinda was breathing shallowly, as if her chest refused to expand enough for her to fill her lungs. Kade drew heavily from the Goddess's current, trying to bathe Erinda in its comfort. Spirit couldn't heal flesh, but it could desensitize pain and maybe induce relaxation. Kade was prepared to use everything it took, for as long as she had to. No matter what happened from this point on, she would never give up on Erinda again.

CHAPTER TWENTY-ONE

A soft scraping sound pulled Erinda from sleep. When she opened her eyes, Myka was brushing cinders back into the hearth. She added another piece of wood to the fire and prodded it into position with an iron poker. Erinda's nose twitched at the scent of woodsmoke.

Myka propped the poker against the wall and picked up a satchel at her feet. She had her tall boots on over her dirty white leggings, and a traveling cloak slung over her shoulders. Erinda raised her head, wincing as her neck and shoulder rebelled.

"Are you going somewhere?"

Myka looked up and pressed a finger to her mouth, nodding over Erinda's shoulder. Erinda turned to see Kade stretched out alongside her. Weary lines etched Kade's face. Her lower lip was split, and one of her eyes was blackened and swollen, but her breath was even and deep.

Gingerly, Erinda slipped out from under Kade's arm, which was resting across her ribs. When she stood up, her exhausted joints nearly buckled. She swayed on her feet, and might have collapsed back onto the bed again, but Myka darted over and caught her.

"You all right?" Myka whispered.

Erinda took a moment to steady herself. Her muscles were weak and sore, but if she focused through the pain, she was able to manage them. She nodded and glanced back at Kade, who looked battered and fragile on the dilapidated mattress.

"She's been working on you all night," Myka explained, keeping her voice hushed. "I woke at dawn and she was only just falling asleep."

Erinda gave her a quizzical look, then spied the stairs and pointed. She held on to Myka's arm for support as they descended to a lower level, where they would be able to talk without disturbing Kade. They entered a large room, which appeared to be a kitchen. Another fire crackled at one end, and a row of dead rabbits was lined up on the table. Myka helped Erinda to a seat on one of the benches, then dropped her satchel on a nearby barrel and started rummaging through it.

Erinda stretched her legs out, flexing them and hissing against the discomfort. Her entire body ached as if she'd been beaten, but everything appeared to move all right.

"What do you mean, Kade was working on me all night?"

"She was doing that glowing hand thing. Mostly on your legs and arms, trying to get them to move. You were dead a long time. You knew that, right? And I guess dead people don't move so well after a while. So you came back, but the Handmaiden was worried you might be, you know…stuck." From the depths of the satchel, Myka produced a ball of twine, and she made a satisfied noise.

"I…" Erinda straightened her elbows, then bent them and rotated her wrists. The movements were stiff and perhaps a little creaky, but everything seemed to bend like it was supposed to. "I don't feel stuck."

Myka busied herself with the nearest rabbit, wrapping the twine around its hind legs. "That's good. She'll be glad. 'Course I didn't get stuck either, after she brought me back, but I wasn't dead as long as you."

"What are you doing?" Erinda asked as Myka climbed atop the table.

Myka grunted as she tossed the ball of twine over one of the rafters, then hoisted the rabbit in the air. "I figure the two of you ought to stay here a few more days. You just came back from the dead, and the Handmaiden looks like she's been through a barbarian gauntlet— which is, you know, pretty much the truth of it. Now that Mardyth's dead and her army is back in Dangar, this place should be safe enough. So I did a little hunting this morning," she finished tying off the rabbit, using a knife to cut the twine, "and it turns out there's a well in the cellar and a creek about a half-league west. Also enough grain to keep a horse happy for a good while." She sat on the edge of the table and picked up the next rabbit to repeat the process.

"But you're not staying?"

"I think someone had better get back to Mondera Temple to let everyone know how things turned out. Especially the captain. Broken ankle or not, I bet if he doesn't get some news soon he'll be on a horse headed for Dangar."

"Talon's injured?" Erinda asked. The last time she'd seen her, Talon had been in bad shape, but it had to be something serious if it had prevented her from joining Kade on her rescue mission.

"Yeah, the healer wouldn't let him leave the temple. Said he'd be fine, but only if he stayed off his leg for a while. He was pretty cranky about it." Myka tied off the second rabbit. When she reached for the third, Erinda picked it up and beckoned for the ball of twine. She tied the legs and handed it up to Myka.

"I think you're right. The temple needs to know what happened. All those people can go back to their homes now, the refugees from Agar, the soldiers. Can you give Talon a message for me?"

"Sure."

"Tell him that I said 'go home.'"

Myka grinned. "Will do." She finished with the rabbits and hopped down from the table, wiping her hands on her tunic. "I think that's everything. You both should be set for the next few days. So, hey, in case I don't see you for a while..." She bent and hugged Erinda around the shoulders. "Tell the Handmaiden I said thanks for everything. This has been every bit the adventure I was hoping for."

"You're not going to say good-bye yourself?"

"Nah. She needs her sleep. And anyway, I'm sure we'll run into each other again." Myka swung the satchel over her shoulder and headed for the stairs. At the first step, she lifted a hand and Erinda waved back. She heard her tromp down the steps, and a faint whinny below.

Carefully, she stood from the bench and stretched her tired body again. Climbing the stairs was difficult, and she made her way back up slowly, using her hands as much as her feet until she'd returned to the room where Kade lay sleeping. Getting a better look at the state of the mattress, she made a face. Recuperating or not, the first thing she was going to do once she had a little more strength was to wash and mend the bedding. But for now...

There were three other sets of bunks to choose from, but she lay back down next to Kade anyway. Kade's golden lashes fluttered. "Rin?"

"Shh, my darling. I'm here. Sleep." Erinda hesitated for a moment, then kissed the uninjured side of Kade's mouth softly. Kade wrapped an arm around her, and slid one leg between Erinda's, so that they were cuddled together as closely as when they were girls. A contented sigh escaped Kade's lips, and Erinda closed her eyes.

This wouldn't be hers forever. She had made peace with that. Kade might love her, but she belonged to the Goddess. And after having met Ithyris, Erinda couldn't bring herself to begrudge that anymore. Ithyris loved Kade as deeply as Erinda did. She was beautiful, powerful, and perfect. Eventually, Kade would return to Her.

But in the meantime, Erinda was going to make the most of every precious moment.

❖

Kade pressed her hands into the small of her back and stretched, eyeing the late afternoon sun. The day had been oppressively hot, and she was looking forward to the twilight that was fast approaching. Erinda had gone to bathe in the creek, but she would be returning soon, and Kade wanted to be sure she was ready. She turned to survey her work.

A blanket was laid out over the plaster of the border tower's roof, and spread with the makings of their dinner. She had sliced the last of their cheese and arranged it around a pile of dandelion greens and wild onions. This was flanked by a small dish filled with mulberries and another of pine nuts. Down in the kitchens, a stew of rabbit, lentils, and leeks simmered over the fire, and even from the rooftop, its perfume made Kade's mouth water. She went to her basket to retrieve a dusty bottle of wine that she had found tucked away in a corner of the tower's cellar. She used her sleeve to polish away the dirt, and set the bottle alongside the other foods.

The past half-moon had gone by like a strange dream. Exhaustion had rendered them both quiet and thoughtful. They had slept, mostly, and talked little other than to coordinate meals and other necessities. But they had also remained constantly within arm's reach of each other, especially those first few days. Kade felt an uncontrollable impulse to maintain physical contact, even if it was just to sit close enough to Erinda that their shoulders brushed, or extend her foot far enough to rest her toes on Erinda's feet. It wasn't so much about possessiveness as it was connection…the reassurance that Erinda was there, that Erinda knew she was there, in the aftermath of something so enormous it couldn't be processed in words. They had died. They had both died, and now they were back, and there was no way to be sure of it except through touch. She felt silly for being so needy, but at least she was not the only one—Erinda seemed to seek out the gratuitous contact as often as she did.

But as the days passed, Erinda's bruises had faded, and the swelling in Kade's eye had gone down until only a greenish yellow stain remained above her cheek. The stitches Erinda had used on the cut across her ribs had begun to itch and pull, and Erinda had promised to remove them for her tonight. They were both healing well, but their provisions were starting to run low. That morning they had agreed that tonight would be their last in this place. Yet Kade still had not found the right moment to tell Erinda that she was leaving the temple.

Over the past few days she had tried, dozens of times, to bring it up. But the timing had never been quite right. And if she were honest with herself, she was a little afraid. What if, once they returned to the palace and Erinda was reunited with her friends, there was no place for Kade in her life? Erinda had already suffered so much because of her. Kade no longer cared what anyone else thought, but would Erinda be able to withstand the ostracism that was sure to come if she took Kade as her lover? Was it even fair to ask it of her?

"You deserve a better life," Kade insisted, even as her vision blurred with tears. She fumbled with the sash of her Pledged robes, which were rumpled after spending the night on the floor. "You deserve someone who can take care of you, provide for you, someone you can love in the open without fear. I can't give that to you." Her voice broke. "After a while, you'd start to hate me."

Erinda sat up in the bed, shaking her head. Her curls bounced around her freckled shoulders. "I wouldn't!"

"You would, and I won't let it come to that. I love you too much to keep you, Rin." Her fingers were trembling so hard she couldn't get the sash tied. The high priestess was probably already waiting for her at the temple.

They were out of time. No matter what impossible fantasy Erinda was clinging to, the idea that they might hop on a horse and ride away together was preposterous. Kade was becoming a priestess today. All she had wanted was to hold Erinda close one last time, to be with her fully and completely in the hours before they said good-bye. But she had never imagined how much harder this would be, after what they had shared last night. This was supposed to be the most momentous, joyful day of her life, and her heart was so heavy she could barely remain on her feet. The grief in Erinda's eyes was unbearable. She never should have allowed things to get so out of control. She needed Erinda so badly, but this was too cruel.

Gently, Erinda moved Kade's shaking hands aside. With slow, deliberate movements, she formed the sash into a neat bow. But her voice was nowhere near as steady. "That's it, then? You've made your decision?"

Kade closed her eyes, tears flooding her cheeks. "I'm so sorry." Leaning forward, she pressed her lips to Erinda's forehead. She heard

Erinda's breath expel harshly, felt the warmth of it against her throat. When she tried to swallow, she ended up in a sob instead. She held the kiss as long as she dared.

"Be happy, Rin."

She turned and ran for the bedchamber door.

The sour knot in her stomach tightened as the high priestess beckoned her to face the assembled worshippers. Slowly, Kade turned, sinking to her knees on a prayer cushion. Behind her came the sound of liquid sloshing in a metal bowl, indicating the shaving implements were being prepared.

Kade searched the faces in the crowd. She spotted her mother and father, beaming at her behind the rows of priestesses. Her brother Jen was next to them, more absorbed in picking his nose than paying attention to the ceremony. When he caught her eye, he grinned and pretended to flick something at her. She cringed, and his grin widened.

Disgusted, she looked away. She didn't really think Erinda would come, not after last night. Especially not after the way she had left this morning. Maybe it was better this way. She was starting a new life, and from today on, she would have to get along without Erinda at her side. Still, the nauseous feeling in her stomach was getting worse.

"Pledged," she heard the high priestess say somewhat impatiently, and realized she had missed the cue to begin reciting her vows.

"*Y'kuranin sora...*" She stammered the first few syllables, then stopped. She had practiced the lines morning and night every day for an entire winter, but the ancient Ithyrian tongue had always given her trouble. Flustered, she started over.

"Y'kuranin sora vai meliaa

"Y'tiriena lo...lo..."

The high priestess sighed and murmured the next line. Kade repeated it, scarcely any louder, but the prompt didn't bring the rest of the words to mind. Panicked, Kade scanned the assembly. Some were starting to appear annoyed, or even amused by her predicament. Others looked back at her with pity. She felt her stomach turn over and knew she was about to be sick right there on the dais, in front of the entire palace temple.

Then a shadow moved at the back of the sanctuary, half-hidden behind a marble pillar. A pair of eyes arrested hers. Kade inhaled.

A sad smile played at Erinda's mouth, but she held Kade's gaze. After a moment, she gave a small nod. The knot in Kade's stomach dissolved.

"Y'kuranin sora vai meliaa
"Y'tiriena lo gulias
"Sherysta yi fuli inrusel, Shaa'Nalusa
"Lurenza y'rastablis sa mihaton..."

The vows flowed freely, as did the hundreds of emotions they exchanged silently across the space of the sanctuary, over the heads of the oblivious onlookers. *I'm sorry. I love you. Don't hate me. Don't forget me. Be happy. Please be happy.*

The high priestess laid a palm full of warm oil against Kade's scalp, and it ran down her temples and dripped over one ear. Then she felt the razor as it was drawn back from her hairline, and the feathery sensation as her hair fell in golden wisps to the floor. Kade closed her eyes and continued chanting. The razor was drawn back again and again, until her head was bare.

When Kade opened her eyes, Erinda was gone. Filmy white fabric was draped over her head, and then drawn over her face and pinned neatly at either side of her cheeks. She looked up to see the high priestess holding out a hand.

"Rise, *Ostryn*."

Beneath her new veils, Kade took a deep breath and accepted her hand.

Sighing, Kade pushed the memory away. If only she had known then how much that decision would cost. At the same time, she couldn't rightly say she regretted it—not when the result had saved the kingdom. She wondered if this was how the Twelve had felt after the Division, once Ithyria was safe in the hands of the Goddess and they had time to contemplate all the things they had lost: Fyn's eyesight, Tabin's face, Olsta's innocence. Yet in the end, every one of them had chosen to stay with Her.

She wouldn't. Not because she had lost any love for Her over the past few moons; if anything, her adoration of the Goddess had grown a hundredfold since she had become *shaa'din*. But Erinda deserved all of her, not just the portions that weren't dedicated to Ithyris. And while her love for Ithyris was deeply spiritual, her love for Erinda was an absolute that she could no longer deny.

Kade moved to the edge of the roof. The tower battlements were low, their tops reaching only to her abdomen, and the walls between rose just to mid-thigh. She leaned between them and looked out toward the creek, shading her eyes against the setting sun. There was no sign of Erinda yet.

Resting her hands on the stone, she eased down to her knees. If she lifted her arms too high, the stitches in her side pulled, so she settled for bending them at the elbows with her palms up. She tilted her head back, and the silver spirit current swept her away in an instant.

❖

The whiteness of the nexus surrounded her, shining doorways flashing on all sides, but the Goddess's surreal beauty was far more blinding.

"Hello, Kadrian."

Whenever She was this close, the spirit current became a symphony under Kade's non-existent skin, and she struggled to catch her breath. The Goddess hovered before her, smiling.

"Lady, I've come to ask…That is, You said that I could…"

How exactly did one make a request like this? Perhaps she should be standing instead. No sooner had the thought crossed her mind than she found herself on her feet. But being face-to-face with Ithyris was worse; Her luminous eyes stole the words from Kade's tongue. Kneeling was probably best after all, she decided, and in an instant, she was back to staring at Her feet in consternation.

The Goddess laughed. "Peace, Beloved. Say what you have come to say."

"Sweet Ithyris, please, I know I promised to serve You for a lifetime. I tried my best, but this isn't…I'm not…I don't think I can do this anymore. I know it's ungrateful, maybe it even makes me a coward…but I'm asking You to release me from my vows."

She heard the smallest of sighs and looked up anxiously, but there was only tenderness in Her expression. "Ah, Kadrian, I wish you could know how greatly your service has honored me. You have never been ungrateful, and most certainly you are not a coward. On the contrary, you have sacrificed so much for my sake that the debt I owe to you is more than I can ever repay."

To Kade's astonishment, She knelt until they were eye to eye again, and took Kade's hands. "You have already done me the service of a hundred lifetimes. Of course I will release you, if that is your desire."

Kade lowered her head. "I am truly sorry, Lady."

"What in the world for?"

"You waited for me for so long, and I'm leaving You alone again."

Ithyris squeezed her hands, a note of mirth in Her reply. "Oh, I will not be alone for long. You see, Kadrian, being with you has shown me how selfish I have been."

"Selfish, Lady?"

"For a thousand winters I have kept to myself in my grief. I was so determined never to harm another of my precious children as Olsta was harmed, and I failed to see how badly they needed me. When my people could no longer hear my voice, they turned to their scriptures and stories to reach me instead. Over the centuries, they've lost so much of what I wanted to give them, so much of what the Twelve had fought for. Also, I am certain my brother Ulrike has only just begun his assault on my lands. Now that you have created an opening in the Division, I must find a way to reach those on the other side who have been kept from me for so long, and I have no doubt that Ulrike will try to reach through to my side as well. So I have decided... You cannot be the last of my *shaa'din*."

"There will be another?"

"She is preparing for me now. I will go to her soon."

Kade wasn't quite sure how to feel about this announcement. Once, she might have been filled with jealousy. Though she hadn't really wanted to become *shaa'din*, had even feared it, in the past few moons she had been more intimately connected with Ithyris than she ever could have imagined. Yet she did not regret her decision, and if Ithyris created another Handmaiden, the kingdom would still have someone to look to for Her guidance and protection.

"Will I ever see You again?"

"Of course. When the time comes, your spirit will return to *Yura'shaana*."

"I mean before that."

Ithyris smiled. "That will depend on whether there is any room left for me in your heart, once you have settled in your new life. I hope so. But even if you cannot see me, I will be with you always. You are in my heart, Beloved, and that will never change."

Kade felt the pull of her Flesh from the other side. This was probably the last time she would ever be able to travel to the nexus at will, and her body was calling her back already. She braced herself against it as Ithyris bent to kiss her cheeks.

"Good-bye, Kadrian. Live well."

The Goddess released her hands and Kade was drawn back along the colorless floor, into the light that would take her home.

CHAPTER TWENTY-TWO

When Kade came to her senses, she was still kneeling on the plaster of the border tower's rooftop. She lurched forward and caught herself on her hands. It took a moment, as it always did after these journeys, to regain equilibrium. The spirit veins were pulsing hard after the surge, like the beat of her heart after a long run. But she felt Ithyris withdrawing, until the current slowed into a faint thrum. The result was similar to how it had been on the other side of the Division, cut off from Her spirit, with only the remnants of Her to draw from.

Ithyris had really let her go. Though she had asked for this, the quieting of the spirit veins brought a twinge of sadness. How long would the current last, now that She was no longer feeding their connection? A few days, perhaps? It would be strange, adjusting to Her absence after all this time.

She became aware that Erinda was standing behind her, a steaming iron pot at her feet. Her shorn curls were plastered wetly to her neck, and her shift, split skirts, and bodice looked damp. They had been laundered, though after their ordeal in Rok Garshluk, they were badly in need of mending.

"Rin…"

Erinda looked down, reaching for the pot handle. "I didn't mean to interrupt," she muttered. "Sorry."

Kade sprang up and helped her lug the heavy stew pot over to the blanket. "You didn't—it's not what you think."

Erinda took a seat on one of the cushions without reply, and began ladling the pot's contents into a bowl. When she looked up, she was smiling brightly, though the cheer did not quite reach her eyes. "It smells delicious. Come on. Let's eat."

Kade sat down, accepting the bowl Erinda handed to her. "I went to see Her, because—" She was cut off by the spoonful of stew that Erinda thrust into her mouth. The flavor of rabbit and wild leek burst over her tongue.

"Good, right?"

She nodded and chewed while Erinda filled her own bowl. As soon as she swallowed, Erinda pressed a slice of cheese to her lips. With a sigh, she bit off one end, and Erinda popped the other half into her own mouth. This was not how their evening was supposed to begin. She had to find a way to explain, but Erinda was doing her best to keep their mouths too full for conversation.

They ate until it seemed like her stomach would burst. The stew was rich, the greens fresh and flavorful, but in her agitation, Kade could barely taste them. Erinda uncorked the wine bottle and tilted it to her lips. She gulped several times, then offered the bottle to Kade with a questioning look. Kade hesitated. Priestesses generally drank wine only as part of specific holidays, and even then in very small quantities. But she was not a priestess anymore. She took the bottle and drank as deeply as Erinda had. The taste was bitter, and burned a little as she swallowed, but the act of drinking itself bolstered her courage.

She passed the bottle back and winced as the movement pulled at the stitches in her side.

Erinda set the bottle down. "Are those bothering you? Let me see."

She leaned over, reaching for the sash at Kade's waist. She had cleaned her nails, each pretty pink nail bed tipped with a neat white crescent, all traces of dirt gone beneath. The sunshine scent of her hair tickled Kade's nose.

The sash came undone in a few tugs, and Erinda peeled her tunic back to reveal the knotted bits of thread dotting her ribs. She skated her fingertips over the stitching, and bent to examine them in the fading light. Damp tendrils of her hair brushed Kade's abdomen.

"These are ready to come out." From beneath her apron, she produced a pair of small iron clippers, tied to her apron strings. She laid one hand flat on Kade's stomach. "Hold still."

The day had been scorching, and the air had only just begun to cool. Still, the warmth of Erinda's hand raised goose bumps on Kade's arms. The sharp tip of the clippers slipped beneath the first stitch and severed the thread with a click. Erinda grasped the knot between her thumb and forefinger and tugged it out. The sensation was no more painful than a pinprick, though her abdominal muscles flinched in response.

Erinda's head came up. "Ah, I'm sorry. This might pinch a bit."

"It's all right." Their eyes met, and Kade felt her face flush. Beneath Erinda's fingers, her ribs expanded and contracted. Erinda's irises darkened to the color of thunderheads, but she turned her attention to the next stitch, snipping it through and yanking it away.

"That's two," she said loudly. "Three. Four. Five…"

She didn't move, but she could feel her heart beating hard against the palm of Erinda's hand.

"Six. Seven. And…eight." Erinda flicked the last bit of thread away and smoothed her fingers over the newly formed scar. "There. Good as new."

When she tried to withdraw her hand, Kade reached up and caught it, pressing it back against her skin. She could feel the vestiges of the spirit current swell at the contact, and allowed it to wash over her hand and up Erinda's arm. Very slowly, she lifted her other hand to Erinda's face, brushing curls behind her ear. The Goddess might be the epitome of feminine beauty, but Erinda's mortal flaws—her secret dimple, the way one eyebrow arched just a little higher than the other—these were Kade's idea of perfection. In the sunset, the curves of her face were highlighted in rose and gold. She was so beautiful, all irresistible softness and wondrous strength. And she was hers. No guilt, no condemnation, no fear. Erinda was hers, and Kade would never give her up again.

Erinda's lips parted, just a little.

If Erinda didn't want to talk, she would get her message across another way. She leaned forward, keeping Erinda's hand trapped firmly against her ribs. Her emotions spilled into the silver current, and she pressed them outward. The space between them narrowed until she could feel Erinda's trembling breath against her mouth.

Then Erinda turned her face away. Kade closed her eyes in frustration.

"Don't do this," Erinda said in a pained whisper. "Please. I can't do this again."

"Rin…"

"Can't we just have a wonderful night? Eat good food, drink wine under the stars. That's all I want. And then tomorrow, I'll be gone before you wake up."

She sat back in alarm. "What are you talking about?"

"We're leaving tomorrow, aren't we? It's a long ride back to Verdred Temple, and Ardrenn isn't exactly on the way. I don't want to say good-bye again, Kade. I'd rather just go our separate ways quietly.

No fuss this time, no…" A surge of anguish rippled through the spirit current, so sharp that Kade winced. "Nothing that's going to make this any harder."

"But I'm not going back to Verdred, Rin."

That seemed to give her pause. "Oh. Then where is She sending you?"

"That's what I've been trying to explain. I'm not *shaa'din* any longer. I'm not a priestess, either." She tightened her grip on Erinda's hand. "Ithyris has released me from my vows."

"She did *what*?" Erinda snatched her hand back, rising to her feet so fast that the hem of her split skirts threatened to topple the wine bottle. "Are you serious?" she exclaimed, her face a mask of fury. "After everything you've done for Her, everything you've been through…you nearly died for Her, and She's turning Her back on you now? How can She do that?"

Shaking her head, Kade stood up. "You don't understand. I asked Her to."

Erinda's arms went limp at her sides, and she stared at Kade wide-eyed. "What?"

Kade reached for her, pulling her into her body. Her tunic still hung open, and Erinda's damp clothes were cool against the bare skin of her chest. She took Erinda's face in her hands and unleashed the last of the spirit current in full force.

"I'm going with you to the palace. You can put me to work in the kitchens, or scrubbing out the chamber pots, or mucking out the duck pond, I don't care. I'll do whatever you want. But I can't live without you anymore, Rin. I love you."

The shudder that traversed Erinda's body was unmistakable. Her eyes glistened, and the intermingled hope and fear that Kade saw there was more than she could stand. She bent and crushed her lips to Erinda's.

Erinda gasped into her mouth. Kade drew the soft fullness of her lower lip between her teeth. She ran her tongue over its satiny surface, then pressed deeper. Erinda's tongue melted against hers like sugar, and just like that, a wildfire spread through her blood, setting the spirit current ablaze. She kissed her the way she'd spent seven winters trying not to think about, using lips and tongue and teeth to communicate what she had never been able to adequately put into words. *You are everything, you are amazing, I don't deserve you, but oh, I want you so much…*

She only broke the kiss when she felt Erinda's tears against her hands. She pulled back, and Erinda was looking at her with such frantic longing that it made her heart hurt.

"Is this really happening?"

She wiped her thumbs beneath Erinda's eyes. "I know you have no reason to trust me. But I swear by the Goddess Herself that I mean it."

"You're sure?"

"I am absolutely sure."

Erinda slid her hands beneath Kade's open tunic. Slowly, she ran them up her chest and around her neck. Her touch sent glittering waves of arousal crashing through Kade's insides, and Kade made no attempt to suppress them. Erinda laid her lips to her throat and Kade made a sound she hadn't known she could make, something like a groan and a gasp and a whine all mashed together. Erinda was giving her another chance. Until this moment, she hadn't been sure that she would.

"If you break my heart this time, Kadrian Crossis, I will kill you."

Her mouth trailed along Kade's collarbone, lips and tongue working incredible sensations against her skin. Kade let Erinda shove her against the battlement. The stone was hard at her back, but her attention was overwhelmed by the feeling of Erinda's body pressed to hers. Underneath the damp fabric she was warm, and strong—Kade had forgotten how strong.

Erinda's hands traveled across her shoulders, sweeping her tunic open. Her nipples hardened in the open air, and Erinda stroked them with her thumbs. Exquisite pleasure arched through her as Erinda drew one tight bud into her mouth. Kade cried out, her hips surging forward. She hadn't expected her to move so fast, but she guessed that Erinda was feeling as impatient as she was.

"Goddess, Rin..."

She captured Erinda's head in her hands, pulling her up to meet her lips again, and in this kiss was everything: the unfulfilled desire of seven winters' separation, the desperate relief of their survival, a promise of the things to come. It began deep and lush, tongues tangling urgently, and softened into a delicate, erotic savoring of lips that barely touched. The silver spirit current encased them both in a haze, and though the flow was self-contained, it moved as easily as it ever had, without any effort on her part. The sheer intensity of it was enough to make Kade lightheaded. She needed to be closer.

Her hands tightened at Erinda's waist, and she spun them both around. Now Erinda was the one pressed against the battlement, and

Kade kissed her feverishly as she tugged at the laces of her bodice. The leather thongs snapped free of their eyelets. Kade wriggled the bodice from Erinda's shoulders and tossed it aside. She broke the kiss long enough to lift Erinda's chemise over her head and at the same time shrugged out of her own tunic. Both garments were sent flying after the first. Then she returned to Erinda's lips, plunging her tongue into the heat of Erinda's mouth. Their bodies came together like merging shadows, the luscious fullness of Erinda's breasts melding against hers, and she heard Erinda's soft, pleading moan. The sound clenched muscles deep within her, so hard that her legs buckled.

She didn't fight it, dropping to her knees on the plaster of the rooftop. She kept hold of Erinda's hips, pressing kisses to her stomach, and fumbled with the ties of her split skirts. They puddled to the ground, followed by her undergarments. She wrapped her arms around Erinda's thighs, sinking fingers into the flesh of her buttocks. She inhaled the gorgeous scent of her, fragrant and heady, and pressed her face to the thatch of curls that covered Erinda's sex.

Erinda moaned again, naked and quivering beneath her hands. She smelled so good, so sweet, and her moisture coated Kade's lips. She put out her tongue to lick it away, and the sound Erinda made nearly stopped her heart. She tongued her again, parting the dainty curls and pressing into the slick folds.

"Kade, oh, my darling, oh…"

Erinda's astonished cries sent a flood of wetness to her own throbbing center. She growled, gripping her even tighter, and took her time exploring this secret, intimate territory. She loved that she could make Erinda cry out like this, get her to tremble in such unrestrained ecstasy. From now on, she would never bring Erinda anything but joy. She would find a way to repay all of the winters of longing and hurt, and she would never let anyone or anything separate them again. Kade stroked her with her tongue until Erinda was shaking so hard that it was clear she could not remain standing, and then pulled her down into her lap.

Erinda's legs folded around her hips, her intimate heat pressed so tight to her pubic bone that Kade could feel it even through her leggings. Beneath her skin her veins rushed with fire. The spirit current expanded, as if driven by the frenetic pounding of her heart. Erinda let her head drop back, panting, and Kade fastened lips to her breast, suckling as she ground their hips together. She slid one hand down, between her body and Erinda's. She ran her fingers through the creamy warmth that awaited her, felt Erinda shudder and writhe against her hand. Her fingers were drenched, and her caresses deepened. Yet when she would have slid inside, Erinda stopped her.

"Together," she rasped. She locked eyes with her and Kade inhaled sharply, the word catapulting her into memories of that night so long ago. She thought of the first and last time they had been with each other like this, cresting with passion at the same time. Having relived it through Erinda's awareness in the current, she knew it had meant the same thing to Erinda as it had to her—that they were one spirit, indivisible, whole. Yes, that was what they needed now, what she needed to be able to give her again. She could not speak, but nodded her understanding.

Erinda shifted, tugging at the waist of Kade's leggings. Kade lifted her hips enough that the clothes could be stripped away, and Erinda pulled them down the length of her legs, her pretty fingernails lightly grazing the flesh of Kade's thighs and calves. When the clothes were gone she brought herself back up Kade's body, the hardened peaks of her breasts brushing Kade's belly, and brought her hand up between Kade's legs. Kade hadn't realized how wet she was until Erinda's fingers glided against her, sweeping over the sensitive knot of nerves like a shock wave. Her stomach went taut as a bowstring, and she reached down to seize Erinda's wrist.

Panting, she pulled Erinda against her, changing the position of their legs so that Erinda was straddling her again. She shifted until she was sitting cross-legged, her knees cradling the soft contours of Erinda's buttocks, Erinda's thighs draped over her hips. She moved her hand down between them, cupping Erinda's sex, and was greeted with a renewed rush of moisture against her fingers.

She let Erinda touch her then, and mimicked every fluttering caress of Erinda's hand with her own. They moved against each other in union, breath coming in audible sighs. This time it was not just pleasure and passion they exchanged; the silver current shimmered between them, trading emotions and sensations with such vivid clarity that Kade couldn't differentiate between her responses and Erinda's, or between the feelings of her flesh and those of her spirit. Unable to wait any longer, she turned her wrist slightly and slipped a finger deep into Erinda's body. A groan escaped from low in her chest at the feel of her, at once both firm and pliant, the wondrous texture and shape of those sacred, innermost places.

Erinda followed suit, entering Kade with the same gentle movement. There was nothing in all the world to compare to this, the feeling that came from being simultaneously surrounded and filled with one another. Erinda rocked and Kade held her, letting her set the pace and choose the most enjoyable angles. Every thrust of her hips drove her fingers deeper into Kade, sending ripples of sensation shattering through the spirit current. Kade had to brace herself against the wall with her free hand, splaying her fingers against the stone to hold them both upright.

She needed Erinda to understand her heart, to know beyond any doubt that this was real. More than anything, she wanted to sweep away all the loneliness, all the sadness of the past seven winters, and fill those places up instead with every wonderful thing that Erinda had ever wanted. It might take a long time to undo the damage she'd done, to make up for the pain she'd inflicted. For the rest of her life, Kade would never stop trying. Her heart was too full, and she could not contain this much emotion all at once. A glowing blue light radiated within her, as dazzling as the Goddess's legendary skin. Suddenly, she understood the reason for Ithyris's permanent state of illumination.

"I love you," she gasped. "Oh, Rin, I love you. I love you."

She felt Erinda's inner muscles constrict around her fingers, so hard that Kade was trapped inside her, and the sweet crescendo that tore through the spirit current swept Kade along with it.

They blazed together, in a flash of brilliant cerulean light. It was the single most extraordinary experience of Kade's life, brighter and more overwhelming even than when the Goddess had first claimed her as *shaa'din*. The spirit erupted from her like an explosion, searing from the core of her being outward. She and Erinda cried out in unison, exclamations of euphoria and wonder. They clung to each other as the surge passed, and the night fell dark around them once more.

They made love many more times that night, brought one another to the peak of ecstasy over and over again, until they were both too exhausted to move anymore. But after that first great release, the current did not return. When Kade awoke the next morning, she found that she could no longer sense the threads of Ithyris's spirit, no matter how she tried. She might have been a little disappointed, except that she could not imagine a more perfect way to have spent the last of Her power.

Though Kade would have much preferred to spend the day in Erinda's arms, their diminishing supplies were a concern that could not be ignored. There was work to be done if they were to be on their way back to the palace. Still, as they packed up the cushions, blankets, and food that had long gone cold from the tower rooftop, she repeatedly interrupted their more mundane tasks to pull Erinda in for long, languorous kisses.

During one of these amorous interludes, Erinda froze, her eyes going wide. She stared over Kade's shoulder, then clapped a hand to her mouth and began to giggle.

"Well, no one will ever be able to forget we were here," she sputtered between peals of laughter.

Kade turned to see what she was pointing at, and her mouth dropped open. After a moment of consternation, she also began to chuckle. Erinda's amusement only added to hers, and soon they were both bent double with laughing.

When the current had overtaken them last night, Kade's hand had been pressed against the battlements. Ithyris's final gift had not just carried them both over the edge. Apparently, it had also scorched a perfect impression of her handprint into the wall.

❖

"You sent for me, Your Majesty?"

Erinda closed the ornately carved doors of the royal chamber, and turned to find Queen Shasta, already fully dressed, smiling at her from the parlor's velvet sofa. To her surprise, Kade was also there, seated to the right of the Queen in a plush brocade armchair. Erinda was brought up short, not just by the presence of Kade but by the sight of her wearing the finest gown Erinda had ever seen her in: pale green silk, embroidered with golden butterflies at the hem and sleeves. The color was stunning with her short blond hair. Erinda could not remember the last time she had seen Kade wearing any color other than the stark white of her Pledged and priestess robes. She was so beautiful that Erinda could only blink at her in a daze.

A grin broke over Kade's face. She stood and crossed the room, and as she walked, Erinda could see that the gown had been made with split skirts. She had heard that Shasta had been working to popularize the fashion of split skirts at court. If everyone looked this graceful and powerful in them, Erinda was sure that every countess, baroness, and lady in the palace would soon be reworking their wardrobes.

"Kade...you look amazing."

"Not even half as amazing as you." Kade put one hand to Erinda's back and bent to kiss her.

That was pure flattery, and Erinda knew it. Her morning ride had left her windblown and breathless. She'd only just managed to pat her hair into some semblance of order and stuff it under her cap before entering the parlor. She hadn't even had time to mop the sweat from her neck, since Panna had met her at the stables with the urgent message that she was wanted in the Queen's chambers.

But whether or not the compliment was warranted, Kade's lips were on hers with a fervency that was most certainly unfeigned. She coaxed Erinda's mouth open and explored her with such tenderness that her heart felt like it might batter free from her chest. Only the knowledge that they had an audience kept her from collapsing into Kade's arms. But the blood rose in Erinda's cheeks, and she pushed her back.

"Kade! Not here. The Queen—"

"Never mind her, Kadrian," Shasta interrupted airily from the sofa. "You may kiss her all you like in my presence. In fact, I rather insist on it. Goddess knows, Erinda has endured the same from Talon and me countless times."

Kade chuckled and bent her head again, but this time she only skimmed Erinda's lips before pulling away.

Erinda turned to Shasta, somewhat flustered, and curtsied. "You're up early this morning, Your Majesty."

"Today is an important day," Shasta said cheerfully. "For more than one reason. Please, sit with me."

Kade laced her fingers with Erinda's and led her to the sofa. She waited for Erinda to sink down next to Shasta, then resumed her spot in the armchair. "Ithyris is creating another *shaa'din* today," she said.

Shasta nodded. "How is Lyris, Your Grace? Is she ready?"

"It's just Kadrian now, Your Majesty. And yes, she seems much more prepared than I was. Truthfully, I believe Lyris will make a far better Handmaiden than I."

Erinda turned to Kade. "Have you told her? About what being touched by the Goddess means?" She lifted a brow, remembering that afternoon in Mondera Temple when she had walked in on Kade and the Goddess while they were busy…*communing*.

Kade winked. "Oh, I've told her. She can't wait."

"Just don't tell Talon," Shasta giggled. "I think she rather likes the idea of her sister remaining safely virginal for the rest of their lives."

"Speaking of Talon, I can't help but notice that the two of you seem pretty happy these days," Erinda said. "May I assume that she's finally come to her senses and let go of all that nonsense about you finding a husband?"

Shasta's eyes lit. "Oh, Erinda, it's even better than that. Believe it or not, the first thing Talon did when she got back to the palace was come find me in the conference hall. She marched into the room, knelt at my feet, and right there in front of the provincial senate she asked me to marry her."

Erinda gasped. "She did?"

"I'm announcing our engagement to the court this evening. Not all the viceroys are pleased, of course, but they'll just have to get over it. Ithyria's going to have an Outlander on the throne whether they like it or not."

"Talon's agreed to take the crown?"

"Well, she's agreed to become King Consort," Shasta said. "The title doesn't require her involvement in kingdom politics, though it's probably impossible for her to avoid them completely. Still, she says she wants us to be a family—her, me, and Brita—and that she isn't going to let my responsibilities as Queen keep us from that anymore. She said..." and here Shasta turned to Kade with a thoughtful expression, "that she'd learned something in Mondera. She said the Goddess's Handmaiden told her that love was more important than any other calling."

Kade inclined her head, and glanced at Erinda shyly. Erinda's eyes filled with tears, and she cleared her throat. "Oh, Your Majesty, I am so happy for you."

"It's all thanks to the two of you," she replied. "Which is why I asked you both here this morning. I have something to give you. I had planned to do it in court tonight, with lots of fanfare, but Talon has assured me you would both prefer a private presentation." She reached a hand to Kade, and laid her other hand on Erinda's.

"Erinda, you are such a dear friend. You have counseled and supported me through the darkest times of my life. I honestly don't know what I would have done without you these past moons. Because of me, you've gone through so much suffering, getting dragged off to Dangar. I can't even imagine how awful that must have been."

Before Erinda could protest, Shasta turned to Kade and continued. "And, Kadrian, you saved my kingdom from a dreadful enemy, at great danger to yourself. Not to mention, you've made Erinda smile like I have never seen before."

Kade's cheeks reddened, and Shasta laughed. "Nothing would make me happier than to see the two of you enjoy a long, peaceful life together, doing what you truly love to do. So, I've asked Kadrian for suggestions. As sad as I will be to lose your company, Erinda, I think you two need a place of your own, away from the court and the temples, to build your own kind of life with each other."

Erinda looked over at Kade, but Kade only smiled.

Shasta squeezed their hands. "I am hereby granting you both shared possession of the baronial estate of Warinsgate."

Erinda knew that name, and her mouth dropped open. "Warinsgate, Your Majesty? Where the royal horses are bred?"

"That's the one. The estate has been in the possession of the crown for several generations, ever since the last baron died. I think it's time to pass it on to someone who will give it the attention and care it deserves. I understand it's a pretty big place, with a manor house, two dozen or so household staff, several stables, and grounds spanning nearly a league in all directions. They tell me there's close to two hundred head of stock there now."

Erinda met Kade's eyes in excitement. Two hundred horses? The Queen was going to give them their own land, and two *hundred* horses? The prospect made her head spin. Though she had never been dissatisfied with her position at the palace, it had never occurred to her that she might one day be offered the chance to work with horses of her own.

Shasta pretended to frown. "Actually, now that I think about it, an estate that size is going to be quite a lot of work. Perhaps you'd prefer someplace else?" But there was a twinkle in her eye as she said it, and Erinda shook her head.

"Oh, Your Majesty, I can't imagine anything better. That is, if Kade wants it too."

Kade's lips curved. "I already told you, Rin, you can put me to work doing anything you want. I'll be happy as long as I'm with you."

"Excellent. It's settled then. Kadrian, can you hand me the little bag, there on the table?"

Kade retrieved a small bag of blue silk from the table, passing it to her. Shasta loosened the drawstrings and turned the contents over into her palm. "As Warinsgate is baronial land, its owners are members of the nobility. These are yours, as its new baronesses." She took Erinda's hand and slid a heavy ring onto her middle finger. A large ruby was secured within bands of gold, which twisted together above the center of the stone. Framed within the bands was a small enameled disk, shaped in a likeness of the royal crest. Erinda held her hand up, eyes wide.

"Your Majesty, this is beautiful. But it's too much, isn't it? I'd be happy with just the horses. Just one horse, even."

Shasta gestured for Kade's hand and placed a matching ring onto her finger. "It's the least I can do. I know how little the affairs of court interest you, so I promise I won't require your presence at court functions. Though I do hope you'll come for visits every now and then. I am sure to miss you terribly."

She rose to her feet and drew Erinda up into a hug. Overcome with gratitude, Erinda could only accept her embrace, mindful not to muss the Queen's carefully arranged hair.

"Panna," Shasta said over Erinda's shoulder, "is the gown ready?"

Erinda turned to see the chambermaid curtsy at the entrance to Shasta's bedchamber. "Yes, Your Majesty."

"Then please assist Lady Erinda as she dresses. Quickly, the ceremony is beginning soon."

❖

The gentle notes of a flute brought everyone in the palace temple to their feet. Standing next to Talon, Erinda craned her neck to see the procession. The flutist was first, a young Pledged with dark hair, who paraded down the central aisle with her instrument at her lips. She was followed by the temple high priestess, two senior priestesses swinging incense burners, and then Kade, whose green silk gown and golden hair were a warm contrast to the priestesses' stark robes and veils.

Erinda watched her as she passed. Something about this ceremony had her a little on edge. Lyris had requested that her *shaa'din* rites take place in the palace temple, rather than at the Great Temple of Aster on the outskirts of Ardrenn. But even though Kade was participating only as a former Handmaiden, Erinda could not help but be reminded of Kade's Pledged ceremony, and that last morning when she'd fled from the bed they had shared to take her vows. Both events had taken place on that very same dais. She felt her heart accelerate and did her best to calm down. Today was different, she reminded herself. Kade was no longer a priestess. She had left the temple and was promised to Erinda now.

Kade reached her spot on the dais and turned toward the crowd. The moment she caught sight of Erinda, such a look of desire came over her face that Erinda felt silly for having worried. The blatant lust with which Kade was staring at her set her cheeks burning, and she looked down self-consciously. The dress that Shasta had created for her was of the same cut as Kade's, with a snug bodice, flowing bell-shaped sleeves, and rustling split skirts. But hers was made of deep rose-colored silk, and the embroidery had been done in the shapes of hundreds of tiny horses, galloping with streaming manes and tails around the hem of the skirt and the edges of her sleeves. Until her hair grew out again, she could not create the braids that she usually wore, so instead Panna had pinned flowers into her cropped curls. Erinda had never worn such fine clothes in her life, and she felt strange in them now. She had been born a palace servant, and had never aspired to any higher station. But with Kade looking at her like that, perhaps the fancy gown wasn't so bad after all.

A murmur spread through the onlookers as another priestess entered. Above her veils, Lyris's olive complexion distinguished her from the others. Her robe was blue rather than the usual snowy white, and she carried a single stick of burning incense, its thread of smoke spiraling toward the ceiling overhead. She moved forward with a reverence that suggested every step was a treasured experience.

Lyris ascended to the dais, where she placed the incense among an arrangement of flowers at the base of an ornately carved statue. After having spent some time with Ithyris in person, Erinda found the statue's beauty underwhelming, to say the least. Then again, she doubted there was a sculptor alive who would be able to re-create the uncompromising perfection of Her features.

Kade moved forward to address the assembly. The past few moons really had changed her. At one time, the prospect of speaking before so many strangers would have held her paralyzed, and she would have been looking to Erinda for help. Now, her voice was strong and clear as it carried through the temple sanctuary.

"Daughters of Ithyris, Children of Ithyria, Your Royal Majesty… we have come together today to witness the birth of a *shaa'din*. Our Divine Lady has decreed that from this day forth, *Ostryn* Lyris shall become a vessel through which She may reach all of Her people. The Handmaiden's face shall not be veiled, and her hair shall no longer be shorn, for she is a warrior consecrated unto Ithyris, and a weapon wielded by Her hand."

As Kade spoke, two of the other priestesses were unfolding a large white-screened partition in front of the statue, and the high priestess was unpinning Lyris's veils. Lyris was offered a shining silver cup, and as she drank from it, Erinda could see spiraling blue paint decorating the backs of her hands. When she handed the Cup of Purification back to the high priestess, Kade took Lyris's elbow and led her out of sight behind the partition. When she returned, she had the blue robe in her hands.

Talon leaned over to Erinda, an odd note in her voice. "Is that what's supposed to happen?" she asked, indicating the robe.

Erinda met her suspicious frown with a grin. "Yes, Captain, it's supposed to happen."

Talon gave a disapproving grunt as she straightened, and Erinda had to suppress a chuckle. It was probably very good for Talon that she didn't know what was coming next.

Kade handed the robe to the high priestess, who began to lead the assembly in a hymn. Kade made her way down the dais steps, coming to stand at Erinda's side. She laced her fingers with Erinda's and kept her eyes on the partition as a faint blue glow began to emanate behind it.

Erinda watched her face for a while, as the blue light intensified and the green of Kade's eyes brightened with tears. Finally, she had to ask.

"Is it hard?" Kade looked down at her, and Erinda nodded toward the partition. "That was you, once. Is it…Are you sorry you chose this instead?"

Kade's grip tightened and she brought their joined hands up, pressing a kiss to Erinda's knuckles. Then she bent until her lips were at Erinda's ear. "Not one bit. I'm so happy, Rin. You have no idea how much."

Closing her eyes, Erinda sighed in relief. All around them, the audience gave a collective cry of amazement as the Goddess's blue light whitened into absolution. But she paid no attention. In the blinding flash that followed, she found Kade's lips with hers, and kissed her softly and deeply until long after the light had receded.

EPILOGUE

A few moons after the new Handmaiden was called into Her service, the first snows fell in the eastern mountains of Mondera. The shift in seasons was particularly important to the people living in the Monderan Outlands, who sent their hunting parties into the foothills to seek what would likely be the last large game to be found before winter.

It was the shaman's daughter who found the stranger's tracks. The marks were undoubtedly human, and female, but too heavy and uneven for an Outlander. She followed them to a small cave, hidden in the rocks, and found within a person unlike any she had seen before, a woman with hair the color of fire and a belly greatly distended with child. The stranger's face was thin, as though she had not eaten well in many days, and her skin was yellowed with signs of infection. The pains of childbirth were upon her with such force that she seemed unaware she had been discovered.

The shamaness was no stranger to the birthing process, and it was not the practice of a shamanic family to abandon those in distress. Laying aside her weapons, she went about preparing a fire, melting snow into water, and covering the stranger with her own fur cloak to ease the chattering of her teeth. She shared the medicinal herbs carried in her pouch, and sang every healing chant she knew. But it seemed nature had already determined this woman's fate. The closer her child came to the world, the weaker she became, until her breathing was so labored the shamaness feared she might die before the baby could be delivered.

At last, the child emerged. The shamaness used her skirt to clean away the birthing membranes. The woman's eyes were still open, and so the shamaness tucked the crying infant into her arms.

"You have a daughter, lady." She did not know whether the woman heard, as a moment later, her eyes closed and she released a final breath. Saddened, the shamaness picked the child up again, drawing it close to keep it warm, and looked it over with curiosity. Such a strange looking thing, with a thick patch of hair the same brilliant shade as its mother's.

"Poor little bug," she said to it. *"Don't worry. Since your mother is gone, I will bring you back with me to my village. You shall be an Outlander now."*

Abruptly, the baby ceased its crying. It gazed up at her with eyes so clear and calm that the shamaness was almost convinced it had understood her. She had no milk to feed it, but there were always plenty of women with young in her village, who would be willing to share. All the child had to do was endure the night.

Outside the cave entrance, the wind whistled, bringing with it the scent of an imminent snowfall. The shamaness laid the baby down near the fire, curled herself around it, and began to croon a lullaby.

About the Author

Merry Shannon currently resides in Colorado with her fiancée and their assorted menagerie of furry companions. She has previously published two novels and three short stories with Bold Strokes Books. Her first novel, *Sword of the Guardian*, won two Golden Crown Literary Awards (Speculative Fiction and Debut Author), and she is a Foreword Book of the Year Finalist and Lesbian Fiction Readers' Choice Award winner for *Branded Ann*. In addition to writing, she works full-time as a social services supervisor, and in her free time enjoys watching Korean drama and playing in the Society for Creative Anachronism. Visit her online at MerryShannon.com.

Books Available from Bold Strokes Books

Twice Lucky by Mardi Alexander. For firefighter Mackenzie James and Dr. Sarah Macarthur, there's suddenly a whole lot more in life to understand, to consider, to risk...someone will need to fight for her life. (978-1-62639-325-7)

Shadow Hunt by L.L. Raand. With young to raise and her Pack under attack, Sylvan, Alpha of the wolf Weres, takes on her greatest challenge when she determines to uncover the faceless enemies known as the Shadow Lords. A Midnight Hunters novel. (978-1-62639-326-4)

Heart of the Game by Rachel Spangler. A baseball writer falls for a single mom, but can she ever love anything as much as she loves the game? (978-1-62639-327-1)

Getting Lost by Michelle Grubb. Twenty-eight days, thirteen European countries, a tour manager fighting attraction, and an accused murderer: Stella and Phoebe's journey of a lifetime begins here. (978-1-62639-328-8)

Prayer of the Handmaiden by Merry Shannon. Celibate priestess Kadrian must defend the kingdom of Ithyria from a dangerous enemy and ultimately choose between her duty to the Goddess and the love of her childhood sweetheart, Erinda. (978-1-62639-329-5)

The Witch of Stalingrad by Justine Saracen. A Soviet "night witch" pilot and American journalist meet on the Eastern Front in WW II and struggle through carnage, conflicting politics, and the deadly Russian winter. (978-1-62639-330-1)

Pedal to the Metal by Jesse J. Thoma. When unreformed thief Dubs Williams is released from prison to help Max Winters bust a car theft ring, Max learns that to catch a thief, get in bed with one. (978-1-62639-239-7)

Dragon Horse War by D. Jackson Leigh. A priestess of peace and a fiery warrior must defeat a vicious uprising that entwines their destinies and ultimately their hearts. (978-1-62639-240-3)

For the Love of Cake by Erin Dutton. When everything is on the line, and one taste can break a heart, will pastry chefs Maya and Shannon take a chance on reality? (978-1-62639-241-0)

Betting on Love by Alyssa Linn Palmer. A quiet country-girl-at-heart and a live-life-to-the-fullest biker take a risk at offering each other their hearts. (978-1-62639-242-7)

The Deadening by Yvonne Heidt. The lines between good and evil, right and wrong, have always been blurry for Shade. When Raven's actions force her to choose, which side will she come out on? (978-1-62639-243-4)

Ordinary Mayhem by Victoria A. Brownworth. Faye Blakemore has been taking photographs since she was ten, but those same photographs threaten to destroy everything she knows and everything she loves. (978-1-62639-315-8)

One Last Thing by Kim Baldwin & Xenia Alexiou. Blood is thicker than pride. The final book in the Elite Operative Series brings together foes, family, and friends to start a new order. (978-1-62639-230-4)

Songs Unfinished by Holly Stratimore. Two aspiring rock stars learn that falling in love while pursuing their dreams can be harmonious—if they can only keep their pasts from throwing them out of tune. (978-1-62639-231-1)

Beyond the Ridge by L.T. Marie. Will a contractor and a horse rancher overcome their family differences and find common ground to build a life together? (978-1-62639-232-8)

Swordfish by Andrea Bramhall. Four women battle the demons from their pasts. Will they learn to let go, or will happiness be forever beyond their grasp? (978-1-62639-233-5)

The Fiend Queen by Barbara Ann Wright. Princess Katya and her consort Starbride must turn evil against evil in order to banish Fiendish power from their kingdom, and only love will pull them back from the brink. (978-1-62639-234-2)

Up the Ante by PJ Trebelhorn. When Jordan Stryker and Ashley Noble meet again fifteen years after a short-lived affair, are either of them prepared to gamble on a chance at love? (978-1-62639-237-3)

Speakeasy by MJ Williamz. When mob leader Helen Byrne sets her sights on the girlfriend of Al Capone's right-hand man, passion and tempers flare on the streets of Chicago. (978-1-62639-238-0)

Venus in Love by Tina Michele. Morgan Blake can't afford any distractions and Ainsley Dencourt can't afford to lose control—but the beauty of life and art usually lies in the unpredictable strokes of the artist's brush. (978-1-62639-220-5)

Rules of Revenge by AJ Quinn. When a lethal operative on a collision course with her past agrees to help a CIA analyst on a critical assignment, the encounter proves explosive in ways neither woman anticipated. (978-1-62639-221-2)

The Romance Vote by Ali Vali. Chili Alexander is a sought-after campaign consultant who isn't prepared when her boss's daughter, Samantha Pellegrin, comes to work at the firm and shakes up Chili's life from the first day. (978-1-62639-222-9)

Advance: Exodus Book One by Gun Brooke. Admiral Dael Caydoc's mission to find a new homeworld for the Oconodian people is hazardous, but working with the infuriating Commander Aniwyn "Spinner" Seclan endangers her heart and soul. (978-1-62639-224-3)

UnCatholic Conduct by Stevie Mikayne. Jil Kidd goes undercover to investigate fraud at St. Marguerite's Catholic School, but life gets complicated when her student is killed—and she begins to fall for her prime target. (978-1-62639-304-2)

Season's Meetings by Amy Dunne. Catherine Birch reluctantly ventures on the festive road trip from hell with beautiful stranger Holly Daniels only to discover the road to true love has its own obstacles to maneuver. (978-1-62639-227-4)

Myth and Magic: Queer Fairy Tales edited by Radclyffe and Stacia Seaman. Myth, magic, and monsters—the stuff of childhood dreams (or nightmares) and adult fantasies. (978-1-62639-225-0)

Nine Nights on the Windy Tree by Martha Miller. Recovering drug addict, Bertha Brannon, is an attorney who is trying to stay clean when a murder sends her back to the bad end of town. (978-1-62639-179-6)

Driving Lessons by Annameekee Hesik. Dive into Abbey Brooks's sophomore year as she attempts to figure out the amazing, but sometimes complicated, life of a you-know-who girl at Gila High School. (978-1-62639-228-1)

Asher's Shot by Elizabeth Wheeler. Asher Price's candid photographs capture the truth, but when his success requires exposing an enemy, Asher discovers his only shot at happiness involves revealing secrets of his own. (978-1-62639-229-8)

Courtship by Carsen Taite. Love and justice—a lethal mix or a perfect match? (978-1-62639-210-6)

Against Doctor's Orders by Radclyffe. Corporate financier Presley Worth wants to shut down Argyle Community Hospital, but Dr. Harper Rivers will fight her every step of the way, if she can also fight their growing attraction. (978-1-62639-211-3)

A Spark of Heavenly Fire by Kathleen Knowles. Kerry and Beth are building their life together, but unexpected circumstances could destroy their happiness. (978-1-62639-212-0)

Never Too Late by Julie Blair. When Dr. Jamie Hammond is forced to hire a new office manager, she's shocked to come face to face with Carla Grant and memories from her past. (978-1-62639-213-7)

Widow by Martha Miller. Judge Bertha Brannon must solve the murder of her lover, a policewoman she thought she'd grow old with. As more bodies pile up, the murderer starts coming for her. (978-1-62639-214-4)

Twisted Echoes by Sheri Lewis Wohl. What's a woman to do when she realizes the voices in her head are real? (978-1-62639-215-1)

Criminal Gold by Ann Aptaker. Through a dangerous night in New York in 1949, Cantor Gold, dapper dyke-about-town, smuggler of fine art, is forced by a crime lord to be his instrument of vengeance. (978-1-62639-216-8)

The Melody of Light by M.L. Rice. After surviving abuse and loss, will Riley Gordon be able to navigate her first year of college and accept true love and family? (978-1-62639-219-9)

Because of You by Julie Cannon. What would you do for the woman you were forced to leave behind? (978-1-62639-199-4)

The Job by Jove Belle. Sera always dreamed that she would one day reunite with Tor. She just didn't think it would involve terrorists, firearms, and hostages. (978-1-62639-200-7)

Making Time by C.J. Harte. Two women going in different directions meet after fifteen years and struggle to reconnect in spite of the past that separated them. (978-1-62639-201-4)

Once The Clouds Have Gone by KE Payne. Overwhelmed by the dark clouds of her past, Tag Grainger is lost until the intriguing and spirited Freddie Metcalfe unexpectedly forces her to reevaluate her life. (978-1-62639-202-1)

The Acquittal by Anne Laughlin. Chicago private investigator Josie Harper searches for the real killer of a woman whose lover has been acquitted of the crime. (978-1-62639-203-8)

An American Queer: The Amazon Trail by Lee Lynch. Lee Lynch's heartening and heart-rending history of gay life from the turbulence of the late 1900s to the triumphs of the early 2000s are recorded in this selection of her columns. (978-1-62639-204-5)

Stick McLaughlin: The Prohibition Years by CF Frizzell. Corruption in 1918 cost Stick her lover, her freedom, and her identity, but a very special flapper and the family bond of her own gang could help win them back—even if it means outwitting the Boston Mob. (978-1-62639-205-2)

Edge of Awareness by C.A. Popovich. When Maria, a woman in the middle of her third divorce, meets Dana, an out lesbian, awareness of her feelings brings up reservations about the teachings of her church. (978-1-62639-188-8)

Taken by Storm by Kim Baldwin. Lives depend on two women when a train derails high in the remote Alps, but an unforgiving mountain, avalanches, crevasses, and other perils stand between them and safety. (978-1-62639-189-5)

The Common Thread by Jaime Maddox. Dr. Nicole Coussart's life is falling apart, but fortunately, DEA Attorney Rae Rhodes is there to pick up the pieces and help Nic put them back together. (978-1-62639-190-1)

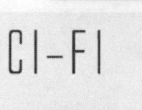